MARY CALMES

A MATTER OF TIME

VOL. 2

Dreamspinner Press

Published by
Dreamspinner Press
4760 Preston Road
Suite 244-149
Frisco, TX 75034
http://www.dreamspinnerpress.com/

A Matter of Time, Vol. 2
Copyright © 2010 by Mary Calmes

Cover Art by Anne Cain   annecain.art@gmail.com
Cover Design by Mara McKennen

ISBN: 978-1-61581-600-2

Printed in the United States of America
First Edition
August, 2010

For all my wonderful fans
who asked when this book
would be in print and
for Elizabeth who made it a reality.

Book Three

Chapter One

THE room was covered in roses. Pale, dusty-rose-colored petals were strewn over everything, the lighting, the colors, all of it giving you that romantic, soft-filtered feeling of femininity. It was stunning. The string quartet, the champagne, the servers in crisp white, it was all so elegant… and completely lost on the rest of the men at the table. They looked wrung out and I understood why. Three days of wedding was an uphill grind, and we were only on day two.

I had no idea who had ever decided that a bachelor party should be the night before the rehearsal dinner, but I was pretty sure that person was a sadist. Having barely recovered from staggering home as the sun came up, Dane's groomsmen had been expected to be sober and high-functioning the following day by five, to be put through the repetitive practice of walking in and out of the church. They were also supposed to be impressed with the lovely room and intimate setting, when all they wanted to do was drink away the remnants of their hangovers. I was glad I had taken the time off from work for my brother's wedding, since if I'd had to keep up my usual schedule of appointments I would have turned instantly to ash. When I was hounded to accompany them out carousing for the second night in a row, I snuck out instead, declining by way of absence, and went home to bed. It was the coward's way, but I could never have kept up. They were all much better drinkers than me, which was saying a lot as I could normally hold my own.

The following morning when I reached the suite with my tuxedo draped over my arm, I was not surprised to find them still in their clothes from the night before. There was one on the floor, one on each couch, one in the wingback chair and Jude, Dane's best man, alone in the bed, drooling. It was a sight to behold. When the door opened and it was Aja Greene—Dane's fiancée and not the man himself—come to roust the boys, I felt really sorry for them. It was her wedding day, and they looked like roadkill. This was not the way to get on her good side.

"Are you kidding me?" she shrieked in the silence.

The moaning and whimpering made me smile as I started pouring coffee and water. I had brought a large bottle of Tylenol with me.

"Hey," Rick Jenner said softly as he gestured me over to him. "What time is it?"

"It's ten." I smiled down at him. "The wedding's not for another eight hours."

"Then why is she screaming?"

"She's not, actually."

"It sounds like it to me."

"Yeah, but you can probably hear paint peeling," I suggested.

He only groaned.

"She's only concerned that you guys aren't gonna look pretty for pictures."

"Owww." He winced, patting the couch beside him. "Sit."

"It was the last shot of tequila off the girl's navel that did it," I teased him. I could only imagine what the second night of debauchery had degraded to.

"How d'ya know?" He tried to smile, putting his head on my leg as soon as I sat down.

I smiled at him as I was bumped from the other side and hands gripped my shoulders.

Lance Simmons and Alex Greene, Aja's brother, had joined me.

"Hey, fellas," I teased them, looking sideways at Lance's profile. "You guys all done barfing?"

"No," he whined, his head on my shoulder. "Tell me what we have to eat for dinner."

"Liver and onions," I cackled evilly.

"Oh screw you," he retched, leaning over to lie down on the couch. The leather had to be cool on his hot face. "Liver, my ass."

"Alex." I called his name softly.

"Mmmm." He barely made a noise, his forehead against the back of my neck.

"Do your eyelids hurt?"

"If I straighten my head, I think it'll explode."

"Your sister's coming."

He whimpered before she yelled, "You guys need to get up!"

Her voice was like getting whiplash—fast and painful. I felt it run down my spine.

"Oh God," Alex groaned from behind me, and we all laughed when we heard the bump as he hit the floor. "I think my eyes are bleeding."

"Guys!" we heard Jude whine from the bedroom. "Will you shut the hell up!"

She whirled around to go see him, and at that moment I thanked God that I was not Jude Coughlin. There was not enough money in the world.

"Do something, J," Rick begged me. "You're the only one she loves."

"J, you gotta make her stop yelling," Alex begged me from the floor on the other side of the couch. "I seriously think it could kill me."

"Is it really liver?" Lance moaned into the couch.

We all heard Jude give out a high-pitched, girly scream from the bedroom.

I couldn't stop smiling.

"I think I'm gonna puke," Rick said from my lap, covering his face with one of the throw pillows.

"I will kill you all if you do not get up!"

"J," Lance almost cried, "make her stop."

"Make her stop," Rick seconded.

"Please make her stop," Alex begged me.

"She's your sister," I reminded him.

"Yeah, but she loves you more than me."

"Do you hear me?" she roared from the other room, obviously still torturing Jude.

"Ohmygod, just kill her," Lance whispered, facedown on the couch now. "Why did you guys let me sleep folded up like a pretzel? I think my spine is broken."

We all heard Jude scream again before there was a crash and a thump.

"I bet she dumped him out of bed," Alex sighed from the floor.

"I'm okay," he called out to us.

"Asshole got the bed," Rick whined. "He deserves what he gets."

"Where's Rick?" she shouted as she came charging into the room.

He whimpered. "J, she's gonna hurt me."

"This is what comes of partying like rock stars." I chuckled. "When you're not."

"Owww," Alex whined.

"Where's the ice bucket?" she yelled from across the room.

"J...." Rick trailed off.

I called to her gently, but loud enough so she could hear me.

Aja Greene came striding across the room to me. "What?" she snapped out.

"How're you this morning, pretty lady?" I smiled wide, looking up at the only other woman besides my work-wife, and best-friend, Dylan Greer that I could say I truly loved. In my life there had been my grandmother, Dylan, and my brother's soon-to-be wife. These were the women who meant the world to me. "You feel okay?"

Her sigh was deep as she passed Lance and slapped him as hard as she could on the ass. He almost howled.

"Yes, baby." She stopped in front of me, shoving Rick up and moving him before she leaned down to give me a kiss. "I feel great."

I lifted my head, and the kiss I received was featherlight on my lips.

"Jory." She smiled, hand sliding under my chin, over my jaw. "Come to my room really fast. I want you to meet my folks, and Dane's people are there."

Which meant that the Reid clan—Susan and Daniel Reid, Dane's biological parents, and his siblings, two brothers and one sister—had arrived to attend the wedding.

"Okay," I said, stifling a yawn and getting up.

"And you guys need to pull it together and get ready," she snarled at the others. "Now!"

The muffled groans made me smile as she took my hand and tugged me after her toward the door. I heard them behind us, and then Rick asked if anyone knew where his sunglasses were. Funny to think that a CEO, a CFO, a partner at one of the major law firms in the city, and a bank manager could so resemble hungover frat boys.

"Look how beautiful," she commented, raising our hands.

Her flawless, smooth, caramel skin against my permanent golden tan: we looked good together. People told us all the time.

"Hey."

I looked at her.

"Did you ever think that your brother would marry a black girl?"

"Are you black?" I asked her.

She smiled wide and I saw the dimples I loved.

"Actually," I sighed, "the minute I saw you, I knew you were the one."

"You lie."

"No."

"Why?"

"You asked him to dance."

"I'm not the only one that ever did."

"No, but you're the only one who ever made him nervous."

She sighed deeply. "I did, didn't I?"

"Yes, ma'am."

"I think we both knew what we wanted."

"Yep. And you're perfect for him."

"Why?" She was fishing.

"'Cause you're smart—school principals hafta be—beautiful, wicked-mean—"

"Mean?" She gasped in mock shock.

"You know you're mean. You nearly killed those poor guys."

"They'll be lucky to live," she growled, brows furrowing.

"You're adorable," I assured her, hand on her cheek. "And you are completely self-sufficient. You want Dane, but you don't need him."

Deep sigh. "Make no mistake, Jory, I need that man desperately."

"Yeah, but you're your own person. Your whole word doesn't revolve around him."

She thought a moment. "No, that's true."

"See? You love Dane, I know that, but you're gonna be Aja Harcourt, not Mrs. Dane Harcourt."

She nodded. "That's true too."

I shrugged. "That's how I knew. All those other women just wanted to disappear inside him. You, we're still gonna be able to see."

She stopped suddenly and stared at me. "You have been amazing since the moment I laid eyes on you."

"I wanted you for my brother," I assured her.

"And I'm so glad you're going to be mine."

"But you gotta be sweet to the one you already have."

She frowned again. "He better shape up, because if he ruins my wedding… so help me God, I will ruin him permanently."

"Okay, now you're gettin' a little spooky." I chuckled.

"Oh Jory." She sighed. "I just love you. Come with me."

And I did.

AJA'S eyes were huge and her mouth hung open. Her mother had an identical expression, as did all her bridesmaids and her maid of honor. It was probably the dancing.

Her father, Judge Greene, and I were doing the twist to Fats Domino music and singing along as we did it. Currently, "My Girl Josephine" was bouncing out of the speakers.

"Miss Aja," I heard her best friend Candace laugh out loud, "look at your father, girl."

"Jory," she called over to me, and I heard the deep chuckle. "Baby, what—"

"Leave him alone," the judge cut her off playfully. "We're busy."

"Kenneth Greene, what in heaven's name are you doing?" Aja's mother asked her husband, her smile making her eyes sparkle.

Instead of answering, he motioned her over. Immediately she went to him, and seconds later he had her in his arms, dipping her low, dancing her around the suite.

Dane suddenly filled the doorway, standing beside the woman who would be his wife by the end of the day. It was funny to see his expression as he looked across the room to where I now danced in a circle of beautiful women. He tipped his head at me, and I smiled back. I watched him put an arm around Aja's shoulders and pull her close before he kissed her cheek.

"Jory." He called my name.

There were hands in my hair, on my back, sliding off my shoulders, clutching at my shirt before I got free to cross the room. As I stepped in front of Dane, he put a hand on the lapel of my dress shirt and pulled me forward into his arms.

"Thank you," he said, face down in my shoulder.

My eyes flicked to Aja's as he let me go and left as suddenly as he'd come.

"What's going on?" she asked quickly.

I coughed once. "Mr. Reid came in here asking questions about you, and your dad took offence."

"I'm sorry, what?"

"It was no big deal," I lied.

"Questions? What kind of questions?"

I shrugged. "He doesn't know anything about you and Dane didn't even invite them to anything but the wedding and reception, so… I guess they wanted to find out about you."

"I see."

"Well, your dad didn't see. You can't really blame him."

She smiled at me. "It's not like my dad to get upset about a few innocent inquiries."

"It was a lot," I defended her father. "I was uncomfortable too."

She nodded. "So what happened?"

"Your dad said that the only family of Dane's he worried about was me." I grinned at her.

"Oh." She nodded. "Since you and Dane are the only Harcourts in the place."

"Right." I smiled wide, leaning close and kissing her forehead. "At least until six o'clock."

She sighed deeply.

"You'll be the new Harcourt down front in the gown, right?"

In answer I got arms wrapped around my neck and she hugged me tight. "What did you do?"

"I went and got my iPod and asked your dad if he still had moves."

I felt her shaking in my arms.

"As you can see, the man's still got it."

She clutched me tighter, her head back as the laughter bubbled up out of her.

When I glanced back at her folks, I was rewarded with the warm smile of her mother.

It had been tense. Dane's parents, especially his father, questioning the judge about his daughter… it had started out so benign, just chatting, before quickly deteriorating into an all-out inquisition. They knew nothing about Aja and wanted to know everything. It had been well intended, but had come off as critical, biased, and almost racist. Dane and I were just walking back from our racquetball game and we heard the raised voices from the hall. We interrupted and Dane insisted on showing the Reids to his suite upstairs, away from the communal one being used so the wedding party could visit with guests or get something to eat before the ceremony. He took his parents, as well as his brothers Caleb and Jeremy and his sister Gwen, so the judge could recover and collect his thoughts. The look Dane had given me as he left had been so pained that I felt my chest tighten just looking at him. The last thing he wanted to do on his wedding day was upset his future father-in-law with people that were of minimal importance to him. The truth was, he simply liked the judge better than his biological family. I had to fix it. I had to restore the ease that the day had begun with; this, then, was what Dane's look had conveyed on his exit. And I had accomplished it by dancing around the suite like an idiot with Aja's dad.

"Jory, what would your brother do without you?" Aja asked me, again squeezing me tight.

"I dunno, but we'll never hafta find out."

"No." She shook her head just barely. "We won't."

"Jory!" the judge called for me.

I ran back to him and he showed me that he could still do the bump. I thought Aja's mother was going to pass out. That everyone was laughing was a very good thing.

THE church was filled with a sea of people that all stood as the bride posed with her father at the end of the aisle. She was breathtakingly beautiful, simple and chic, and the pride on her father's face made everyone smile. Dane's parents and siblings sat in the front row on the right, Aja's mother and grandparents on the left. Her extended family filled the first three pews, and after that were family friends and friends that were like family. Dane and Aja now shared a lot of the same people, those that would be spending their lives with them. The nearest and dearest of all were there with the groom on the stage as they waited for the bride to join them. Candace Jacobs stood, regal and stunning, head raised as she watched her best friend in the world walk toward the man she loved. All Aja's bridesmaids were perfection in their strapless pewter mermaid gowns—long, graceful lines with upswept hair, flawless, smooth skin, resembling delicate, graceful swans. They were luminous.

Jude was resplendent in his Armani tuxedo, and stood beside Dane proudly, looking as though he had stepped from the pages of a magazine. I had never seen him look better. Dane's friends had come together to stand at his side, all of them crisp and pressed, simply gorgeous, causing a stir when they had walked out to take their places on the stairs, descending down to me. I had worried at being included, not wanting to tarnish his moment being, as I was, without the same height, breadth of shoulder, or chest. Dane had not worried. He was less concerned with the perfect picture and more with his brother on stage with him. Aja, with the same desire, had drowned my objections.

And as I watched them, their hands entwined, speaking the words that would join them forever, I was thankful to be there, sharing their moment. It was humbling to be at the beginning of a new life, the one they would share together. I closed my eyes and breathed when they were presented. Mr. and Mrs. Harcourt, husband and wife. The picture etched in my mind forever of Aja lifting her head to receive his kiss, her eyes filled with him, his hands on her face, drawing her close as he bent to seal their lips together. Her arms went around his neck and he clutched her to his chest. They were stunning together, the picture of what love looked like. There was an eruption of applause when they parted and were introduced as husband and wife, a thundering sound that consumed the silence from seconds before. I could not imagine a more perfect moment.

THE reception was lavish, money that I could not even dream of having being spent to give Aja the day she had dreamed of since she was ten. There were six courses of food accompanied by wine and champagne and any beverage a guest could request. People were in awe of the orchestra and the full dance floor and the thousands of candles that cast a warm glow through the room. The first dance for the bride and groom was fluid precision and mesmerizing to watch. They went naturally together, blending seamlessly because they fit. When Aja danced with her father, no one did anything else but stare at the dashing man and his daughter. Dane floated across the floor with Aja's mother, and the same was true. Obvious from the way they all hugged afterwards that this was a union that had both their approval and support. Not surprising, as it was hard to imagine any parent not wanting Dane for a son-in-law.

I knew that Mrs. Reid had wanted the mother-son dance with Dane that he had given to Aja's mom. In the end, Dane had invited his birth parents, along with his sister and two brothers, to come to his wedding, but it was me, without benefit of blood, who stood at his side. I was the one with the same name; I was the one he hugged tight after the ceremony. I was the one his wife called her new brother and her parents saw as the entirety of the family that he brought to the marriage.

I listened to the speeches. I was moved by Candace's words to the bride, laughed at Jude's to Dane, and when Dane and Aja stood and thanked the crowd for coming and celebrating with them, I was so happy for them that I stood and gave them the standing ovation with everyone else. When all seats had been retaken, Dane took a breath as Aja leaned into his side. I waved to the photographer and he caught it before they moved apart. I had a feeling it was going to be one of the best of the night. Before anything else happened, Alex stood and directed all attention to the screen at the side of the dance floor. When the curtain drew back, the images and the music began the montage of Dane and Aja, their families, their friends, and their times before meeting and after. The last shot was of Dane on his knees in front of Aja as he held a rose up to her. They both looked at me, in an instant remembering the trip to Carmel and the picture I had snapped. I was pleased with the tears in the bride's eyes and Dane's clenched jaw as Aja's favorite Stevie Wonder song filled the room. The applause came like a roar as the guests went wild. Aja's mother was up and out of her seat in one fluid movement, rushing from her table to mine to take me in her arms. She understood at last why I had needed to go through her photo albums with her. When she let me go, I turned to the bride and groom and gestured for them to take the floor. Dane led his wife past me, his hand lingering on my cheek for a moment before he walked by.

After midnight the orchestra retired and the DJ came in to keep the dancing going until the wee hours of the morning. Jackets and bow ties were shed, high heels were discarded, and the serious dancing began. I would have joined in but there were small details that needed attention. I had to hand out the "swag," as Aja called it—going from table to table to personally make sure everyone got a keepsake from the wedding—coordinate with the catering manager, and arrange for all the disposable cameras on every table to be picked up.

When I felt the arms wrap around my waist, I turned in her embrace and found the bride.

"Come dance with me." She smiled.

I smiled back and we went together to the floor. Always, the two of us together could not remain serious for even a minute. In her dress and my tuxedo, it translated to an over-the-top waltz. There were spins and dips and we basically had everyone laughing and clapping and calling for an encore when we were done. She told me over and over how much she loved me, and when Dane came to part us, instead of taking her into his arms, he wrapped an arm around my neck and led me from the crowd back to the table.

We sat together, leaning forward, elbows on knees, talking quietly.

"So, it goes without saying, but still… I have the woman I love, the brother I love, friends I love… there is no one more blessed than me."

I looked into his dark gray eyes, saw the warmth there, and nodded. "I'm sorry Mr. and Mrs. Harcourt couldn't be here today to be with you."

He nodded. "They are."

"They would be so proud of you, Dane."

His eyes absorbed me. "My family, the people who mean the world to me… are Aja and you."

I smiled at him.

"I need you with me always."

I nodded. "Same here."

Hand on the back of my neck, he squeezed tight before he let go and stood. "Love you," he said as he walked away. He barely got it out.

I sat back and watched him go, and there came a sudden feeling of absolute peace. I let my head fall back, my eyes close, and just breathed.

"Take that."

I heard the click of a shutter and opened my eyes to find Aja hovering on the other side of the table with Candace and another bridesmaid. I glanced at the photographer before returning my gaze to the bride. "What're you doing?"

She let out a deep breath but said nothing.

"Jory," Candace said, drawing my attention. "Baby, I had no idea you were so pretty."

I chuckled and looked again to Aja.

"You are, you know."

"What?"

"Beautiful," she told me, motioning me over to her. "It's funny because you worried about standing up with the others, and the truth of the matter is that, Jory honey, you are the beauty of the bunch."

"You love me." I smiled wide, wrapping her up in my arms. "You're a little biased."

"I do love you, but that doesn't make you any less gorgeous."

I chuckled and squeezed her tight and she buried her face in my shoulder.

CANDACE bumped the bouquet into Jude's girlfriend's arms when Aja deliberately threw it at her an hour later, and the look on his face when he realized she had was priceless. The surge to the door to watch Dane and Aja leave in the Rolls Royce limousine pushed the wedding party from the front to the back. There was no way for any of us to even get close. Dane held up his hand for me and Aja blew me a kiss. I had my orders. In the three weeks they would be gone on their honeymoon, I had to coordinate movers. All her things, all his things needed to be in the new house in Highland Park by the time they got back. It was all me. I had promised to get it done, even with my busy schedule. My brother was counting on me.

People started to trickle out and the music changed to oldies that everyone could dance to and sing along with. I went and said good-bye to the Reids, gave Caleb a hug, and was surprised when Dane's father made a point of saying how much he appreciated me putting a photo of their family in the montage.

"Of course." I smiled at him.

He patted my back as I was squatting between his and his wife's chairs.

"Jory, you're such a good boy," Mrs. Reid sighed, the tears welling in her eyes. "Dane certainly picked a wonderful brother."

I leaned up and kissed her cheek and her hand stayed pressed to the side of my neck until she could breathe without crying. I thanked them all for coming, and Caleb told me how lucky Dane was to have me. I told him that I was the lucky one.

I worked my way slowly through the crowd, doing the last check, moving from table to table before I found the catering manager to thank him. Finally done, I changed back into jeans, a long-sleeved T-shirt, and Converse sneakers and headed toward the door. I weaved through the crowd to say my last good nights to the wedding party and quickly kissed and hugged all the women. I found Rick, Lance, and Alex sitting together and stopped at their table.

"You wanna wait and catch a ride, J?" Rick asked me.

I smiled at him and shook my head.

"What're we gonna do without him?" Jude asked as he walked up to lean on the back of one of the empty chairs. "He's the first to fall."

"We were always together," Rick said softly, looking around at all of us. "It's weird. It's like the end of an era or something."

"I feel like I should mourn my friend."

I smiled at them as I hooked myself up to my iPod.

"You think it's funny, J?" Rick asked me.

"No." I took a deep breath, stepping away from the table. "But you gotta grow up sometime."

"I'm not ready to get married," Rick insisted. "And I definitely don't want to be anybody's father."

"Okay," I agreed, my eyes slipping over each of them in turn. "You guys take it easy. I'll see ya round."

"Gimme a call, J," Rick insisted. "I'll kick your ass at some racquetball or something."

"Sure," I lied before I pivoted around and headed for the door.

It was nice that, outside, it was crisp but not cold, a beautiful night—or early morning now—for the first week of October. It was funny, but unlike his friends, I felt nothing but contentment for Dane and a sort of peacefulness for me. I had seen my brother through a milestone in his life. I was very grateful.

Chapter Two

THERE were a great many things I was good at. Picking out screws at the hardware store the following Sunday night was not one of them. On the phone with Chris, I told him for the millionth time why I should have stayed home with Dylan and he should have been the one looking in bins marked with fractions. They all looked the same to me.

"Don't be such a whiny bitch," he snapped at me.

I grunted.

"C'mon, boy, use that Y chromosome for something," he teased me.

"You're hilarious," I grunted at him. "What are you doing anyway?"

"I'm watching TV and making your dinner."

I chuckled. "Very domestic."

"Just hurry up. If I don't get the damn crib put together today, my life is gonna be hell."

"Fine, I'm coming."

"Don't forget the half-gallon of paint and the staple gun."

"I won't."

"And that blue tape that you use when you're painting."

"You mean the painter's tape?"

"Screw you, smart-ass," he grumbled as he hung up.

I was smiling as I turned and stepped into someone.

"Sorry."

"Jory."

My head snapped up and I was face to face with Sam Kage. He reached instantly to steady me, but I was faster and stepped back before he could.

His hands went deep into the pockets of his jeans. "Hey."

I stared up into his eyes.

He took a quick breath. "How are you?"

"Good. You?"

"Good," he nodded. The way he was looking at me, uncertain and curious at the same time.... Funny. "What's it been? Three years?"

"Somewhere around there," I agreed with him.

We were silent several minutes before he squinted at me. "You know, this might sound weird, but you don't seem that surprised to see me."

I smiled at him. "No. I saw you like a year ago at a street fair downtown."

"You did?"

I nodded. "Yeah, and right after that I did some work for your brother's firm and he caught me up on the events in your life." I spoke fast. "Not that I asked—he was just making conversation."

"Was he?"

"Yeah."

"Huh. So then you know I've been back for a while?"

"Yeah."

"But you never...."

I shrugged. "No, but you didn't either."

His eyes narrowed. "No... I didn't."

"Okay, so, I'll see ya." I smiled again, stepping around him.

Hand on my arm, he stopped me, shifting back into my path. "What is it you do now?"

"Oh," I said. "Well, I don't know if you remember my partner, Dylan Greer, but—"

"I remember her," he assured me.

"Yeah, well, she and I have our own business now. It's called Harvest Design, and we do logos, branding, company concept, identity, that sort of stuff."

"Sounds good. You like it?"

"I do. I mean, it's not like a million-dollar business or anything, but we do okay."

"Dane set you up?"

I was irritated instantly. He thought maybe I had borrowed the money from my brother to start my business because I was such a charity case? "Actually, no," I said curtly, realizing he was still holding onto my arm. "Dy and I took out a business loan together and had it paid off within three months of being open."

"That's great."

Like he cared. I rolled my shoulder and his hand dropped away.

"Sorry," he said under his breath.

I held up the tape and the plastic bag full of screws. "Well I gotta jet. I'm in the middle of a project, but it was—"

"What're you doing?"

"I'm helping Chris build a crib."

"Chris?"

"Dylan's husband."

"Oh," he nodded. "Is this their first child?"

"Yeah." I smiled. "We're finishing up the nursery today so I gotta get there."

"Sure," he agreed.

"I'll see ya." I sighed before turning and jogging away.

I didn't care if it looked like I was running. I wanted to put the distance between us. I had closed and locked the door on Sam Kage and the mess my life had been a long time ago. I wanted it to stay that way. Obviously he did as well. If he had wanted it any other way, the first time I saw him—after the time I had seen him in the hospital—would not have been as he strolled, laughing, with friends and a woman I didn't know. His life, I was sure, was as he wanted it.

"Jory."

I turned and there was a stranger.

"Hi." He smiled sheepishly. "Brandon Rossi. Do you remember me?"

I shook my head. "No, sorry."

He cleared his throat. "I was at Bigelow and Stein when you and your partner did the logo for their new community outreach program a few months ago."

"Oh, that's right." I smiled wide. "They ended up with the big scary clown on their logo. Bigelow and Stein, the home of the killer-clowns."

"You don't like clowns huh?"

"They're creepy as hell."

The smile made his eyes twinkle behind the wire-rimmed glasses. "Well, I for one didn't understand what you guys were saying about the tree until I saw it in print."

I nodded.

"C'mon," he chuckled, reaching out, giving me a pat on the shoulder. "I just didn't get it. I couldn't see it in my head like you could. I'm not an artist."

"Neither am I," I said adamantly, laughing at him. "But like I said, clowns creep me out."

He scowled at me, but the smile tugged at the corner of his mouth. "Don't make fun of me. I'm not at all creative. That's why I became a lawyer."

"Oh, I think the interpretation of the law is plenty creative."

"Sarcasm." he nodded. "Super."

He had warm eyes and a great smile that I didn't remember seeing before. "So what brings you to the hardware store on a Sunday night?"

He cleared his throat. "This confession will hopefully not scare you."

"Uh-oh," I teased him. "What?"

"I was across the street and I thought I saw you run in here. You're driving a really ugly green Jeep and—"

"The Jeep is not ugly," I defended Chris's pride and joy. "And it's not green. It's gunmetal. You just can't tell at night."

He snorted. "It's green. It's like greenish-brown and—"

"You know nothing about color."

"I do too."

"Oh yeah? What's your favorite color?"

"Black."

"Uh-huh."

"Yeah but not black as in the absence of all other color, but black as in lots of paint colors mixed up together to make black."

"I see," I said like he was nuts.

"You're not freaked out that I saw you and followed you in here?"

I shrugged. "You just wanted to say hi and give me a little crap about my ride. That's all very understandable and kinda nice."

He nodded and I watched his eyes slide over me. "You think maybe you'd like to grab some dinner with me?"

"I can't tonight," I said quickly. "I'm putting a crib together, but I will take a rain check if that'd be okay?"

"Yeah, that's okay." he smiled, pushing the glasses up on his nose. "Is dinner tomorrow all right, 'cause if it's not we can—"

"Tomorrow night's great," I cut him off. "Why don't you call me at work and we'll figure out where we wanna go."

His smile was huge. "That's perfect."

I nodded. "Okay, so I'll expect to hear from ya."

"You will. Thanks."

I squinted at him. "Thanks for what?"

He shrugged. "Saying yes."

I grinned at him and I heard his breath catch. It was very flattering, his reaction to me.

"I'll see ya soon."

"Yes, you will," he said from behind me as I walked away.

As I was pulling out of the parking lot, I saw Sam getting into an SUV with blacked-out windows that was even bigger than his old one, close to Hummer size. I stopped and called over to him. When he turned, I smiled wide. I just couldn't resist.

"Is it big enough, Detective?" I teased him.

The smile I got in return was the same crooked one I remembered. "No."

I nodded as I flipped on my radio and Fontella Bass came screaming out. "Did your mom tell you about her job?" I yelled over the music at him.

"Her what?"

I waved at him before I pulled out into the street and drove away.

Hours later I told Dylan all about seeing Sam and my date the following night with Brandon Rossi. She pretended to go into labor, which scared the hell out of both her husband and me. It was just plain evil. I was still harping on her about it as we walked into work together the next morning.

"I could do it again." She waggled her finger at me. "So don't push me, J."

"Do what again?" Sadie Kincaid asked me as she walked into our office with two coffee cups.

I loved our perky little receptionist form Kenosha, Wisconsin. She was funny and smart and had a scathing sense of humor that matched Dylan's perfectly.

"She pretended to go into labor again," I told her.

"Why?" She looked at Dylan. "Did the bakery only have one chocolate chip muffin?"

"Oh for crissakes," she snapped at us. "Fake your water breaking one time and you're branded for life."

We both laughed at her.

"Oh no," Sadie moaned suddenly, walking over to me. "What did you do to your beautiful hair?" she asked me as her fingers slid through it.

"I got—" I stopped and looked at Dylan. "What color is it again? Baby's Breath Blue?"

"Yeah."

I looked back at Sadie. "I got Baby's Breath Blue in it. I had to do the ceiling of the baby's nursery. Chris screwed up the corners."

"I see." She smiled at me and there was something different about the way she did it, almost loving. Dylan's sigh brought me back to her.

"What?" I asked her

"Nothing," she chuckled before she sighed deeply looking at me.

They were both being so weird. "What?"

"I said, nothing," Dylan snapped at me. "Let's look at the proofs we did for Trotter."

We spent most of the morning going over current accounts, and then our work ethic dissolved into office-chair races by ten. We took a cab to meet a new client for lunch, and on the way back Brandon called me. I told him I had been getting worried that he was blowing me off.

"No, Jory," he murmured into the phone. "That will never happen."

"You are very good for my ego, Mr. Rossi," I chuckled.

"I'm going to be good for you, period," he said flatly. "How about Brava at seven?"

"That sounds great. I'll meet ya there."

"Okay." Long exhale. "See ya there."

When I hung up, Dylan was scowling at me. "What?"

"Who is this guy?"

"I think we did the logo work for his old law firm. I got the idea he moved."

"From where? You didn't say where he was in the first place."

"He was at Bigelow and Stein."

"I don't remember anyone but Chelsea Connors from Bigelow and Stein."

"That's because you only remember the people who write us the check at the end of the job."

"So what?"

"That's not good business."

She only grunted as her frown darkened. "You need to let me meet this guy."

"Oh, I don't think so, crazy hormonal lady."

She growled at me.

"You see, that's what I'm talking about right there."

Dylan, Sadie, and I were coming back from our afternoon yogurt break when we turned the corner and found Sam Kage leaning against the locked glass door of our office. I shoved my half-eaten bowl at Dylan and sprinted down the hall toward him.

"Hey." I smiled quickly. "What're you doing here?"

"I talked to my mom and I talked to Michael." He nodded slowly. "It was interesting."

I heard Dylan and Sadie walking into the office behind me but I didn't turn and say hi to Sam. I didn't want to extend the visit.

"Jory?"

"Sorry. You said the talk was interesting, how so?" And I could have kicked myself for talking to him in the parking lot the day before. There were times when I blurted things out because I craved praise. I really was far too externally motivated for my own good. I liked to be told how great I was. Not all the time, but enough that it was a problem. In this instance, if I had kept my big mouth shut I would have not had the follow-up visit from Sam Kage.

"Hey."

I looked up, realizing that, as usual, my mind had been drifting. "Yeah?"

"You got my mom her job." He stared at me. "She's the host of Date Night Friday Night on Channel Ten."

And I had needed him to know it, which was just plain lame. "They wanted a concept from me and Dy and I gave them her."

He nodded. "She loves it, ya know."

"I know."

Every Friday night they screened a classic romantic movie, like *From Here To Eternity*, and Regina gave out tips on what to cook or what wine to serve. It was fun and she loved it. The reviews were really good. People loved her and made a point of staying home with their loved ones and watching her and the movie.

"I had no idea. I mean, I've been back a year and she never once told me that you're the reason she got the job in the first place."

"Why would she? It has nothing to do with you."

"She could have at least mentioned it."

I shrugged. What he found odd I saw nothing wrong with at all.

"She misses you. She said she hasn't seen you in almost six months."

"We're both busy," I commented. "I'll call her, though. Maybe we can grab lunch soon."

He nodded.

I walked farther down the hall, away from the office. When I turned to face him, he was closer than I thought, having followed right behind me. Before I could take a step back, he grabbed a handful of the front of my turtleneck sweater.

"What?"

He just looked at me as his hand dropped away.

I tried to keep things light. "What'd Michael say?"

"He said his firm hired you and that you and Dylan were phenomenal. He didn't really get a chance to talk to you alone much, and he was sorry about that."

"Me too."

He took a breath and stepped closer to me. "Can I talk to you?"

"We are talking."

"I mean I'd like to sit and… I just wanna sit, if that'd be all right."

I stepped back slowly. "I'm not trying to be a dick or anything, but why? I mean, what's the point?"

He cleared his throat. "You must have questions about what happened and—"

"No, I know what I need to." I forced a smile. "A couple of detectives came to see me when I got out of the hospital."

"Oh yeah? Tell me what you know."

I took another step back from him. "Well, I know you got to Maggie's place that night in time to save her and in time for her to tell you that she was a diversion to get you away from me."

He nodded.

"Except the detectives didn't know about you and me, of course, they just said that Dominic used her to get you over there."

His eyes didn't move from mine.

"There was actually no mention of our relationship in any official report."

He nodded. "No, there wasn't. If there had been, I would've been thrown off the force."

"So that was good."

"Yeah."

I cleared my throat. "So, how is Maggie?"

"I have no idea. I never saw her again after that night."

"She never called?"

"I have no idea. My life went a little bit crazy after that."

"Yours?" I arched a brow for him.

His smile was quick. "Okay, you win."

We were silent a moment, just our eyes locked together before I looked away.

"Hey." His voice so soft I barely heard it. "Look at me."

I was nervous and edgy and I had no idea why. Why the weird reaction to Sam Kage? "So I heard that Dominic went into protective custody and then into the witness protection program, like my friend Anna. Do you know where either of them are now?"

He shook his head. "No. I did hear that Anna got remarried, though, and she's expecting a child. They told me that when Dom went in. You should be happy for her."

I nodded. "I am. I really am."

"What are you thinking?"

My eyes flicked back to his.

"I can always tell when your brain's workin' overtime."

I smiled at him. "It's just weird… I used to think I'd always know Anna, just run into her from time to time, ya know? Funny how nothing turns out like you think it will."

"Yeah, it is."

"So you just came by to—"

He took a step closer to me. "If you saw me that day in the street, why didn't you come talk to me? That seems strange, that you didn't."

"You were with a lot of people and I didn't wanna intrude."

He nodded, easing forward again. "And you saw my mom, you saw Michael... why not ask about me?"

"They told me without me even having to ask." I sighed, leaning back against the wall to put distance between us.

"I guess they thought you cared. Sorry about that."

"I did care," I said softly. "I still do."

His eyes were locked on mine.

"They said you were working homicide now. You like it better than vice?"

He nodded.

"Good, I'm glad you're happy. I wish nothing but the best for you, Sam, you know that."

He exhaled slowly. "I do know that."

"So, see?" I grinned as I walked by him back toward the office. "Everything worked out."

"Hey."

I turned at the door.

"Would it kill you to eat with me?"

I smiled at his phrasing. "No. When?"

"How 'bout tonight?"

"Sorry, I've got a date. How's tomorrow?"

"Date, huh? With who, that guy from the hardware store yesterday?"

"Yeah. How'dya know?"

He shrugged. "I saw ya talking... I figured, 'cause the way he was lookin' at ya."

"Okay," I chuckled.

"So you're just dating right now? Nobody serious? I figured by now there'd be somebody serious."

"I'm picky." I smiled at him.

"What about Aaron Sutter?"

My head snapped up. "How do you know about Aaron?"

"I'm a detective," he said, giving me the crooked grin.

"That's right," I said over my pounding heart.

"So what happened there?"

I just looked at him, feeling my brows draw together.

"What?" He chuckled. "We're just shootin' the shit, right. Spit it out."

I shrugged. "He wanted me to move in and I thought it was too soon."

"You guys still friends?"

"No." I shook my head. "It was an all or nothing deal, and when I picked nothing that was pretty much it."

"I find that hard to believe."

"Some people stay gone, Sam," I teased him, turning to duck back inside my office.

"J."

I leaned back out.

"Can I get your number so I can give you a call?"

"Your mom's got it," I told him. "I'll see ya."

"Yep," he said as I closed the door behind me.

"Jory!" Dylan yelled for me from the other room. "Get your ass in here and explain to me why in the hell I just saw Sam Kage!"

"Who's Sam Kage?" Sadie asked me softly. "The hot guy in the hall?"

I waved my hands at Sadie to shut her up.

"My God, Jory, that man could do whatever he wanted to me."

"You're not helping," I whispered at her.

"Jory!" Dylan almost screamed. "Get in here now!"

I groaned and went to explain to my best friend why shrieking was no good for either her or her baby. I had to talk really fast to convince her that hurling her Rolodex at me wasn't an acceptable solution either.

Chapter Three

IT TURNED out that the place where Brandon had invited me to meet him was a block from his office. All the lawyers hung out there after work, swapping stories, getting drunk, and dancing badly. At the table I was sitting at with my date, they were talking about a case at work and I was drinking. There was not one attempt to include me in the conversation or segue into a new one. After a few more minutes ticked by, I pulled my phone out of my leather racing jacket and posed the question to Dylan, Evan, and my pal Tracy: Why was I attending happy hour instead of being out on a date?

When I looked up, the waiter was back and I ordered another Mojito. I slipped him a twenty and asked him to separate my bill from the rest of the table. My phone gave out a catcall whistle to let me know I had messages, and I found out that Evan thought he was showing me off because I was so pretty. Dylan thought he was the kind of guy that needed the approval of his friends on who he could or could not date, and my buddy Tracy said that he was out to make his friends jealous because I was not only hot but also talented and successful. I told Evan that he was on crack, sent Tracy the same, and agreed with Dylan. The man for me would not have cared what his friends thought, as Brandon so obviously did.

"Are you okay?" Brandon asked, leaning in beside me, hand on my leg. "Can I get you another drink?"

Maybe his friends had to see me first before he even decided whether to waste time taking me out to a real restaurant or not. I sent that back to Dylan.

"Jory?"

"I'm good." I sighed and saw that I had a picture from Dane of he and Aja on some beach, drinking. They were both smiling into the phone.

"Good."

It was rude to sit on my phone and text, so I sent Evan one last message asking him if he and Loudon wanted to have dinner with me on Friday. I got a yes back with a promise that Loudon had another friend for me to meet. I couldn't stifle the groan. The last guy Loudon McKay, Evan's partner of the last two years, had me meet ended up having a cat with some kind of weird skin disease. There was ointment that needed to be applied every four hours. I had run like hell.

"You all right?" one of Brandon's friends asked me.

"Super," I grunted, shoving my phone back into my jacket as it hung on my chair.

The music changed from whatever weird electronic down-tempo crap they had on to classic seventies. I was very happy. When I started singing along, I looked down the table and saw the girl at the other end signing along with me. The shy smile was very appealing. So were the dimples. And she knew all the words for "Rich Girl" by Hall and Oates, just like I did. I waved and she waved back.

I got up and walked down to the other end and squatted down beside her chair. She turned to look at me, one rusty-colored brow arched up high.

"Hiya."

She smiled slowly and her fingers brushed the hair out of my face. "Hiya back."

"Would you like to dance with me?"

"I would."

She took the hand I held out for her and I led her to the dance floor.

"I'm Jory." I smiled at her.

"Aubrey."

"Beautiful name, beautiful lady," I said as I dipped her low.

She didn't giggle, she laughed, and it was deep and throaty. "Right backatcha, pretty boy."

I chuckled as I brought her back up to her feet and we started to dance. It was fun, and she followed me as we moved around each other like idiots. Twenty minutes later she called a time-out for alcohol and I followed her back to the bar. It quickly became a routine: dance a little, drink a little, repeat again and again. We both lost track of how many we had. I bought a round, then her, then me again... and there was still more dancing until we took a long break to sit down and put our numbers in each other's phones.

The dance music came pounding out of the speakers and we went back to the floor. It was fun and I didn't care what had gotten me there anymore, I was just looking forward to getting to know my new friend. I saw us shopping for matching sequin tube tops or something equally ridiculous. When I spun her around and dipped her in my arms, she laughed so hard I thought she was going to pee.

When we were both tired out and liquored up, we decide to sit for a while. I had her in my lap when her date, Adam Myers, came and grabbed her arm. She yanked out of his grasp and when he did it again, harder, she lost her balance, slipping off my legs to the floor.

"What the hell are you doing?" I yelled at him, kneeling down on the ground to make sure she was okay.

"She is embarrassing me, and you are embarrassing Bran. God, do you guys not understand that this is where everyone at our firm hangs out after work? From the associates on up, this is where we go."

I looked at Aubrey, and she shrugged.

She pointed back at him over her shoulder. "I just finally gave in because this guy's been asking me out for a month and half."

"Are you okay?" I said, helping her to her feet, checking her over, realizing she looked no worse for wear. It was more a bump than a fall.

"Yes, honey," she sighed, smiling at me, standing up, and straightening her wrap shirt.

Straight woman, gay man... we were a match made in heaven.

"Where do you work?" I smiled back at her.

"At a company called Barrington. We do—"

"I used to work at Barrington." I smiled wider. "But I left to start my own business. I run Harvest Design now. I work with—"

"Oh shit." She laughed and launched herself at me. "Jory, I'm Abe."

I pushed her back so I could look at her. "*You're* Abe Flanagan, who's coming to help me while Dylan's out on maternity leave?"

"Yes." She nodded, laughing, grabbing me again and hugging me tight. "Holy shit, the world is just a teeny little place."

I nodded slowly. "Yeah, it is. C'mon, let's go get some food."

"I'll get my bag," she said, pulling away.

But as she turned, Adam barred her path.

"What?"

"One of the partners at my firm is on his way over here and you need to wait and meet him."

"Like hell I do," she said like he was high.

"Jory."

Brandon grabbed a handful of the front of my shirt. "Could you not try and completely embarrass me?"

"Shouldn't have invited me if you didn't wanna be embarrassed," I told him. "You can't take poor white trash like me and Abe anywhere."

Aubrey giggled, ending with a snort, which made me start laughing.

"Shit," he whined, looking at Adam as Rick Jenner stepped in front of all of us.

I instantly understood that Brandon Rossi and Adam Meyers worked at Riley, Jenner, Knox, and Pomeroy. They were petrified, and Rick wasn't even looking at them. The twinkling green eyes were all for me.

"Hey." I smiled at him.

"Hey," he grinned back, completely at ease. "What brings you to the lawyer haunt, J?"

"I brought my friend Abe."

He turned his attention to Aubrey Flanagan and his smile widened. "Well, hello there, Abe."

She smiled wide at him. "Hello back, um...."

"Richard Jenner, Attorney At Law," he said fast, making his voice deep and serious.

"I hate lawyers," she baited him, again arching that gorgeous copper-colored brow.

"Really." He smiled, and it was wicked as he took her hand and drew it through his arm.

"Yes, really," she breathed as he eased her close to him.

"I can fix that."

Her eyes narrowed and I saw his jaw clench.

"Call me Rick."

"Okay," she said, her eyes absorbing him, the thick black hair, the cleft chin, the laugh lines in the corner of his sparkling emerald eyes. "How do you know Jory, Rick?"

"He's the little brother of one of my best friends in the world."

Adam and Brandon went absolutely ashen, and I bit my lip so I wouldn't smile.

"How do you know Jory, Abe?" he asked, vastly amused, just staring at her, riveted.

"We work together," she said, her eyes meeting mine.

"That's right," I assured him.

"Well, you guys want to come with me and get some dinner?"

"Actually," I said quickly." I've gotta go, but Abe is free."

"Well, not free," she teased me. "But dinner sounds like heaven."

Rick's smile was warm and he was obviously taken with her... with the energy that you could feel, taste in the back of your throat, the passion that radiated off her and the glowing smile that lit her face. The girl just had it. That *it* factor, where she was so animated, so there in the moment that you just knew that if you missed her it would be a shame. I was crazy about her already. I loved her hair—long and curly, the color of copper, red and gold at the same time, completely wild—and her freckled skin and smiling rosebud mouth. When she took the lacquered chopsticks out of her purse and put up her tresses, pieces tumbled out, stray curls falling down the back of her long neck and forward into her lovely pale blue eyes. Rick reached out and twisted a piece around her ear. He was drowning in her after only moments.

"I should cut it all off," she sighed, looking down and then quickly back up into his eyes. The long lashes looked like they had been dipped in gold.

"Oh no," he assured her, taking her hand again, this time slipping his fingers between hers, keeping her close to him. "Never."

She grunted. "We'll see, Mr. Jenner."

"Yes, we will," he said quickly, pointing at me. "You're good?"

"Yessir," I said quickly, because I knew he wanted out. He was desperate to get the lady alone. Take her to dinner so she could see what a gentleman he was. Have her ride in his car so she could see he had money. Hopefully show her his house so she could see the life he could provide. At twenty-six, I knew love at first sight when I saw it. Cupid had just hit Rick Jenner with a Mack truck. It was funny that it usually happened that way. Some guy went along dating for years, a real catch—like my brother Dane, the eligible bachelor of the century—then suddenly he met the girl, the one that would be the mother of his children, and usually within six months they were married. Guys went from player to dad in like a year after meeting *the one*.

As I watched Rick walk out with Aubrey Flanagan on his arm, talking a mile a minute to her, I had an overwhelming feeling of accomplishment. It had nothing whatsoever to do with me, in actuality Adam had been the instrument of love and not me, but still, I felt good. I had introduced them after all. It was my lap she had been in.

"Jory."

I looked up at Adam. "Hey, I—"

He clapped my shoulder hard. "Thanks, man, you saved my life."

Funny that he had no idea how amazing the woman was that he had just let walk out of his life.

"No problem," I said softly, pulling on my jacket, turning to leave.

"Jory."

I let Brandon walk around in front of me.

"What a screwed-up evening. I'm so sorry for—"

I shook my head, pulling out my phone as it rang for the second time. "Don't worry about it." I smiled at him. "Thanks for inviting me. I'll see ya round." I finished before I stepped around him and answered my phone. "Hello?"

"J?"

"Oh hey, Sam," I said like I talked to him every day. Even after three years apart, I knew the man's voice as well as my own.

"Sorry to bother you while you're on your date and all but—"

"No, it's okay. I'm done."

"You're done? Whaddya mean you're—"

"It's a long story."

"I'd love to hear it."

I grunted instead.

"So then, you're doing what now?"

"You mean tonight?"

"Yeah."

"Nothing."

Quick breath. "Okay, so can I take you to eat?"

"Sure, but I'll buy. What do you want?"

"Where are you?"

"I'm downtown. You want just like a sandwich or something?"

"That sounds great. I'll just change and—"

"You're at home?"

"Yeah."

"Where's that now?"

"Don't laugh but it's in the exact same place."

"Oh, that's right, Jen told me that."

"Jen?"

"Yeah." I smiled. "You know… your sister, Jen."

"You still talk to Jen?"

"Off and on. Rachel too."

"Jesus Christ. Nobody says shit to me about anything."

"Why're you mad?"

"'Cause I just… I wanna know when somebody in my family sees you."

"Why?"

"I just do!"

That made no sense. "But it has nothing to do with you."

"It has everything to do with me! My whole family's still crazy about you."

"I wouldn't say they're—"

"I would. Shit. Nobody—"

"Did you know that Dane and your dad and Michael golf together?"

There was a long pause. "I'm sorry?"

I chuckled.

"What'd you say?"

"I said your dad and Michael and Dane golf together. Did you know that?"

"No, I—"

"Yeah. Just every three months or so."

"For crissakes, J, nobody tells me anything!"

"Why would they?"

"Why would they what—mention that they all see you and I'm the only one who doesn't? Oh I dunno, lemme think."

I had to laugh. He was so indignant. "You were gone a long time, Sam, we all got used to you not being around."

"But I've been back more than a year and nobody said shit to me."

"They probably didn't want to make your new girlfriend uncomfortable by talking about me."

There was a quick pause. "What?"

"Oh no, I'm sorry. Your wife then."

"What the hell are you talking about?"

"I saw a woman with you that day at the street fair. I assumed while you were undercover you probably met someone and—"

"You know you watch way too much TV. Undercover doesn't work like that."

"Huh."

He chuckled and it was a warm sound. "You sound disappointed."

"I'm a romantic at heart."

"I know," he sighed heavily. "Lemme come get you."

"So who was the girl?" I asked before I could stop myself.

"I dunno—probably one of Jen or Rachel's friends... why?"

"No reason."

"You sure?"

I would not be drawn back in. "You know what, Sam, maybe this isn't such a—"

"No, it's fine. C'mon."

"You don't get to decide what's fine or not, Sam," I said fast.

"No, I know," he sighed. "But just c'mon."

I was silent, thinking about what I should do.

"Please, J. Just eat with me."

What could it hurt? "Okay, fine. Do you know Carmine's?"

"Yeah, sure."

"Great. I can meet you there in fifteen minutes?"

"I'm leaving now," he said and hung up on me.

I walked to the curb as I heard my name called. Brandon Rossi was jogging toward me as I opened the door of the cab.

"Jory, please don't—"

"Thanks again for inviting me," I indulged him as I got in the cab and closed the door behind me. I didn't look back.

I WAS leaning against the wall to the side of the hostess station, where I had checked in, when I felt a hand on the small of my back. It was a very familiar place to touch, and when I looked up from texting Dylan I found Sam.

"Hey."

"Hey." He smiled back, gesturing me close.

"What?"

"I dunno, what do I hafta do to get a proper greeting from an old friend?"

He was right. I pocketed my phone and stepped into him, reaching up to wrap my arms around his neck. I squeezed tight and, instantly, he hugged me back. He buried his face in my shoulder, his arms holding me close, pressing me against him, and he breathed in deeply before the long exhale.

"It's good to see you, J."

I hugged him because I used to love him and he felt good in my arms.

"I missed you," he said, and the shiver ran through him fast.

Better to gargle glass than respond.

He pulled back and looked down at me, into my eyes. "How are you?"

"I'm fine," I said, stepping free.

"You look good," he said to the floor.

"Yeah?" I fished because he was not one to dish out compliments.

"Yeah," he said under his breath, his eyes flicking up to mine. "Really good."

"And you look tired," I passed judgment as I looked him over. "Maybe we should do this another—"

"No," he cut me off, his brows furrowing.

"Have you been sleeping?"

"I wanna sleep with you," he said slowly, his voice deep and gravelly. "Come home with me."

It took me a second to respond, as my heart was in my throat, but I forced a dry chuckle. "Just like that?"

"Could we maybe have a summit meeting tomorrow? Right now I'm beat, I want you to come home with me and lie down so I can lie down with you."

I watched his eyes, heavy-lidded, as he stared down at me.

"I swear to God I haven't really slept since I saw you last."

"I thought you would have...." I trailed off because I had started speaking without thinking.

He let out a deep breath as I took a step back. "Would have what?"

I shook my head.

"Talk to me."

"I just figured you'd go back to your life."

"Meaning what?"

I cleared my throat. "C'mon, let's eat." I smiled, gesturing to the hostess who was trying to get my attention. "I'm starving and I had a lot to drink."

"You did?"

"Oh hell, yeah."

"Tell me all about your date."

I smiled as we followed the hostess to the table. We were in a booth toward the back, and I wondered if Sam had requested that or if she was just trying to tuck us away because we looked like trouble.

"So talk," he ordered me, sliding over until his knee bumped mine.

I chuckled as I recounted my adventures at Brava.

"The girl sounds nice."

"She's the kind of girl you need."

"I got what I need right here," he said flatly.

I tipped my head to look at him. "It's been a long time, Sam."

"So what? You told me there was nobody special."

"Maybe I lied."

"Well, I don't see a ring on your finger."

Ridiculous argument. "Gay men don't wear—"

"Oh the fuck they don't," he dismissed me. "Who says what they can or can't do?"

"Sam—"

"You're gonna wear a ring for me."

I rolled my eyes and turned my attention to the waiter. I ordered a club sandwich and soup and Sam ended up having the same. Alone again, Sam slid closer, putting an arm around the back of the seat.

"Listen, J," he began, the deep sigh making me smile. "What?"

"Nothing."

"What? C'mon."

"I just never in my life thought I would see you again."

"That is funny," he squinted at me. "'Cause I never once doubted that you would."

I was silent before I went at him from another angle. "Sam, isn't your life good right now?"

"Yes, it is."

"See, so why you wanna—"

"Only you give me this much crap," he cut me off. "You're the only one who fights with me."

"We're not fighting."

"But you're trying to, and you're the only one I know who does."

I squinted at him.

His deep rumbling laughter, "I don't scare you at all, huh, J?"

"Are you kidding?" I scoffed.

His big lopsided grin then, eyes twinkling as he stared at me. "I scare a lot of people, J."

"Okay," I indulged him.

"Hey."

"What?"

"You cut your hair."

"Yeah." I smiled at him. "Long time ago." My hair, that used to hit my shoulders, was now short like everyone else's. It was still longer on top, strands fell into my eyes, got tangled in my lashes occasionally, but it was not the mane it had been.

He made a noise in the back of his throat and I looked at him.

"Sam?"

"It's just good to see you," he said, his voice deep and low, his eyes so very dark.

I couldn't speak around the lump in my throat.

He chuckled softly. "Nothing to say?"

"It's good to see you too."

He reached out and ran the back of his fingers up and down my throat, stroking over my skin so lightly. "Eat your food so I can take you home."

"You don't know where I live," I teased him, trying to steady my pounding heart. The familiar response to Sam Kage flared through me.

"No, baby." He exhaled. "You're coming home with me."

"Sam—"

"J—"

"I'm not your baby," I assured him, brushing his hand away. "I'm nobody's—"

"You belong to me," he said flatly. "Always have, always will. Deal with it."

I was silent.

"Speak... you look like you've got—"

"Screw you, Sam. You left me. You left, period, and it's fine 'cause I understand why ya did but... make no mistake, I will never step back into that shit with you again. I'm done."

"Is that right?"

"Yeah, that's right. In fact, I have a date on Friday."

He nodded. "Huh."

"You don't get to decide my life for me, Sam."

"Okay." He grinned quickly. "Don't flip out right here. Eat your food."

I was stunned and it probably showed on my face. He was being so reasonable, and if I was being honest, I was disappointed that he wasn't going to fight with me, for me. It was for the best, but still, it stung that he would give up so easily.

He made the conversation I was used to providing, telling me about his family and what it had been like to come home after two years away to his old life. He had friends to reconnect with and a job to relearn and all that had taken time. He wanted to focus on all his external priorities before he came for me.

"I'm sorry, what?" My thoughts had been drifting but I had caught the last part.

"You heard me, J."

"You're actually sitting there telling me that you want us to get back together."

"Yep. I told you what I wanted before we sat down."

"Yeah, but I thought you were just playin' around."

"No, you didn't, but you're pretending you did."

He still knew me well. "Okay, but just a second ago you… I thought you were letting this go?"

"When did I say that?"

"But—"

"I wanted to wait to see you until I had my life back. Now I do, so here I am."

I squinted at him. "Life doesn't wait until you're ready, Sam. You—"

"Are you done?"

"No, I'm not done. You think you can just—"

"With your food, dumb-ass," he cut me off.

"Oh… yeah." I deflated, reaching into my jacket for my wallet.

"I invited you, I'll buy." He smiled at me.

"No, I said I would. I'm not a charity—"

"Anything to fight me," he teased me, leaning forward to kiss the side of my neck.

I tried to slide away from him, but his hand under the table, like a vice on my thigh, kept me where I was. His lips on my skin were scalding. When my eyes flicked to his, he smiled lazily. It was very sexy.

"Three years look good on you, J."

To keep from responding to him, I tried to provoke him. "You don't want me, Sam. You're just like all those other guys that just wanna get laid."

"Is that all I want?"

"Yeah."

"Huh."

I shrugged.

"It's lucky you're pretty because you're not real bright."

I stood up, pulled two twenties out and dropped them on the table. "I'll see ya."

He coughed and I looked at him. The smile had fallen out of his eyes.

"I can get home my—"

His voice was low and flat. "So you know, if you try one of your usual dramatic exits, I will grab you, throw you over my shoulder, and take you right outta here."

I just stared at him.

"If you don't want to be the floor show that they'll be talking about for years, I suggest you stand there and wait for me and walk out of here like a grown-up."

I crossed my arms and waited.

He smiled up at me. "You're cute when you pout."

I smirked at him, and the snort of laughter almost made me smile back.

Outside the front door I realized I was faced with his monster car, the SUV from hell.

"Okay," I sighed, shoving my hands down into my pockets. "So it was good to see ya."

His scowl could not have been any darker. "I was serious inside. I wanna take you home."

I shrugged. "Well I was serious too, so… no."

We stood there staring at each other, and when he finally took a step toward me I took one back.

"I can make you if I want."

"Sure," I agreed.

The muscles in his jaw corded tight. "Can I just say something before you walk away?"

I stared into the smoky blue eyes and he stepped closer, his hand lifting, going to my chest and settling over my heart.

"I want you, only you, and not just for tonight."

I was silent.

"Did you hear me?" he asked, his hand sliding around behind my neck as he stepped in against me, staring down into my eyes. "I want you."

"But—"

"I did what I said I would. I made sure you were safe and then I came back. I figured out what I can do, what I can't, and it took a while longer than I thought."

"Sam, you—"

"But now I'm done. I've got everything I want except the one most important… I want you."

"But you've been back, Sam, and you never came to—"

"I came as soon as I could."

"Bullshit." I tried to step back, but even though I was bigger than I used to be, more muscular, I was still no match for his strength. His grip was like steel and he had me.

"I did. Everything had to be settled and now it is."

I shook my head, tried to pull back again.

"And I'm lucky 'cause that guy Aaron pushed too fast too hard and you ran."

My head snapped up. "That was just 'cause it was—"

"Don't say it was too soon, J, 'cause we both know you've got no problem with too soon when you know something's right. You didn't love him, so you didn't move in. Simple as that."

I just stared up into his eyes.

"You know who's right for you and who isn't."

"Sam, you can't just come back after three years, tell me you're ready for your life to start, and have me back. It doesn't work like that. I'm different, you're different... just let it go."

He raised his other hand, cupping my face as he stared down into my eyes. "I can't. I want you back... I need you."

I lifted my head out of his hands and stepped away from him. "There's no way. You almost...." And I was going to confess that he had almost killed me when he left. I had been so desolate at being abandoned. Only Dane and my friends and work had moved me through all the heartbreak and the loneliness and the grief. I could never go back there and open myself back up to the pain. I was stupid but I wasn't a masochist.

"I almost what?" he pressed me, reaching out for my jacket only to have me step just beyond his fingertips. "Tell me."

"Nothing," I sighed, trying so hard to smile even though my eyes were blurring. "I'll see ya."

I turned and found I could breathe again as I started down the street.

"J!"

I swung back around to look at him. He was standing there, hands in his pockets, his jaw clenched, just staring at me.

"Can I call ya?"

I nodded, because words were beyond me.

"Okay." He smiled and I turned away before he could say another word.

It took everything I had not to run.

WHEN I was halfway home my phone rang, and I smiled when I checked the display.

"Hey." I was happy to hear from him because I'd thought I never would again. It had been six months of silence that I thought was permanent.

"Jory," he breathed.

"When did you get back?" I asked, keeping it light.

"Couple days ago."

"How was Hong Kong?" I asked Aaron Sutter. "Did the hotel go up on time?"

"Of course," he said, and I could hear the smile in his voice. "This is me we're talking about."

"Sorry." I chuckled. "So tell me everything."

"How about I tell you over a late dinner?"

I hesitated. "Really?"

"Yes."

"But I... I thought you didn't wanna see me."

The cough was barely one. "Listen, I did a lot of thinking while I was away and I realize that you were right... there's no reason in the world for us not to be friends. Just because we want different things shouldn't make us strangers. We spent a year and half together, why would we just throw all that away? It makes no sense."

"This was my argument," I reminded him.

"I know, and I'm sorry for the things I said. I just… I've never asked anyone to live with me before, and I was certain that you would say yes. The no never even entered my thought process."

I sighed deeply. "I'm sorry too. I wish I could've said yes."

"Well, so you know, there's not a time limit on the offer."

"But you said—"

"I know what I said. I'm telling you now, if you change your mind… please tell me. I would love to know if you do."

"You sure?"

"Absolutely."

"Okay."

Long exhale of breath from him. "Good… now, when will you eat with me?"

"When do you want me?"

"Tonight. I have a new chef who makes a wonderful risotto."

"No, I ate already. How 'bout tomorrow?"

"How about now?" he chuckled. "I'll eat and you can tell me all about Dane's wedding. I'll meet you at Serenade instead."

"That's a cocktail bar, Sutter. What're you gonna eat?"

"Are you kidding? They make great steaks there, J. Don't worry, I'll eat."

I let out a quick breath. "Okay."

"Yes? You'll meet me?"

"Sure."

"That's great. I thought I'd have to fight with you."

"No, I'm all argued out."

"Why? What happened?"

"Do you remember me telling you about the police detective I was involved with a while back?"

"The one you were in love with? The one who left you?"

I stifled a groan. The one who left me sounded bad. "Yeah, that's him."

"Yes, I remember."

"Well, he's back and I saw him tonight and—"

"And he wants you back."

"Yeah."

"Of course he does. Makes sense."

"Does it?"

"Yes," he answered. "So can you be there in half an hour?"

"Probably sooner, I'm still downtown."

"Great, I'll see you in twenty minutes."

"Yep," I said and hung up my phone. I was surprised when it rang again. "Hello?"

"Hey."

"Sam. What—"

"Do you still drink tea?"

Weird question. "Yeah."

"Good. How 'bout I make you some?"

"When?"

"Now."

"I can't. I'm meeting Aaron. We're gonna catch up."

"You left me to go see him?"

"No. I left you because there was nothing else to say. Aaron just got back from Hong Kong and wants to hang out. It'll be good. I could use the diversion."

"'Cause of me."

"That's right."

"I see."

"I'll talk to you—"

"Don't hang up." He cleared his throat.

"Why? What's the point of—"

"I don't want you to go sit and talk to Aaron Sutter. If you're gonna sit with somebody, sit with me. I'm the one who wants to talk to you."

"Yeah, but Aaron just wants to—"

"What happened to some people stay gone?"

"I guess, in my life, everybody comes back."

He laughed, and the sound buzzed right through me.

"So I'll—"

"Listen, lemme see you tomorrow, all right?"

"No. How 'bout Saturday or Sunday?"

"How 'bout Thursday instead?"

"Sam."

"C'mon."

"Sam, I'm on my way to see—"

"Yeah, I know. Just call me when you're done talking to him, all right?"

"No, that'll be like midnight or—"

"I care. Just call."

"Sam—"

"Where are you going? His place?"

"No, to Serenade," I told him before I thought about it.

"I know where that is."

"Yeah, but don't—"

"Call me soon so I don't show up, all right?"

"Oh for crissakes, Sam, you can't just—"

He cut me off when he hung up. It was just plain rude. I tried to stop scowling before I got to the bar.

When I turned the corner onto the street where Serenade was, I saw Aaron leaning against the side of his black Mercedes in his charcoal cashmere topcoat, looking like some ad in a magazine. Immediately when he saw me I got the smile that lit his eyes. As always, I noticed the warmth in them. Aaron's beauty came not as much from physical appearance as from what radiated from the inside. He was the kind of person people instantly liked, instantly wanted to touch and be close to. He brought it out in everyone, and it was from there that my initial attraction had sprung.

I had met Aaron Sutter when Dylan and I had done some corporate identity work for his company. They wanted to create a logo that embodied their commitment to the culture of the area they built in, their commitment to the environment, as well as speaking to the ideal of their mission statement, which was their constant striving for excellence. Dylan and I had been unable to come up with something that hit every concept they were shooting for, but Aaron had insisted on taking us to lunch anyway. Later that same day he came by the office when I was alone and asked me to dinner. I turned him down flat. I did not mix my business and personal life. He told me it was all right since I didn't work for him, but I held my ground and gave him the second no of the night. When he left, I was relieved. I was not in a place where I could date anyone. I wasn't ready to do any more than I was—going out and going home with a different stranger every night. Having returned to the club scene six months after Sam left, I was in an endless cycle of drinking and one-night stands. I was toxic, and it wasn't fair to subject a nice guy like Aaron Sutter to that.

Aaron might have been nice, but he was also relentless. I got constant calls from him. Would I like to go to the ballet with him? Would I like to go to a baseball game with him? There was an art exhibit opening, there was a new club opening, a new restaurant downtown… would I go with him? The answer was always no, but he was so gracious about it, never angry, never resentful, only hopeful each and every time he asked, promising me that surely next time I would say yes. I told him he should concentrate on someone worth his time and he assured me I was.

I saw him at a club on Halloween, dressed like a gladiator, and I was falling down drunk. I stumbled over to say hi and he ended up taking my hand and sitting me down in his lap. It had to have looked funny since I was dressed like a pirate, but his hand tangled in my hair felt good, as did the arm around my waist anchoring me to him.

"Please, Jory," he said, rubbing his cheek against mine. "Let me take you somewhere, anywhere. I'll take you to the movies and buy you popcorn. It doesn't matter, I just want to spend some time with you. Please. I'll do anything."

And I gave in, because he was so honest and Sam wasn't coming back. A year had come and gone without a word. I was holding onto a dream and I was lonely and depressed and just a wreck. Dane was on me constantly to start dating instead of just sleeping around. His new girlfriend, Aja, had lots of prospects she was dying to set me up with. It was time, and I took the plunge. Five dates later when I realized that it was me who was going to have to make the move to get us in bed, I invited him over for spaghetti out of a jar and lots of red wine. He told me how great everything was and I rolled my eyes. The man had his own chef and my food was good? It was ridiculous, but the way he watched me, never took his eyes off me, told me all I needed to know.

When we were sitting on the couch watching a movie, I eased him over against me so his back was pressed to my chest. His sigh was long and made me smile. When I slid my hand down his abdomen to his belt buckle, I felt a slight tremble run through him. When I undid first his belt and then the snap of his jeans, he scooted up higher so I could reach him more easily. The zipper went next, and then my hand slipped under the waistband of his briefs to find him already hard. He bucked up into my hand, and his head went back on my shoulder.

"Jory," he moaned out, kissing over my jaw as my hand moved on him. "Please, can I get in your bed?"

"Later," I said, shoving him off me. "First we see what you think of my blow job."

"What?"

I liked that his voice went out on him, and I liked how he could not keep his eyes off me. The panting and writhing that followed, how he begged me... I liked all that too. When he cried my name and had to have me in his arms, all that was good and nice... it just didn't satisfy me.

When I made love to Aaron Sutter, I never had to clench my jaw so I wouldn't scream his name. I tried not to draw a comparison to Sam Kage. It was pleasant enough and Aaron was a very considerate lover. I had appreciated him and when he told me that none of his lovers ever had any complaints, I believed him. Such an attentive, compassionate man could never be called bad in bed. The thing was, I craved dominance and strength. I craved Sam. I wasn't careful or inhibited when I was in bed with Detective Kage, I was myself, and he knew the things he could do to me. So, whereas Aaron would have worried if he were too rough, not wanting to ever hurt me, Sam knew better.

"Jory?"

I looked up and realized that my mind had been drifting.

"Come here."

I jogged over to him and didn't stop, lunging at him instead, wrapping him in my arms.

"Oh." He laughed softly, his face buried in the side of my neck. "Somebody missed me."

Turning my head to lay it on his shoulder, I let out a deep breath. I felt his hand on my hair, felt the other clutching my back, the way he was trying to press against me, and I understood instantly that this was a huge mistake. I pushed out of his arms.

"What?" He looked at me, his hand on my arm. "Why are you—"

"Let's go in," I suggested, taking a step toward the entrance.

"Sure." He forced a smile, his hand sliding down my back.

The lounge was not as crowded as usual since it was Monday night, but it wouldn't have mattered if it were. Aaron Sutter was given the same preferential treatment as Dane or Rick Jenner. Money bought clout, and if you were a patron of a certain place, when they saw you they moved fast to take care of you. The manager was fast getting to us and we were seated at a private table toward the fireplace, away from the noise of the bar. I ordered a Jack and Coke and sat there staring out the window as Aaron spoke to the waiter.

"Hey."

I looked back at him resting his chin on his hand, just absorbing me with his eyes.

"It's a nice jacket."

"Thanks."

"Why don't you take it off and stay a while?"

I smiled and shed the racing jacket, hanging it behind my chair.

"You look good," he said softly.

"You too."

He breathed in deeply. "So tell me all about Dane's big day, any juicy stories? Any women charging down the aisle after him, screaming about not holding their peace?"

I smiled wide. "No, nothing like that."

"I'm sure Aja was stunning."

"Yeah, she was."

"All right then, speak."

I told him all about the wedding and the reception and had his eyes watering with laughter over Dane's groomsmen and the sorry state they were in. I drank and he listened and ate. I told him about the date I had been on with Brandon Rossi earlier in the evening, and all about Aubrey Flanagan and Rick Jenner. I listened when he told me his war stories from Hong Kong, and how badly he had mangled Mandarin while he'd been there. He had studied the language for a year before going, but in actual practice, he stunk. I was laughing as I listened to him tell me about the food he'd ended up eating because he got his nouns mixed up.

"I really missed you," he said, suddenly serious, his eyes locked on mine.

I smiled at him because it was a nice thing to say.

"Did you miss me at all?"

"Yes," I said, because I had missed him—just not like he wanted.

"Come home with me."

My eyes flicked to my empty highball glass instead of his face.

"Jory."

I finally looked across the table into the clear, turquoise blue eyes.

"You're a mess," he chuckled. "Let me take care of you."

"I'm good," I assured him.

"You drink too much, Jory."

It was an old argument that he was never going to win. I knew my tolerance, even though no one else seemed to believe me. At Dane's wedding, for instance, I had one glass of champagne with the toast and that was all I'd had for the entire night. People mistook me for an alcoholic, and that wasn't the case.

"And I don't want you to end up in some guy's bed because you fell in."

This was what our last conversation had degenerated into when we broke up. He was sure I would end up in the gutter without him, as that was, apparently, where I'd been when he found me. He had wanted to know why I didn't want my life to be good, why I couldn't let myself have nice things, and why I couldn't leave the self-destructive party-boy behind. It was time to grow up and start a life with someone. Time to make a commitment to being a boyfriend and a partner… I wouldn't be young forever. Drinking until all hours of the morning, sleeping with nameless men, how was that good for me? He was offering me a life people would kill for, why would I ever turn him down?

"Jory?"

I groaned, grabbed my leather jacket, and stood up. "This was a mistake, Aaron. It's too new. Maybe we can hang out down the road, but not right now."

"I haven't seen you in months."

"Maybe it needs to be a year," I sighed, pulling out my wallet, looking for the bill I needed.

"What are you—wait." He put up his hand as I tossed a twenty on the table. "Just wait. I'll drive you, just give me a—"

"Aaron!"

And I used to hate the way his friends always just showed up and interrupted us, but at that moment they were a godsend.

"Jory." His friend Todd reached for my arm. "I thought you were history, man. I thought Aaron finally tossed the trash out."

Oh! That was so my cue to walk out. "He did, Todd," I slapped his arm hard, turned and walked out of the lounge.

Jacket on, I stood outside for a second and breathed in deeply. What a weird, fragmented night. I needed to go home and go to bed and start fresh the next morning. Everything tilted for a second and then my head cleared. I felt the hand on my shoulder before Aaron stepped around in front of me.

"What?" I sighed, rolling my shoulder so his hand fell off.

"Jory," he grabbed my face in his hands, "I want to take you home with me. Let me."

"After all that? After what you said?"

"What did I say?"

And I realized he hadn't said much of anything; it was just a record that played over and over in my head. He thought of me one way, and it was all he saw and all I heard.

"You don't want me, Aaron," I sighed deeply. "You don't even see me."

"Jory," he said, leaning in to kiss me.

I pushed him back and stepped away. "Let's just take a break, all right. You need to find yourself a nice boy that needs a home. I've already got one."

"Jory, I just want to take care of you."

"That's not what I need."

"You don't know what you need!" he shouted at me. "You're so hung up on me having money that you can't see what I'm really offering you."

I stared directly into his eyes. "Oh, I know exactly what your offer is."

"Fuck you, Jory," he snapped and spun around and left without another word.

I watched him walk back inside.

"Nice mouth on the rich boy."

I looked up the street and there, parked three cars down, was Sam Kage. I jogged over to him before I even thought about it.

"You bring that kind of language out in everybody you know, huh, J?"

I smiled at him and shrugged. "What can I tell you? People go all poetic when I'm around."

He sighed deeply before he grabbed hold of my jacket and yanked me up against him. I let my head fall back on my shoulders as I stared up into his beautiful eyes.

"He thinks I drink too much."

"'Cause ya do," he agreed, his hand warm on my skin, his thumb stroking my cheek. "But that ain't the way to get you to stop, taking you to a fuckin' bar. I'd keep you home in bed."

I let out a snort of laughter as my eyes drifted closed and I leaned into his hand.

"Baby," he said softly, and his lips brushed over the side of my neck. "Get in the car."

"Not tonight," I said, stepping back from him, my eyes opening. "I gotta work tomorrow."

He took a step closer and I took another back.

"J," he warned me, reaching for my jacket.

I sidestepped him, doing a half-spin so he couldn't get a hold of me. "I really gotta go," I smiled at him, walking to the curb, hailing a cab. "But you take it easy."

"You're leaving me?" He was dumbfounded.

I waved before I got in the cab and was immediately halfway down the street. I gave the driver my home address and slouched down in the backseat. My phone rang minutes later.

"How 'bout I take you to breakfast in the morning?"

I smiled into my phone. "No, Sam. I don't eat breakfast."

"Then lunch. Meet me for lunch at The Chop House. I'll get you a steak."

"I have a lunch meeting tomorrow already."

"Dinner. Lemme feed you. Please, J."

"Sam, I can't just—"

"Why you gotta be so difficult?"

"Hey."

"What?"

"It's fun, you know, flirting with you, but really… we should stop."

"Why?"

"'Cause what's the point?"

"The point is very simple. You belong to me."

"No, I don't."

"Yeah, ya do. I'm the only one that'll put up with your shit, because I love you."

I could barely breathe.

"And you know you're a pain in the ass."

"I—"

"Jory—c'mon… you throw temper tantrums, you second-guess everything, you have no patience at all, you want things to be instantly perfect without any work, you never listen, you jump to conclusions, you create more drama than ten people put together, you drink too much, you're oblivious to shit that goes on around you, and if things go wrong your first instinct is to run away as fast as you can." He sighed deeply. "You're a fuckin' mess and you can't deny it."

"You've been gone a long time, Sam. I'm not like that anymore."

"The hell you're not."

"I'm not, but if you think I'm such a piece of shit, then—"

"I never said that. I said you were a pain in the ass and you are. Ya know ya are," he let out a long-drawn-out breath. "But so am I. That's why we're made for each other."

"Sam—"

"Please lemme see you. I gotta see you."

"Sam, I—"

"I'm crazy about you… you know that."

"Sam—"

"We'll just hang out. No pressure, okay?"

"Sam—"

"Let's have dinner tomorrow. I'll be there at six."

"No," I told him.

"We'll just hang out," he repeated, his voice softer, lower.

I sighed deeply. "It's not a good idea, Sam. It never—"

"We'll talk about it tomorrow."

"Fine," I yawned. "We'll talk tomorrow. Call me if you want."

"I'll see you at six," he said and hung up.

But I knew him and his job. There was no way he would show.

Chapter Four

MY PROBLEM was that I had the memory of an elephant. As I laid in bed for hours thinking about Sam Kage, all I could remember was how I had felt when he left. So as much as my heart did leaps and flips thinking about him… my brain kept it together. No way, no how was I letting him near me ever again. It would break me a second time.

When I finally fell asleep, I felt content in my resolve and in the fact that I wouldn't see him again. Sam was great at promising things he couldn't deliver on, so I put him out of my mind and concentrated on work. It was the last thought I had before I fell asleep. Well, second to the last. Sam's voice telling me he was crazy about me was the very last. My idiocy knew no limits.

Dylan was sick the next morning and so she called to get me to come over and work from her place. I took scones and hot chocolate for her, extra strong coffee for me. We were done working by eleven and spent the rest of the day shopping for baby clothes. You had to be really disciplined to be self-employed, and lately we weren't really cutting it.

I went back to the office around four and returned calls and e-mails and set appointments for the following week. I was on the phone when Sam came through the front door. He was unannounced, as Sadie had already left for the night.

"Wow," I said, trying not to smile as he stopped in front of my desk. "What're you doing here?"

"You said we could eat."

"I didn't really think you'd make it."

"Why?"

"'Cause of what you do."

"I have to make time for you, J."

I stared at him as the phone rang on my desk.

"You gonna get that or just look at me?"

I answered the phone because I hated the smug tone in his voice.

"Jory, it's T," my friend Tracy said nervously on the other end. "Listen, I know it's late notice, but Wes just called and flaked out on meeting me."

"Where are you?"

"I'm at Shane's birthday party, at the Hyatt."

"I'm not dressed for a party."

"You always look good, J. I just need a wingman."

It was a choice of spending time with Sam, or taking the easy way out and cancelling going to a party with my friend in need. It was an easy choice to make. "Fine," I agreed.

"Thanks, man—I owe ya big. When can you be here?"

"In like fifteen minutes."

"Have I told you lately that I love you?"

I hung up on him and looked at Sam. "I'm sorry, but duty calls."

He nodded. "When you're done, then."

"It might be late. Let's try again tomorrow."

He shook his head.

"C'mon. I'll meet you at Dundee's for dinner after I go to the gym. Say seven-thirty?"

"Okay."

I got up, smiling at him. "Thanks, Sam, I—"

"C'mon, I'll drive you."

"Oh no, that's okay. I can—"

"I'll drive you."

"It's not necessary."

But by the heavy hand on my shoulder I knew that, to him, it very much was.

THREE hours later I told myself I shouldn't care. The man didn't belong to me. And yet every woman that walked over to Sam Kage and put her hand on his shoulder annoyed me. Every man that leaned on the bar next to him and checked him out irritated me even more. The fact that he was just sitting there—having told me that since he was at a bar he might as well have a drink—minding his own business, was slowly driving me crazy. To try and numb the growing pain in the pit of my stomach, I was drinking.

When my friend Tracy walked up behind me and put his hands on my shoulders, I rolled them so he'd have to let go.

"What's with you?" he snapped at me.

"Nothing," I said absently, standing up. "I think I'm gonna go, though. I saw Scott and Jerry, you don't need me anymore."

"Yes, I do," he said, shoving me back down into the chair. "I need you."

My eyes darted to Sam and I saw him leaning back against the bar, long legs crossed at the ankles. He was the picture of ease, and I was all tangled up just looking at him.

"Jory, honey, just come dance."

"I don't feel like it." I forced a smile, draining my third Chivas and water. "I just wanna sit."

"You gonna let somebody sit with you?" he asked, tipping his head toward the seat beside me, where my leather racing jacket lay. "There's plenty of guys dyin' to come over here, but you are definitely not being real inviting right now."

"Oh no?" I grinned up at him, the alcohol slowly seeping through my veins. "I feel pretty good."

"Yeah, I bet," he nodded, leaning down to rest his forehead on mine. "But the way you're acting is not friendly. Your whole vibe right now is 'fuck off'."

"Is it?"

"Yeah, I've counted nine guys that've tried to sit down and they've all been shut down hard."

I grunted, reaching up to put my hand around the back of his neck. "You wanna be number ten, T?" I sighed, letting my eyes drift closed. "You wanna take me home and fuck me?"

"Jory, you are such a cocktease," he snapped at me, pulling back as I chuckled. "We both know you'd never even let me kiss you."

I started on my fourth drink, which the waiter had dropped off. "There's always the first time."

"Jory—"

"Excuse me."

We both looked up at the tall, dark-haired man hovering over us.

He pointed at the chair where my jacket was. "Can I sit there?"

"Sure," I said, grabbing my drink, snatching my jacket off the chair, and leaving fast. I walked to a different table, higher and with barstools around it, and sat down.

"Jory, you're such a prick," Tracy scolded me as he walked up beside me and leaned on the table. "That guy was really hot and he totally wanted to talk to you."

"Whatever," I grunted, leaning my chin on my hand to look at him. "So you wanna go get something to eat? I'm starving."

"Jory, I'm here to pick somebody up. Unlike you, it's work for me. I—"

"No, it's not," I assured him. "There's no guy in here you can't have." I said, looking around, my eyes finding Sam Kage. "Except him. You can't have him."

He chuckled. "You can't have him, either, J. He's straight."

"You think so?"

"Look at him," he said like I was nuts. "Yeah, J, he's got the whole *breeder* vibe goin' on."

I checked out Sam Kage and my stomach did a slow roll.

"Even you might let a guy like that sit with you, huh, J?"

"Maybe I would," I said, as Sam caught me staring and smiled.

"Oh shit," Tracy moaned, watching Sam lever himself off the bar and start across the room, his eyes on me the whole time. "You know him?"

"Yes, I do."

"God, Jory, how hot is he?"

"You have no idea," I assured my friend.

He shivered as Sam Kage stepped in beside me, hand on the back of my neck.

"I want you to come outside and get in my car now."

"I can't do that," I told him. "I'm here with friends."

"This is bullshit. You made a date with me first."

"And something came up."

"This is not something. This is you blowing me off."

"Then go."

"No."

"Sam, you—"

He growled. "Just come talk to me outside for a second. It's hot in here."

"It is a little," I agreed, looking up into his dark eyes.

"C'mon."

"What are you still doing here?"

He smiled slowly and I saw the flash in his eyes. "You're still here."

"Jory, introduce me to your friend." Tracy asked, interrupting us.

"I'm not his friend," Sam corrected him. "I'm way more than that."

I watched his eyes get huge. "I'm sorry?"

"He's not," I told Tracy.

Sam yanked my head back and stared down into my eyes. "The hell I'm not," he said as he bent to kiss me, his hand tight in my hair.

I shoved him away and in the process lost my balance, nearly falling off my barstool. It was perhaps the most uncoordinated, ungraceful thing I'd ever done, but he caught me, crushing me against him and patting my ass before he set me on my feet.

I was sputtering as he laughed at me. "You can't just—"

"I love it when you get all worked up." He smiled lazily. "You get all flushed and your eyes go all dark and wet... it's really something."

I deflated. How was I supposed to remain indignant when he was looking at me like that? Like I was the most amazing thing he'd ever laid eyes on?

Gently, he ran the back of his fingers under my chin. "Put your jacket on. I wanna go."

"I—"

"C'mon, baby," he said softly, pleading.

I felt drugged, and when I looked at Tracy I saw the completely enraptured smile.

"T?"

"God, Jory, he's crazy about you."

"Yes, I am," Sam agreed, taking a handful of my dress shirt. "Just come talk to me."

"No, there's no point," I said, grabbing my jacket and my drink, ready to move again.

"Hey, pretty boy."

I looked over at the next table and there was a guy sitting there smiling at me. He was young, covered in tattoos, and his shirt was open, revealing toned pecs and six-pack abs. The only word that described him was hot, and the look he was giving me said that he was more than interested in getting to know me.

"C'mere. I wanna talk to you."

But there was no way I could walk away from Sam Kage, even if I wanted to, even if I was trying to prove a point. There was just no way.

"Not a chance, man," Sam said to the guy, his voice deep, menacing.

I sighed and looked back at Sam. "What do you want?"

"I told you... I want to talk to you outside."

The way he was looking at me, how dark his eyes were... he would not take no for an answer. We would stand there all night if I argued with him. "Fine."

I followed him through the crowd, moving slowly until we made it to the front door. Outside, I stood in front of him and waited.

"Let's go eat. I know you're starving."

"I'm not—"

"J, you drank your dinner. Lemme feed you."

I just stared at him.

"C'mon," he chuckled. "I promise to lay off."

I continued to study his face for a second and nodded before suggesting we try the diner around the corner. He gave me a lopsided grin and started walking. It was nice when he started talking about nothing, making conversation about the last movie he'd seen, how he'd spent last Saturday cleaning his mother's rain gutters, and about a case at work where a guy had shot his best friend in the foot over a golf club.

"I am continually surprised by the things people do," I told him.

"You and me both," he chuckled, holding open the door for me so I could step inside the family-run diner where pot roast was the special of the day.

Dinner was really nice. We laughed and talked and he kept our conversation light. When I was having a cup of hot chocolate with marshmallows for dessert and he was having a slice of pecan pie and coffee, he caught me staring.

"What?"

"Nothing."

"C'mon, J," he said softly, coaxing, leaning close to me, his knee bumping against mine under the table, his arm behind my head, draped over the back of the booth. "Tell me."

I shrugged. "It's just you. You look exactly the same. You haven't changed at all."

"I've changed a lot," he assured me. "I promise you."

I didn't want to delve. It sounded like a dangerous topic of conversation.

As we walked back toward the club, he asked me if he could drive me home.

"It's probably not a real good idea."

"Why not?" he asked as we reached his huge SUV.

"I thought we were having dinner tomorrow and—"

"I don't wanna have dinner again," he told me. "I want you to—"

"I thought you said you weren't gonna push?"

"Fuck this," he growled at me. "I'm done with you saying no."

I walked a few feet away from him. "It's not gonna be like you want, so maybe you should just give up."

After a minute of staring at me, he nodded.

"I just can't, Sam." I said, swallowing hard, the lump in my throat almost painful.

"Okay."

I let out a deep breath and turned to walk away.

"Hey."

I stopped and looked over my shoulder at him.

"I'll see you around, all right?"

I smiled at him and continued down the street. I wasn't sure how to feel. Relieved? Sad? Steeped in regret, vindicated, or hopeful? Hard to imagine that I would ever fall in love with another man the way I had been in love with Sam Kage. It was, however, not necessarily a bad thing. To be in that deep was really scary.

Chapter Five

I WAS in early the next morning, and by working through lunch and staying after Sophie left that night, caught up on three days' work. Dylan was very impressed when I called her that evening, even though she worried when I didn't eat.

"You're too thin now, Jory," she sighed into the phone.

"Okay," I indulged her as I ate the PowerBar in my desk.

She promised to try and be in the following day if she felt better, but I told her not to worry, I'd call if I got in any trouble. I made her play guess-who, to figure out who I had accidentally run into.

"I hate this game and you know it," she complained. "Who'd ya meet?"

"Abe—your friend, Aubrey Flanagan."

"Really? How funny."

"I know, it was totally random."

"Well, that's great. Didn't you just love her, isn't she awesome?"

"She is."

"But don't love her more than me, okay?"

"Could you be more hormonal?" I asked her. "Like that's even possible."

"Good."

"That reminds me, I gotta call her."

"That's my cue to get off the phone." She yawned and then burped.

"Lovely."

"Sorry," she sighed. "My stomach's all screwed up."

"Because it's been taken over by an alien."

"You're funny. You should do stand-up."

I smiled into the phone.

"God, I'm so sick of being sick. I need to have this kid already."

"It's just a couple of weeks more, Dy. Just rest."

She appreciated me trying to rally her spirits and told me she loved me before she got off the phone. I called Aubrey immediately afterwards. My pinch hitter promised to be in the office the following Monday morning at eight sharp. I told her I didn't do sharp, I did *ish*, as in nine-*ish*.

"Ish?" She giggled.

"So ish," I assured her. "Dylan and I might be a little laid-back but still... eight in the morning is just obscene."

"Okay, partner," she sighed into the phone. "Nine-*ish* it is."

When I asked how her date had gone with Rick Jenner, she said it wasn't over yet. Apparently they had been inseparable since they'd had dinner.

"Have you even gone home yet?"

She had no comment.

I chuckled and she groaned.

"He's a good guy," I championed my brother's friend.

"He's a phenomenal guy," she corrected me, "and so damn hot."

I grunted. "I'll take your word for it."

"And speaking of hot guys... who was the gorgeous guy I saw you leaving The Corner Diner with last night?"

"I didn't see you."

"No, I know. I yelled but you were too far away, but who cares! Who was the guy?"

"Sam."

"Oooh," she purred. "Do you realize you just sighed when you said his name?"

"I did not."

"Oh, I think ya did. Who is he?"

"He's a police detective."

"Well he's totally yummy. I approve."

"Stop."

"And can I just say what a stunning couple you guys make? I mean holy shit, drop-dead, could-not-take my-eyes-off-of-you-guys gorgeous."

"No, we don't but you and Rick on the other hand... really beautiful."

"Well, thank you very much." She squealed suddenly, and her throaty laughter filled my ears.

"Whatcha doin', babe?" I teased her.

"Shut up." She laughed more. "Richard Jenner, go away, I'm trying to talk to Jor—"

A second later she was gone and I smiled wide. It would be interesting to find out what Dane thought of his friend's new girl when he got back from his honeymoon.

I WAS already home that evening when my friend Sloan called and invited me to dinner with her and her boyfriend Derek. Because I had turned her down the last five times she'd called me, I accepted and went to meet them at a steakhouse downtown. When I met them outside the restaurant and was introduced to three other people, among them Parker Strom, I understood that I was being "fixed-up." I dragged Sloan to the bar with me, where she confessed that because she loved both Parker and me she hoped we would hit it off. I stifled a groan.

When we rejoined the group, Parker had a glass of white wine for me. I took it to be polite, even though wine gave me headaches. He stood close, asked me what I did, and complimented my leather racing jacket. I was listening to him answer all Sloan's questions about his job, his house, his car and his plans for the holidays. She was obviously interviewing him for me, letting me hear his answers, tell me himself that he was a catch. A hand on my shoulder made me turn and when I did, I found myself faced with Aaron Sutter.

"Hey." I smiled at him.

"Jory." He smiled back, hand closing on my jacket. "What are you doing here?"

"Just having dinner with friends."

"Great." His eyes were locked on mine. "Eat with us."

"There's like six of us, Sutter," I teased him, smiling wide. "How can you—"

"I've got a private room upstairs," he said, hand on my bicep, easing me closer to him. "Come on, I feel like crap about last time. Treat your friends, eat with me."

And it would be a treat, for anyone. Unless you lived under a rock, everyone knew Aaron Sutter. People saw his name splashed all over newspapers, read articles and saw his picture in magazines, understood that he was rich, powerful, and connected. Partying with him was Cristal and caviar, nothing but the best. So there was no reason to say no when someone was offering to make a normal Wednesday night into an event. It was assumed that dinner would just be the beginning. The expressions given him were ones of wonder as he led the entire entourage through the crowded restaurant, one arm draped over Sloan's shoulder, the other hand tight on my bicep.

Up the marble staircase to the second floor was a private room that had its own tiny dance floor and was set up like someone's living room instead of a restaurant.

"This is amazing," Parker said, watching Aaron as he mingled with his friends.

"Yep," I sighed, motioning the waiter over to me, passing him the full glass of wine and ordering a Chivas and water. "It's all first class with Aaron."

"He's even better-looking in person."

The man was handsome, period. Live or in print, he looked exactly the same.

"Don't you think so?"

"Sure."

He stepped in closer to me. "So listen, before this evening goes on any further, I would like to get your number so I can call you and ask you out on a real date."

"Who's going on a date?"

We both turned to find Aaron beside us, his hand on the back of my neck, fingers sliding up into my hair.

"I...." Parker began but faltered, and I saw him watching Aaron's obvious show of possessiveness. "I wanted to thank you for inviting me, Mr. Sutter."

"Aaron," he corrected gently. "And I'm sorry, did you want to ask Jory out?"

He swallowed nervously. "I did, yes."

Aaron nodded before he excused us both, leading me toward the table. "Sit with me."

I chuckled. "That was kind of an asshole thing to do, don't you think?"

"No," he said. "He needs to know that if he wants you, the line forms behind me."

I smiled at him. "C'mon, Sutter, order us all something to eat already. Everybody's starving."

"Yes, dear," he said, smiling, pulling me closer.

It was fun, as it always was when Aaron was the host of his own party. He didn't order off the menu but instead rattled off selections that the chef would prepare only for him. And normally I took offence to the making of assumptions about what I wanted, but I wasn't in the mood to argue and so let him tell the waiter what I would have.

"Lemme take your jacket."

I took it off and passed it to him. When he complimented the dress shirt underneath, I gave him a look.

"What?"

"I look the same as always, Sutter, don't screw with me."

He scowled at me.

"You, on the other hand, look great," I assured him, my hand fixing the collar of his dress shirt under his V-neck sweater. "But you always do."

"Do I?"

"Quit fishing," I grunted.

"I just like it when you notice."

I stared into his eyes and tried to understand, again, what it was that wasn't there. Why I wouldn't just change for him and be the way he wanted. Anyone in their right mind would. The man was perfect and yet... not for me. He wasn't perfect for me.

"Try the wine, J," he urged, moving a piece of hair out of my eyes.

"I thought I drank too much?" I quipped, annoyed suddenly for no reason.

"Please... I don't want to fight." He sighed, his fingers stroking over my jaw. "I just want to feed you and maybe, hopefully... take you home with me."

I let it go and tried the red wine. He was looking at me expectantly, and I felt a familiar knot twist in my stomach. Always I could be counted on to let him down in these instances. He thought I knew wine and food and I didn't. He imagined me a connoisseur because he was and all his friends were, but the truth was that I had simple tastes, always had.

"You like it?"

"Yeah, it's great."

"What's wrong?"

"Nothing," I said, turning to look at Sloan, asking her to repeat her question about Dane. She wanted to know about the wedding, and I was more than willing to give her details.

Later, when a plate was set down in front of me, Aaron drew my attention to him with a hand on my knee.

"Try the steak, J. It's Kobe beef, you're gonna love it."

And I did like it when I tried it, but I didn't want to be told that I *had* to love it. As usual, I realized I was nitpicking at him and tried to stop. When my phone rang I excused myself to the opposite side of the room before I answered it.

"Jory."

"Sam," I sighed because I was so happy to hear his voice.

"Well," he said softly, "that's the best greeting I've gotten so far."

"Yeah?"

"Yeah. You sound good. Where are you?"

"I'm at dinner."

"Dinner? What is it, like ten now?"

I laughed at him. "Don't be so regimented, Detective. Dinner's whenever you want it."

"If you say so, but I gotta tell ya, you keep some weird-ass hours."

I smiled into my phone. "Very true. Why are you calling?"

"You said I could."

"Yeah, but—"

"You know the other night, when you said that all I wanted you for was to fuck, that was messed up. You knew it was crap even when you were saying it."

"I don't wanna talk about—"

"'Cause the first thing I want is your heart."

Jesus.

"I want you, period."

"Listen, maybe you shouldn't call—"

"Where are you having dinner?"

"It's not—"

"Jory, come sit down," Aaron said as he walked up beside me. "Your food's getting cold."

"Who's that?" Sam asked me.

"I'll talk to you later," I said quickly.

"You don't wanna hang up," he warned me. "'Cause I can find your cell phone, J, no problem."

"Oh yeah?" I baited him and clicked it off. "Good luck." When I turned to go back to the table I stopped instantly, as Aaron was standing right there, barring my path and smiling at me.

"What?"

"Your temper, Jory," he sighed, his fingers sliding over my jaw. "It's really something."

I moved past him to go back to the table at the same time that the waiter finally dropped off my Chivas and water. I thanked him, drained it before he could leave, and quickly ordered another one before I even sat down.

"Jory, don't ruin the evening just because you're pissed off at whoever was on the phone."

"I'm not ruining anything," I said, cutting into my steak again. "Just drop it."

But Aaron never could. "Why don't we go?"

"I'm eating," I told him, "and all my friends are here, having a good time. You should too."

"How can I, when I know if you keep drinking that you might go home with someone else instead of me?"

"Don't worry about it. I'm not going home with anyone."

"Please," he shook his head, "you always go home with someone, Jory. You're predictable that way. I used to watch you when you were out, and you never left alone, every night a different guy. I'm sure nothing's changed."

I turned to look at him as the waiter dropped off my second drink. "What are you talking about now?"

He searched my eyes with his. "Before we started dating, I'd see you at the club, picking up a different guy every night. You'd leave with them, and then the next night if the same guy came near you, you ignored them until they got the message. Nobody ever gets a repeat performance from you. You're a one-night stand kind of guy."

I nodded, feeling my face get hot. People were listening and pretending they weren't; some of their faces showed embarrassment and others were just disgusted. Parker looked surprised. He was probably wondering why Sloan would have wanted him to date me, since I was so obviously just looking for my next hook-up.

"C'mon, you know I'm right. You never sleep with the same guy twice, that's not how you operate. You sleep with them and forget them."

"Is that right?"

"Yes," he chuckled. "And I bet it's been even worse since we broke up. You're like the biggest slut in Chicago, and you know it."

He was right to some degree. Before him, after Sam, there had been a lot of men. And before Sam, there were too many to count. So I did sleep around a lot, but when I *was* with someone, I was monogamous. My first instinct was to loyalty and wanting to belong to someone. If Sam wanted me, I would....

I jerked hard, startling Sloan, who was sitting on the other side of me.

"Jesus, Jory," she chuckled, sliding her chair away from me, closer to her boyfriend, Derek, who was sitting beside her. "Just because you're drunk, don't spill on me."

But I wasn't drunk. I hadn't even finished my second drink yet. But everyone thought I was or would be.

"Did you hear me?" Aaron asked.

What was I doing, thinking about Sam?

"Are you all right?"

"Yeah I'm... fine."

"Look at me."

I did as he asked.

"It used to piss me off, seeing you go home with all those guys after turning me down. It took me forever to get you to say yes."

I heard his words, but I wasn't actually thinking about what he was saying. I wasn't emotionally connected at all.

"When we finally got together... God, Jory, it was like winning the lottery."

I was a prize, then.

"Jory...."

I looked into his eyes, saw how hungry they were, how dark.

He leaned close to me so he wouldn't be overheard. "You know people look at you and think you're hot, but they have no idea how great your body is."

Always, this had been Aaron's need—for everyone to admire his things, to covet his possessions... and I had been one of them.

When we used to go out with his friends, he would buy me a shirt or a sweater, a gift he'd say. And I would put it on only to find that it was a size too small. "Your body is gorgeous," he told me. "You should show it off more." If we were lounging by the pool, he'd run his hand over my stomach in front of his friends, tell them that you could scrub laundry on my abs, sometimes yanking down the side of my swim trunks to trace the V-line from my hip to my groin. I would shove him off me, head for the house, and he would catch me, say he was sorry, never meaning to embarrass me. I was just so beautiful, what was he supposed to do? I told him I wanted to be treated with respect. And he would promise to, even as his hand slid over my ass to the catcalls and whistles of his friends. The end result was logical; the people who mattered to him thought our relationship was a joke. They were sure that all I had to offer was what you could see.

We would go to expensive places, and Aaron was reminded by his friends to buy my drinks or my meal since I couldn't possibly afford it. My age was a constant source of amusement, my lack of a financial portfolio and property cause for concern. It was understood that he was slumming with me because I had a hot body and I was good in bed. And when we broke up, leaving that part behind had been a huge relief. Funny that Dane's friends never made me feel bad about myself. Maybe because they were all self-made men, not one of them a trust-fund baby like Aaron's ubiquitous posse.

"What are you thinking about?"

I shook my head, gulping down my drink.

He leaned in close and I felt his warm breath in my ear. "Jory, I know you're back to the clubs, sleeping with any guy who asks... so I'm asking... come home with me. Choose me tonight... please."

But it was over, and going back was just plain stupid. Just being with him, seeing the sneering looks from his friends, hearing him criticize me was annoying.

He turned my face to him. "I'm not trying to make you feel bad."

"Yeah, ya are," I said, lifting my chin out of his hand and pushing back from the table. "But it's normal for you and these assholes, so I'm not upset. I'm just done."

"But I don't care that you're like that," he went on, because he wasn't really listening to me. "I just want you to—"

"I know what you want," I said as I stood up and put on my jacket.

"What are you doing?" he asked suddenly.

It seemed obvious. "I'm leaving."

"Why?" he asked, reaching out to grab hold of my wrist.

"I forgot how bad you and your friends make me feel about myself," I told him, yanking my arm free of his grasp. "I'll see ya later. Thanks for dinner."

"Jory—"

"Bye," I yelled at the table, smiling before I turned and left the room, dodging the waiters coming in to serve more food and drinks. I made it down the staircase to the restaurant and then snaked my way through the crowd to the door. On the street I felt instantly better, less claustrophobic, like I could breathe.

"Jory!"

I turned and found Aaron.

"Where are you going?"

"Home."

"Why? What did I say that's not true?"

"Nothing," I said, turning to leave.

"Jory!" he snapped, grabbing my arm tight, holding on. "I hate these damn dramatic exits. Just for once, stay and fight. You always run."

I shrugged. "So find someone who'll stay. It doesn't seem that hard. You get tons of guys hitting on you all the time, just pick one already. That guy Parker thinks you're plenty hot."

"Jory—"

"Lemme go, Aaron," I said tiredly. "I'm not the guy for you and you're definitely not the one for me. Let's just call it a day."

"God!" he roared, the frustration just rolling off him. "Why do you have to fight me all the time? Why can't you just listen to me, since all I want is the best for you? You could be so happy! I could show you so many things and places and—"

I peeled his hand off me and took a step back. "I don't need that."

"What do you need? Do you even know?"

I didn't, but I knew for certain it wasn't Aaron Sutter. I had to trust in order to love, and I didn't trust Aaron. He wanted to change me, and I was afraid if I stayed with him I would lose myself along the way.

"Jory? Tell me the kind of guy you need and I'll be that guy."

I shook my head. The only man I had ever loved so completely that every wall in me had come down was Sam Kage. And it was because he was strong enough to never break under the strain of being with me. I was a mess and he had been my rock. I needed that, I needed to be able to surrender and just be. But it would sound desperate and codependent if I gave voice to it, so I just stood there silently.

"Jory, please. I thought about you every day I was gone."

When he took a step forward I took another back. I wasn't going to let him touch me anymore… there was no point. I had my doubts that we could even be friends.

"Jory… honey."

And Sam was an even worse prospect, because as much as I wanted him, he was no good for me. It was funny—the guy I didn't want would stay forever, and the guy I did want would end up leaving me again, if I allowed him the chance. I needed a drink.

"That's your answer for everything."

I hadn't realized I'd said it out loud.

"What you need is to come home with me and spend the weekend. We need to talk."

I was overwhelmed suddenly with sadness. This was really good-bye, and I was ending forever yet another failed relationship. My track record was total shit.

"Jory." He whispered my name, trying to step in close to me, reaching for my shoulder.

I stepped back, turned around, and ran. He yelled my name more than once.

I wasn't ready to go home. I really needed to just sit somewhere, have a drink, and clear my head. Someplace quiet where no one would bother me. And I knew exactly where.

IT TURNED out that I was reaping some serious karma for God knew what. Or maybe it was someone else's karma and I was just caught in the cross fire. There was a drug raid at my favorite piano bar, due to the fact that the owner of the club had apparently been moving quite a bit of cocaine in and out of his place for some time. And vice detectives had picked tonight, Wednesday night, to bust him. So I was sitting on the ground in a long row with everyone else that had been inside when the police came swarming through the front door. There was a barricade of black and white cars blocking us from the other side of the street, where a crowd had formed. It was the cherry on the cake of my day. When someone gently kicked my foot, I let my head roll back so I could look up. Turned out I had been wrong: here was the cake topper.

"Hi." Sam Kage smirked down at me. "What brings you to this den of iniquity, J?"

I groaned and his smirk changed into a full-blown evil grin. He was enjoying this to no end.

"Since when do you do drugs?"

"I don't and you know it." I shot him a look. "Don't be an ass."

"Better watch how you talk to me," he said, crouching down in front of me. "You could be in a lot of trouble here."

I stared into his eyes. "What are you even doing here? You don't work vice anymore, you're a homicide detective now."

He didn't answer me.

"Sam?"

"Get up."

As soon as I was on my feet he grabbed me hard, fingers digging into my shoulder, before he walked me away from the others, down the street and around the corner to his car. I pulled free of his grasp and turned to face him, but before I could say a word, he shoved me up against the side door and pinned me there. He held me still with just one hand on my chest.

"Jesus, Sam," I barked at him. "What the hell are you—"

"Shut up," he cut me off, stepping forward so we were only inches apart.

The heat radiating off the man was amazing. I caught my breath, I couldn't help it.

He made a noise in the back of his throat. "Some things never change, huh, J?"

I wasn't going to give him the satisfaction of speaking to him.

"Look at me."

I lifted my head to look up into his eyes and found that he had bent toward me at the same time. When he spoke, I felt his warm breath on my face.

"What are you doing here?"

"I just wanted to sit and relax a little before I went home."

He nodded, dipping his head lower, inhaling me. "You're shaking, you know."

I knew. Nothing I could do about it.

"Maybe I should search you for illegal substances."

I swallowed hard, trying to get my body to calm down.

"Or maybe I'll just put you in the back of my car and fuck you 'til you pass out."

Just the thought of him holding me down had me desperate for it. When I caught my breath, his knee wedged between my legs and then his thigh as he leaned into me.

"Listen, I want you to meet me around the corner at the River Road Bar." His voice was deep and sexy, sending ripples of heat through me. "You go there and wait, and as soon as I'm done here, I'll meet you."

But my brain kicked in and my head cleared.

"Did you hear me?"

I had no intention of meeting him anywhere. The illustration of his power over me was terrifying. No other guy could get me panting and writhing in seconds. No one else had such dominion over me. I wanted to run away as fast as I could.

He grabbed a fistful of my hair and yanked my head back hard, uncaring about whether or not it hurt. "Do not even think about ditching me."

"No."

He kissed the base of my neck. "Your heart is beating so fast, baby."

I shivered hard.

"Fuck it, get in the car."

"You're on duty," I reminded him.

"No, I'm not," he told me. "I was just driving home and heard the call. I figured I was close to where you were, so I could check in on you after."

"How did you know where—"

"I can track your phone, I told you."

Police Detective. I forgot sometimes. "Lemme go," I ordered. "You're hurting me."

"I am not," he said, his hand moving from my hair to my throat. "I could never hurt you."

"Get off me," I snapped, wriggling in his arms, trying to lever myself off the car.

He stepped back and I moved quickly away from him.

"Walk to the bar, J. I'll be there in fifteen minutes."

I turned to go, but before I was out of his reach he grabbed hold of my shoulder and spun me back around to face him.

"God, what?"

His expression was dark, brows furrowed, jaw clenched. "Be there."

I just stared at him a long minute before I started walking backward.

"You're not gonna meet me there, are you?"

I shook my head.

"Why?" he yelled down the street, the space between us significant enough that even if he bolted he wouldn't reach me.

"'Cause of what you just did."

"That's bullshit and you know it."

I shrugged.

"You loved every second of that."

And if we were being honest, I had, but we weren't being honest. He stood there watching me and I turned and walked away.

My body was flushed and hot now that Sam had ignited my libido, so I caught another cab and headed toward one of my usual haunts to pick somebody up. I needed a stranger with no strings attached to quench my desire.

At the lounge they were playing Billie Holiday standards, and the singer had a deep, sultry sound to her voice. I ordered a snifter of Hennessy and sat at the end of the bar, listening. When I drained my glass, another one was right there to take its place. Turning my head, I found a very handsome man smiling at me.

"Finally, you show up."

"I'm sorry?" I smiled at him.

"You don't remember me?"

I didn't.

"You picked me up here like a month ago."

I had no idea who he was. "Sure."

He smiled slowly. "You don't remember, but that's okay... I remember you."

I took a sip of my drink.

"But you haven't been around in a while, and you wouldn't give me your number."

I nodded. I hardly ever gave out my number.

"I kept thinking if I hung out here, I'd bump into you again."

"And now you have."

"Now I have."

"Is that a good thing?"

He nodded, leaning forward. "It's a very good thing."

"You live around here?"

He nodded. "Yep, real close."

"Thanks for the drink."

"You finish it, then you can have another at my place."

And I was ready to take him up on his offer. My body was basically throbbing with pent-up desire and he was as good as the next guy. At least we liked the same kind of music. It was something. So I smiled at him and would have continued our flirty conversation, but the hand that slid up my left thigh turned my head in the opposite direction. Sam Kage was there, leaning on the bar, staring at me and just waiting.

I was stunned. "What are you—"

"Excuse me," the guy began, leaning in close to me. "I was talking to—"

"Fuck off," Sam said flatly before returning his eyes to mine. His smile was huge. "He's with me."

And because it was Sam Kage talking, the guy disappeared. I turned my head to say something nice to my admirer but he was gone. The detective was just too big and scary.

"Look at me."

I exhaled sharply and dragged my eyes to Sam.

"Can I sit?"

I shrugged.

"It's nice in here," he said softly, sitting down on the barstool beside me, pushing my drink out of my reach. "You like this kinda music, huh?"

"I don't come here for the music." Which I didn't. It was a meat market and that was why I was there. "I came to pick somebody up."

"I see."

"What are you doing here?" I asked quickly, my voice coming out sharper than I wanted.

"You're here."

"But we both know that this isn't—"

"Lemme drive you home."

"Absolutely not."

He leaned close to me, invading my personal space, his knee against mine. "Why not?"

"How did you even know I—"

"Did you know I'm a police detective? You know I find people all the time?"

"Shit."

He chuckled. "You can't ditch me, J. Come home with me."

"Sam, you shouldn't waste your time."

"I don't consider any time spent with you a waste."

"But Sam, you—"

"What, honey?" he said, looking at me, his eyes locked on my mouth.

"It's doomed to fail, Sam."

"I don't accept that," he said, his hand slowly reaching for me, giving me time to move away if I wanted.

"You don't really care, Sam… not really."

"I don't?" He touched my chin lightly, tipping it gently up so he could run the back of his fingers down my throat. "'Cause… I think I do. Because, unlike all the rest of these guys, I wanna keep you."

I lifted my head away and he let me. "You just wanna fuck me."

"Oh I wanna do that too," he chuckled warmly. "But that's only part of it."

"How can it be? Sam, you don't even know me or—"

"You have no idea about anything," he said, searching my eyes. "I dream about you."

I looked down at the bar.

"It's killing me that you won't just give in."

I closed my eyes and leaned my forehead into my hand.

"And you'll let some stranger take you home and fuck you, but me... me you won't let near you. How does that make any fuckin' sense at all?"

"A stranger won't hurt me."

"I won't either."

I scoffed, smiling wide as I lifted my head up and looked him in the eye. "Fuck you, Sam."

He shrugged. "Go ahead, vent at me—I don't give a shit."

I drained the drink the guy had bought me in one gulp and slid off the barstool. I was halfway to the front door before my arm was grabbed, hard. I froze as he walked around in front of me.

"Let me drive you home."

I moved by him and took a deep breath as soon as I was back outside.

"Do you care that I missed you?" Sam said as he appeared at my side.

"No."

"Liar."

"Sam, I can't do this, I won't," I said, shoving my hands in my pockets. It was cold and late and I could see my breath when I spoke. "I'd have to be crazy." I walked faster, hoping he'd just let me go.

He grabbed me again, yanked me around so fast I almost fell. "You've always been crazy."

"Let go!" I tried to twist free but he had me. The harder I pulled, the harder he held. He was going to leave bruises on my skin.

"No."

I stopped fighting and stared up at him. "Just go away."

"Why?"

"Why?" I repeated, "Well, for starters, how about that bullshit in the street? You think it turns me on to be treated like some piece of ass that you—"

"Yeah," he cut me off, his eyes full of heat. "I think you get off on the idea of me making you do whatever I want. You're dying to submit to me."

I shook my head, tried to tug my arm free, but he wasn't letting me go.

"We both know you want me." His voice was calm but the muscle in his jaw was flexing. "And I want you, J, with me—not just in my bed."

I stared up into his eyes. "If you wanted me so bad, if I was so important... why'd you never call me or write me or send me a damn e-mail? You left for three years, Sam, three goddamn years! You can't expect us to just pick up where we left off after all this time just because you're ready. That's total crap!"

"I was gone, I was out of the country for two years, J. I didn't talk to anyone. I—"

"Fine. You've been back a year then, you even said it's been a year. So... why am I only seeing you now? We meet accidentally at a hardware store and you're what, overcome with emotion, and now you've gotta see me again? It's bullshit."

He grabbed my other arm and shook me hard. "I didn't know what to do. I never know what to do about you. When I got back, I went to see you and you were with that guy Aaron."

I was stunned. "You saw me with Aaron?"

"Yeah," he said, letting me go, letting me take a few steps away from him. "You looked happy and you deserve to be happy, so.... But I had to check, and then I saw he wasn't around anymore and you... you give yourself away. Why do you do that? Why do you go home with anybody who asks, J?"

I looked away because I couldn't tell him.

"Do you have any idea what it's like to watch you go home with a different guy every night?"

"See?" I said, shrugging, still staring off down the street. "I'm trash, Sam... why even bother with me?"

"Look at me."

But I didn't.

"Look at me," he growled, grabbing my arm, yanking me back to him.

I tried tugging free, but his grip was like iron, no way was I going anywhere.

"You're not trash, it's just that none of those guys are right for you."

I had no snappy comeback because what he thought was exactly how I felt. Silence seemed the best option, so I went with it.

"I think you wanna belong to me, and if it ain't gonna be me you don't want anybody."

I turned back to look at him. "That's crap and you're full of shit."

He shook his head, reached out and put a hand on my cheek. "Nope, I'm right."

"Sam—"

He closed the small distance between us. "Why are you trembling?"

"'Cause it's cold out here."

"But that's not why," he said, running his fingers over my jaw, smiling.

"Sam—"

"You need me bad."

How did he know? My skin felt prickly, itchy, my muscles tense, I could barely breathe. Everything in me was ready, waiting for him. I ached for him even as my flight reflex was choking me. I wanted to run away at the same time I wanted to stay.

"And I don't just mean in bed."

He knew me so well... even after so long, he still knew me.

"Your eyes are a mess, J."

I wanted to give in but I was drowning in fear. He could shred my heart so easily.

"I'm sorry I didn't come for you the minute I got back."

"You don't hafta—"

"But I'm here now."

"Sam, you—"

"Jory!" he yelled at me. "I'm right here."

I shook my head.

"I want you back."

Everything blurred as my eyes filled. "You can find another guy."

"I don't want another guy, I want you."

"You're no good for me."

"Yeah, I am, and I can't wait to show you."

"Sam," I sighed, "do you really think that after all this—"

"I don't want anybody else to have you from this second on, I can't... I won't."

I opened my mouth to tell him it was too late, but I was off my feet and in his monster SUV before I even realized I was moving. The door was locked behind me and I sat there, waiting, while he got in. When he slid in behind the steering wheel he immediately turned and smiled at me. He looked very smug.

"Stop." I tried not to smile, so close to just giving in. "Lemme out."

"You're drunk, you can't even walk."

"I'm so not drunk."

"I wanna take you home."

I groaned and he chuckled.

"C'mon, baby."

"I am not your baby."

"Yeah, ya are," he said, smiling lazily. "You know ya are."

"Sam—"

"You never stopped belonging to me."

"That's crazy."

"Nope. It's the truth."

"And so what?" I was exhausted already.

"So lemme take you home."

"Fine," I threw up my hands in defeat. "Drive me home."

"Okay." He smiled, starting the car.

"Wait, to *my* home," I clarified.

"I don't know where you live."

"Are you kidding me?" I muttered. "You're unbelievable."

He started laughing.

"You're lying. I know you know where I live. You're a detective, after all."

"It's outta my way." He shrugged, his laughter giving him away. He was so lying through his teeth. "You can come to my place instead."

"No."

His smile went from smug to wicked that fast. "Like you can do shit right now."

I groaned again, but I couldn't stop smiling. It was insane that I could still feel this way... still crazy about Sam Kage after all this time. He had ruined me for other men. It was ridiculous.

"Jory... baby," he sighed deeply, reaching for me to put a hand around the back of my neck and pull me forward. "Stop fighting with me. Just give in."

"Sam—"

"I see how you look at me… you want me."

"Of course I want you, Sam, but that doesn't mean I should."

"Baby—"

"This scene is so familiar. Me in your car, you promising things will be different this time, me believing you…. We've done this before and it never works out. We need to call it a day."

"You're fighting so hard 'cause you're so scared of getting hurt."

"No, I just—"

"Baby." His voice was so warm, so soothing and gentle. "Stop… give in… I love you."

"No, you're just trying to—"

I felt his warm breath on my face a second before he kissed me. The wave of heat flooded me, and when his tongue pushed between my lips I opened for him. His mouth sealed over mine and I felt his hand slip around my throat to keep me there. The noises of pleasure that came out of him made my stomach flutter as he pushed in deeper, his tongue tangled with mine, tasting me, taking his time, devouring me. It lasted so long, the heat, the need, just building… and I felt his hands on me, one tangled in my hair, the other sliding up under my shirt, now rubbing circles on my back. He would kiss me for hours if I let him. When I tried to pull back, he leaned with me until I put my hands on his chest and shoved hard.

"What?" he asked, his voice full of gravel, his eyes heavy-lidded and so, so dark. No way to miss how turned on he was—a study in lust.

"Drive me home."

"After that kiss… after the way you just responded… no. No way."

"Sam, c'mon. I don't wanna make—"

"Just come home with me. I wanna talk to you."

"I know exactly what you wanna do," I assured him.

"Just c'mon. I promise to keep my hands off ya."

"You're so full of shit right now."

"Just right now?" He winked at me.

I leaned back in the seat.

"So?" He teased me.

"You're gonna do whatever you want anyway."

"This is true."

When I closed my eyes I felt his hand on my thigh. "You said you'd keep your hands off me."

"Yeah, I lied."

And I knew that, of course.

HIS apartment looked exactly the same. I walked it, reacquainting myself with where everything was. The teacups I bought were still in the cabinet. It was funny.

"Weird, right?"

I looked around, then back at him. "Yeah," I said, looking at all the same framed pictures on the shelves next to the TV.

"Take your jacket off."

I threw it on the couch and continued my inspection.

"You want some water or something?"

"No, but I appreciate the concern for my sobriety."

He chuckled before he crossed the room and reached for me, cupping my face in his hands.

"What are we doing here, Sam?" I said softly. "It's too late."

"It's never too late." He smiled into my eyes, his fingers sliding over my jaw, my lips. "Can I kiss you before I put you in my bed?"

"What?" I pulled away from him but he moved with me, hands fisted in my shirt.

"I want you," and his voice was husky, filled with need.

"Well, you can't have me." I told him, and even to myself I sounded pitiful. There was no power behind my words. The promise was empty.

"Oh no?" he asked, his strong hands gentle as they slipped over my throat.

"No," I said again, making no attempt to move an inch away from him. "It's too late."

"Is it?" His voice was so low, I felt my chest heave just looking at him.

"Yes," I protested weakly, and I couldn't even imagine how lame I sounded.

"You're lying." He smiled slyly. "You're hard for me right now."

I lifted my chin to protest and his mouth came down and covered mine. I trembled in his arms because the kiss sent a charge straight to my groin. He burned me up, and I was reminded that the man really knew how to kiss me. No one before or since had been able to deliver a kiss that I could feel race through my entire body like liquid heat. It was annihilating, all that desire and passion directed at me; he was so big and strong, the force of him overwhelming as he crushed me in his arms and kissed me hard and deep. I wasn't passive; I tangled my hands in his hair as the sensations raced through my body. I ravaged his mouth. When I thought my head was going to explode, I broke the kiss to take in some air.

"Jesus, you taste good," he panted, his forehead against mine.

I put my hands on his chest and tried to push him back away from me. He didn't budge.

"Baby," he breathed against my mouth, his hand under my chin, his thumb on my bottom lip, sliding over it. "Kiss me again."

And it was useless not to because I wanted to so badly. I burned for him, so I lifted my chin and his mouth was on mine, sucking, biting, kissing, claiming my lips. He swept his tongue inside my mouth and I hit the front door before I realized he'd been moving me backward into it.

"Better," he growled. "Now I've got you."

I shivered with just the sound of his voice as he kissed his way down my throat to my collarbone.

"Can't wait," his voice was so low, so full of need.

"Sam," I got out. "Maybe we should slow—"

He grabbed hold of my shirt and yanked it open. I heard the buttons as they bounced off the floor. His mouth was all over me, my chest, my nipples, down over my abdomen, biting, licking, and leaving a wet trail that made me shiver when the air hit it.

"God, baby, your skin," he groaned out, his hands on my belt buckle, fumbling with it fast, before moving to the snap of my jeans and my zipper.

"Sam... I...."

My jeans went down, my briefs following. His effect on me obvious, I moaned loudly as he knelt in front of me, hands on my hips, and took me inside his hot mouth, swallowing me down his throat. I was frozen to the door, my hands and fingers splayed behind me as the desire tore through me. I wouldn't last, couldn't last, too turned on from earlier, this now a continuation of foreplay he had begun in the street.

"Sam...." his name coming out as a whimper as I stared down at him.

He looked up at me, leaning back to smile, and it was wicked and dark. "Gonna make you scream my name. Make you mine all over again. Never gonna leave me ever."

Like he had to do anything to get that. I'd never wanted anyone the way I wanted him. Instantly, I had gone back to where his touch was like air I needed to breathe.

He rose after long minutes, spun me around, and shoved me face-first up against the door. He kicked my legs apart and I heard the crinkling of foil behind me.

"The condom's got lube on it," he breathed into my ear, sending a shiver through me. He nibbled and licked his way behind my ear and then down the side of my neck. "Gotta have you, gotta show you you're still mine."

"Sam," I could barely think, let alone form words.

He pressed himself against me and sucked on my shoulder, hard. His skin was so hot. When he pushed himself inside me, filling me, I thought I would die.

I heard him catch his breath, felt his hand like a vise on my hip, the other around me.

"Baby," he growled into my shoulder before he bit me. "You feel so good."

It went way past good. I was in heaven. His mouth was wet on my skin; his one hand stroking me sent waves of pleasure through me.

"So good," he rasped out. "Jesus, J, you're so tight and hot."

"Don't stop," I begged him and I felt his teeth on the back of my neck.

He drove into me over and over, as hard as he could, and I braced my hands on the door.

"Mine," he growled, his voice so sexy, so raw. "My baby."

I trembled under him. Just imagining him fully dressed, standing behind me, and me practically naked, the dominance and submission, only he had ever been able to make me do what he wanted. He could be rough with me, but he would never hurt me. He was made for me.

"I love the little noises you make when you're happy." He licked my shoulder, the side of my neck, tasting me, biting me, all the time thrusting so deep, his hands restless as they moved over my skin.

"Sam," I breathed.

"How do I feel, baby?" His voice was so low and sensual it shot right through me.

"I missed you," I answered breathlessly, trying so hard to think.

"'Cause you love me." His hand was on my stomach, pressing me back against him.

"No," I managed to get out.

"Yes," he insisted, clutching me tight, his fingers digging into my abdomen, feeling the muscles working.

"I'll always love you," I placated him.

"No, you love me. Not like over, like forever."

"No."

"Say it."

"No."

"Say you love me."

"No."

"Yes. Say my name and tell me."

"No."

"Yes."

"No. I won't go down this road with you again."

"You're already on it."

"The hell I am," I chuckled because it was ridiculous that we were having a conversation while he had me pinned up against his front door. Only he and I could ever be this stubborn. "It's just for tonight."

"Bullshit," he growled at me, sliding his hand over my ass. "You're mine."

I struggled halfheartedly because I was ready to start screaming right then and there. My heart was pounding so hard I could barely hear him.

"Now, say my name and tell me."

But I was lost in my body's reaction to him, all my muscles tightening at once, clamping down... my head rolled back on his shoulder, my palms pressing against the door as I cried out.

"Jesus God," he roared, as my legs went out from under me.

The sizzling heat raced through me, but Sam held tight, clutching me to him as his body bucked and shuddered, so deep inside me that we were fused together.

"Christ... I could die from this," he whispered into my shoulder.

So could I. The mix of the pleasure and pain was excruciating and intoxicating at the same time. I never felt better than when I was with him.

"Jory... baby...."

I had to concentrate on staying vertical.

He let me go as my breathing evened out and then slowly, gently, turned me around to face him. Not that I could bring myself to look at him, since for all my protesting I had surrendered so quickly. I had no willpower at all.

"Jory...." he said before he tipped my chin up and kissed me, long and hard. I made whimpering noises in the back of my throat because I couldn't help it. He deepened the kiss until I thought my heart was going to burst.

"Say you love me, J, tell me the truth." His breath was warm on my face before he wrapped me in his arms, holding me tight to his pounding heart.

"Sam...."

"Say it," he ordered, running his fingers up and down my spine.

I looked up at him, bumping his chin with the top of my head. "You know I love you. Don't be stupid."

"And that's why Aaron got a no," he persisted, his hand slipping up the back of my neck, his fingers buried in my hair.

"That's why," I agreed, my voice ragged. I sounded drugged. "I need to—"

"Lie down?" He teased me, easing back to look down at my face.

"I—"

He chuckled. "Let's get your shoes off."

I watched as he knelt and pulled off my boots and socks, slid my jeans and briefs over my ankles, and then rose and grabbed me, throwing me over his shoulder. He carried me to his bedroom. I hit the cold sheets that he pulled back and he stood there, looking down at me as I hurried to cover myself with the blankets.

I watched him strip out of his clothes to slowly reveal the rippling muscles and big, hard body that I knew. The man was massive.

He smiled down at me wickedly. "You look good lying in my bed."

"It's only for tonight."

"Whatever you say." He smiled down at me before he lifted the covers and slid in beside me.

The heat in his eyes made me catch my breath.

"I'm keeping you. If you were smarter, you'd get that this is a done deal already."

My brows furrowed and he bent to kiss the bridge of my nose.

"You're so adorable."

I tried to push him off me but he was too strong, his mouth slanting over mine, his tongue slipping deep into my mouth.

"Jory... baby," he sighed as he pulled back to look into my eyes. "I love you so."

I wrapped my arms around his neck and pulled him back down to me. And his weight on me felt like coming home.

"I know you're scared I'm gonna go away or something's gonna happen 'cause our track record is for shit, and I know you have no reason in the world to trust me, but you just... you have to, is all. I can't be without you. I think about you all the time."

I just stared up into his beautiful eyes.

He shook his head, just barely, brows furrowing like he was dismissing something. "Knock it off. You love me, who're you kiddin'?"

"Sam, I—"

"You're not gonna love anybody but me, you know you're not."

"I'm not?"

"Fuck no."

He was so eloquent. I couldn't keep from smiling.

"I'll just tie you to the bed."

"That'll go over well with your superiors," I said, rolling over on my stomach, closing my eyes, my body getting heavy.

His hand slid down my spine and before I could slip away to sleep, his lips followed the same path, and then his teeth. A moan rose up out of me.

"I missed all this gold skin."

I was so relaxed, so sated, so ready to sleep.

"You gonna stay here with me forever?"

I sighed deeply.

"Good," he said, his hand sliding over my ass before his mouth closed on my right cheek.

"Stop."

"Why?"

"'Cause you're gonna kill me."

He bit me hard, and it stung before he swirled his tongue over it, sucking and bathing it at the same time. He would leave a huge mark.

"Feel good?"

Of course it did. "No."

"Liar," he said, and I could hear the smile in his voice before he rolled me onto my back.

"Sam," I gasped out as he slid his hands down my legs from ankle to thigh, holding me down, allowing only for the writhing but no escape.

"Baby, you're never gonna leave me."

I could only look at him with narrowed eyes as he leaned over to his nightstand and pulled another condom out of the top drawer. He used his teeth to rip the wrapper open.

"Maybe I'm not ready to go again."

He chuckled, and it was deep and husky. "You're always ready for me."

Which was true.

"Put your legs over my arms."

In his bed we moved slower, taking our time, and it was as gentle and loving as the first had been rough and mauling. I went from consciousness to sleep so seamlessly I didn't remember making the transition until my phone woke me in the middle of the night.

I heard it from inside a dream, and woke to the reality of it going off in the living room of Sam's apartment. With him plastered to my back, holding me tight even in sleep, it was hard to get untangled. After several minutes, I managed to get free of both him and the covers on the bed. I staggered around the rooms that were both familiar and alien at the same time and found my phone where I'd left it. My jeans hadn't moved; they were still crumpled up by the front door. It was like a neon light pointing to my surrender.

"Crap," I grumbled before I answered, raking my hands through my hair, trying to wake up. "Hello?"

"Jory," Chris said. "It's Chris."

"I know." I yawned. "What's wrong?"

"Dylan."

"Dylan what?"

"She's in the bathroom and she won't come out. We need to go to the hospital—I think maybe she's in labor, but she won't.... Her mom and dad are here, my folks are here, her sister... I—she won't come out, and Jory, I need you now. Right now!"

"Okay," I rubbed my eyes. "Okay. I'm coming. I'm coming. Hold tight."

I was pulling on my boots, zipping up the first one, when the light came on. Sam shuffled over to the couch and leaned on it. He was naked, clearly not awake, and his hair was sticking up in tufts. He looked adorable, all sleep-tousled and bleary-eyed.

"What are you doing?"

"I gotta go."

"No," he whined. "You promised you'd stay here with me forever."

I chuckled, pulling on the second boot. "I never said any such thing."

The noise he made in return was half-whimper, half-moan.

"Sam," I said softly, standing up, pulling on my shirt, realizing it was useless since I could no longer button it. "Shit. I need a sweater or a T-shirt or something."

"I need to get my gun," he grumbled, opening his eyes wide to try and wake up. "A bullet will slow you down some."

"Sam," I said as I walked past him back to his bedroom. "Dylan's in labor, she needs me."

I was alone in the bedroom for several minutes before I heard him fumbling around behind me. When I turned to look at him, he had his underwear and jeans back on.

"What're you doing?"

"What?" he grunted, scowling at me.

"You're not going anywhere. Go back to bed."

"Tell me again who called."

"My friend Dylan, my partner—she's in labor and it sounds like maybe she's having a bit of a meltdown," I explained, continuing with rifling through the drawers in his armoire. "I need to get over there and help her poor sweet husband before he has a meltdown too and they're both scarred for life."

"Dylan called or her husband?"

"Her husband."

"Okay."

I found a long-sleeved gray T-shirt. I held it up. "Who's is this?"

"It's Jen's or Rachel's." He yawned, smiling slowly. "They were here a lot while I was gone."

I arched a brow for him.

"Not like that," he snapped at me. "Jen doesn't bring guys here anymore."

"That you know of."

"Screw you, J," he said with mock anger before he suddenly gave a snort of laughter. "Did you see the front of that shirt, baby?"

The word "Diva" was large and airbrushed on in pink metallic ink. But I would have to deal with it; there was nothing else in Sam Kage's closet that was going to work. He was six-four, I was five-nine, he was a mountain of hard, bulging muscle, I was small and lean, and none of his clothes were going to fit me. It was this or nothing, because my dress shirt no longer had buttons.

"Maybe next time you won't ruin my clothes," I complained.

"Sorry," he shrugged, but he obviously wasn't.

I yanked the tag off, turned it inside out, and pulled it on. It clung to me but it covered me. "Okay," I said, raking my fingers through my hair a few times. "I gotta go. I'll call ya."

"The fuck you will," he snapped at me. "Just wait, I'm going with you."

"No, Sam, you can't do that. Dylan hates you—you bein' there won't help."

"It'll help."

"No, it really won't."

"Listen," he said, walking over to me, his hand heavy around the back of my neck. "You're mine. I go where you go, and anywhere that you go at three in the goddamn morning I go too."

He had no idea what he was even saying, but it was very cute, and so I wrapped my arms around him, squeezed tight, and told him to button his jeans and find a shirt. I slapped his ass hard when he turned away from me.

He muttered to himself all the way back down the hall.

THERE were hurried introductions made when we arrived at Dylan and Chris's apartment and I called Sam my boyfriend because it was easier than the explanation would have been. His smile over the title was huge.

"It's only for tonight," I told him.

"Whatever you say," he grinned back.

We all took turns trying to extricate Dylan from the bathroom. I tapped on the bathroom door and tried to talk my best friend and partner out. She wouldn't budge. Her husband was so sweet, I thought Dylan's mother was going to cry, his own mother giving him a look like he was the second coming. The door didn't even crack. Her father tried, then Chris's father tried, and then her sister went with the funny, sarcastic approach. We all laughed, even Sam smiled, but nothing from Dylan but her screams as the contractions ripped through her.

"Can I try?" Sam asked me from where he was leaning next to the china cabinet. Arms crossed, ankles crossed, he looked very calm.

"Sure," Chris invited him with a sweeping motion of his hand. "Come one, come all."

Sam pushed off the wall and moved across the room to the door. He tapped gently and we all watched him, riveted.

"Hey, Dylan—it's me, Sam. You know, Detective Kage. The one you fuckin' hate."

I really needed to work on his swearing.

"Don't you have something you wanna say to me?"

And the reaction was instant. The door slammed open and she came roaring out of the room. "How dare you even speak to him again, you selfish sonofabitch! I hate you for hurting him, I hate you even more for leaving, and I hate you most of all for coming back! You... don't... deserve him! Get the hell out of his life, you poisonous manipulating asshole!"

The room was silent except for Sam, who stepped close and took her chin in his hand and lifted it so he could look down into her eyes.

"Oh ho, the lady's a tiger."

She breathed deeply, staring up at him.

"Feel better?"

She shivered once, and there was water on the floor beneath her.

Sam didn't even flinch.

"My water broke," she said in the tiniest voice I had ever heard.

"Yep," he nodded, the lopsided grin there that I loved. "So let's go to the hospital."

"I can't walk," she said, looking at her husband, then her dad, then me.

"It's okay," he said, and scooped her up in his arms. Like she weighed nothing at all.

There wasn't another man in the room that could have lifted her, even if he had help. He was at the door seconds later, holding her cradled against his chest, her arms wrapped around his neck, her face lying on his shoulder. Even nine months pregnant, she looked tiny and fragile in comparison to the big and strong that he was. The picture of them together would be forever ingrained in my memory.

"J, get a trash bag for Dy to sit on in the car and the bag she packed for the hospital. C'mon, Chris, let's do this."

Chris seemed rooted to the spot he was standing in and just stared back at Sam.

"Let's go, buddy," Sam coaxed him.

"But I was going to drive her in—"

"I'm a cop. I have a cool blue light and a siren in my car. Who's gonna get you there faster?"

"Okay, you win," he agreed, rushing around the house, hurrying everyone out as we all followed Sam down the stairs.

Four flights down carrying a very heavy pregnant woman and he wasn't even winded as he put her gently in the passenger seat after I spread the trash bag. The SUV was huge, but all the parents still had to take a separate car. Three in the backseat was all the room there was.

"Why do I need the trash bag?" Dylan asked as Sam pulled away from the curb, blue light going off like a strobe. "My water already broke."

He chuckled, reached out and touched her cheek, petting her. "Oh sweetie, you're so pretty."

She had to smile—no way not to.

"That's amniotic fluid, dear, it doesn't stop until the baby's out."

"Oh," she said, looking over her shoulder at Chris. "Did you know that?"

"No."

She questioned her sister Roxanne and then me. None of us had any idea. When she turned back to Sam she explained that she thought there was just one big gush like in the movies.

"Nope," he assured her.

"How come you know so much?"

Talking kept her mind occupied and Sam knew all about diversionary tactics.

I was surprised at the amount of things Sam knew about babies. He had himself delivered four when he was a uniformed officer: one in a bank during a robbery, two in cabs, and one in the back of his squad car. All his sisters had kids and had recounted their birth stories to him and the rest of his family in grisly detail. He had Dylan laughing as he talked about his sister Jen's birth video and how it had accidentally turned up at the local video store. When she had a contraction he made her count through it, and told her how well she'd done when it was over.

As we were all climbing out of the SUV in front of the hospital, I felt a hand on my back. I was faced with Roxanne, and she was smiling at me.

"You keep that man, Jory," she sighed deeply. "Gorgeous and built like that.... God! Those arms of his and the way he carried Dy.... Christ. Does he have a straight brother?"

I laughed, because basically, before me, Sam *was* that brother. Chris caught my arm and pulled me in beside him as we walked behind them through the parking lot.

"I wish I could carry her like that."

"He's just big, so he can."

"I wish I was too."

He sounded so sad and I got it as we stopped at the nurses' station and they looked up at Sam, all doe-eyed and sighing. It was so romantic, the man carrying his wife into the hospital, able to stand there forever bearing her weight, and so gentle as he lowered her into the waiting wheelchair. They were disappointed to learn that Chris was Daddy instead of Sam.

Dylan made them wait to take her as she grabbed Sam's hand and pulled him down so they were level. His eyes glowed as he looked at her.

She sighed deeply. "I hate you."

He nodded, tipped his head toward me. "I know. He hates me too."

"Don't think we've bonded, because we haven't bonded."

"Okay," he said, leaning forward, kissing her forehead as he rose to tower above her. I realized then she was still holding his hand.

We all sat down to wait and Sam put his arm across the back of my chair and his hand in my hair. When he kissed my temple before getting up, I found all eyes on me.

"What?"

"Jory," Dylan's mother smiled at me, "you and Sam make a beautiful couple."

"Thank you."

"You do," Roxanne chimed in. "And I don't mean this to be taken the wrong way, but he's very much a man's man and you're prettier than most women I know. It fits. It makes sense that if a man like that is gay, a man like you would be his partner."

I wasn't sure how to take all that.

"Like I said," Dylan's mother spoke softly, "you make a striking couple. He so obviously adores you."

That part I liked hearing.

Sam returned with hot chocolate for everyone, and when he took his seat back beside me, he slouched down low, laced his fingers with mine, and closed his eyes.

"Sam, they'll be out any minute," I assured him.

"It's her first baby, right?"

"Yeah."

He chuckled. "Wake me when she delivers."

"Wait, what?"

He snickered, raised my hand, kissed the palm, and then settled back and sighed deeply. I thought it would be like the movies. No such luck.

It was still faster than it could have been, and ten hours later Mica was born. He was wrinkled and he had a lot of hair and I could see his Japanese ancestry very clearly. Dylan pointed out that all babies were born looking Japanese. When I looked at Sam as he held the baby, he nodded.

"Okay, so I get it," Dylan sighed, watching Sam hold her son as I sat beside her in the hospital bed. "He's absolutely beautiful and gorgeous and every other word you wanna use, but seriously, you need to watch yourself and not get too involved too fast. Go slow."

"I can't," I confessed seriously. "I'm already in love with Mica."

She rolled her eyes. "Please don't make me smack you. I don't have the energy."

"Okay." I smiled at her. She was radiant. I had never seen her look better.

"We both know I'm taking about Sam Kage."

I grunted.

"Jory, honey… please take it slow with him this time."

Too late, I thought but said nothing.

She sighed heavily, her head on my shoulder, her hand in mine. "Thank you for rescuing me. I was a little out of it."

"It was Sam."

"Make no mistake," she kissed my cheek. "You make him like this."

Like she could know what my effect on Sam Kage was. I watched him pass the baby to Dylan's mom, and his eyes were on me.

"You know it's really a big deal that he was here with us," Dylan told me. "It feels like he's going to be permanent this time, doesn't it?"

And I didn't tell her that I had been thinking the exact same thing.

"What are you wearing?" She had finally noticed the inside-out Diva T-shirt.

"Just never mind."

It was nice to see her laugh.

MY EVENTFUL night ended with Sam and I cooking breakfast together at four in the afternoon, having been up since three in the morning. Sam checked in at work, having called out earlier in the day, and I got hold of Sadie and told her that I'd be back in the office the following morning. She was still at the hospital visiting Dylan, and told me that she had checked e-mail and phone messages and had rescheduled all my appointments for the following week. The office was closed on account of the baby. I told her Aubrey Flanagan was coming in on Monday, and she responded truthfully that she couldn't care less. She just wanted to hold Mica.

Sam made omelets and we sat and talked. Afterwards I did the dishes. He passed out on the couch around six and I left to go home and shower and change. I made sure to leave a note.

Chapter Six

THE knocking on my front door brought me from my bedroom in only my jeans. I was surprised to find Brandon Rossi on my doorstep.

"Hey," I said, pulling my T-shirt on as I looked at him. "What's up?"

"I called your office earlier and your assistant said you were all out today."

I was guessing Sadie had routed the office phone to her cell for whatever reason. "Yep. We're closed due to the baby."

He gave me a ghost of a smile. "I have no idea what that means."

I grinned back. "My partner Dy, she had her baby last night."

"Oh, well, give her my congratulations."

"I will."

"Your assistant gave me your address, I hope you don't mind."

"No," I lied. I would have to talk to Sadie about that.

He cleared his throat, smiling sheepishly. "Look, Jory, I just wanted to come over here in person and say how sorry I was about the other night. Adam and I just completely lost track of what we were doing."

"Sure." I smiled at him. "Don't worry about it."

"But see, I really wanted to spend some time with you, and Adam, he... he's crazy about that girl and—"

"Adam's done, man." I smiled slowly, seeing a familiar head of hair appear as he climbed the stairs. I loved his hair... the golden brown waves, how thick it was, and all the colors in it, streaks of copper, wheat, and bronze.

"What do you mean by that?"

"I mean that Aubrey Flanagan is now dating Rick Jenner. Adam needs to let it go."

"Are you kidding me?"

"No." I smiled over his shoulder at Sam. The way he was looking at me with his dark eyes brought back the night before. I felt the heat in my face.

"Are you okay?" Brandon asked. "You're all flushed."

"Fine," I said.

"What?"

"What?" I was listening now.

"Jo—"

"Excuse me," Sam yawned, stepping around Brandon to walk past me into my apartment. He slapped my ass hard on his way by and I couldn't contain my gasp or the smile that followed.

"Who's that?"

"That's Sam." I rubbed the bridge of my nose. "So, I'll see ya round. Thanks for coming by to apologize, that was really nice of you."

"Jory." He reached for me as I tried to retreat into the apartment. "I want to take you—"

"C'mon, Brandon," I said softly, brushing his hand off my shoulder. "You can see I've got company, so—"

"So I'll call you later." He smiled and turned to go.

"Don't do that," I called after him.

He turned to look at me. "What?"

"Don't call me. We're not gonna be friends and we're not gonna date, so there's no point."

He stood there staring at me. "Wow. I had no idea I only had one shot at impressing you."

"Bra—"

"God, Jory, you should put that on cards and pass them out when you meet people."

"Whatever," I said, closing the door.

But he hit the door before it clicked shut and it was just dumb luck that it caught my lip and split it.

"Crap," I groaned, pressing the back of my hand to my mouth.

"Jory," he said, reaching for my face. "I just wanted to say some—"

"What the fuck is going on?" Sam roared from the kitchen.

It was completely accidental, but Brandon wouldn't even live long enough to explain. I looked at him with wide eyes. "Run."

"Jory, I—"

"Run." I panicked as I heard Sam moving behind me in the apartment.

"Baby, are you... what the fuck!" His voice dropped low, turning to ice as he charged toward me.

Brandon hit the doorframe, bounced off of it, and ran. I heard his feet pounding on the wooden floors outside in the hall and then there was silence.

"Sam," I called him before he could get out the door. "I need you."

He was back in front of me in seconds, his hands on my face, frowning.

I grabbed hold of the lapels of his topcoat and looked up into his eyes.

"I will beat that fuck 'til there's nothing left."

I chuckled. "It was an accident."

"What the fuck was he doin' over here anyway? And how'n the hell does he know where you fuckin' live?" he growled at me, hand on my throat, so gentle as he looked me over. "We gotta ice that."

"Stop swearing," I told him. "And I'd like to point out that you know where I live too."

"So what? You belong to me. Of course I know where you live."

I nodded, smiling up at him.

"Shit," he glowered at me, grabbing and dragging me into the kitchen. Sam's ministrations were almost more painful than the bump that had caused the split lip.

When he was done, I stood and stared at him.

"What?"

"I was going back to your place."

"Yeah, the note covered that," he grumbled.

I smiled at him before I left for my bedroom to pull on a sweater. While I was fastening my belt buckle he leaned in the room, holding on to the doorjamb.

"You should have woken me up. I would've driven you over here."

"It's fine."

"I woke up and you were gone... I didn't like it."

"So that's why you came? Just couldn't wait for me to come back?" I teased him. "Or maybe you thought I wasn't coming?"

"No, I just wanted to talk to you and I couldn't wait."

"Wait for what?"

He walked slowly into my bedroom. "I like your place."

"Thanks." I smiled at him. "It's bigger than the old one."

He nodded. "So what now, J?"

"Whaddya mean?"

"I mean... was I gonna sleep over here with you? Were you planning to spend the night at my place? Were we getting dinner and then doing our own thing? I dunno what's going on 'cause you're not talking. I've told you how I want things to be, but you haven't said anything."

I stared into those dark, smoky blue eyes of his.

"J?"

I took a deep breath. "I was planning to pack a bag and sleep at your place tonight, if I wouldn't upset your morning routine too much."

The light that came into his eyes was very satisfying. "No, you wouldn't upset anything. That'd be great."

"Okay." I smiled at him. "Sit down and talk to me while I pack."

He watched intently as I put things into my duffel and afterwards carried it out for me as I followed him down to his car. When we were inside but he didn't start the engine, I turned to look at him.

"What?"

"Last night you said it was just for the night... did you mean it?"

I looked at him, studying his face. "Obviously not."

"Don't be funny, okay? I know this is really fast for you so I'm trying to not push, but it's killin' me 'cause there's stuff I want you to say and... I'm not sure what to do. Should I leave you alone for a little while or what should I do, J? Tell me what you want me to do."

"This is fast, Sam, you know it is. I mean, I just saw you Sunday, now it's Thursday night, and—"

His phone rang, cutting me off. He ignored it, intent on me. I couldn't. "You better get that."

He answered while I looked out the window, trying to figure out what I was going to do. I was split right down the middle. Half of me wanted to throw caution to the wind and beg him to move in with me, the other wanted to run away as fast as I could. I was terrified to lose him and terrified of getting hurt again. When he cleared his throat, I looked back at him. The crooked grin made me smile.

"What?"

"Well, this oughta be the clincher," he sighed.

"What? Tell me."

"That was my mom calling to remind me that I'm already late for dinner."

"Dinner? Don't you guys usually do the Sunday thing?"

"Yeah, but Mike's girlfriend is a stewardess—"

"Flight attendant," I corrected him.

"Whatever, Mr. Politically Correct," he grumbled. "I'm just telling you that his girl flies like every Sunday, so the only time to catch her is in the middle of the week. My mom wants everybody to meet her so... we got Thursday night dinner at the Kages."

"Oh."

"Don't sound so excited."

"No, I didn't mean anything." I moved to get out of the SUV. "I'll let you go and maybe after, if you want, you can pick—"

"Hey," he said softly, taking hold of my arm, leaning me close enough so he could put his hand on my face. "I'm not going without you."

"Oh no, Sam, you—"

"Listen, I know you're scared to go over there, 'cause what does that mean, right? It's too fast and you're starting to panic."

"No," I lied even though he had hit the nail on the head. "I just think—"

He tilted my chin up and looked down into my eyes. "It's fast 'cause it's right, and make no mistake, I need you to go with me."

I stared at him and he leaned close and kissed me. It was so soft and so tender and I tried to deepen it, to draw him down, but he resisted.

"You can hurt me a little, Sam," I breathed against his mouth. My split lip didn't even hurt.

"I already did," he said softly. "Never again."

And I knew he meant when he left. "It's okay."

"It's not," he said, his eyes absorbing my face. "But I have the rest of my life to make it up to you."

"Sam—"

He cleared his throat. "C'mon, baby, get your belt on—we gotta hurry."

"Why?"

"'Cause my mom's making her world-famous casserole for Mike's new girl and we don't wanna miss the carnage," he almost cackled.

"That's not funny," I assured him, scowling. "Your family is big and loud and scary. Poor girl."

"It's a little funny," he argued, evil smile for me. "And don't kid yourself, you love my family."

"I love you," I said, turning the heater up.

"What?"

Too late I realized what I'd said. And I had voiced it before, but not without him asking me, pressuring me. The words had simply tumbled out and I could tell he was very pleased.

"J... what?"

"What?" I looked at him. I was hoping to play it off like nothing.

"Say it again."

"Say what?" I asked innocently. Maybe he'd let it go.

He smiled evilly. "You know, what ya said."

No chance he was letting it go.

"C'mon," he prodded me. "Say it again."

I stared at him and he leaned over the emergency brake to give me a quick kiss.

"I love you." He breathed down the side of my neck.

I nodded. "I love you too."

And the smile on his face when he leaned back, so wide, so arrogant, so relieved, so smug, was not to be missed. I had created a monster with four little words.

EVEN though it was Thursday night instead of Sunday, there were enough people there that we needed to park the usual half a block away. With an arm draped over my shoulder, Sam led me through the front yard and around the side of the house to the steps that led to the back door of the large two-story, A-frame, redbrick home. I followed him into the kitchen, and as soon as I was inside I smelled the food.

"Jesus, what is that?" I said, breathing it in. I was almost salivating right there.

"It's the Mousalia." He smiled at me. "I told you it's world famous."

"It smells like heaven."

He winked at me before he yelled. "Mom! I'm home."

"What did you bring me?" she asked from the other room, and I could hear her laughing at her own joke.

I heard so many other voices laughing along with her that all at once I was scared. What if she was mad at me? What if everybody hated me now, what if they all thought that time away from me had turned him back into a straight man? Maybe their son's gay lover wasn't the guest they were looking forward to seeing at their table, for a special middle-of-the-week-night edition of dinner.

"Sammy, get in here," Thomas Kage called out. "The game started on ESPN already."

"What's wrong?" Sam asked me quickly.

"You first."

"There's nothing wrong with me." He grinned slowly, devilishly. "You're the one who's freaked out."

"And if I am?" I asked, my voice rising just a little.

He reached out and put an arm around my neck, easing me up against him. He kissed my temple. "Aww, baby, everybody already loves you. You're golden."

I smiled up at him and he bent and kissed me.

"C'mon, baby."

I followed him into the living room.

"Look what I brought you, Mom."

Regina Kage was a stunning woman just sitting doing nothing. When she smiled, you saw the movie-star magic. When she smiled, you got that she was luminous. She was smiling now. Her eyes darted back and forth between us and settled on me.

"Jory," she said, "oh my goodness, finally." Her breath caught as she rushed across the room to me. She threw her arms out wide and I stepped into them, hugging her tight. "Finally."

She chanted the word with so much feeling and relief that I felt stupid for even doubting my reception. The woman loved me, it was obvious.

"Oh my sweet boy," she cooed into my hair, rubbing circles on my back. "My sweet-sweet boy." And then she said something into my shoulder that I couldn't hear before she pulled back to look at me. "Everyone, come see," she called to the women sitting in the living room. "My boy is home!"

And I looked over at Sam as he shrugged and people surged around me.

Jen came and threw herself into my arms, kissing and hugging me tight before stepping back to introduce me to her new boyfriend, Doug Yates. He was nice, had three kids of his own, and was a construction foreman. I liked him right away, and the fact that he didn't care one bit that I was gay was a big fat point in his favor. He cared more about Sam than me. He was just as intimidated by Detective Kage as everyone else that ever met him, careful of his size, the muscles, and the quick temper. Me, he cared nothing about at all.

Rachel mauled me and her husband Dean was very pleased to see me. There were other cousins to see, and the men greeted me with outstretched hands, the cool-guy head tip, or a yell. The women quickly invaded my personal space. I kissed and hugged them all and they pointed out the main attraction to me—Beverly Stiles, Michael's new girlfriend. She was meeting the extended family for the first time. My heart went out to her. She looked like a deer caught in the headlights.

"J," Michael said, smiling crazily at me as he breezed into the room. "Hey, buddy, I missed ya."

When he was close enough, he surprised me by reaching out and grabbing me into a tight guy-clench. "Sammy missed ya, too," he said softly, his voice catching. "More than a little. Maybe now my brother can stop being such a prick."

"Michael!" Regina had overheard him and she was clearly mortified.

"Aww, Mom, you know it's the God's honest truth!" he grumbled at her, letting me go. "He's been a total asshole the whole time Jory's been gone."

"Yes, I know, but your words, Michael, Mother of God!"

"But Mom, we both know he should do a helluva lot of ass-kissin' or—" He stopped and looked at me. "And no offence there, J, since maybe that's something you're into or—you know—I dunno… but the point is, whatever it takes, Sammy should just do already, 'cause I can't deal with him when you're not around. He's a total dick." He was adamant.

"Michael!"

"Amen," Levi Kage chimed in, walking up to stand behind me. "How ya doin', Jory?" He held out his hand for me when I turned around. "I hope you're planning to stick around this time."

I took the offered hand and was pulled into the same guy-clench I had gotten from Michael. It was the hard handclasp, the shoulder-to-shoulder jerk, followed by the sharp back slap. It was slightly painful, so I knew it was sincere. I got many more handshakes as many of Sam's cousins flowed through the room.

Minutes later, I leaned over the back of the couch and reached out a hand to Joseph, Levi's brother. Funny to think that I had met all the guys years ago but it seemed like only yesterday. He stepped close so I could reach him and we shook hands.

"It's great to see ya."

"You too."

He nodded, staring at me hard. "Do me a favor and just hang out, okay?"

"Yeah, I'm going to."

"No, I mean like, stick around for a while. Not just for tonight."

I nodded. It was very nice.

"Seriously," he said, suddenly so quiet and still. "Sammy looks like himself again, ya know?"

I shrugged. "He looks the same to me."

Michael squeezed my arm as he walked by. "That's what he means."

I smiled, gazing after both of them as they left the room.

"Jory," Thomas Kage, Sam's father, called out to me from over near the TV. "C'mere!"

I moved quickly because you just did as he ordered.

He glanced up at me, but only for a second. Some game was on. "Jory."

"Sir."

"You stick around this time, Jory, all right?"

It wasn't my fault. "Sir, I—"

"Ah!" he cut me off sharply, loudly, leaving no room for protest. "Just do as I say."

"But it wasn't my—"

"Ah!" He did it again, and I realized what an annoying sound it was. "Just promise me. That's all I want to hear. I'm not interested in excuses."

I sighed deeply. "Yessir."

"Good," he said quickly and gestured to Michael's new girlfriend, whom I hadn't noticed until then, sitting beside him. "Did you meet Beverly?"

"No sir."

"Beverly, this is my son's partner, Jory."

She rose off the couch and gave me her hand.

"More friend," I corrected him, smiling at her.

"Partner!" Sam's dad yelled at me.

I shot him a look. Now I knew where Sam got his temper.

"You have something to say?" he dared me, finally looking from the television screen to my face. "Go ahead, speak."

"No sir," I whispered, drawing Beverly away from him, turning to look at her face.

"Good," he grunted, like everything was settled.

"I'm so happy to meet you," she said sincerely, clinging to my hand.

I saw the wide-eyed fright in her eyes and smiled tenderly. Poor thing, they were scaring the crap out of her. I knew that, for people who weren't used to big families, the volume in the house, the yelling, and the way people just came and went, could be a little daunting.

"Same here," I told her. "So how long have you and Michael been going out?"

"About five months," she said quickly, turning and smiling after him as he walked through the living room. "And I have to say that this is like the first time I have seen his brother not look mean."

"Mean?"

"Yes."

"Really?"

"Oh yes," she assured me firmly.

"How so?"

She thought a moment. "I think the scowling is my favorite. And the way he never speaks to me and how gruff his tone is when he does."

"Really?" I just couldn't get over it. "Well, you have to cut him some slack. He's a police detective and—"

"Oh, I know all about his job." She dismissed my argument.

"So you understand why sometimes he can come off—"

"It must be very stressful to be a detective," she agreed, "I'm not debating that with you. But it doesn't really explain his mood since I've met him."

"Oh. What does?"

"Well, I thought maybe it was because he was lonely."

I shrugged. "That would seem reasonable."

"So I asked Mikey, and he agreed with me that we would set him up with some of my friends."

Mikey? "That's really nice of you guys." I nodded, thinking how I could get Michael alone so I could strangle him. Set Sam up? Was he high?

"It was," she smiled sheepishly. "But the second you walked through the door, he leaned over and told me to not worry about it anymore."

"Oh?"

"Yeah. I think I know what Mikey wants now."

"And what is that?" *Not to be called Mikey?*

"Oh please!" She giggled. "He was worried about his brother and thought maybe I could help him do something about it. But now that you're here... he wants you and Sam to be together."

"You think?"

She laughed because she knew I was teasing her. "Jory, ohmygod, could Mikey like you any more? Could any of them? My goodness, it's like Christmas around here right now."

"It's 'cause—"

"I had no idea Sam was gay," she said in a low voice. "Nobody tells me anything."

"Well, he—"

"Holy crap," she said softly before I saw her glance warily around the room. I put an arm around her shoulders. "There are a lot of people here."

And I realized that, to her, we were just talking. She didn't care for a second that I was gay or Sam was. It was a tiny detail to her, a momentary "huh," merely something she hadn't known or considered. In her universe, where Michael was the center, the situation with Sam and me was meaningless. I loved the fact that no one cared at all.

"Beverly."

She turned to look at my face.

"Everything's gonna be all right. It must be a good sign that the extended family was summoned over here to meet you."

"I guess." She was unsure, and it was clear from her voice.

"No, I'm sure it was."

"Oh God." She flinched.

I smiled tenderly. "It's okay. You must always tell yourself, the more the merrier."

"Uh-huh."

"So, are you guys getting engaged?"

"Oh, don't I wish," she replied honestly, and I doubt she even realized what she'd said to me. "No, it's just he wanted me to meet his whole family and so did his mom, which is nice, I guess, but... I mean, I've been here a few times before, met his folks of course, and Sam and his sisters, but not... everyone."

"It'll be okay," I told her, patting her arm.

She whimpered.

"Why don't you come in the kitchen and help Regina and me?"

"Are you sure that's the right thing to do? I mean, I want her to like me but I don't want to push."

"Believe me, that's the way to do it. I'll help you clean the kitchen after the meal is set out. That's a step in the right direction, big time."

She grabbed my arm. "Thank you thank you thank you. You have no idea how crazy I am about this man. I have to make his family love me."

"It's easy." I smiled warmly, speaking from experience. "Just be yourself."

"Were you yourself?"

I thought about it a minute. "Yeah, I was."

"Did you know you wanted to be with Sam from the moment you laid eyes on him?"

"I don't know if—"

"Me too," she jumped to the conclusion even after cutting me off. "I want to marry Mikey," she confessed. "I'm in way over my head, Jory."

I put an arm around her shoulders and squeezed gently. "Well, I think he'd be lucky to have you," I said supportively, realizing that I meant it. This was a really nice girl. I hoped that Michael was healthy enough to realize what he had.

Beverly Stiles was just a little shorter than me, so just under five-nine, with shoulder-length brown hair and big cornflower-blue eyes. She did her makeup with the heavy black eyeliner on top that made your eyes look like a cat's. The lipstick was pale and lined dark, and she had an amazing tan for the middle of winter. I was thinking at least two trips a week to the tanning salon.

"And how long are you going to be around?"

"What?" My mind had been drifting.

"I asked you how long you were planning on staying around."

This was a very good question.

"I hope for a long time, 'cause I need you."

"Me too," Sam said quickly, his voice deep as he walked up beside me.

"Hey." I smiled up at him. "Say hello to Beverly."

"Hi there." He smiled at her, his hand slipping around the back of my neck. "Hope you're not put off by the volume in here today."

She was stunned, you could tell. Like a lot of people, she had thought she'd seen Sam and knew what he looked like. "No," she gulped, and I saw her pale, looking at him.

"It's good to see you again," he said honestly, moving his hand to massage the back of my head, his fingers buried in my hair. "My brother looks really happy."

She nodded, and I watched her melt under his warm eyes, his gentle voice, and trace of a smile. She wondered, like everyone else, how in the hell he hadn't commanded more of her attention before. Had he always looked like that? Was she so blinded by Michael that she had missed his gorgeous brother?

"I've never seen you look better," she told him sincerely.

Automatic smile in response instead of the cold, disapproving look I knew she was used to. "Thanks. You want something to drink? I'll grab it for you."

"No." I put up my hand. "Let Beverly get it Your mom will like that."

"What?" Beverly asked anxiously, turning from Sam to me.

"I've watched Regina—she likes her boys to be served, not to do the serving." I told her. "Really, go in the kitchen and tell her you're there to get Michael a drink, and one for Sam as well."

"Oh, okay." She nodded, moving around me fast. "Thanks, Jory."

I watched her go as Sam stepped behind me and wrapped his arms loosely around my neck. He leaned down and kissed my ear as his father yelled for the prodigal son to come into the living room and watch football with him. Like I even did that.

I sighed heavily. "What's with him pushing my buttons tonight? He's never been like that before?"

"Ask me what he said every time I came over here," he whispered in my ear, giving me goose bumps.

"What?" I smiled as the heat raced along my skin.

"He said, "So, dipshit, when you gonna go get your boy?""

"Are you kidding?" I was stunned. He called me Sam's boy?

"Yeah. He's embraced my alternative lifestyle very quickly."

"Is three years quickly?"

"More like two," he said, pressing a kiss into the crook of my neck. "You smell so good."

"Quit."

"You wanna see my old room?"

"No."

"I think ya do."

"No." I smiled, but I didn't laugh. It was a victory for me.

"How 'bout my old bed? It doesn't creak much."

"Sam—"

"My dad is crazy about you. Everyone is."

I let out a deep breath.

"You're the only one everybody likes, in fact."

He sounded odd, so I turned my head to look at him.

"Huh." He was really thinking about what he'd just said. "That's really interesting. Everybody else has a problem with at least one other person in the family."

I smiled at him as he looked down into my eyes.

"Except you."

I arched a brow for him.

"Funny."

But I was likable. Dane always said so.

I HAD never been in Sam's room before and I had no idea why. Maybe because I'd never been invited, and to go without being asked seemed like an intrusion. But he had offered, so I was there, alone, looking at his bookshelves, at the pictures tacked to the corkboard, at trophies and a letterman jacket hanging by itself on a hook behind the door.

"In case you missed it," he said from behind me. "I wanted to come up here with you."

I hadn't even heard him open the door. "I know, I just wanted to see what you were like when you were younger. Where'd ya keep the porn?"

He chuckled and walked up behind me. I felt him there like a wall of heat, and when he kissed the crook of my neck, I tilted my head so he could reach more. Instantly, his arms wrapped me up, holding me tight against his chest.

"We should've stayed home."

"Why?"

"'Cause all I can think about is last night."

"And?"

"I wanna go back to bed."

I felt my heart flutter and I trembled hard. I couldn't help it; my body just reacted to the sound of his voice, the low, throaty quality of it that just dripped sex.

"Your body was always beautiful, but now...." He put a hand in my hair. "Damn, baby."

I couldn't take it. "Sam," I barely got out.

He turned me in his arms, bent and kissed me in one fluid motion. His mouth was sealed over mine, his tongue sliding over my lips as I opened them for him. One of his hands was on the small of my back, the other one lower on my ass, kneading, caressing me through my jeans. My hands were in his hair, holding him close to me, kissing back with every drop of need in me. I was hungry for him and he wanted me just as bad.

"Wow, that's hot."

We broke the kiss, flying apart, both of us facing the sound of the voice at the door.

"Oh, don't stop on my account." Rachel smiled first at her brother and then me. The twinkle in her eyes was absolutely evil. "You two go right ahead."

"Aww," Jen said from beside her. "You guys are adorable together."

"Uh," Sam groaned. "Talk about a buzz kill."

Rachel's arched eyebrow, Jen's clasped hands held to her heart, and Sam's scowl—it was all too much. I dissolved into laughter. I loved Sam's family.

Another groan from him and I could barely breathe.

"He's so cute," Rachel said, smiling at me.

"Oh yeah," Sam exhaled. "He's a goddamn riot."

Later on, after everyone ate and I helped clean for almost two hours, Beverly at my side making points the entire time, I went and found Sam. He was watching more football with his dad, stretched out on the recliner, and I sat down on the arm of the chair. I felt his hand on my back, and when I looked down at him, he patted his chest. I sank down on top of him, my head under his chin, one arm under him, the other draped across his chest. I was so comfortable and he was so warm. I fell asleep with him stroking my back.

I woke up because Sam's dad yelled.

"Shhh, you'll wake him up," Sam whispered harshly.

"And so what if I do? Maybe he'll give me better answers then you."

"Mom," he called for her.

"Thomas," I heard Regina soothe him. "Leave your son alone. He's done well today. He brought his boy back home and I'm sure he's not stupid enough to let him go again."

"Mom," he groaned, and I felt the sigh come up out of him.

"What do you want me to say, darling?" she asked him patiently. "That whatever this boy wants you to do, you should do, so he never leaves you? Why you let him go in the first place is completely beyond me. Didn't you know you loved him?"

"'Course."

"But not how much. You had no clue how it would feel to lose him."

No answer, he simply took a deep breath.

"I knew. He's the best thing that ever happened to you."

"Mom," he began, groaning. "I didn't leave him. I had a job to do and I needed to keep him safe and—"

"You deny it?"

"Deny what?"

"That he's the best thing that ever happened to you."

"No, but I'm trying to tell you why I—"

"There's no but, my love. Before him you were a wild thing with no one to care for you. All those women and not one that could keep a home for you."

"Mom," he complained. "There weren't that many—"

"I prayed for a wife for you every night," she interrupted him. "And now I know the Lord, he heard my prayers, he just knew better than me what was best for you. I understand now because when I see the way Jory looks at you, my heart hurts with joy."

"Okay, Mom."

"He's an angel straight from heaven."

"Yes, he is," he agreed, and I felt his fingers trailing through my hair.

"You are so happy when he's with you. Everyone said to me tonight, Regina, your son is radiant."

"I'm sure they did, Mom."

"Sarcasm is not lost on me, Samuel."

"Christ."

"Sam!"

"Sorry—sorry, I just—"

"Be quiet. Just sit there and hush."

"How come no one's on my side?" he grumbled, shifting so he could kiss my forehead.

"What's your side?" Michael asked.

"That I had to go and—"

"But you're the man," Thomas argued in his medieval mindset. "As soon as you got back you should have gone to him, told him how things would be. This is your place, Sam."

"It doesn't work like that."

"Why?"

"'Cause I don't own him, Pop."

"No?"

"You know I don't. Jory does what he wants to do."

"And so now he wants to be with you?"

"Yes. I think so. I hope so."

"You don't know?"

"I told him how I wanted it to be but… he's gotta say."

"He doesn't say, you say, and he's here now, so whatever you do, you keep him."

"Aww, man, it's not my fault I had to go. I—"

"But it is your fault that it took so long to come back. You should thank God Jory did not find someone new. Where would you be then?"

"Who cares whose fault it was?" I heard Michael throw in. "It only matters that it's fixed now."

"Christ, I wasn't in *that* bad a shape."

"Don't take the Lord's name in vain!" Regina scolded him.

"Mom, that wasn't taking—"

"You sure as shit were," Michael interrupted him. "I mean, you know it's gotta be bad when even Beverly, who barely knows you, can see the difference."

"Oh yeah? What can you see?" I heard Sam bait her.

"No, Sam, I only meant that—"

"Oh no, little girl, you're in it," Thomas explained to her. "Say what you think."

"Okay." I heard her voice shake. "I just mentioned to Mikey that you look really good today. It's like I said earlier, I've never seen you look better."

"I see."

"Are you upset with me?" she asked slowly, her voice very small.

I pressed against him, squeezing him tight, before slipping a leg between his. I wanted to listen, but I was just too sleepy. I kissed his throat and then snuggled back down, my head over his heart, letting out a contented sigh.

"No," I heard him answer before I dropped off again. "I've got my boy back, there's no way I could be pissed at anyone right now."

"So what are you going to do now, Sammy?" I heard Jen ask.

She must have walked into the room.

"Whatever he wants me to."

"Oooh, that's a nice answer." She laughed and everyone joined her.

I woke up much later and looked around the room. Thomas was yelling at the TV and Regina was smiling at me. I turned and saw Michael, with his attention on the screen, and Beverly sitting quietly beside him.

"Oh I'm so sorry." I yawned, smiling at Regina. "I missed everybody."

"It doesn't matter," she said cheerfully. "There will be other times for you to see them."

My face must have given her pause.

"Jory?"

"Regina," I hedged, "I don't know if—"

"What?"

"I don't know if Sam and I are gonna—"

"What?" Thomas snapped, turning to look at me, and I had Michael's attention as well.

"I have a job I love and a life, and I think that Sam—"

"Since when do I care what you think?" Thomas asked dryly. "I don't care. It's Sam's fault you went away in the first place, but if you leave again it's all on you, Jory."

"Thomas!"

"Regina, do you hear what he's saying? He's going to leave your son."

"No, that's not what I'm saying. I just...." I shook my head, rising up off of Sam, awkwardly getting to my feet. I was all tangled up in him and almost took a header into the coffee table before I found my legs. I moved to stand over Thomas. "I'm not saying I'm leaving him, it's just moving too fast and—"

"Wait," Thomas put up a hand in front of me. "Do you love my son?"

This was a thousand times worse than how I had imagined it. I looked over at Regina and she looked as though someone had slapped her.

"I don't know if I—"

"You don't love him?" Michael asked pointedly.

"No, I love him, I—"

"It's one or the other," Thomas said solemnly. "Which is it, Jory?"

"Jory?" Regina prodded me.

"I just, it's like a minute old, ya know? He just comes storming back into my life and... I need a second to breathe. I can't promise you anything right this second."

They were all staring up at me and I felt terrible. Here they were, ready to welcome me with open arms, and I was on the fence.

"What the hell's going on?" I heard Sam growl behind me.

"Listen," Thomas said quickly, rising up in front of me and grabbing me into his arms in one fluid motion. I was crushed against him as he whispered into my hair. "He needs you and you need him. Don't let something as insignificant as time change your heart. When it's right, you know, and I think you do."

I trembled in his arms and he rubbed the back of my head like I'd seen him do with his grandchildren.

"Seriously, what the hell is going on? Why're you cryin', Mom?"

"I'm so happy. Jory's home."

"Mike?"

"What?" he snapped at Sam.

"Are you crying?"

"In your dreams, asswipe."

"Mikey, don't curse in your parents' home."

"Sorry, Bev," he apologized. "I meant to say asshole."

"Mikey!" Beverly yelled.

"Michael!" Regina yelled.

"Sorry, Mom. Sorry, Bev," he apologized to both of them.

"Oh," Regina clapped her hands. "I'm so happy."

"Christ."

"Samuel Thomas Kage!"

He groaned.

"Don't take the Lord's name in vain!" Thomas bellowed at his son, finally letting me go. "You stay with us, Jory. This family needs you," he said sincerely, his eyes all soft and liquid.

"That's such a nice thing to say."

"I know," he said arrogantly. "Now, this Sunday we're having deer for dinner. My brother Joe will be back from his hunting trip."

Eating Bambi. I felt my stomach roll. "Great."

He patted my face.

"Jory dear, come help me in the kitchen." Regina smiled, getting up off the couch. "Who wants cake?"

I turned and looked down at Sam. I couldn't stop smiling. What a weird twenty-four hours this had been.

"Baby, I'm sorry," he said worriedly, standing up in front of me. "We can go slow and—"

"Why?"

"Why?"

"Yeah. What's the point?"

He was searching my face. "But you've been such a basket case about me coming back into—"

"And I'm still worried, Sam, but what am I gonna do, just live in fear that something's gonna go wrong? I mean, c'mon—something will always go wrong, we just gotta roll with it this time. I mean, I don't know if you feel it, but... and maybe it's as simple as we're both older, I dunno, I just...." I took a steadying breath. "I'm at the job I'm gonna keep, ya know, and I have Dylan and Chris and friends that have stuck around, and of course Dane and now his wife Aja and... I just didn't have you, and now you're here so... and I've got your family's blessing... I figure," I shrugged, "I'm good to go."

He gave me a crooked grin. "So you're saying what? You'll move in with me?"

"No." I shook my head. "That part we do need to take slow."

"Then what?"

"We can date."

He scowled at me. "I don't wanna date you, I wanna live with you."

"Well, you get to date me." I smiled at him. "You gotta start somewhere."

"I want you to move in with me."

"Let me explain something to you," I began, "you can keep saying that, but it's not gonna change anything."

Just the very corner of his lip curved. "Oh no?"

"Let's see how it goes, Sam."

He nodded. "It's gonna go so great, you're gonna be begging me to move in."

"We'll see."

"But you won't see anyone else," he was clarifying, making sure. "I'm the only one you're sleeping with from now on, right?"

"Right."

"Okay," he said. "I'll take it, it's a start."

I just looked at him. He'd take it; like he had a choice…. The man was hilarious. Of course he'd take it; it was all he was going to get right now.

He put his hands on my face. "You mean it, right? There's only gonna be me."

Did I mean it? I searched my heart just to make sure nothing felt weird. I purposefully tried to think of our worst times, but all that came to mind was us having breakfast in the middle of the afternoon. Just the two of us together in his apartment, sitting and eating, being together and talking about the events of the night. It felt comfortable and right. There was only good stuff, nothing bad.

"Yeah, I mean it," I told him. "And God help you when Dane gets back from his honeymoon."

"I don't give a shit about Dane Harcourt." He grabbed me roughly, and his arms were around me as he lifted me off my feet. "I just care about you, J. I'm gonna make you so happy this time. I swear to God."

I smiled, wrapping my arms around him, holding him tight. "What? You love me?"

"I do," he said, and I felt the shiver run through his huge frame. "You know I do."

"Yeah?"

"Fuck, yeah."

I really needed to work on the swearing. "Yeah, well. I love you too." I sighed in his arms. "It's exhausting, but I do."

"I know, baby. I know."

Chapter Seven

I HAD been frantic all Friday, trying to catch up and do my job as well as Dylan's, so that when Sam called and said he was coming to pick me up for lunch I had to turn him down. I was buried, and it was a nice change that he understood. He had things to catch up on himself. I told him I would see him at dinner. I was surprised when he showed up at noon with Chinese food. It was really nice, and the make-out session on the couch was even better. When I was shoving him out the door two hours later, he looked sad until I passed him the extra set of keys I had for my apartment. His smile lit his eyes.

"What?" I smiled back.

"These are keys to your place, right?" he asked, rolling them in his hand.

"Yeah. You should have a set."

The muscles in his jaw clenched tight. "Thank you."

"Are you okay?"

He nodded.

"Good," I said, leaning up to touch his face. "Me too."

He grabbed me tight and kissed me hard. Who knew a set of keys could make the man so happy?

THAT night Sam had arranged for me to meet his partner and her boyfriend for the first time. I wanted to make a really good impression, but I was so nervous that I did what I always did when I was either worried or bored—I drank. By the time Sam got to the restaurant with his guests and collected me at the bar, the hour head start that I had on them made it impossible for me to be anything but funny and charming as all hell. I was good tipsy and a fun drunk, and so people were always torn between worrying about me getting wasted and the fun they had when I was. When I was drinking I was the life of the party, and I realized that was how I wanted to be when I met Sam's partner. I wanted her to love me.

Chloe Stazzi was warm and kind and her boyfriend Jason Cozza was one of those strong, silent types. That I got him laughing surprised both her and Sam. After that I could do no wrong. We went to sing karaoke after dinner and I got Jason up on stage with me. Chloe fell out of her chair watching us sing "Love Will Keep Us Together" and then dancing around on the stage. Sam was very pleased with me, but when he bought the next few rounds, I noticed I had a Long Island Ice Tea without the Long Island.

"What's going on?" I asked him, trying to focus my eyes.

"You're done," he assured me. "You drink too much, babe, and if I'm gonna stop swearing, you're gonna sober up."

"Me? I drink too much?"

"Yeah." He smiled evilly. "Ya do, and even though you're cute as hell, we're gonna cut this off."

And as I waited for the lecture and the scowl, and waited, I realized that it wasn't coming. He wasn't passing judgment on me; he was just stating the facts.

"You're not mad at me?"

"Why would I be mad?" he asked, reaching for my hand and tugging me forward to stand between his legs. "You ready to let me take you home with me, hotshot?"

I stared down into his eyes.

"Your face is all flushed and your pupils are huge."

I was stunned. There was no yelling, no growling, and no threats… just Sam talking to me.

"What?"

"Nothing." I shook my head. "I'm ready to go."

"Good, 'cause just watching you is killin' me," he breathed, standing up, his hand going to the back of my neck, massaging as I let my head fall forward.

I leaned into him and I heard the deep chuckle.

"I love the purring."

"I think maybe I'm hungry again," I said, suddenly ready to just sit and talk to him.

"Me too," he agreed, his arm wrapping around my neck. "Come with me. Let's find Chloe and Jace and see if they wanna grab a late dinner."

At the car Jason told me he loved me, and I quickly returned the sentiment. Chloe groaned loudly and laughed before giving me a big kiss and telling Sam I was a keeper. Something about me being as big a pain in the ass as her man. I liked her so much. I was glad that Sam had me meet this partner, and it was a nice way to spend a Friday night. I wanted everyone in his life to adore me. I was surprised when they didn't wait for us but instead drove away.

"Wait," I said, pointing after them. "Did you ask them if they wanted to eat?"

"No dear, you did."

"I did?"

There was a snort of laughter from him. "Yeah."

I looked up at his face. "What'd they say?"

He shook his head "They told you no like five times. You never listen when you're fucked up."

"Don't swear." I yawned. "Say wasted instead."

"Fine. You never listen when you're wasted."

I grinned wide. "Chloe liked me."

"Yeah, she did."

"Her boyfriend's nice."

"Her boyfriend barely looked at her. He paid more attention to you."

"You think so?"

"Yeah, I think so."

"Sam, he just—"

"You move nice, by the way," he said with his smoky voice, and I felt the shudder pass through me just from the sound. "Cold?"

"No, I'm fine."

"I wouldn't get too attached to Jason if I were you."

"Whaddya mean?"

"I'm thinkin' he's done."

"Like how? You think he's cheating on Chloe?"

"Maybe not cheating, but you can tell just from watching them that he's not that into her. I mean, I'm not saying he has to throw her down and screw on the floor of the bar, but I don't think he touched her once all night."

As we walked to the car I thought about what he had said. Could I roll back the night in my head and see disinterest from Jason? I made the argument that some people just weren't that demonstrative.

He grunted.

"Okay," I chuckled, "but for example... obviously, because we were in a straight club, you—"

"Even if we were in a gay club, J, which for the record I might never go in... I'm not usually into the whole public display thing."

"This is what I'm saying." I yawned quickly. "Maybe Jason isn't either."

"Yeah, but I never take my eyes off you when we're out."

I snorted out my laughter. "We've been out all of once at this point."

He shook his head. "No, even from before... I never take my eyes off you."

"Why's that?"

"Well, for one," he said as we reached the car. "I like looking at you, and for two, if someone other than me tries to get close to you without my permission, then we've got a problem."

"Whatever," I chuckled.

"We both know it's true."

I let him open the door for me, and as I climbed in he went around. I leaned across his seat to unlock the driver's side door and then put on my seat belt.

"That's nice, you know?"

I turned to look at him. "What?"

"That you always unlock the door."

I smiled at him. "It's common courtesy."

"To some people it is."

I nodded. I needed to accept compliments better.

"Okay," he said as he pulled the car away from the curb. "About Jason, I know it's different when it's new and you're hot for each other twenty-four seven, but I can't imagine that there will ever come a time when I'm sitting with you and don't feel the need to touch you. I think when you're in love, even over time, that you still like that physical contact with the other person."

I nodded my agreement, because he had just told me he loved me again.

"So ya know, he doesn't need to maul Chloe in public, but you'd think he'd at least wanna stand close to her or make sure no other guy was hittin' on her."

"Maybe he figures since she's a cop she can take care of herself."

"He's still a guy, he should at least get jealous."

I shook my head.

"Okay, so you disagree, but I know people. He's not into her."

"Maybe not."

He let out a long breath. "It's probably been hard on the guy, ya know?"

"Hard how?"

"Hard to be alone so much."

"What're you talking about?"

"All the long hours, J. Being the spouse or partner of a cop is a rough gig. You hardly ever see them and you worry all the time if this is gonna be the day that they don't come home. I mean, most people don't have the potential to die every day when they go to work, unless they're in the military or something."

I turned to look at him. "This is all very comforting."

He chuckled and his hand went to my leg. "C'mon, J, you knew it was like this. I mean, as much as I can I'll be around, but the whole home every night deal ain't gonna be me. You're gonna have a lot of time alone, and during that time I don't want you out drinkin'."

"What?" Talk about a weird transition.

"You heard me."

"I don't drink every night, Sam."

"Yeah, but when you do drink, you drink too much."

I scoffed at him. "I'm a social drinker."

"Not anymore. We're gonna skip this scene for a while."

I grunted. "Like you get to say what I do."

"Oh, I get to say," he said smugly, reaching out to slip his hand under my chin, draw me close to him. "Remember who you let back in your life, J."

I lifted my chin out of his hand and sat there scowling at him.

"You are fuckin' adorable."

"Stop swearing," I grumbled at him as he laughed at me.

AS I sat across from him at the diner, slouched down in the booth, I was struck by how easily we had both fallen into our old patterns. Back together for not even two full days and acting like we had never been apart. It was a little overwhelming, but I was trying not to dwell on it and freak out.

"What are you thinking about?"

I needed something that would give me a second to breathe. "Oh, I know," I said more to myself than Sam. "Tell me how many women you slept with while you were gone."

"Why would you wanna know that?"

"Because I do."

"Fine," he shrugged. "None."

"Any guys?"

"Yeah."

"How many?"

"I dunno, a few."

It was irrational, but I was very happy.

"Why are you smiling? That makes no sense at all."

"I just didn't wanna be the only guy you ever slept with, Sam."

"Why the hell not?"

"'Cause if I was, you'd always be curious about what it would be like with other men. This way, you know."

"Yep, I know."

"And what do you know?"

"That it's not the same as sleeping with you."

I stared at him, my gaze unwavering. "It's not?"

"No, J."

"How come?"

"It was just sex, J. I fucked those guys and left. They were all one-night stands."

"You ever let any of them top, Sam?"

"What? Oh, fuck no."

"Don't—"

"Swear, I know. Whatever."

"I was just wondering."

"It's not me, J, it's not how I'm built. That will never happen."

"Okay."

"Why? Do you have the urge to fu—do me?"

"Nice save," I teased him.

"Answer the question."

"No, Sam," I told him sincerely. "I don't have the urge to do you. That's not how *I'm* built."

"Have you ever?"

"What? Topped anyone?"

"Yeah."

"Lots of times."

"And you didn't like it?"

"No, I didn't."

"Okay."

"Okay," I let out a breath. "So these other five guys... did you—"

"I fucked them and forgot them, J. End of story."

"Really. Simple as that?"

"Simple as that."

"Did you use protection?"

"No, J, I just fuck around without a condom," he snapped irritably, shooting me a look like I was an idiot.

"Sorry, it was just a question."

"A stupid one," he qualified, still scowling.

"Okay, now I know."

"Like I would ever do that with some stranger."

I smiled down at the table because he was so indignant.

"I didn't spend the night with any of them."

I couldn't have said anything if I tried.

"And you?"

I took a breath. "What?"

"Don't be an idiot, answer the goddamn question."

I took a deep breath. "After you left I was a little messed up. I slept with a lot of guys."

He nodded. "And then what?"

"Then for a while there was Aaron."

"Uh-huh. Who else?"

"No one worth mentioning."

His eyes were dark. Clearly he didn't like my number of conquests. "Where did you meet Aaron Sutter?"

"Why do you care?"

"Just answer the question."

"When I was working at Barrington. Dylan and I did some work for his company."

"What does he do?"

"He builds and manages hotels all over the world."

"Rich."

"Very."

"Huh. And so what?"

"You know the story. He wanted me to move in, wanted me to travel with him, just go places with him and be around."

"He wanted to be your sugar daddy."

"No." I shook my head. "He wanted me to be his partner."

"But?"

"But it was too soon. I wasn't ready."

"It was a year later, J, when were you gonna be ready?"

"His question exactly." I smiled lazily, pushing my half-eaten piece of apple pie away from me.

"And?"

"And I dunno. I liked him, I enjoyed being with him—we had a lot of fun... I dunno."

"You know."

I did, and Sam knew me too well to not get it out of me. "He wants me to be what he wants me to be, and I don't feel like changing just to please him."

"Nobody can change anybody else, it's not possible."

We were in complete agreement on this one point.

"Was he good in bed?"

I groaned. "How is that your business?"

"Was he?"

"Yeah," I answered too quickly.

His grin was instant and evil, staring at me with heavy-lidded eyes. "You lie. He didn't do for you at all."

"You have no idea what you're even—"

"The hell I don't," he almost cackled, leaning forward, pointing at me. "I bet he was one of those gentle, considerate guys, huh, J, the kind who asks what he can do first. Tell me I'm wrong."

"Aaron was—"

"Lousy in bed," he chuckled, getting up only to take a seat beside me in the booth.

"Go back over there," I grumbled, pushing on his chest, trying to get him to move.

His thigh was pressed to mine and he leaned against me, his warm breath on the side of my neck, his lips hovering over my skin.

"He was the sensitive type, huh, J?"

"Yes," I snapped at him, trying to scoot over. "And a lot of guys get off on that."

"I'm sure that's true," he said, letting his voice drop to almost a whisper as he slid his hand down over my groin. He cupped me through my dress pants, and I sucked in my breath hard. "But you don't, baby. You like it when I hold you down and do whatever the hell I want."

"I like it when you're gentle," I corrected him, even as I pushed up into his hand and tipped my head so he could reach my neck.

"You like it gentle after, but first you like to be manhandled and wrestled down on the bed. Being thrown up against walls, pinned there, done hard—you crave that and I know, 'cause I'm the one who gets off on doing that to you. Any guy who ain't strong enough to physically force you to do what he wants doesn't stand a chance of being in your bed for long."

"No, I—"

"You need a guy that can overpower you, J, plain and simple."

"You think you know me so well."

He kissed up the side of my neck to behind my ear. When I shivered, he laughed at me. "I do know you and Aaron Sutter can kiss my ass. I'm the only one that can give you what you need. Tell me I'm wrong."

I kept quiet.

"See," he said, biting the side of my neck before he kissed it hard. "There's only me for you."

I wanted to climb in his lap, but we were in the middle of a restaurant. "Take me home."

"Okay," he said, his voice husky and deep. "Tell me first, can I keep you?"

"I already said yes." I smiled at him as he pulled his wallet from the breast pocket of his leather jacket and took four twenties from it. I watched him get up and stand beside the table. He looked really good, and I had told him so when he met me at the bar in the restaurant hours ago. In his black jeans and boots, dark brown cashmere sweater and leather jacket, he was stunning. You saw how big he was; tall, with his broad shoulders, lean hips, and long legs. The sweater was tight, clinging to all the defined muscles in his arms and chest.

"Hey."

My eyes moved from the bulging biceps back to his face. "What?"

"Focus, willya?"

"Sorry."

"I need you to say stuff."

"Like what?"

"I need ya to say that even though it's fast, it's okay. Say you're gonna stick around," he said, his gaze locked on mine. "Say you'll wear a ring if I get you one."

I licked my lips and noticed how his attention was drawn there, to my mouth. The man definitely had it bad for me. "Sam, you—"

"Please, J." He cleared his throat, his voice dropping lower. "It's making me sick, thinkin' about you having doubts about us."

I sighed deeply, standing up beside him. "I don't have any doubts."

"Are you sure?"

"I'm sure. I'll expect you to be around until you aren't anymore."

"I'm not going anywhere," he said, draping his arm over my shoulder, pulling me close to him.

"Okay." I grinned, patting the rock-hard abdomen as I lifted my head to look at him. "So move in."

I groaned, trying to pull away.

His arm was suddenly an anchor holding me beside him. I couldn't move. "You say we're in this together, I've got keys for you at home… just move in."

"Sam—"

"Move in." He was insistent. "I want you to live with me."

I shook my head. "If anybody's moving anywhere, you're moving in with me. Your place is cursed, Detective."

A surge of heat fired his eyes. "You're on. I'll be happy to move in with you."

"Wait, that's not what I said."

"When can I move in?"

I had a feeling that this was going to be a daily conversation until I relented. "J?"

I stared up into his eyes.

"I could move in this weekend."

"No," I chuckled. "It's too soon."

"How 'bout Monday?"

I groaned.

"I wanna kiss you."

I smiled at him. He was adorable.

"But I'm just not comfortable doing that in the middle of this diner."

I made a noise. "Please, like I'm into the whole public display thing either. You can kiss me in the car," I teased him, grinning lazily. "The windows are tinted, after all."

I watched the muscle in this jaw clench. "Okay. I'll kiss you in the car."

And he was as good as his word, even though I was much more than just kissed. I was mauled in the SUV, driven to a secluded spot, stripped naked, and pulled into his lap. It was where I had wanted to be all night.

THE thump woke me. I reached for the light beside his bed and the room came into dim focus.

"Where are you going?" I croaked out, finding Sam putting on his hiking boots in the Empire chair across from the bed by the window.

"I gotta go to work. Go back to sleep, baby."

I checked the clock on the nightstand and saw the time. "It's three in the morning. Come back to bed."

He smiled suddenly and his eyes sparkled in the low light. "I would like nothing better, believe me, but duty calls."

"Just go later," I pleaded, yawning, barely awake and groggy.

"I can't, baby."

"But Sam—"

"I left you a set of keys on the kitchen table."

"Okay."

"You know, you could just move in and then you wouldn't have to carry two sets."

"That's very logical of you."

"That's me, logical."

I stared at him and when both boots were laced, he got up and crossed the room to me.

"You know, I was thinking," he said, sitting down beside me, rubbing my arm. "I really rushed you into all this and I didn't even think about what was going on with you."

I squinted up at him. "And?"

"And I'm sorry," he said softly, leaning down, kissing my throat. "But I can't have it any other way."

"That actually makes me really happy."

"Good, 'cause like I said, I hafta have you with me."

I stared up at him.

"So you really should move in, 'cause you're gonna hafta start cooking."

It took me a second to process what he was saying. "I'm sorry, what?"

He chuckled, then leaned in and kissed me so hard and so deep I got light-headed.

"You cook on Tuesday, Thursday, and Saturday. I cook on Monday and Wednesday and Friday."

"What?" The kiss had muddled my brain.

"And Sunday my mom cooks." He went on like I was following him.

"Sam... what?"

"Yep. It's perfect. We can't afford to eat out every night so... I'll be home between six and seven. I'll call if I'll be any later."

"Okay."

"So your ass needs to be here."

"What?"

"Since you need to cook." He grinned at me.

"I'll be here."

He was silent a minute.

"What?"

"Just happy," he said, his hand trailing down my chest, then lower under the blanket, gently rubbing circles on my stomach.

"Me too."

"Are you?"

"Yes."

The growl that came out of him, pure contentment, made me smile. I understood at that moment how much he loved me, needed me, and truly wanted me around.

"So feed me," he said, kissing me again, his tongue instantly deep inside my mouth, tasting me, moving lazily because he knew I belonged to him.

I whimpered at the loss when he pulled back. I wanted him to stay.

He rose over me, his hand in my hair before he leaned back down and kissed my forehead. "Stay outta trouble, J. I'll see you tonight."

I could only nod, I had no voice.

"You know, moving in would be so much more convenient."

My smile came on its own. The man was determined to drive his point home.

"Or I can move in with you."

"Give it a rest."

"What? I'm just thinking of you."

"Like hell you are."

The bed lifted as he stood up, and I watched him go. I stayed awake for a while even after I heard the front door close.

End of Book Three

Book Four

Chapter One

MY PHONE woke me at eight.

"It's Saturday morning," I complained to whoever it was.

"Oh, *now* you answer your phone? What about last night, asshole? You totally blew us off."

I processed the voice, tried to think of what I was supposed to have done on Friday night instead of being out with my boyfriend, Sam Kage, his partner Chloe, and her boyfriend Jason. It took me a couple of minutes for my brain to kick in and remember. "Oh, Ev," I groaned. "You had a guy for me to meet."

"That's right, I did," my friend, Evan Rheems, scolded me. "C'mon, Jory—if you didn't want to go all you had to do was tell me. You know I would never make you meet somebody who's not cool."

"Oh no? I have two words for you—Mark Benassi."

There was a long silence before, "Screw you, J, that's not—one pervert does not negate my entire record of great hook-ups."

I chuckled because he was being very defensive. "You suck at setting me up and you know it."

"But that's no excuse to—"

"I'll make it up to you," I soothed him. "How 'bout I take you and your lovely boyfriend Loudon out for dinner tonight? I promise to—"

"No," he grumbled. "We've gotta pick up Loudon's mom at the airport. She's in from Ames for a week."

"Ames?"

"It's in Iowa."

"Oh." I couldn't stifle the laugh. "Well, I am sorry I blew you off. I didn't mean to, but Sam's back and I—"

"What?"

"Sam."

He caught his breath. "What?"

"Evan," I warned him.

"You know another Sam?"

"We both know I don't."

"Oh God."

"Stop."

He was starting to breathe hard. "So *the* Sam."

"Yep."

"The police detective Sam."

"Yes."

"As in the-guy-I-hate Sam?"

"You don't hate him."

"Oh no, I'm sure I do hate him."

"Well stop, 'cause he's gonna move in," I said, deciding at that moment that he could. What was I waiting for, a shining light from heaven? Just because Sam Kage had come charging back into my life after a three-year absence did not mean that I was not still madly in love with him. He was, in fact, the only man that I had ever loved. To make him wait through a period of dating to move in with me was a stupid waste of time. The man wanted to be with me—who was I to say no?

"Jory!"

"Sorry, Ev," I smiled into the phone.

"He's moving in?"

I chuckled.

"Jory… catch me up."

"It's too early for this." I laughed, because he was starting to hyperventilate. "Sam Kage is back and I'm gonna live with him since I love him. So you don't hafta worry about me anymore, you don't hafta set me up on blind dates anymore. Call me when Loudon's mother leaves and we'll all have dinner, okay? Okay. Bye," I said and hung up.

It took him all of twenty-three seconds to call back.

"What?"

"What? Are you kidding?" He was yelling. "Are you kidding?"

"Evan, don't have a—"

"Sam Kage? Are you kidding?"

"You're repeating yourself."

"Sam Kage?" He wheezed. "Ohmygod… Sam Kage?"

"Evan, you know I love him."

"He nearly killed you last time, and I mean literally almost killed you! It was his fault you were shot and kidnapped and—"

"Evan, you—"

"Ohmygod are you serious? Sam Kage!"

It took me a half an hour to get him not to pass out, and the phone was finally taken away and I was talking to his boyfriend Loudon, who had to have me explain the whole story to him before he could offer his partner any solace.

Three years ago I had witnessed a murder and met Sam Kage, the detective, who was working the case. Since I had refused to enter witness protection, Sam became the man in charge of keeping me safe. In the middle of it all, we had fallen in love. But being gay and a vice detective was hard for Sam, and as a result, it was a roller coaster for me. We were apart and together so many times, and all the while I was running from men who wanted me dead instead of on the witness stand. The end came when Sam's partner at the time, his best friend, Dominic Kairov, had kidnapped me. The Internal Affairs Division was investigating Dominic and it turned out that he was working for the men trying to kill me. He was a dirty cop, and he had kidnapped me to tie up loose ends. But Sam knew his partner, knew how his mind worked, and so was able to find me before I was killed. In the chaos of that moment, though, the moment when he found me, I ended up taking a bullet meant for my lover fired from Dominic's gun.

I spent eight days in ICU with Sam never leaving my side. But once I was no longer critical, he left to track down the people responsible for both the contract on my life and for Dominic's initial corruption. Dominic had started off as a good cop and a driven vice detective. Sam was determined to make those people pay for hurting me and corrupting his best friend. The task had taken him from me. He had promised to return, but without a word for three years I had given up hope of ever seeing him again. And then he was suddenly back and ready to pick up where we'd left off.

I had fought him off much longer than I would have thought, almost a week, before succumbing to the pull of my heart, the needs of my body, my brain buried under an avalanche of emotion. It was hard to try and explain to anyone else how I could still love Sam Kage after all we had been through, but I tried to make Loudon understand over the phone. If I could get through to him, he would in turn get through to Evan. As usual, in direct contrast to Evan's drama queeniness, Loudon was his logical, thoughtful self. He would reserve judgment until he met Sam. As soon as his mother left, they would have us over for dinner, as inquisitions needed to be performed in private. In the meantime, there would be a moratorium called on blind dates for me. When he hung up the phone, even after all the talking, I was still able to roll back over and go to sleep. It was a gift.

I HAD gone home to shower and change and was getting ready to leave my apartment when I heard Sam come through the front door. I had given him a set of keys the day before.

"Hey," I called out from the bedroom, straightening my tie, buttoning up my suit jacket. "I thought I wasn't gonna see you until tonight?" He had left me at three in the morning, called out to some crime scene.

He appeared in the doorway; I saw him in the mirror, but he didn't say a word. He just stood and stared at me. After a minute I smiled as I turned around to look at him.

"What are you doing here?"

He looked me up and down, absorbing me, his eyes pained, his jaw clenched.

"Sam? What's wrong?"

He moved suddenly, really fast, and as soon as he could reach me, yanked me forward into his arms and clutched me so tight he squeezed the breath right out of me.

"Sam, you're scaring me."

He held on, pressing me close, his face buried in my hair.

"Honey, what's wrong?" I soothed him, laying my head on his chest. "Please tell me."

He shoved me out to arm's length, his hands digging into my biceps. He was tense and worried and his breathing was shaky.

"Sam?"

"Listen to me." He dragged in a breath. "Do you remember back when that whole thing was going on with Dominic, and during that time your old apartment got broken into?"

Did I remember that? It was blurry. "Yes," I said after a few minutes because I sort of did.

"And the new tenant got killed? You remember all that?"

That I remembered. "Yeah, but that was just Dominic. He killed that guy because he thought he was me."

He shook his head. "No, J. I know Dom. There's no way he makes a mistake like that."

I stared into his eyes. "Okay, so then maybe it was one of Roman's guys." Roman was the man who had wanted me dead. He had been there the night I witnessed the murder. That I could place him at the scene was the reason I needed to be eliminated. "I remember you saying that they thought I was dead but there was a leak that turned out to be Dominic and—"

"No. When we tapped Roman's father's phone, we heard someone call him—it turned out to be Dominic—and tell him that you were still alive. We thought they killed that kid in hopes that it was you, but it turned out they were just reporting on the second failed attempt on your life. Neither Dominic, Roman's old man, or Roman ever knew anything about the murder in Oak Park."

"Oh." The hair was starting to stand up on the back of my neck.

He was searching my eyes.

"You're sure about that?"

"Yeah, we're sure."

"Okay." I tried to smile. "So why the sudden interest in something that happened three years ago?" He was staring holes in me and holding on so tight.

"'Cause we found another guy this morning, cut up just like that kid was."

"Cut up?"

"Yeah. Just like the first and the two others."

"Others?"

He ignored my question. "We found your driver's license in his wallet."

I was suddenly freezing.

"When did you lose your wallet, J?"

I racked my brain. It had been ages. "I dunno, right after you left, at least three years ago."

"I figured. It still had the Oak Park address on it."

"Sam, what's going on?"

"I'm not sure," he breathed, letting me go, walking to my bed and sitting down on it. "All I do know is that it has nothing to do with the Brian Minor case at all."

Three years ago my friend Anna was married to Brian Minor. He was an abusive asshole, and when she had finally decided to leave him, she had called me for one little favor. She needed me to go to her house and pick up her dog. It had seemed like a nothing errand, and because I wanted her out, I went to her home without hesitation.

When I got there, however, my world turned upside down. Brian Minor shot someone in front of me and thus made me, in the span of seconds, witness to a murder. I would have been killed myself, but it so happened that this was the night the vice detectives had decided to finally bust my friend Anna's husband for extortion, racketeering, and a list of other crimes. They saved me, and I ended up flat on my back in the middle of the street with Anna's beagle, George, licking my face. It was the first time I ever laid eyes on Sam Kage. Towering above me, he was scowling down at me with his gorgeous steel-blue eyes, asking me who the hell I was and what the hell I was doing there.

"Jory?"

"Sorry," I said, looking at him. "So are you gonna get in trouble for being with me, since it sounds like I might be in the middle of another case?"

"No. It's been three years and I went away. Nobody's around who cares anymore."

"Cops care, Sam."

"My partner Chloe doesn't give a shit that I'm gay. My new captain doesn't either. It's different now, you gotta trust me."

I nodded. "If you say so, but—"

"Jesus Christ, J, who gives a shit about me?" he yelled, raking his fingers through his hair. "You're the one I'm worried about! You're the one everybody… shit! Did you fuckin' hear what I said? We found your license on this guy, J. Your goddamn license!"

"I heard you," I said softly, walking around in front of him, stepping between his legs so he had to lean back and sit up straight, tilt his head up to look at me. "Tell me about the others."

He took a deep breath. "Well, besides Trey Hart—"

"Is he the one that was killed in my old apartment?"

"Yes."

"Sorry, go on."

"All in all there have been four murders."

"Okay. Tell me about them."

His sigh was deep. "Well, for starters, they've stretched over a three-year period."

I looked at him. "And?"

"And nothing. Four men are dead, but because it seemed random and the gaps between the killings were so long… no one made the connection."

"Until now."

"Until now."

"Why now?"

"The FBI got involved when you were kidnapped the first time by Dom. I guess they stayed involved, and when we pulled that kid out of that dumpster this morning, it hit somebody's radar in Quantico."

"What does that mean?"

"The profilers say that the murders are the work of a serial killer."

"How can that be?"

"All the men were killed the same way and they all looked alike."

"But you said it was random… you said there was a lot of time between."

"Which is why no one here took notice of it, but the feds… the feds, they load everything into computers and there's guys that watch this stuff and look at patterns and time and everything else and crunch the numbers, and so if they tell us we have a serial killer on our hands, we gotta believe them."

"Okay." I tried to absorb everything he'd said. "And who are the guys that got killed?"

"Two of them were hustlers."

"What about the others?"

"The others were just regular guys."

"Yeah, but who were they?"

"The guy today was a teacher, here in Chicago for an art seminar from Pittsburgh, and Trey Hart, the first guy, was a student who'd just moved here from Atlanta. They were both random guys, and if you add them in with the rent boys, I mean, it's like, shit… it fits no pattern at all… it makes no sense."

"If they're so random, then besides Trey and the teacher—who was he?"

"Glenn McKenna."

"Okay, so besides Glenn and Trey, how do you or the department or the FBI know that they have anything to do with each other?"

"Because the common thread is you."

"How?"

"One of the rent boys lived in the same building as you, just not at the same time."

"Which building?"

"The one your brother owned, across from the jazz club."

"Okay, it's weird but it's still just a coincidence."

"Maybe," he allowed, "but the other hustler, he was employed by the catering company that worked Dane's engagement party."

My brother, Dane Harcourt, was a prominent architect in the city, one of the top in the country; all his events were huge, sprawling affairs.

I shook my head, raking my fingers through my hair. "It's just weird, Sam, nothing else. I think you're looking for things that aren't there. I mean, some guy who lived in my same building but not even when I was there, some random waiter at a party Dane threw… it's crap."

"The FBI profilers don't think so. The only connection they find between the murders is you."

"So am I a suspect then?"

"No, they believe you're the target."

"And how come none of this was in the papers or on the news?"

"The murders all made the news and the papers, J, but they're so spread out—three years between the first and the last—no one in the press has made the connection."

I nodded. "But they might."

"They might."

"Okay, but have you checked out all the—"

"Baby, it's not my case. It'll never be my case, 'cause I'm way too close to you. It's all about you, so I hafta stay on the outside looking in. All I can do is ask Hefron and Lange what they've got and what I can do. If they hadn't called me this morning, I would still have no idea what was going on."

"Will they talk to you?"

"'Course. We're all detectives, and they're friends of mine."

"Will they still be your friends once they find out about you and me?"

"They already know about you and me, J, that's why they called me, and yes— they're still my friends. You're not the only one with good people in his life."

"I didn't say I was."

We were quiet for several minutes.

"Sam."

"What?"

"I remember you saying when Trey was killed that whoever did it wrote something on the wall about me. What was it?"

"A word."

"What word?"

"Just… it doesn't matter."

He really didn't want to tell me. I felt like my stomach had dropped out of my body. "What was the word written in?"

He just looked at me.

"Was it written in blood? In Trey's blood?"

"In his blood, and something else."

"What?"

"I don't wanna talk about this," he almost yelled. "Just help me figure out who would wanna hurt you."

"I dunno, Sam, it still seems like it could all just be a weird coincidence."

"Jory—"

"I mean, everyone but Trey obviously. I still think Roman's guys were—"

"Jory, come on," he sighed wearily. "Your license was on the victim and the resemblance was good. I mean, he could've been your brother."

I arched a brow for him. "He was as pretty as me?"

"Don't fuckin' joke around! This isn't funny! Watching those guys pull that kid outta that dumpster today… fuck! If I hadn't just left you I would've fuckin' lost it right there."

"Sorry," I said softly, running my fingers through his hair, watching it curl. "So what now?"

"Now you work from home. If Aubrey wants to see you, she—"

"No," I shook my head. "I won't be a prisoner in my own—"

"Goddamnit, J! How stubborn are you gonna be? Do you get that not only is there some whack job out there killing guys that look like you, but whoever the fuck it is has been stalking you for the last three years, maybe longer? Do you fuckin' get that?"

"What're you—"

"Whoever killed the teacher today stole your wallet or had somebody else do it a long time ago. I mean, do you get how fucked up it is to steal something from your intended victim years in advance, only to plant it on your current victim? That is twisted as shit and really, really spooky."

"Why kill other people? Why not just kill me?"

"Maybe he can't. Maybe something's preventing him."

"Him?"

"The chances of it being a woman are very small. Plus, from what we know about the killing wounds... the force... a woman couldn't have done it."

"Oh."

"So it's more than likely a man, and he's probably a good size guy from the damage that we've seen inflicted on the victims."

I nodded quickly.

"So you've gotta go into protective custody and—"

"Oh, fuck that, Sam!" I shouted, stalking out of the bedroom and down the hall.

"Jory!" he shouted, and I heard him striding after me before my arm was grabbed and I was yanked around to face him. "Goddamnit, you need to—"

"No, Sam. I am not gonna go through that again. I will not have my life flipped upside down because of something I didn't do. It's not fair and I won't do it."

"Jory—" he began, his voice rising.

"And then what?" I asked, walking away from him, turning at the couch to look back at him. "You're gonna bail 'cause you gotta go look for my stalker? You won't be able to protect me if you're so close to me?" I ranted, throwing up my hands. "That's bullshit too. If you wanna go—then just go. If it's another all-or-nothing proposition for you—fuck it. I don't want this again. Once was more than enough."

We were silent, just glaring at each other.

"You're right."

"About what?" I said when I could breathe, crossing my arms.

"When I left the first time, it was an excuse. I wanted you, but I wanted my life to stay the same too. I used running down that drug connection as a way out."

"You ran away."

"Yes, I did."

I nodded. "If you're gonna run again, please do it now before I get in too deep."

"C'mere."

I crossed slowly back to him, like I was walking to the electric chair, and when he could reach me, he grabbed hold of my lapel and yanked me forward.

"Like you're not in too deep right now," he smiled slyly, his hands on my face, raising my chin for a kiss.

I melted against him, my hands on his forearms, kissing him back, deep and slow, wanting to make it last.

"I want you to stay home with me today, all right?"

"No, I need to get things together for Abe on Monday and I might see some clients this afternoon to make up for Wednesday—Thursday—whatever day, and there's just a lot to—"

He unbuttoned my suit jacket and his hands eased it off my shoulders. I heard it fall softly on the back of the couch. He wasn't listening to me, but I had things to do. My business partner, Dylan Greer, had delivered a baby days earlier and I needed to prepare the office for Aubrey "Abe" Flanagan, who was going to be helping me out until Dylan got back from maternity leave. Even though it was Saturday morning, I had calls to make, e-mails to send, there was no way that I could just blow off my responsibilities to spend the day in bed with my very hot boyfriend.

"Sam...."

My tie was worked gently loose and slid off, joining my suit jacket, before his fingers started working the buttons down the front of my shirt.

"Sam, I can't—"

"I could just rip it off like I did the one the other night, but I figured you didn't wanna explain two of them to your dry cleaner."

I let my head fall back and he kissed my chin and jaw as he got me out of my clothes. The shirt he let fall to the floor before he smoothed his hands up my sides, raising my arms. I leaned back so he could drag the T-shirt up and over my head.

"Don't need this," he said, balling it up and tossing it onto the floor.

I stared into his eyes, marveling as always at the color, the deep smoky blue now absolutely molten with desire. Impossible to miss the need there, and it was a great big turn-on knowing that I was the one responsible. I got him hot, just me, and that power was intoxicating.

"I'm not going anywhere this time, J," he said, his voice so low and sexy, a seductive heat in his gaze, his hands on my back moving over my skin causing my trembling. "I'll protect you. I won't let anything happen to my baby. I can't. What would I do without you?"

I could feel my body vibrating under his touch as a line was kissed down the side of my neck, over my collarbone to my chest.

"So beautiful."

Me? Was he kidding? I wasn't the one that looked like he was carved out of living stone. Not an ounce of fat on the man anywhere, just rippling muscle and warm, smooth skin. Between his size—six-four—and massive build, he was absolute fantasy material, but instead of me worshipping him, he was standing there looking at me like I was the ideal.

"All that gold skin and your deep, dark eyes... Jesus, J, you kill me."

I swallowed hard as he bent and kissed me.

"I can't be away from you anymore," he said, his breath warm against my lips. "You know I used to wake up and want you, and go to sleep wishing you were there, and then I'd get up and go to work and the whole thing would start all over again."

I just stared up at him.

His chest constricted and his eyes showed me how vulnerable he felt. "I won't leave you again, ever. I promise."

"And you'll take care of me?" I asked playfully, leaning in to kiss him thoroughly, to suck and lick and make his breath shaky, his eyes cloud with passion. "Love me forever?"

"Yes."

He was at my mercy and I loved it. Who was dominant now? "You ready to scream my name some more?" I asked as I got my hands under his sweater, under the T-shirt beneath, my fingers sliding over his hot skin, over the hard, defined muscles in his back, moving around over the sculpted pectorals, down the chiseled, bumpy plains of his abdomen, the deep groove to his navel. "God, Sam, you're beautiful."

He suddenly grabbed me, my feet leaving the floor as he hugged me tight to his body before walking me back down the hall to my bedroom, and pinning me under him on the bed.

"Lemme tell you who's gonna be doing all the screaming."

I shuddered and my breath came out in huffs, the whimpering that he was after. He rolled me over on my stomach and then pulled me up to my hands and knees. I heard him getting undressed, his movements frantic, and the nightstand rattled when he yanked open the drawer.

"Listen to me," he growled in my ear, which covered me in goose bumps. "I got tested two weeks ago and I'm clean. I've never been with anyone but you without protection, but I wanted to be sure. So… we're done with the fuckin' condoms."

I could only nod as he slid lubed fingers deep inside me.

"Say yes to me."

"Yes."

His mouth was on the back of my neck and he pushed inside me with one powerful thrust. I cried out as his slick hand slipped under me, wrapping around my cock, and he bit down into my shoulder.

"My beautiful baby."

I felt like the vibrating that was deep inside me resonated out, and I was shaking beneath him.

"Say my name!" he demanded, and his voice was barely his—more guttural, raw, filled with heat and lust.

"Sam," I said.

"I will take care of you," he promised, pounding down into me. "Say it!"

"Just you."

A hand tangled in my hair before my head was snapped back hard. "Tell me you belong to me."

"I'm all yours, Sam. I belong to you."

He devoured me then, his mouth, his hands, flipping me over on my back like I was weightless, wrapping my legs around him, driving down into me while I called his name. The power exerted over me, the absolute possessiveness, the need in him to dominate me, drowned everything else.

LIGHT, tender kisses were placed between my shoulder blades as his fingers trailed up from the small of my back to the nape of my neck and back down. Over and over, so gentle, causing slow heat to build in me.

"How ya feel, baby?"

"I feel good."

"Yeah?"

"Mmmm."

"I've got it bad."

"What's that?"

"Needing you, wanting you."

"I'd be lying if I said I was sorry."

He pressed his hot mouth into the middle of my back and kissed hard, sucking, and ending with a bite. It felt amazing.

"You like leaving marks on me." I grinned into my pillow.

"Yes, I do, and I love the noises you make when I do it." He dragged his stubbled cheek over the small of my back and I nearly came up off the bed. "That feel good?"

My whole body was tingling. "Yes," I managed to get out.

"You know," he sighed, kissing my shoulder and the side of my neck, his hand sliding down over my ass and squeezing. "You're the only person I ever wanted to actually eat."

"Go ahead," I exhaled deeply. "Eat me."

"Christ," he groaned. "I've never loved anyone the way I love you, Jory. It scares the shit outta me, I swear to God."

"Just stay with me."

I heard his breath hitch. He sounded like he was in pain.

"Lay down and hold me."

Instantly he was spooned around me and I was wrapped up in hot, sleek skin and muscle. He buried his face in my shoulder and his chest and groin were pressed to my back and ass.

"I need to get up and make some calls." I smiled as my eyes drifted closed.

"No, just rest."

"I haven't even done anything," I chuckled before I let out a long yawn.

"Well, you're going to rest because you're not leaving the apartment. I packed a bag, so I ain't leaving either. I'll order Chinese when we wake up and have it delivered."

I laughed. "We're just gonna hole up here, huh?"

"When we get up, we're gonna talk. You're gonna hate it."

"I could never hate talking to you."

His deep, rumbling laugh put goose bumps all over my skin. "We'll see."

HE WAS right. Being interrogated, especially since I was in love with the guy doing it, really stunk.

"I don't know," I growled at him, covering my face with the pillow.

"Think, J," he ordered, pulling the pillow away from me, propping himself up on his arm, resting his chin on his hand as he stared down at me. "Who hates you?"

"You, obviously," I groaned, rolling away from him to lay on my stomach. "For crissakes, Sam, you've been drilling me for like two hours already and we're just going around in circles. I don't know, okay?"

His hand slid over my ass and he squeezed hard. The motion gave me hope.

"Sam?"

"What?"

"You wanna drill me hard?"

"Quit," he patted my ass before his hand slid higher, to the small of my back.

"Maybe I should put your name on me, huh? Ink it right there where your hand is?"

"What? A tramp stamp—hell, no. If I put my name on you, it goes on the back of your right shoulder where I bite you every time I've got you down on your hands and knees." I felt him tremble against me.

"Let's go do it," I said, laying my head down on the cool sheet.

"Yeah? I can put my name on you?"

"Yes, Sam."

Instantly I was pulled over next to him, the heat from his skin sending a shiver down my spine.

"You think it's a joke? Do you have any idea how bad I want that?"

I rolled my head so I could see his eyes, and I was surprised at how dark, serious, and hungry they were. "I had no idea."

His eyes stayed locked on mine. "I don't know how to let people know that you belong to me."

"I tell them." I smiled at him, reaching out to run my fingers over his jaw. "You don't worry about that."

His sigh was deep as he looked in my eyes. We stayed like that for a while, just staring at each other.

"What are you thinking?"

"I just wonder if you'll miss it."

"What's that?"

"The milestones that come with being straight."

"Like what?"

I shrugged. "Like the big, beautiful wedding my brother Dane just had. You're never gonna have a Disney moment with me, ya know?"

"Explain that."

"The whole finding your princess deal, Sam," I rolled over on my back and stared at the ceiling. "You're never gonna have the happily ever after with me."

"No?"

"C'mon, none of the great movie moments happen between two guys. That's not how it works."

"No?"

"No," I promised him.

"I think you're wrong. I think, in real life, magic happens every day," he said, rolling over on top of me, staring down into my eyes. "But even if it doesn't, who cares? I don't need a happily ever after, J, I just need the ever after part. The adjective can be whatever. Up and down ever after, sometimes rocky ever after, crazy ever after—I don't give a shit. As long as you stick around, we'll just do the best we can, day after day."

The tears welled up in my eyes and he got blurry.

"Jesus, you've got a soft heart," he chuckled, wiping the tears from my temples. "And baby... don't let anyone ever tell you you're not a princess."

"Oh screw you, Kage!" I shoved him away from me.

When he held me down and kissed me breathless I thought my heart would stop. But it turned out that beating for Sam Kage was its main function.

Chapter Two

AS I walked through the market pushing the shopping cart later that afternoon, my phone went off. Chinese food had not sounded good after all, so we had opted to cook.

"Hello?"

"Jory."

"Hey," I smiled into my phone. My brother sounded really good. Why he was calling me when he was on his honeymoon I had no idea, but I was always happy to hear from him. "What are you—"

"I need you to pick Aja and me up at the airport tomorrow morning."

"Ohmygod." I stopped walking, standing up straight from leaning on the cart. "Why? What's wrong, Dane?"

"Aja's dad had a heart attack yesterday."

"Oh no, oh Dane, I'm so sorry."

"No, it's okay, he's okay, but we just both think we need to be there."

"Sure, of course," I said on an exhale. "Tell me what—"

"He doesn't even want us to come home early," he said tightly, "but I've got other things on my mind, so it's good that we're cutting this short."

"Oh yeah? Like what?"

"Oh, I dunno... Detective Kage, for instance."

There was a heartbeat of silence. "Oh shit."

"Oh shit is right! What the hell are you thinking?" The last came out in a roar.

It made sense that Dane was livid with me. The last time he had seen Sam Kage was three years ago. I had taken a bullet for the man and then Sam had left me alone in the hospital to heal. To Dane—who had taken care of me afterwards, been there when my boyfriend was not—it looked like a cold, heartless bastard had been allowed back into my life. To him I was insane, my logic drowned in a sea of desire.

"Are you even thinking?"

"Dane, I—"

"May I have the phone?" I heard Aja ask.

"No, I need to—"

"Jory," Aja came on the phone. "Hi, honey."

"I'm so sorry about—"

"It was a teeny-tiny-itty-bitty little heart attack," she soothed me. "He's going to be fine. I just want to see him for myself, you know?"

"'Course."

"But I must say, I have never seen Dane like this," she said softly. "Who in the world is Sam Kage?"

"He's—how did he even find out?"

"Rick Jenner has a new girlfriend, I guess, and she somehow works with you?"

"Aubrey Flanagan, yeah."

"Well, apparently she saw you and this Sam guy somewhere—"

Oh yeah. "Crap, I forgot about that."

"Jory, what is going—"

"Dylan had her baby."

"Oh how wonderful! I'll get her something as soon as I get back."

"Where are you now?"

"We're already in New York, we're taking the red-eye out tonight."

"I'm really sorry about your dad."

"No-no, it's okay. He's okay. I think Dane's more upset about you and… tell me all about this Sam person."

"He's just—see… I'm sure Dane thinks he's gonna hurt me, 'cause I was in trouble the last time Sam was around, but I love him, and now with these murders, he should know that with Sam here that—"

There was a sudden gasp of indrawn breath. "Ohmygod, what did you say?"

I filled her in on what Sam had told me, without all the gory details.

"Ohmygod," she cried and I heard the phone hit the floor. There was rustling and I heard the word murder repeated, this time muffled.

"Are you kidding me?" he yelled into the phone.

"Wait—"

"Jory, goddamnit! I leave you alone for two weeks and you—"

"Dane, it's not like—"

"Is he there?" he asked as Sam walked up to the cart and dropped French bread in.

"Who's on the phone?" Sam yawned, his eyes soft as he looked at me.

I shook my head and lied to my brother. "No."

"You're lying. Put him on."

"Who is it?" Sam's brows furrowed suddenly.

I moved the phone away from my mouth. "Dane."

He grunted and held out his hand. "He wants me, right?"

"Yeah, but—"

He wiggled his fingers for the phone. "Just c'mon."

"He's pissed off," I told Sam.

"Who's pissed off?" Dane snapped at me.

"Not you—I mean yeah, you—you're the one who's pissed off."

"I most certainly am," he assured me icily. "Put the detective on the phone."

"Jory," Sam said sternly. "Gimme the fuckin' phone."

I passed it to him and he took a breath before he said hello. I would have loved to eavesdrop but he walked away after mouthing the word "spaghetti" at me.

I finished the shopping as fast as I could, and when I was finally done and through the line, I pushed the cart outside to find Sam leaning against the passenger-side door of his SUV.

"You all done talking?" I called over to him.

"Yep."

I winced. "So what?"

"Oh he's pissed." He grinned at me. "And he's terrified about those guys getting killed. He says as soon as he gets home you're moving in with him and… Anna?"

"Aja. His wife's name is Aja."

"Oh." He shrugged, "Well, whatever. You're not going."

"I'm not?" I teased him.

"Hell no. You're staying with me."

"You mean you're staying with me," I corrected him. "At least I live in a security building."

"You know what I meant. Get in the fuckin' car."

"Stop swearing."

"Fine," he agreed.

"Hey."

He looked at me over the hood of the SUV.

"Thank you for talking to him and not getting mad. I know how he can be."

"No, J, he's right about everything. I know how it looks. It seems like I'm back in your life for like two seconds and you've got trouble again. It must hardly seem worth it."

"It's worth it to me." I smiled at him.

"Oh I don't care if it is or isn't," he dismissed my concern. "I'm not going anywhere."

"Do you have any idea how happy you make me when you talk like that?" I stared at him.

"Get in the car, for crissakes," he growled at me. "I'm hungry."

We were unloading the groceries when Sam's head snapped up and he looked at me. "What?"

"Whatever happened to that doctor you used to date?"

"Who?"

"The one you set up on a date with that guy on the pier that time."

I racked my brain. "Oh, Nick Sullivan."

"Yeah, him. You still talk to him?"

"That's amazing that you remember that."

"Hafta have a good memory when you're a cop."

"I guess so."

"Back to the doctor."

"What'd you ask?"

He groaned. "Do you still talk to him?"

"No."

"No?"

"No."

"Why not?"

I shrugged. "I dunno," I said, stepping back from the SUV as he slammed the rear door. "We just sort of lost touch."

"Why?"

"I think after he and Kai broke up—"

"That was the guy you set him up with."

"Yeah. That lasted over a year."

"Wow. Impressive matchmaking skills you got there."

"No. If they were so great, they'd still be together."

"You did your best, J. At some point it depends on the two people involved."

"I guess."

"Go on. They were together and when they broke up, what?"

"Well, after that Nick wanted to see me, and when I wouldn't that was it."

He nodded.

"What made you think of Nick?"

"I dunno, J. The doctor was around a long time and he'd sure as hell know how to cut somebody up, wouldn't he?"

"There's no way," I assured him. "Nick Sullivan is not a killer."

"I'm gonna check on the doctor anyway."

"You do that." I grinned at him.

"I'm gonna go with you to pick up Dane and Aja."

"The hell you are." I laughed at him. "I don't want you to miss Sunday dinner with your mom." Every Sunday Sam had dinner with his huge family in the suburbs. I didn't want him to miss it because of me. "Besides, Bambi's on the menu, remember?"

"What?"

"You remember. Your uncle is bringing back deer from his hunting trip."

"That's right."

"See, so—"

"My folk's will live. They just saw us two days ago," he sighed. "Besides... this is way more important."

"You're insane," I assured him. "It's gonna be a bloodbath."

He walked by me and kissed my forehead. "I gotta back up my partner."

"Yeah, but Dane might just murder you."

"He can try."

I shook my head as I followed him up the front stoop of my building.

HE WAS doing the dishes, since I had cooked, and we were talking about what he'd done for the first two years after he left. It was interesting to hear him talk about going all the way to Columbia and how he had slept in tents and the conditions for the DEA team. He had enjoyed it, following the lead as far as it went and busting all the people along the way.

It had all started the night I had seen Brian Minor murder Saul Grant in cold blood. Among the people in the room at the time, along with me and Brian, was Roman Michaelev. Dominic, Sam's old partner and friend, had worked for Roman's father, Yuri. Because I could put Roman in the room when Saul was killed, Yuri had put a contract out on my life. When Dominic was busted, he had turned state's evidence against Yuri, and he had in turn rolled over on his boss, a man named Dario Ruiz. Sam had left me to run down the drug connection that connected Chicago to Moscow to Columbia. It had been a domino effect after Dominic told what he knew, including how he had shot Roman to death in front of me. For a nice normal guy, I had seen two men killed. All those people—Dominic, Yuri, and even Anna Minor—were all still in the witness protection program, would be for the rest of their lives. They would live out the remainder of their days as other people, private citizens, in different states.

I asked Sam if he ever worried that Dominic would come back to take revenge on him.

"No, babe."

"Why not?"

"It doesn't work like that."

Apparently it wasn't like the movies; people actually kept really good tabs on you in witness protection, and in Dominic's case, it was prison for the rest of his life if he ever came near anyone he knew. I asked Sam what he would do if he ever accidentally saw Dominic on a plane somewhere. He told me he would cross that bridge when and if he ever came to it.

"You know, I never got a chance to tell you how sorry I was about Dominic." I sighed heavily. "I mean, he was your best friend for half your life."

"Yes, he was." Sam gave me a slight smile, reaching out to put a hand on my cheek. "But he tried to kill me, and he tried to kill you and he hurt you...." He took a settling breath. "And I'm not the forgiving kind."

I nodded.

After several minutes of silence, Sam told me that he had a question for me.

"Sure. What?"

"Do you know why Dominic shot that guy we found in the body bag?"

"What are you talking about?"

"We found a guy in a body bag when we raided the place where you were held. The ballistics on the gun matched Dom's, so I know he shot him, but I never could figure out why and he wouldn't tell me."

"No?"

"No. He said to ask you. So I'm asking you."

"Dominic told you to ask me?"

"Yeah."

I nodded. "That was Marco, right?"

"That's right, Marco Danov. What happened to him?"

I looked at Sam.

"Somebody broke his nose before they killed him. Did Dominic do that?"

"No."

"Who did?"

"I did. I broke his nose."

"You did."

"Yeah... he tried to...." I stared at Sam until he got it.

"Oh. But he didn't? He didn't hurt you?"

Neither of us wanted to be reminded of what the word *hurt* entailed. Better to leave it alone.

"No, I... he fell and then I ran and Dominic was pissed and... I heard the shots but I wasn't sure that Dominic killed him."

Sam nodded, his jaw muscles working as he looked at me. "He did."

"Well, it was because he thought he'd lost me, not because of anything else. Dominic even suggested that I...." Too late, I thought about what I was saying.

"Suggested that you what?"

I shook my head.

"C'mon, Jory, just say. It was a long time ago."

I let out a deep breath. "Okay... he was just trying to make me feel like shit and I knew that at the time but... he suggested I give this guy a blowjob to get some more blankets. It was about him trying to screw with my head, nothing else."

Sam nodded and wiped his hands on the dishtowel before he walked out of the kitchen.

"This is why you never talk about this kinda crap," I said to myself, folding the towel and laying it over the sink before I went to look for Sam. I found him stretched out on my bed, hands folded behind his head, staring up at the ceiling. "What's wrong?"

"I didn't protect you from any of that. If I was smart, I would have taken you with me to see Maggie and he would have never gotten his hands on you."

"Oh, I doubt that," I assured him and he rolled his head to look at me. "One way or another, Dominic was gonna get me. If it hadn't been that night, it would've been the next or the one after that. It was inevitable."

"So you're saying what... I won't be able to protect you from this psychopath that's after you now? You think it's inevitable that he gets you too?"

"No," I said, leaning on the doorframe. "That's not what I said. I said Dominic getting me was inevitable. He was too close to you, Sam, he knew you too well, knew how you would react, exactly what you would do... there's no way he wouldn't have been able to get me. It was just a matter of time."

He rolled his head back so he was again staring at the ceiling.

"Listen, I want some pie. How 'bout you?"

"No, I don't want any fuckin' pie."

"You owe a quarter."

"What?" He was irritated, it was clear in his voice as he looked back at me.

"I put a jar on the counter and you owe a quarter from now on every time you swear. It's out of hand and needs to be stopped."

"Oh fuck you, J, I ain't gonna—"

"That's fifty cents. Pay up or sleep on the couch. Your call."

"Fine, I'll sleep on the couch."

"Maybe you should go sleep at your place."

"Don't push me."

"Or what?"

"Or maybe I will."

"Fine." I shrugged, turning to walk away. "I'm going for pie. I'll see ya later."

When I got to the front door and opened it, his voice reached me.

"If you set one foot out of this apartment, I will beat your ass!"

"Fine!" I yelled back and stalked over to the couch so he could hear me stomping and the floorboards creak before I tiptoed backward to the door, reversing my steps, and closed it silently behind me. I didn't make a sound when I locked it. I was outside on the curb when he yelled down at me.

"Goddamnit, Jory, you better get your ass back in—"

I waved at him and cackled as I did it.

He leaned further out the window. "I am so not playing with you. " His voice was cold even from that far up and really should have scared me.

"You can kiss my ass, buddy," I said, and slapped it for him just in case he missed it.

The window was slammed shut and I ran.

In jeans and sneakers I could move pretty fast. I wondered, though, if he'd get in his oversized SUV or run after me. I just wanted some pie. I was worried that if I ran too fast he'd miss me, so I jogged to the end of the street and crossed and then again until I could see the diner where I was headed. I heard the squealing tires behind me and knew the answer to the question. He had brought the monster car.

The motor was loud and when he came up beside me he revved it up to where it was deafening. I turned and looked and he had the passenger window rolled down.

"Get in the car!"

I shook my head, pointed down the street. "I'm getting pie."

"You better—"

"If you stop the car, I'll run." I grinned at him. "And I'll make it before you can get out, so why don't you just be a good boy and meet me at the diner."

"If you set one foot in that diner, I will drag your ass out, throw you in the car, and—"

"And what? Beat me?" I gave him an exaggerated shiver. "Oooh, baby you know what I like."

He growled his frustration.

"You don't own me, Sam." I smiled over at him. "We're partners, and if you're feeling like shit you don't just close up and go into your cave and sulk or whatever, you talk to me. That's how a partnership works. I share, you share, we share. That's it. 'Cause if you're gonna want to be alone... I'll leave you alone." I finished, arching a brow for him.

He stopped the car and I stopped walking.

"I don't want you to leave me alone."

I shrugged. "Well then."

He motioned me to the SUV.

"I want pie."

"Diva... I will take you for pie."

I smiled wide, zipping my hoodie further up my chest and walked quickly to the car. He opened the door for me and as soon as I was in the seat, his hand was on the back of my neck.

"What?"

He pulled me close and stared down into my eyes. "Don't leave the house without me. You could get hurt... all right?"

I climbed over the emergency brake and into his lap, straddling his hips, grinding my groin into his stomach. "You gonna hurt me, Sam? 'Cause I would seriously love that."

His hands went to my face, and I realized how cool it was that we were behind all the tinted glass so we could fool around in the middle of the street.

"What got into you?" he asked, staring at my mouth.

"I want pie, and then I want you to take me home to bed."

He half-grunted, half-growled before pulling me close for a kiss.

My throaty moan made his body quake under mine, and his hands grabbed hold of my ass and squeezed tight. No doubt in my mind that he wanted me. After the scorching kisses that were shared, I told him to just forget the pie and take me home. He ran in and got two slices of Key lime to go.

Even as I was carried into my apartment, my legs wrapped around his waist, his hand patting my ass, I noticed the two quarters in the jar on the counter. I put my hand on his cheek and smiled at him.

"What?" he asked as he put the bag with the pie in it down on the counter. "I don't wanna sleep on the couch."

I shook my head as the tears welled up in my eyes.

"Oh for crissakes," he grumbled, leaning in to kiss me. "Like I ever wanna sleep without you."

I wrapped my arms around his neck and squeezed tight, my mouth ravenous on his. His deep rumbling laughter, sounding so content, was not lost on me.

Chapter Three

THE only part that was fun was watching Aja. Her eyes went from Dane to Sam, back and forth, watching them both, wanting to miss nothing. It was like watching tennis or volleyball, except the only thing flying between them were words. When Dane yelled, she winced; when Sam roared back, she flinched. I just breathed whenever anyone posed a rhetorical question to me. Obviously they wanted no answers, they just wanted to be loud. When Aja sat down beside me on the couch, I leaned my head on her shoulder. When she chuckled, the room went silent.

"Sorry," she whispered, hand up, gritting her teeth. "Continue."

And they did: Dane yelling, pointing at Sam, Sam with his fingers laced on top of his head, Dane attacking, Sam defending, both just livid. I had never seen Dane so mad.

"Wow," Aja said softly, talking into my hair. "The man really loves you, Jory. I've never seen him this way. I hope he never gets this mad at me."

I grunted.

"But I hafta say… it is sexy as hell. Look at those beautiful dark gray eyes," she purred. "I can't wait to love all that right out of him."

"Gross," I groaned, slouching down further beside her.

But it was funny, watching two grown men yell at each other. And while Dane had an inch of height over Sam, being six-five, Sam had the muscle over Dane. My brother with his jet black hair and gray eyes was built tall and lean like a swimmer. Sam with his copper-colored hair and slate blue eyes had the big, muscular frame of a defensive lineman. He had, in fact, played football all through high school.

Aja giggled, returning my attention to her before she leaned sideways on the couch and kissed my temple. "May I say that I used to think that Aaron Sutter was a gorgeous man and I loved you guys together? I was sad when it was over."

My ex-boyfriend, Aaron Sutter. It had lasted a year and a half. "Yeah, well," I sighed. "Sometimes things don't—"

"Let me finish," she cut me off and pointed at Sam. "That man, however, is beautiful. He's the kind of man I would have gone after myself, all tall and buff and fine… look at his arms—damn."

"Shut up." I grinned in spite of myself.

"I bet he's solid all over."

"Quit."

"And his ass is—"

"Stop."

"I'm just saying… I get it, and the way he looks at you and touches you… Aaron had it bad, but that man there is head over heels in love with you. I would not let that go either, not for anyone. Not even for Dane."

"I appreciate the vote of confidence here before I die."

She giggled again, careful to not be too loud. "The thing is, Sam loves you but so does Dane. And before I met Sam I wanted you as far away from him as possible too. I thought he brought whatever it is back into your life, but from what I'm hearing, this has nothing at all to do with you being a witness."

"No, it doesn't."

"So Sam's just trying to keep you safe, and since Dane wants that too, when they get tired of arguing over who knows what's best for you, they should come to some kind of mutual agreement and understanding."

I wasn't convinced. As I was sitting there, I noticed her wedding ring. "God, that thing is huge. What is that, like a carat or something?"

She grunted. "You, my darling, know nothing about diamonds. That is four carats of icy goodness."

"Icy goodness?" I teased her.

She smiled wide. "It's my only bling."

"Yeah, it's enough."

She made a low noise of appreciation. "Yes, it is."

"So-owww," I groaned, having shifted so that my shoulder hit the back of the couch. I was being so careful to keep the pressure off it.

"What did you do?"

"Nothing. It's a surprise for Sam. I figured he'd need the pick-me-up after this."

"What is it?"

"I put his name on the back of my right shoulder."

"You got a tattoo?"

"Yeah."

"Really?"

"Yeah, today at lunch. He had to go to work for a little while so… I went and did it."

"How very Hollywood of you," she teased me. "Can I see?"

"Wait, I wanna know how your dad is."

"Oh, thank you for asking, baby, but he's fine. Doctor said he'll be just fine."

"I'm glad."

"Me too. He didn't even have to spend any time in the hospital."

"Good."

"So, again, can I see the tattoo?"

"You wanna go to the bathroom with me?"

She waggled her eyebrows at me and we got up.

"Do me a favor," Dane barked at me. "Go get us all something to eat."

I looked at him and his eyes were cold and dark, Sam looked much the same, brows furrowed as he stared at me. "Sure."

"C'mon, Jory," Aja said gently, walking over to Dane to take his hand for a minute, her eyes suddenly on Sam. "You two play nice while we're gone."

"Yes, ma'am," he said quickly, his voice low and husky. His eyes softened when he looked at me, and I got just a slight curl at the corner of his mouth.

She patted Dane's ass and then grabbed my hand and tugged me out after her.

We took a cab to toward Hubbard and Clark because there was a Thai place I wanted to try. Once we were on the street, she told me all about the honeymoon and how romantic it had been and how much fiddling with his ring Dane did.

"He'll get used to it." I smiled at her as she walked arm in arm with me.

"I know, it's just funny to watch him. I like seeing women see the ring too. Ooh!" She said suddenly. "I've got something to tell you."

"What?"

"I saw Clarissa Connelly on the plane to New York."

"Really?" I smiled wide, remembering the woman that had been dating Dane the night he met Aja. She had told everyone that she would be the one to get him to the altar. "And?"

"I made sure she saw the ring."

"Evil," I snickered. "You're just wicked mean."

"What? I can't help it if she couldn't keep her man."

"And can you keep him?"

"Oh no, you didn't just ask me that question." She laughed, pinching my side.

"I—Aja!"

I yanked her back against me as a van came to a squealing stop on the sidewalk in front of us and the side door was hurled open. We both saw the gun at the same time.

"Get in the van!" the man yelled at us.

And it was stupid, but my movement was instinctive. I grabbed Aja's hand and ran. I heard the gunshot and then we were behind the van, next to the rear right tire.

"Jory!" she screamed and the back doors flew open. I yanked her sideways and a guy jumped out but missed us.

"Go-go-go!"

We ran across the lanes of cars, heard the blaring horns, squealing tires, and the crush of metal. We didn't stop and look, we ran. There were gunshots, but we ran. I took her down an alley, across another street, through a parking lot and we huddled together behind a trash-filled dumpster.

"Call Dane," I ordered as I kept lookout.

"Ohmygod, Jory, they're really trying to get us."

I would have laughed at any other time "Just call him—hurry up."

"Baby, we're really in trouble here."

She was obviously in a little bit of shock.

"Hurry," I said and heard my voice get panicky.

I saw the van streak by on the street and I stopped breathing. Alone I could outrun them, but not with Aja.

"Dane," Aja almost shrieked. "No-no-no, listen-listen—somebody just tried to grab me and Jory. Listen! We're on the street, we're running and I don't know what—"

"Shut up," I yelled as I saw the van suddenly reverse in the street and start racing down the alley toward us. "Run!"

I grabbed Aja and ran. I took a chance and we dived across the alley to the opposite side. We hit the bagged garbage and rolled off under wooden stairs that ran around the back of an apartment building. I scrambled to my feet and a bullet hit the stairs behind me. Ducking down, I tugged on Aja's hand and pulled her around the corner of the building.

"Dane, tell Sam we're—shit! I can't see the—ohmygod, there's a white van and—"

"Shit," I yelled because I saw the van, and yanked her the other way, doubling back, heading for the subway. "Aja, just stop talking and run!"

I felt the change instantly: I was no longer pulling her, she was right beside me, her feet pounding the pavement with mine, dropping my hand and keeping pace with me as we both ran as fast as we could. We flew by so many people and crossed behind an apartment building when the van was suddenly there and I had to pull up fast or slam into the side of it. Aja grabbed me as the door flew open and the gun was inches from my face.

I put up my hand. "Just me, not her."

"Both of you now or you're both dead!" the voice snarled back.

Aja clutched me tight as I took a step toward the open door. Never-never-never get in a car. Better to try anything, fight wildly, recklessly, then to succumb to another's power and get in the car. I saw the gun and clawed for it, got my hands around the wrist that held it and fought hard.

"Aja, run! Run!" I shouted at her, and she listened because I heard her fumbling behind me and then felt the bump as she pushed away from me and, when I turned to look, saw her running down the road. She was flying, arms pumping, legs a blur, and then my face was covered with a rag. I heard the slide of the door, felt the jolt as I lost my balance, and then nothing.

"JORY, open your eyes. Please-please-please...."

My eyes fluttered open and it was dark except for a slight glow across the room. When I tried to lift up, I realized my hands were tied behind me. It was all too familiar.

"Shit." I focused my eyes and was stunned to see Caleb Reid lying on the floor beside me, his eyes wide open, staring at me. "Caleb?"

"Jory," he said, obviously relieved. "Thank God you're all right."

"Caleb." I was trying so hard to wrap my brain around it all. "What the hell?"

"Jory, are you okay?"

"Yeah, I'm okay," I assured him as I struggled to sit up. "What's going on? Tell me."

"I dunno—I dunno," he almost whined, his voice rising. "I was in town on business, but I didn't even bother calling Dane 'cause I knew he was still on his honeymoon and—" He stopped suddenly as the door slid open and a man appeared there. The light was behind him, which made it impossible for either of us to see his face. "What do you want?" Caleb yelled at him.

I saw the raised gun.

"Facedown, you fucks!"

I did as I was told, moving as fast as I could.

"What the—get off me! Get off me!" Caleb screamed, and it sounded like he was being dragged out of the room. I listened to him yell until I couldn't hear him anymore.

"Please don't hurt him," I pleaded.

I felt the foot squarely in the middle of my back. There was scrambling above me.

"You should worry about yourself," the man warned me, grinding his heel into my back. It hurt like hell but I didn't make a sound. "Don't do anything stupid."

I nodded.

"I'm already pissed at you for making me lose his wife. You better hope he'll pay for you, little brother, or you are royally fucked."

It was about money. Somehow I was relieved.

"Just sit tight and don't fuck up."

I nodded again.

"Good," he said and was gone. The door was slammed shut and I heard the chain and the lock on the other side. The room was pitch-black. I put my cheek down on the cold floor and waited for my breathing to become regular. I was terrified for Caleb even as I rolled to my side and realized I was really light-headed. Something was wrong, and as the wave of nausea went through me I wondered briefly if I was more hurt than I knew. I must have dozed then, because the shouting jarred me awake.

"You crazy piece of shit," a man roared, and something hit the other side of the door really hard. "You never told me you were fuckin' around with Sam Kage!"

There was a muffled sound from the other side and then the bang, again followed by a low moan.

"You don't fuck with a cop, man, especially not a goddamn detective! How stupid are you?"

No sound, just silence until a sort of light hammering began.

"Let's just dump the guy and walk away before—"

A sharp crack then, and glass shattered.

"No! Get rid of the goddamn—"

And there was a firecracker sound and then a low thud and nothing after that but thundering silence. That silence that you almost hear things in but is really just your own heart beating. All alone in the dark, I was terrified that I would never see anyone ever again. There was nothing to do but wait and see, so I laid there and waited for what came next. It was scary to have my eyes open and see no more than I would if my eyes were closed. I tried not to think about it too much.

I MUST have nodded off again because the door opening woke me up.

"Jory?"

"Caleb," I said. "Come here. Did they hurt you?"

"No." His voice cracked and I could hear how raspy his breathing was. When his hands touched my face, I realized he was untied.

"Ohmygod, you're loose—why're you loose?"

"He untied me before I talked to Dane."

"You talked to Dane?"

"Just for a second."

"And?"

"And it's a ransom. He wants ten million, Jory. Five million apiece or Dane doesn't get either of us back ever. He said Dane would have nothing to bury."

"And?"

"And what? That's it. I was told that as long as I behaved he wouldn't shoot you. If I do something stupid—you get hurt, not me." I felt his hands cup my face. "I don't plan to be any trouble, so you're gonna be just fine."

"Caleb—"

"No, Jory," he said flatly. "We are going to do whatever is asked of us. All they want is the money. We're gonna be perfect and they'll get their money and we'll get to go home."

"Okay."

"Okay," he said. "Okay."

"What'd Dane say?"

"Dane said the guy could have the money."

"Why do you sound weird?"

"Nothing."

"Caleb, please just say."

"No I just—I... I figured Dane would pay for you but... I didn't think he'd agree to pay for me. I'm nothing to him, Jory. Nothing at all."

"You're his brother, you idiot."

"Yeah, but not like you."

And I knew what he meant. Three years ago, Caleb Reid had appeared to tell Dane a very strange story. Caleb's parents, Susan and Daniel Reid, were actually Dane's birth parents. And while Dane had known he was adopted, he was not ready to receive the Reids with open arms. I, on the other hand, had started out working for Dane Harcourt, but after five years he had decided that he didn't just want to run my work life but my personal one as well. I had gone from being his assistant to his brother after one trip to his lawyer's office. And while Caleb, Jeremy, and Gwen were all now his siblings too, I was the only one Dane had chosen. I was the one who had stood up with him in the church when he got married and I was the only one who shared his name besides his wife. I knew Dane would do anything to get me back, but the kind of man my brother was, I never doubted that he would put in the same effort for Caleb. He was the only one that was surprised.

"Dane thinks of you as his brother too, Caleb," I assured him.

"Yeah, but I didn't really get that he thought so before today."

"Why not, why wouldn't he?"

"I guess I just—"

"Did somebody get hurt?" I cut him off.

"When?"

"Before. I think one of the guy's got shot."

"How do you know?"

"I heard it."

"I dunno, J. I didn't see anything."

"Shit."

There was a silence before Caleb gasped.

"What's wrong?"

"Did you hear that?"

"Hear what?" I was instantly terrified.

"Jory, there's somebody in here," Caleb whimpered.

"What?" I almost cried out and then the back of my head exploded and I didn't hear anything.

THE sharp bump woke me because my head hurt and it rapped me against the floor really hard. I realized the bouncing was from movement, and from the tiny light I figured out I was in the trunk of a car. My hands were still tied, but the zip ties had loosened and I was flexible. I got my arms to slide over my hips and got my ass over my hands. I was bent like a pretzel but the outcome was that I got my hands in front of me so I could use them. I immediately went to work on the taillight, like they tell you to do in every book on self-defense ever written. Get the light out and wave to people on the highway. If there were small things to drop out the hole, you were supposed to do that too. I worked as fast as I could. There was the copper smell of blood, and I hoped that it wasn't Caleb's or mine. Not that Caleb was with me, which was scary since I had no idea where he was. But I pushed that out of my head and concentrated on getting the taillight shoved out. It was an old car and everything was rusted so it was harder than it would have normally been. When we stopped suddenly, I had just enough time to put my hands up so my forehead hit them instead of the trunk. The ride changed then from bouncing and quiet to smooth with a hum. We were off a dirt road or something to an actual paved road.

I tried really hard to get the taillight out but it was no use. By the time I got myself rolled over and turned around to try the other one, we had stopped. I heard voices, and there was a sudden knock above me.

"Make a sound and Caleb Reid is dead."

I froze. He had to be in the backseat or somewhere close.

"Did you hear me?"

"Yes," I rasped, whispering before clearing my throat to speak louder. "Yes."

"Good."

I laid there listening for anything, trying to feel if the car was moving at all, wanting to call out to Caleb but afraid of being heard at the same time. The mixture of tension, adrenaline, and fear made me have to pee. It was painful, and I rolled over on my back and was faced with the rusted metal trunk.

I heard the laughter before the car started; the motor was gunned and I was bounced hard before I got my hands up to shield my face. I was thrown side-to-side and there was yelling and blaring music. I rolled into a ball and tried to protect as much of my body as I could.

The ride went on for so long, the steady hum of the tires with only an occasional bump, that I fell asleep. I tried really hard not to, but I kept jerking hard only to realize that I had been drooling. When the car came to a sudden stop, the brakes squealed and I was hurled up against the back so hard that I was winded. Trunk thrown open, I blinked at the light and the bewildered faces looking down at me. They stared and I stared back. I absorbed their faces.

"Oh shit," one of the guys said. "That fucking guy was a goddamn kidnapper!"

"Shit!" Another yelled and I heard their pounding feet on the pavement as they ran away.

I wasn't sure what to do. After several minutes of looking up at the slowly lightening sky, I sat up and looked around. The parking lot of the liquor store was deserted except for a homeless guy in the corner with his shopping cart and three guys standing around talking next to the side of the building. I was somewhere downtown—I could hear the subway rattling close by—and because my surroundings weren't completely alien, I started to calm down. I crossed my legs, sat in the trunk, and tried to figure out the best thing to do.

I had no cell phone, no wallet, no money; the nearest hospital was blocks from me and getting a police officer in a deserted part of downtown first thing in the morning would be a miracle. When it started to snow, I climbed shakily out of the trunk. I didn't think I should leave the car—every episode of *CSI* I had ever seen told me not to—but neither did I want to be a sitting duck if the kidnappers came looking for me. Although the chances of that happening were not likely. It was the most ridiculous situation ever. The kidnapper had gotten carjacked. Hysterical.

I took deep breaths as I walked through the parking lot and around the corner to the sidewalk. The front was boarded up and there were old flyers for bands performing in the city pasted up all over it. When I looked further down the street, there was a closed auto body shop and across from that a closed key shop and a store that sold vacuums. Across the street was a hotel that boasted rooms for ten dollars a night, fifteen if you wanted to shower. There was not one light on in any window. There was nothing open anywhere, no signs of life at all, everything was deserted. Pieces of trash blew across the street and into the gutter. It was cold and dark and a little gloomy. I walked toward the end of the street and checked to see where I was. Finding that I was close to La Salle wasn't bad. I could get home, it would just take forever as I was miles from my apartment. I would check the car first, see if on the off chance the keys were still in it.

When I walked back and saw the keys dangling from the ignition, I started laughing. It was just absurd. Between the kidnappers and the carjackers, it was a toss-up over who were the bigger morons. I was hopeful that, because Caleb was a smart guy, he too had been able to escape. I got in, closed the door, and drove out of the parking lot.

It worked out great, since driving the kidnapper's car I could take all the evidence with me. I parked it in front of the police station downtown. It was a noisy, crowded zoo, but I stood in line and waited my turn. When I finally made it to the desk sergeant, I asked him to call Detective Sam Kage downstairs for me. I was informed that the detective was out but that his partner, Detective Stazzi, was free to see me. I asked to go upstairs, but he told me to take a seat instead. I walked to the waiting area and slipped down into the first chair I came to. I heard my name minutes later and lifted my head in time to see Chloe flying across the room to me. She was yelling at people to get out of her way and the two other men beside her—big guys, big like Sam—parted the crowd for her. When she knelt in front of me, hands on my face, I smiled at her.

"Hi."

"Jesus Christ, Jory," she breathed, her eyes all over me. "Where did you come from?"

So I told her about the kidnapper's car I had parked out front and all about Caleb and me and how worried I was about him.

She nodded and smiled, used a very soft voice when she talked to me, and had several blankets brought for me. She was very concerned about my body temperature and how big my pupils were and the fact that I was talking a mile a minute. When she suggested that I go to the hospital with her I agreed, since I wanted to make her happy. I told her I was only doing it for her.

"Thank you, honey." She smiled at me, looking at the other two men with her, moving me toward the door, her cell phone in her hand.

"Are you calling Sam?"

"Yes, honey."

I nodded. "Will you call Dane and tell him to meet me at the hospital?"

"Yes."

"Is Aja okay? I saw her running, but I just—"

"Aja's just fine. You're the one we were worried about."

"I was worried about her and Caleb. I tried to—"

"Jory, everybody's been looking for you. You're the one we were worried about. We weren't sure if you were hurt or—"

"I'm a little bumped up but... will you tell Sam I'm sorry?"

She nodded, steering me toward the door. "Of course. Now stay with me, okay? Open your eyes for me."

I was closing my eyes?

"Jory... sweetie...."

But my legs went out from under me and even her calling my name didn't help. I couldn't see anything at all.

I WOKE up at the hospital, and even though Chloe wanted me to go in on a gurney, I wouldn't. The wheelchair was out of the question as well. I shuffled along beside her, unsure of my feet, and when I looked up and saw him at the emergency room entrance, I smiled.

I saw his chest constrict, heard his sharp intake of breath as he stood there, frozen, taking me in, absorbing me with his eyes. The muscles in his jaw were cording, as were those in his neck. His eyes were ravaged and I felt terrible, standing there knowing that I was the cause.

"I didn't mean to get kidnapped," I said when I was close enough for Sam to hear me.

He charged across the remaining few feet that separated us and I got my arms lifted in time to receive him as he crushed me to him, his face buried in my shoulder. He took deep breaths as he clutched me tight.

"Jory." He shivered hard.

"Sam," I sighed, listening to his heart hammering in his chest, drawing the heat from his body and pulling it into mine. He was so solid and strong, I just wanted to lean and be held. "Say something good."

"I love you." He kissed the side of my neck, my shoulder, slipped his hands up under the back of my sweater to caress my bare skin.

The warmth of his voice, the tenderness of his touch sent heat racing through my body. The man didn't just love me—I was his home. He couldn't do without me.

"Why didn't you fuckin' call me?" he growled, stepping back to look at me.

I realized how much I needed him close to me. When I reached for him, he shook his head.

"I didn't have a phone," I said in way of an explanation. "I went where I thought you'd be. That was smart, wasn't it?"

He cupped my face in his hands and looked into my eyes.

"Right?"

"Loving you is gonna fuckin' kill me."

I smiled into his beautiful eyes and he pulled me back to him and kissed me long and hard. I was so lost in kissing him that, when he ended it, I moaned loudly.

"God, Jory, I was so scared. Nobody knew where you were and... baby, you can't just—"

I pulled him down for another kiss, my mouth devouring, my tongue tangled with his.

"Stop." He shoved me back, but clutched me tight at the same time, making sure I didn't fall. "You scared the shit outta me."

I put my hands on the side of his neck. "I'm sorry."

"We gotta get you checked out and—"

"I'm okay." I smiled, leaning my forehead against his lips. "I just need to sleep."

"Baby—"

"Is Caleb okay? I was so scared when—"

"Baby," he cut me off, cupping my face in his hands. His palms were so warm; I realized how frozen I was as I shivered hard. "You need to let me take care of you."

"He's really out of it," Chloe said from behind me. "You should get him inside."

Sam didn't respond, concentrating on me. "Jesus, J, your pupils are huge."

"Oh yeah?"

"Did somebody hit—"

"I got hit in the back of the head," I told him before I smiled up into his eyes. I felt like I was floating and I was pretty sure Sam was the reason. 'Cause I loved him. "But it doesn't really hurt anymore, I just—"

His hand went to my hair as he leaned my forehead into his chest. "Oh shit, J, there's a huge bump back here."

"I'm okay," I said as I tipped my head back and kissed his chin. "I'm so glad to see you. I missed you."

"J," he said sharply, shaking me a little. "Baby, open your eyes."

I realized when I did that I was suddenly looking down a long tunnel at him. "Sam, I love you."

"Jory! Baby!" he yelled at me and it felt like there was a dip, like I was riding a roller coaster, that drop in your stomach just before you start down. And then there was nothing at all.

I GROANED as I opened my eyes. "Crap."

"J?"

I rolled my head to the left and there were Sam and Dane and Aja.

"Hey, baby." Sam smiled at me, his voice soft, gentle, reaching out to put his hand on my cheek. It was so warm and I leaned into it. "How ya feel?"

I grunted. "I feel like shit. What's wrong with me?"

"You got a mild case of hypothermia, a concussion, and you're really dehydrated. They've given you three IV bags already."

"Oh yeah?"

"Yes, baby. You were really out of it before."

I nodded and looked at Dane. "Sorry. I'm really sorry I worried you."

He walked around the bed and leaned over and took me in his arms. I breathed him in and he held me tight, his face in my hair.

"Dane, please—"

"You saved Aja and you're home safe. I couldn't ask any more of you."

"You're not mad at me?"

"Mad at you?" He exhaled deeply, rubbing my back. "No, Jory, I'm just thankful. It's all I am."

"You sure?"

"Jory, you're amazing. The only reason I yell at you and worry about you is because you're my brother. If you… if anything ever… I…."

I relaxed in his arms and my eyes drifted closed. The lips that touched my cheek were featherlight and soft, like the petals of a rose. I smiled slowly. "Aja," I sighed, opening my eyes with great effort, her lovely face my reward. "Hi."

"Jory." She smiled even though her eyes were filling fast, her bottom lip trembling. "Oh baby, I was so scared."

"Don't cry."

But she couldn't speak because the tears had drowned her voice.

"Dane, lemme hold your wife," I sighed.

He threw his arm around her, pulling her in close so we were both in the circle of his arms, holding us both so tight. "I can't lose either of you," he barely got out.

"You won't," Sam assured him, his hand rubbing circles on the small of my back. "But I think you need to put J back down before he passes out."

And I didn't hear what Dane said back because the room did a sharp tilt to the left and I was dumped into a black pit.

THE hand was slowly smoothing the hair back from my face, over and over, gently, lovingly. It felt really good.

"Are you awake?"

I made a noise.

"Open your eyes then."

I opened them just barely and saw Sam sitting there, looking at me.

"How do you feel?"

"My whole body hurts."

He nodded. "I bet."

The three-day-old stubble, how soft his eyes were, the way his hair was sort of sticking up, the shy, crooked grin that took the ice out of his dark, smoky blue eyes, infusing them with heat... all of it made my heart hurt. "You look so good."

He just stared at me. "They want you to spend the night in the hospital for observation because of the concussion."

"I wanna go home."

"I knew you would, that's what I told them. Dane's fixing it now."

"Good," I sighed deeply, "because I just wanna sleep with you."

"Baby—"

I felt the sting of the tears behind my eyes. "I missed you."

"I missed you too, love."

"That's even better than baby." I smiled up at him, letting out a deep breath of contentment. "I can't wait to go home."

"Okay, baby," he said, and put his head down on my chest, over my heart.

I trailed my fingers through his hair as I looked out the window. I watched the snow gather on my window. Gray, cloudy days being my favorite, I was comforted by the darkness.

SAM gave me a choice. I could either be carried down to Caleb's room or I could ride in a wheelchair. I rode,, and when I reached his room and saw him, I was so relieved I started shaking. Caleb had been grazed by a bullet that hit his leg, but other than that he was in great shape. He actually looked much better than my own bruised and battered appearance.

"I was so worried about you," I told him, holding his hand, trying not to cry.

"I know." He sighed, hugging me tight. "You care so much about me."

And I did. We were friends, and family, sort of. I stayed with him as long as Sam let me. I found it sad that Caleb didn't have anyone to sit with him. Sam assured me that it was not going to be me.

Once we were home and Sam had the car parked on the street in front of my apartment, I swung the door open to get out.

"Don't move, J."

So I waited for him to come around, and when he did I jumped down. Before I could walk away though, he scooped me up into his arms.

"Oh hell, no." I squirmed to get him to drop me. "I'm not a girl, Sam. You can't carry me like—"

"I'm carrying you up to that apartment," he told me, "and if I put you over my shoulder you're gonna be sick. So today you're going like this."

"But Sam, I—"

"No, J, just stop talking."

I sighed, realizing he was going to have his way since there was nothing at all I could do about it.

He rubbed his chin in my hair as he carried me up the front stoop and inside the door that led into the foyer of the building. I let my head drop onto his shoulder and felt him tighten his hold.

"Caleb's gonna be all right, isn't he?"

"That's the fifth time you've asked me."

"No, I know," I said. "I was just worried about him."

"You're the one that got hurt, J, he should be worried about you."

"He got shot." I was incredulous. "I didn't even—"

"He was grazed by a bullet, that's it. You, on the other hand...." He took a settling breath. "You were choked and hit and kicked and—"

"I'm fine," I cut him off before he got worked up. "You can see I'm fine."

"Well, so is Caleb," he snapped at me. "He's in better shape than you."

I was going to mention again that Caleb Reid had been shot, but Sam didn't seem all that receptive to the reminder.

"Caleb was way luckier than you," Sam said, letting himself in with the key to the security door. I told him I could get up the stairs myself, I didn't need to be carried, but he didn't even slow down. "Just let me take care of you... please."

"Why don't you just put me down?"

"I don't feel like it. I like holding you," he said as he effortlessly took the stairs even with my added weight.

I squeezed him tight and felt the deep breath he took when he reached my front door. My apartment was just as I'd left it days earlier. It was so good to be home.

"It's cold in here," he commented as he locked the door behind him.

"The radiator just hasn't kicked on yet." I yawned. "But it will."

"Yeah, and you'll be frozen by then."

I couldn't stop yawning. My eyes were watering, I was so tired. "I need a shower so bad."

He carried me to the bathroom, and after I promised not to pass out and hit my head on the tile or the faucet, he went to get a fire started while I stripped out of my clothes and washed away my days of captivity.

When I was towel-drying my hair, he came in with sweats and socks and a long T-shirt for me. He watched me as I changed.

"What?"

"Nothing." He shook his head. "I'm just glad to see you."

"Where are you going with my clothes?" I asked as he put my jeans and sweater and boots in a plastic bag.

"It's evidence," he told me. "I'm gonna call someone to come pick them up."

"Okay," I said weakly, "I'm gonna go lie down."

"You should try and eat something."

But just the thought of food was nauseating. "Maybe later," I said, walking away from him.

My bed felt amazing and I sank down onto it. I was almost asleep by the time he came back, but I felt the bed dip as he lay down.

"Come here."

I lifted up and he pulled me into his arms so I was lying with my legs between his and my head on his chest. The steady beat of his heart was very comforting, as was his warmth.

"Did you miss me?"

"I more than missed you," he said, his hands in my hair, on my back, petting me.

"Yeah?"

"I don't sleep the same when you're not with me. I figured that out when I was gone all that time. You're the only one who makes me forget about everything else so I can just... be."

"You know, for a big tough silent-guy type, you say a lot of really good stuff."

"Yeah well, I try."

"No, you don't." I smiled, my body getting heavy. "And that's the best part."

"J, you—"

"Wait," I said, rolling over on my stomach away from him, reaching between my shoulder blades to pull my T-shirt off and over my head. "Look."

"J, I'm trying to… oh shit." I heard him deflate.

I smiled into the pillow as I felt his warm hands sliding over my back.

"Jory… baby, you put my name on you."

"Yes, I did," I said softly. This was the first time Sam was seeing my tattoo. I hadn't gotten the chance to show him before everything happened.

"I don't…." he trailed off, and that made me very happy.

The tattoo was simple, just large black letters, but it was special because I had taken a piece of paper with his signature on it with me to the tattoo parlor. They had used a projector and enlarged it and then traced it on my skin. The result was as though Sam himself had signed his name directly over my right shoulder blade. There was no mistake to whom I belonged now.

"How did you do this?"

I grunted as his hands slid up and down my spine, down over the small of my back and lower, over my ass, massaging, kneading my skin, taking the tension away with each pass.

"Jory?"

"Do you like it?"

"Yeah," he said simply, his voice hoarse, kissing the tattoo gently, and then tracing the same path as his hands, down my back to my ass. "I was so scared, J. I've never been that scared even before."

I rested my head on my hands, tried to roll over without success. He wanted me down.

"There's bruises on your back and your ribs."

"One of the guys roughed me up a little."

"There was blood on your clothes," he said tightly.

"Don't think about it anymore."

"No."

"I'm home now."

"I know, I just… we're no closer to stopping this guy."

"We?"

"Yeah. Me, my partner, the department, the feds… all of us."

"You'll figure it out, Sam."

He cleared his throat. "You know Dane asked to talk to you when he talked to Caleb, but the guy said no."

"You were scared I was dead, huh?"

"No, 'cause Caleb said you were okay, but… I wanted to talk to you."

"'Course." I shivered as his hands started back up my back.

"Feel good?"

"You know it feels good."

"I missed rubbing your tight little ass every morning."

I concentrated on breathing.

"I missed everything about you."

"I'm sorry I scared you."

"Honey, you have no reason to be sorry."

"I just feel… weird. I think maybe I'm a little out of it right now."

"Baby, you are so out of it, you have no idea. Everything that's happened and you're this calm, talking to me, rambling on about how funny it was that you were carjacked after being kidnapped… Jory, honey, you should be terrified."

"But it's just so stupid, Sam. C'mon, that shit is funny as hell."

"You're in shock, baby."

"I am," I asked, rolling over onto my side.

He instantly spooned around my back, holding me close so I was wrapped up in warmth.

"Sam." I sighed as I closed my eyes, suddenly so tired.

"You know after this you're gonna do exactly as I say, right?"

"Okay." I felt his hand slide up my neck as he leaned my head back.

"Thank you for putting my name on you, J, it's like the sexiest thing I've ever seen in my life."

And I could feel how turned on he was by the way he pressed against me, the way his hand slipped down under the elastic waistband of my sweats and then under and inside my briefs. I sucked in my breath as his warm hand closed around my shaft.

"Sam," I tried to breathe.

"Shhh," he soothed me as he shifted around me, rolling me over to my back, moving down my body, dragging my clothes with him to my knees.

"Sam," I called his name as my back bowed and I arched up off the bed.

At the same time I was swallowed in tight, moist heat, I felt strong hands on my hips, anchoring me under him, looked into the eyes locked on mine. And I knew that, for him, the way I was responding told him I was all right. For Sam there was no substitute for action, as for him, words were cheap. He could ask me if I was all right and I could lie. My body could not. When I shuddered and clutched at his hair, he was happy. I saw the glint in his eyes as his name tore out of me, and afterwards, as I lay there only able to watch him, exhausted beyond anything else, he took a deep, settling breath.

"Believe me Sam… I love you."

He nodded, staring down at me in that possessive way he had. "I know."

"I need to take care of you," I said, smiling, shifting to rise up off the bed.

His hand on my abdomen stilled me. "Stay there, close your eyes."

And I thought maybe he was going to say something else, but he only looked at me. I tried to wait but it was a losing battle. I was out seconds later.

IT WAS light when I woke, and he was sitting in bed beside me, reading. I lifted my head and, without looking at me, he patted his chest. I moved closer and he reached for me, tucking my head under his chin. The sigh came up out of me, rising, and I felt his soft, rumbling laughter before he rubbed his chin in my hair. He said he loved me and I closed my eyes again.

"What time is it?"

"It's around nine."

"At night?"

"No, love, in the morning."

"God, I slept a long time." I yawned languidly, feeling too good to move, knowing I should.

"Yeah, ya did. You needed it."

"I should get up and make you something to eat."

"Just lie still and let me hold you."

I wrapped my arms around his neck and snuggled against him. He hugged me tight and kissed my eyelids. I was so peaceful, my body so heavy, I felt drugged by his closeness, by his attention.

"Love you." I yawned.

"I know, baby. Go back to sleep, you're safe. I'm here."

He had no idea how comforting it was.

Chapter Four

WE HAD a full house. Dane and Aja were there, as well as Sam's family; Dylan had come to check on me, leaving her husband Chris at home with their newborn baby; Aubrey Flanagan dropped by with her new boyfriend, Rick Jenner; and Sam's partner Chloe was there, as well as my friends Evan and Loudon. And even though the reason for it was scary, I loved seeing Aja sitting with Sam's mother and his sisters. Fun to watch Evan talking to Dane, Sam's brother Michael, and Rick. Nice to eavesdrop on Sam's father chatting with Loudon and Aubrey, and listening to Dylan and Sam in the kitchen with Chloe was a treat. It should have been a dinner party, as well as everyone was getting along. When the doorbell rang and Sam let strangers in, I realized that these were the detectives working my case. There were six all together, four from the FBI and two from Chicago PD. I was surprised that Sam didn't take me in the other room with them, but he merely made everyone quiet down while he introduced them to me.

Sam's friends from the department were James Hefron and Neal Lange. Hefron was tall and balding, with broad shoulders and a wide chest. His eyes were dark brown like mine, and his brows looked permanently furrowed. In contrast, his partner Neal Lange had bright green eyes and a slight build. His smile was quick, his dimples deep, and his hands moved continuously. He seemed restless, but in an eager way instead of a fidgety one. Hefron took a seat as Lange took up space on the coffee table directly in front of me. The FBI agents just stood and looked at me, one of them passing me the morning newspaper, where my kidnapping had made the bottom of the front page. It was spooky to see my name in print.

"Oh shit," I groaned.

The agent chuckled and introduced himself. I didn't catch his name, I wasn't really listening, but I shook all four of their hands and thanked them for trying to help me. I was still looking at the article in the paper. At the time it went to press I had still been missing. I was hoping none of my friends saw it. At least there was no picture of me. I looked really bad in black and white, my coloring didn't come through at all.

Someone coughed softly and when I looked up, I found Neal Lange staring at me.

"Jory," he said softly, staring into my eyes. "I wanna talk to you a little bit here, all right?"

"Sure."

"Okay." He forced a smile. "Over the last few days, as we talked to your brother and to Sam, and after we went back over the old case files from the murder in Oak Park and the others, we were able to piece together something that we didn't really see before."

I was confused.

"You look confused." He smiled at me.

"Aren't you here about the kidnapping?"

"In a roundabout way, yes. We're here about the murders."

"Why? I don't think they have anything to do with me."

"They do in that you are the intended victim but don't as the violence is not actually directed at you."

"What does that even mean?"

"Well, actually, this whole thing, the murders, the kidnapping... we believe that all of this has less to do with you and more to do with your brother, Mr. Harcourt."

"Dane?"

"Yes."

"How? Why?"

"Whoever this guy is, he wants what your brother has. He wants to hurt Mr. Harcourt and he can accomplish that by striking at the people Mr. Harcourt loves. The perpetrator was specifically targeting you because, initially, you were the most important person in Dane Harcourt's life."

"But not anymore."

"No. Now there's Mrs. Harcourt as well."

I shivered. "And Caleb."

He scowled at me, but said yes.

"Why do you look like that?"

"Right this second we're not really sure how Caleb Reid fits into all of this. You fit, Mrs. Harcourt fits, even if Mr. Harcourt's friends had been targets, which they haven't... they would fit, but we're uncertain about Mr. Reid. It raises questions about how well this person really knows Dane Harcourt."

I looked at him. "How'dya mean?"

"Well, Mr. Reid is Mr. Harcourt's brother, but they are not close."

"Right."

"And who knows that, Jory?"

"I'm—"

"Who knows that Mr. Reid is related to Mr. Harcourt but is not privy to the extent of their relationship?"

"A ton of people."

"Not really. Only someone close to Mr. Harcourt would know."

"I guess."

He nodded. "So technically we would be looking for someone that knows Mr. Harcourt only superficially. He knows the people your brother knows, knows names, but nothing more."

I shivered. "So you're thinking that the kidnappers know somebody that knows Dane, or they are people that know Dane like an acquaintance."

"Exactly," he agreed, rubbing his forehead. "But that's a lot of people. Mr. Harcourt's close circle was easy to go through and eliminate suspects from. The wider circle will take much longer."

"I see," I said. "So you think Caleb was taken because—"

"We think Mr. Reid got taken by mistake," he cut me off. "Or because it was easy… we're not sure what went on there. We're going through what Mr. Reid remembers, trying to piece something together."

"I dunno about your theory." I stared into his eyes. "What are you basing any of this on? It sounds really far-fetched, like a—"

"The first victim that was killed, the one in your apartment… that was right around the time that Mr. Harcourt made you his brother."

I waited and tried to breathe. Instantly, I was creeped out.

"The second victim was killed when Mr. Harcourt had his big fortieth birthday party. It was huge, the mayor went and—"

"How do you guys know about his birthday party? It wasn't like it was—"

"Jory," he interrupted me. "We're detectives, Jory, this is what we do. We look for patterns."

"But—"

"Listen to me… the third victim was killed right after Mr. Harcourt's engagement party, and the fourth was found just a couple of weeks after his wedding."

"It seems really random. I mean, if some guy wants to hurt Dane, why not just kill me? Why kill guys that look like me? On top of that, why try and kidnap Aja and me? Why not just her?"

"We think that the brunt of the psychosis is focused on you, but with the opportunity having presented itself to take both you and Mrs. Harcourt… we believe it was too good to pass up."

"But—"

"This was the reason for Mr. Reid being taken as well… opportunity."

"But wouldn't it stand to reason that he would want to take Aja?"

"It's reasonable, but we doubt it was actually planned, which was why it was so easy for Mrs. Harcourt to get away. He really wasn't prepared to take both of you. Not really."

"You think it was just luck that let Aja get away?"

"Poor planning, your heroics, and some luck, yes."

"Well, the guy is obviously a moron," I scoffed. "I mean, leaving me in a car to be—"

"Make no mistake," Lange shut me down hard. "This man has murdered four people. He has been cunning enough to kill them and leave no trace of his identity, only the similarity of the killings being enough to link them. He has left no DNA evidence at any of his crime scenes, he's a complete unknown."

I noticed when he stopped talking how quiet the room was. It was like everyone was holding their collective breath.

"And the only reason I'm letting all these people know what's going on is that my partner and I have eliminated as a suspect each and every one of them. They also need to help us keep an eye on you, as you have refused protective custody."

"I'm not living in fear, no matter what."

"Jory, we don't want you to be afraid, we just want you to be aware of—" Lange began.

"We're not saying that you should be—" Hefron chimed in.

"Can I just say that compared to the first time… this was a walk in the park?"

"Jory," Sam warned me.

"What?" I snapped at him, standing up. "It was. You guys forget I've been kidnapped by a cop."

The room was so silent everyone could hear the refrigerator cycling.

"Can I speak to you, please," Sam said before he stood and yanked me after him, his hand like a vice on my bicep as he walked me into the bedroom.

He shoved me away from him before he closed the door behind us.

"What?" I asked, exasperated.

"You think this is a joke?"

"No, but I think whoever this guy is has got nothing on Dominic Kairov so fuck him."

He shoved his hands deep into his pockets.

"Do you want me to be afraid, Sam?"

"A little bit, yeah."

"Well fine, I am a little bit, but not much more. As long as I'm more careful, I'll be all right."

We were silent for several minutes.

"So can we talk about something else?"

I was stunned. "You're not going to yell at me?"

"No."

"Oh."

"Do you want me to yell at you?"

"No," I said quickly.

"Okay, so while I was gone, I thought a lot about you and what my life would be like if I had never met you and—what? Why're you looking at me like that?"

"'Cause you're really not going to yell at me."

"Can we get off that, please? I have something to say."

I put up my hands. "Sorry, go ahead."

"Okay."

I waited.

He stared at me.

"Sam?"

"When this is all over, I want us to fly up to Canada with everybody and get married."

I wasn't sure I heard him. "I'm sorry, what?"

"I want to marry you. I don't feel like going to Massachusetts or anywhere else so… Canada."

I couldn't stop staring at him.

"We can go to Quebec after and hang out. It's beautiful there."

"Like a honeymoon."

"Exactly like a honeymoon."

I wasn't sure if he was being serious.

"Why are you looking at me like that?"

"Am I looking at you weird?"

"Yeah."

"Are you serious?"

"Yes, I'm serious. Why wouldn't I be serious?"

"I dunno I… I dunno."

"Listen, you need to marry me."

"But Sam, I don't need you to prove anything to me. We don't need to—"

"Who said anything about proving something? I want to be married. I always have. Just because you're not a woman doesn't mean what I want has changed. I wanna wear a ring. I want you to wear a ring. I wanna stand up in front of my family and your family and our friends and make a commitment to you, because I don't ever plan to leave you, and I want everyone to know that. And I want strangers to see a ring on your finger and know that you're taken. It's important to me."

"I can see that."

"I went down and picked up a domestic partnership agreement, but we gotta both sign it and have it notarized so—God, what?" he asked, exasperated. "Can you stop lookin' at me like that?"

"How am I looking at you?"

"Like I'm crazy or something."

"I'm just stunned is all."

"Why?"

"I just never expected this."

"You're looking at me like I grew another head."

"Sam, that domestic partnership agreement is like a legal affidavit and—"

"Yeah?"

"Sam, if you do that then everyone will know that—"

"I know!" He raised his voice, grabbing my arms, shaking me gently. "That's what I want."

"Sam, what if being openly gay is hard on you—on your career?"

"J, I'm not expecting it to be any other way."

"Yeah, but—"

"I don't give a shit. I want everyone to know you belong to me. It's the most important thing."

The knock on the door drew our attention. Aja poked her head into the room.

"You guys need to come back out here."

"Be right there." Sam assured her.

She smiled at us both before she closed the door.

I turned to leave but Sam caught my shoulder and stepped around in front of me.

"What?"

"So will you marry me?"

Such a simply spoken question, that I had never thought to hear. Being gay, I figured marriage wasn't an option for me. All my friends thought it was something stupid that never worked out, that only straight people did. It was a heterosexual not a homosexual agenda. I had never had an opinion past it not affecting me one way or another. But into my life had come a very traditional man who never once hadn't thought of marriage as a milestone in his life. Even with our many talks about how his life wouldn't be like he had imagined, he still held fast to the idea that he would be a husband.

"Jory?"

I stared up into his eyes.

"You want me down on one knee?"

I shook my head.

"At the hospital, the doctors were explaining to Dane what they were doing with you. If you'd been really hurt, they would've asked him to make decisions about you. I hated that. Just standing there like I was invisible… I want to be the person that decides. I want to be the only one they let in if you're ever hurt. I want to be your husband."

My eyes blurred and I felt the tears on my cheeks.

"So whaddya say?"

I assumed it was a given. Of course I would marry him. I would do anything with him he ever wanted.

"J?"

I was completely overwhelmed; any words were out of the question.

"Aww, babe," he said, hands on my face before he bent and kissed me.

My arms wrapped around his neck and I kissed him back with everything I felt but couldn't say.

He clutched me tight, breaking the kiss to smile against my mouth. "So what's your answer?"

"Yes, Sam."

"Yes, Sam what?"

I took a deep breath as I stared up into his eyes. "Yes, Sam Kage, I will marry you."

His scowl was instant. "Jesus, that was like the longest goddamn minute of my life."

I laughed at him as he grabbed me and kissed me breathless.

"I love you, Jory."

"I know." I smiled up at him.

When I was kissed again, I forgot about everything else but the man in my arms. Nothing mattered except that I was loved. I suddenly understood the depth of what Dane felt on his wedding day. To have everything you wanted all at once was very humbling.

I WAS sitting on the couch watching Sam and Aja play a video game while Dane stood by the window on the phone. Everyone else was gone.

"I think everyone got along really well, don't you?" I asked Sam.

"Yep."

"Did you enjoy meeting Sam's family?" I asked Aja.

Nothing.

"Aja?"

"Oh, are you talking to me?"

"Yes, I'm talking to you."

"Sorry," she said quickly, her eyes never leaving the screen.

"So?"

"So what?"

"Did you enjoy meeting Sam's family?"

"I did. I'm looking forward to going over there this Sunday. It sounds like fun."

"Sam, that was nice of your mom to invite Dane and Aja."

"Yep."

I rolled my eyes. Talking to the walls would be more interactive. I got up and crossed the room to Dane, who raised a finger when I started to say something to him. I needed to give him a minute. I padded into the kitchen and started to make some tea.

Now that no one was talking to me, I started thinking about what had happened. I had been gone four days, Caleb six, and because we had both gotten away, no ransom had been paid. Apparently, the night the car was stolen the kidnapper had been taking us to the drop-off site, where we would have been exchanged for the money. The kidnapper had taken Caleb with him at gunpoint to walk to the pay phone, and when he got back, the car was gone. He ran off after that, leaving Caleb alone to walk the streets looking for help in Oak Lawn. I had told Hefron and Lange that I was sure there had been a second guy at some point, but that after hearing them argue about Sam, I was fairly certain one of them had been shot. Whoever the dead one was, he had wanted to let me go rather than tangle with Detective Kage. Hefron and Lange did not blame him. Sam's reputation was decidedly brutal. He was an excellent detective with a menacing demeanor. Everyone had agreed on that point.

I put the kettle on to boil and walked into the other room, even though I heard a knock on the front door. Let someone else get it. I took a seat on my bed, and that was where Dane found me minutes later.

"Hey."

When I looked at the doorway, he tossed something at me.

I caught it, realized it was an iPhone, and looked back at him.

"I got the same one you had and I went ahead and cancelled both your credit cards and ordered new ones. The only thing you need to do is go get another driver's license."

"Thanks."

"You're welcome," he nodded, walking into my bedroom and sitting down beside me. "So Sam said you agreed to marry him... that's good. I look forward to being his brother-in-law."

"I'm glad."

"You don't look that happy."

"No, I'm happy about that. I just… I want this whole thing to be over already."

"I'm so sorry, J. If it wasn't for me, you—"

"Please," I groaned, lying back on the bed. "You have no control over the scary people in the world—believe me, I know. Some psychopath has got it out for you for whatever reason… that's his problem, Dane, not yours. You'd hafta be crazy to think that you have any control of anything but yourself."

"That's very good advice."

"That's not advice, it's just… logical." I said, fiddling with the new cell phone in my hand. "Thanks for this."

"You're welcome," he said, putting his hand around the back of my neck.

"Did you like Aubrey Flanagan?"

"I did, and more important than me liking her—Rick likes her."

"I know, right? It's nice."

"It is," he said, his fingers massaging my neck, the base of my skull.

I closed my eyes and breathed.

"Oh, this is interesting," he said quietly. "Sam found that doctor you used to date. Remember?"

"Nick Sullivan."

"Yes."

"And? What about him?"

"He's married now."

"Oh yeah? To who?"

"Sam says to a very beautiful woman named Jenna."

I smiled slowly. "He's married to a woman? That is interesting."

"I told you."

"I wonder what made him do that."

"You know, Sam came out late. Maybe the reverse is true of Nick Sullivan."

"Maybe," I said thoughtfully, wondering.

"He lives in Lake Forest with his wife and two kids. Sam said he asked about you."

"That's not surprising. We were close once."

"That's weird, isn't it?"

"What's that?"

"Being close and then not."

I turned my head to look at him. "I don't emotionally connect with many people. I've slept with a ton of guys, but I can count like two before Sam that I ever even gave a crap about, and Nick Sullivan wasn't one of them."

"Oh no?"

"No."

"I remember a Kevin that came to the office a couple of times."

"Yep." I smiled at him. "Kevin Wu, I liked him a lot."

"And Aaron Sutter, of course."

"Of course."

"So nothing for Nick Sullivan."

"Friendship isn't nothing."

"It's not love."

"No. Did you love all those women you slept with?"

"Not one." He eyed me.

"Except the one you married." I smiled at him.

"That's right."

"Do you believe there's only one soul mate for each person?"

"Yes, I do," he said gently, leaning me against him, arm around my shoulders. "And so do you. You're a hopeless romantic."

It was true. "You should go to the hospital and see Caleb."

"I'm where I need to be. I'm with my brother and my wife."

"Caleb's your brother too."

But he wasn't listening anymore. He got up to get the kettle when it whistled and I was left on the bed, staring out at the sky. It was snowing steadily and the white flakes were building up on my windowpanes. Days like this, I was always thankful to not be homeless. I was thankful to be warm and safe and inside.

"J."

I looked up at Sam as he walked into the bedroom.

"Baby, the Reids wanna come over and see you, if that'd be okay."

"Why don't I go to the hospital tomorrow and see Caleb, and I'll see them at the same time?"

"You tired?"

I nodded and went back to looking out the window. When Dane brought me a cup of tea I thanked him and put it on my nightstand before I stretched out on my bed. I didn't remember falling asleep.

IT WAS dark when I woke up, and when I called for Sam there was no answer. The kitchen light was on and that was where I found a note from him; he had just run out to pick up dinner. He would be right back. Since he always wrote down the time on his notes, after I checked the display on the microwave I realized he'd been gone maybe ten minutes. It explained the fire blazing away in the living room. There was a weird ring, and I realized that it was my new phone. I would need to put all my downloads from my computer into it as soon as possible. A generic ringtone was just not me.

"Hello?"

"Jory?"

"Yeah. Who's this?"

"You're so lucky, Jory. How many lives do you have?"

"I'm sorry, who is this?"

"Jory, if it wasn't for you, I'd have what I want."

I felt the hair stand up on the back of my neck and a chill raced through my body.

"Jo… ry," came the singsong voice. "I'm going to kiss you when you're cold."

I hung up and threw the phone on the couch and stared at it. When Sam walked into the apartment minutes later carrying a large brown bag, I was sitting next to the fireplace, my knees pulled up to my chest, my arms wrapped around my legs.

"Hey." He smiled at me. "You're up. Are you hungry, 'cause I went and got your… J? You all right?"

I shook my head, pointed at my phone. "He called."

"Who called?"

"The guy… the guy called."

"The kidnapper called?" he asked calmly as he walked to the couch and picked up my phone.

I nodded.

"What'd he say?" He asked as he dialed my phone.

I stared at him a minute, waiting for him to freak out.

"J?"

"Um, he asked me how many lives I had and he told me that if it wasn't for me he'd have everything he wanted. He said he'd kiss me when I was cold."

He nodded. "Is that it?"

"Yeah." I shivered even though the heat from the fire was warm on my back.

"Okay," he said very clinically as he started speaking into my phone. "I need a trace on this number right now—see who called it in the last five minutes and then have Hefron or Lange call me back on my phone. Yep—okay."

I closed my eyes and put my face down on my knees. The idea that the guy could just call me, that he knew my number… it was just so creepy. I heard Sam barking orders at people and fumbling around in the kitchen before he started yelling. For some reason his anger and volume was comforting, and when I heard him swearing I didn't scold him like usual. I just sat still and silent, listening to the crackling of the fire when the room finally fell silent.

"Hey."

I lifted my head to look up into his face.

He pointed at the front door. "That's locked, I'm here, I have a gun, and you know besides that I'm a really strong guy."

I had no idea where this was going.

"So you know when I'm here, you're safe, right?"

"I know."

"Good," he said as he dropped to his knees in front of me. "So come here and kiss me."

I unwrapped myself and reached for him as he pulled me to my knees in front of him, his hands all over me, tugging my T-shirt off over my head before he eased me down onto the rug in front of the fire. My sweats were next to go, and the briefs underneath. I lay there naked, staring up at him as his eyes swept over me.

"Stay," he said before he got up and left me there, vulnerable and cold. And I wondered if it was a test to see if I'd move. Did I trust what he'd said? Did I trust that there was no reason for even a sliver of fear to touch me as long as he was there?

I heard him and turned to look and he was back, wrapped up in one of the blankets off the bed.

I smiled wide. "What're you doing?"

"I'm here for you," he said softly as he crouched over me, opening the blanket to reveal both the lube from the nightstand and the fact that he was completely naked.

"I see." I grinned lazily. "Something you want?"

"Yes, baby… there's something I want."

"Whatzat?"

He leaned over and wrapped me in his arms, and the contact with his warm, sleek skin made me gasp. I wrapped my legs around his waist and moved around under him until I was where I wanted to be.

"I'm thinkin' maybe there's somethin' you want too, J," he said softly, his hands on me, drawing me into his arms, his lips on my throat.

I arched my back, lifting for him and begged him to just make everything else disappear. And he was magic, so it did.

Chapter Five

I WAS standing outside getting the mail, after being on the phone with Caleb Reid for half an hour, when I heard the roar of Sam's SUV behind me. Even though I was in nothing but jeans and a tank top, I waited for him. It was nice that, as soon as he saw me, the smile was huge. I watched him parallel park his monster vehicle, which I was always amazed that he could do, and saw him climb down out of the cab.

"What are you doing out here?" he called over to me as he started across the lawn.

"Just enjoying the view," I said, hearing the alarm chirp as he pocketed his keys.

He gave me a look like I was crazy, gesturing around at the gray sky, barren trees, and slushy sidewalks. "What view, baby?"

I pointed at him. Just looking at him made me happy. The swagger in his walk, the fluid way he moved, the confidence easy to spot, and the heat that just radiated off the man. I should have been embarrassed that I was standing there sighing like a lovesick schoolgirl, but I had no pride where the man was concerned.

His wicked grin nearly stopped my heart.

"Hi, baby," he said as he reached me, hand instantly on my bicep, rubbing gently. "Let's go inside. Before you freeze."

I looked him up and down. He looked really good. "Jeans to work today?"

"I'm undercover."

"Oh." I nodded, unable to take my eyes off him.

"Baby, you're not even wearing any shoes," he scowled, turning me around, gently shoving me toward the front door of the building.

"I'll live, Sam," I chuckled, letting him move me through the door, grab my hand, and tug me toward the stairs. "I promise I won't freeze to death before your eyes."

He leaned in close to me to kiss the side of my neck. His warm breath made me shiver. "See—you're cold, you shouldn't be out here in just—"

"You're making me shiver, not the cold."

He nodded as we started up the stairs. As we walked down the hall, my neighbors, Lisa and Steven, came out of their apartment. Odd that they were there in the middle of the day. Maybe it was a little afternoon delight.

"Jory," Lisa called out to me, smiling big.

"Hey." I smiled back at her, not making any move to stop.

"Hi." Steven stopped Sam, putting out his hand when he was close enough. "I'm Steven Warren, this is Lisa Tate—we live across the hall."

"Good to meet you," Sam said, taking his hand, shaking it. "I'm Sam Kage."

"I've been seeing you around a lot, Sam." Lisa smiled at him. "Are you the man in Jory's life now?"

"Yes, ma'am," he said huskily, and I saw her take breath. The man was very masculine and very hot; she'd have to be blind not to notice. "I'm the old... new guy."

She chuckled. "Sounds like there's a story there."

"Yep, there is." His wicked grin, and she lit up like a Christmas tree.

"Well, I'm so pleased. Jory's a wonderful guy—he deserves to be happy."

"Thank you," I said gently as Sam shoved me forward.

"Nice to meet you," he said absently, kissing the side of my neck. "Hurry up."

I didn't turn back around.

Once we were inside the apartment, I locked the door behind us and watched him walk through the living room to the kitchen.

"You didn't leave the house dressed like that this morning. I would've remembered."

"You didn't see me this morning—you were dead to the world. I was hoping you'd sleep a lot longer."

"You should change before you go back to work."

"Why?" he asked me as he shed his peacoat to reveal an open short-sleeved shirt over a T-shirt that could have been mine for how tight it was. All you saw were bulging biceps and rippling abs, the material clinging to him like a second skin. The gun holster with the Glock in it just added to the whole presence of the man. He was dangerous and sexy and I felt the blood racing to my groin. I had trouble breathing.

"Christ."

He was pulling lunch out of the brown paper bag he'd carried in and wasn't paying any attention to me at all. It was all I could do not to cross the room and lunge at him.

"Where were you working undercover at—an escort service?"

"What are you talking about?" He glanced up at me as he laid everything out. "I got Italian—you're not eating real well so I thought some fettuccine, since it's your favorite and... what?"

"What?"

"I dunno—you're lookin' at me all weird."

"Am I?"

"Yeah. Are you all right? Do you need to lie down?"

"I—"

"Do you need me to hold you down?" he teased me, smiling wickedly, one eyebrow arched.

"Sam—"

"What, baby?"

"Can you come here, please?"

He moved fast, crossing the floor to me, and I liked that—loving that he was eager to be close to me. "What's the matter, J?"

I didn't answer, instead leaned up and kissed him, capturing his bottom lip gently between my teeth.

The soft growl from him made me smile. He was a very sensual creature, my detective, and I enjoyed that to no end.

"I think you need me." I smiled up at him, my hand on his belt buckle.

"Stop, you'll be sorry."

"Never sorry. Ravaged before lunch hopefully, but never sorry."

"J... you're tempting fate," he said, his hands moving to my hips, his fingers slowly slipping under the waistband of my jeans, around front to the fly.

"God, I hope so."

"You should be more careful." He tipped my chin up with his nose, leaning in to kiss my throat as he undid the buttons on my jeans.

"Sam." I shivered.

"Shouldn't have teased me... warned you not to," he growled in my ear before he let out a soft groan when he cupped my ass. "No underwear—definitely tempting fate."

"I didn't want you to go to work today."

"And I didn't want to go," he told me. "Look at me."

When I lifted my head to look at his face, he bent and kissed me. He wasn't gentle, the kiss instead deep and claiming. I barely got out his name before I was dragged to the kitchen table, spun around, and bent over it, facedown. My jeans were yanked to my ankles, the tank top roughly pulled off.

"Don't you move." It was a threat.

I didn't want to move, and so stayed there, frozen, as he rifled through a drawer behind me.

"Did you know I keep lube in the kitchen?" he asked cheerfully as I heard the pop-top open.

I had to smile at him in the middle of our torrid sex scene. The man was just too cute. "What?"

"You're just always prepared, Sam."

"I'm trained to be that way," he said with mock seriousness.

"I love you."

"I love you too," he said before he bit the back of my neck.

The moan that tore out of me went right through him, arousing him like I knew it would, his hands hard and demanding on my body. Sam loved all the noises I made, loved my submissiveness and how I craved him. I loved how rough he was with me, manhandling me, how he bit and licked and kissed me, my skin under his hands driving him wild with a need to mark it all as his.

"Look at you," he breathed against my ear. "Head thrown back, trembling, all ready for me—you're so beautiful, J, and you're mine."

"Please, Sam... please."

I didn't have time to think before he moved, his slick hand around my cock, taking hold of me, his mouth on my shoulder, on his name, biting down gently, his chest pressed to my back. I cried out when he thrust forward, sliding all the way into me.

"Jory," he groaned and it came from his gut, down deep. "Baby."

"Sam," I whimpered, arching back into him, impaling myself deeper, grabbing the hand he had braced on my hip and using it to pull his arm around my neck. I wanted him to clutch me tight, hold me close.

He drove into me, forcing me down onto the table, bending me in half and lifting me off the floor as he thrust deep. I called his name and he told me to yell louder, kissing down the side of my neck, his body molding to mine.

His name bounced off the walls of our apartment.

Afterwards he gathered me close and kissed me until I thought my head was going to explode. I was sure, I told him, that not having air caused brain damage. He couldn't have cared less. He pulled me down on the couch, still naked, into his lap. I felt so good. I never wanted him to leave.

"I had no idea tight jeans made you so hot, J. I'll hafta file that away for future reference."

"Sam, I just—"

"God, I love having you in my lap."

I just stared at him.

"You know what the sexiest thing about you is?" he asked me, massaging my ass, pulling me forward over his groin so I could feel the rough texture of his jeans.

"My ass?" I teased him, as he kissed my nose and my cheeks and my forehead.

"No," he said, pulling back to look at my face. "Your eyes. They're like never completely open, always like half-open... like you just got fucked, like minutes before, you were in bed."

I smiled at him. "That's lovely, thank you."

"You're being sarcastic but I'm serious."

I grunted.

"It's sexy as hell, your bedroom eyes."

"As long as you think so."

"And your mouth—you have the most beautiful lips...."

I put my hands flat on his chest, feeling the sculpted muscles under my palms.

"And your skin and your ass."

"See," I scoffed. "I knew you'd get around to my ass eventually."

"But seriously," he said, hands on my face as he eased me forward, tilting my head at the last moment so he could kiss up my throat. "Your eyes kill me. They burn me up every time."

I trembled under his hands. The man was so sexy and he had no clue.

"Tell me something I don't know."

"I got a call from Aaron Sutter today."

"You did?"

"Yessir, I did." I smiled at him.

"And?"

"And nothing. He just wanted to make sure I was all right and he wanted to apologize for the fight we had the last time he saw me."

"What else?"

"Nothing else, he just apologized. It was nice of him."

He nodded. "I don't want him around, Jory."

"He won't be."

"He didn't want to see you?"

"I told him that I'd be back to work next week and that he could gimme a call then."

"And he just let you blow him off?"

"I didn't blow him off. I just told him that we could talk next week."

He smiled before clutching me to him, pressing me to his chest, his hands on my back. I wrapped my arms around his neck, holding him tight. His warm skin felt like heaven.

"It's nice that he was worried about you, J, but I repeat, I don't want the man around," he said as his fingers slid up the back of my neck into my hair.

"I know, don't worry."

"You belong to me, I say when and if he can see you."

I snuggled in tighter against him. "I should hate that, but I don't."

"Hate what?"

"You telling me what to do."

"Like I fuckin' care what you like or don't."

He was adorable. "Don't swear."

The back of his fingers slid under my chin and when it was lifted, his mouth settled over mine. He kissed me lazily, his tongue tangled with mine, and I was content not to move and let him.

"Hey, hold this."

I couldn't stifle my chuckle as I was passed the lube. "You are seriously scary."

"You talk too much—lift up," he said as he pushed his jeans and briefs down to his knees with one hand and took the lube from me with the other.

"Don't you hafta go back to work?"

"After."

When I was lowered over him, I watched his head roll back on his shoulders, the way his chest constricted, and the slight tremble that ran through his frame. There was a sense of power that came with knowing that I caused all that. His reaction to me was honest. He couldn't fake it.

"You like me." I smiled, looking at his closed eyes, watching him wet his lips, hearing his shaky breath. "You like doing this to me."

His hand ran down my abdomen to my cock; the fingers stroking me felt incredible. "My beautiful baby," he said softly. "Love being inside you."

I loved it too.

"You're never gonna leave me."

And there was something solid and comforting about his declaration, because I tended to test the limits of what I could do and he was telling me that whatever drama or stunts were thrown his way, he would endure. He was strong, I wouldn't wear him down. I couldn't get him to stop loving me like every other guy had before.

"Kiss me."

And when I did, when I slanted my mouth over his, kissing him hard and deep, I heard the sigh of contentment come up from his gut.

"God, I love you," he groaned.

I told him the feeling was mutual.

A HALF hour later, after I had him cleaned up and changed into a long-sleeved button-down shirt over the T-shirt, I walked him back down to the front stoop. I received a bruising, thorough kiss that left me breathless, and waved like a crazy person when he got to his car. I heard the chirp of the alarm and then the SUV exploded.

It was so fast. It was there one second, gone the next—the flame turning into a fireball that blew over the top of the next car, dying in the snow beyond it. I heard dogs barking and every car alarm on the street blaring as I ran in my bare feet across the lawn to the sidewalk, to the street. My heartbeat was pounding in my ears, I was conscious of my panting breath and the way my heart felt—like a knife had been driven through it. There was a smell like rubber burning, the truck itself now a charred, twisted piece of metal. Sam was lying on his back in the street and I fell to my knees beside him. I put my head on his chest, but I couldn't hear anything. I touched him everywhere at once, checking for signs of life. It was unreal and I kept looking around for something that I could point to and know I was dreaming. I had bruises on my skin that he'd put there just a half hour ago, my lips were still tender from his kisses, and now he barely had a pulse as he lay there, unconscious and bleeding in the street. I rifled through his peacoat, but when I found his cell phone it was smashed, the display black. I started screaming then, yelling for someone to call 911. I should have run back inside, I should have left him to get help, but I couldn't. I couldn't leave his side. I could only sit there.

Chapter Six

SAM had changed things and not let me know. So when they came to tell me that he was bleeding internally and that they were going to operate, they actually wanted my permission. They had done something—MRI, CTI, letters I didn't really understand but that meant something—and still they couldn't really know how much damage had been done until they cut him open. They wanted my permission to cut him open. I wanted someone else to decide what to do, but there was only me. I had to fill out forms and sign on the line with the word "consent" under it. I had talked to his parents and his captain and his partner and it was all too much for me until Dane showed up. He had a way of dealing with madness, and so he sat with me and made everything calmer for a little while.

Regina Kage sat on one side of me, Aja on the other, while Dane paced along with Sam's dad and Michael. Soon the waiting room was full and still there was no word. We had to wait and see and it was slowly driving me insane. Dane went back to my apartment with a police escort and got me shoes and socks and my heavy fisherman sweater. He made it back right before I froze to death, still in the tank top and jeans that Sam had seen me in last. The socks and my boots were the most needed; hard to go barefoot in a hospital, since they kept the temperature at meat-locker cold.

I sat there for nine hours staring at the ceiling tiles, three more watching people get coffee from the machine, remembering that Sam and I had just been there together not even a month ago, when Mica was born. I let Regina tell me everything would be all right, I let Aja put her arm around my shoulders and hug me tight. Sam's captain came and squeezed my hand; Chloe put her hands on my face and promised me that Sam was way too tough to die. Dane just looked at me, saying nothing because he didn't know anything yet, the realist that he was unable to give me false hope. Somehow that was the most comforting, because it wasn't the time to be sad yet, or worry. We had no idea what was going on, the time for panic would be later, if at all. No reason to get ahead of myself.

Swarms of policemen came and went, there were reporters that spoke to his captain outside the hospital about the incident, and the FBI guys lingered on the edge of the circus. One of the reporters got upstairs with a cameraman and tried to talk to Sam's family and me, but he was dragged away by uniformed policeman before he could get too close. Apparently the captain didn't mind answering questions about Sam's service record, his time on the force, or his injuries, but his relationship to me was not for public knowledge. And even though Aja said it shouldn't matter, I thanked the captain anyway. Dane told me later that there was another FBI agent coming, but I didn't listen to who it was or when he would show up. The only thing I could do was wait to hear about Sam. My mind could focus on nothing else. I stared out the window and tried to picture my life without Sam Kage. I couldn't see it, and took that as a good sign.

Almost everyone was asleep when the surgeon finally emerged early the following morning. I was up and out of my chair so fast that I upset Regina and Aja, who were asleep on either side of me. I reached him and stood there, holding my breath as the others crowded around us. I waited for my life to either begin or end. Dr. Kohara didn't look at anyone but me.

"He lost a lot of blood, Mr. Harcourt," he sighed deeply, looking absolutely weary. "But we're confident that he'll make a full recovery. He's got a very strong heart, he's in good physical health, and he's a fighter."

I nodded, too overwhelmed to speak.

"We had to remove his spleen and I know that sounds scary, but it's really not. I'm sorry we had you wait so long without word on him, but even though it was critical at the beginning, he really came through so much better than we could have hoped."

I nodded.

He smiled slightly. "He's going to heal well. He didn't sustain any traumatic damage to his brain or spine. He's a very lucky man, it could have been so much worse."

I couldn't stop nodding.

"You can come in and maybe one more person, but that's it."

I grabbed his hand, squeezed tight. "Thank you—really… thank you."

He nodded, his eyes on mine, and suddenly smiled. "What's your first name?"

"Jory."

He sighed, his hand going to my shoulder. "I thought it might be—he said it a lot."

I felt the smile on my face.

His smile deepened. "Something about a swear jar?"

"I'm working on him."

"Well, that's good. All of us should have someone trying to help us be better."

I felt like the tears were just waiting to drown me and him and everyone else for miles.

"Come on—who's coming with you?"

I reached for Regina's hand and she grabbed mine tight. We followed after Dr. Kohara together.

The room sounded like a pet store full of chirping birds, but it was the machines whirling and beeping, little alarms going off, things pinging, all of it there to monitor different parts of the man's anatomy. I was glad he didn't look small in the bed. He looked the same, just still, and the fact that he was breathing on his own, no machine hooked up to his face, made me very happy. His right cheek was scraped and there was dried blood in splotches everywhere. He had a bandage over his right eyebrow, lots of IV tubes coming out of him, and that weird clip thing on his middle finger that kept track of his heartbeat. I put another blanket over his feet because I didn't want them to get cold.

"His color is good." Regina sighed, her smile brilliant. "Oh, Jory, he looks so good."

She took the hand without the monitor on it as I leaned up to his forehead and kissed him gently. When I pulled back, I voiced the thought that had been screaming in my head for the past twelve hours.

"This is all my fault."

"I'm sorry?"

I looked over at my boyfriend's mother. "The guy—he went after Sam to get to me. I put Sam in danger. This is all my fault."

"No-no-no," she shook her head. "This is no more your fault then it is Dane's. This man wants to hurt Dane so he goes after you, and in getting to you now, he's gone after Sam. It's—"

"Okay," I placated her. "You're right."

She let me soothe her and I was glad, because it would have been harder if she didn't trust me. I didn't need her checking on me. I needed to be able to leave without anybody realizing it. I knew what I had to do even though I didn't really want to do it.

I went back out of the room and sent Sam's father in while I thanked everyone for being there. I told them all how he looked and how he was breathing all by himself. I spent the next half an hour hugging them all good-bye and telling each of them how much it meant that they were there. It was tough arguing with Dane because he wanted me to go home with him and Aja. Even though there was a police car permanently sitting on the street in front of my building, he felt like it still wasn't safe enough. Regina came out of the room and wanted me to come home with her. I promised to be there tomorrow, but I wanted to stay at the hospital. Everyone understood. Back in the room with Sam, I held his hand and told him how much I loved him.

"You know, I get it now…. When you left me that time in the hospital, I mean—I know you had to leave 'cause you wanted to keep me safe. There was more to your—being gay was a brand new thing and it was hard for you and… you had to figure out that part, but now I get the whole leaving to keep me safe 'cause I'm gonna go too." I smiled at him. "I gotta find this guy Sam—I can't let anyone hurt you again. My heart won't recover from any more of this shit."

I leaned up and kissed his lips, and when I pulled back I stared at his face a long moment, engraining it in my memory. It would have to last just for a little while.

I went home and packed a small duffel bag at nine in the morning. I turned all the lights on in the apartment, left one on in the living room but then turned off the one in my bedroom an hour later. I went out the window to the fire escape and took that to the alley behind my building. The cops never even saw me leave.

Chapter Seven

MY PLAN was simple and logical, because the way I figured it I had one course of action left open to me. I had to retrace my steps and start from where the car had been abandoned. Because if I could find the place where the carjackers got the car, perhaps from there I could work my way back to where I'd been held. It seemed reasonable. So I went back to the vacant lot beside the liquor store and staked it out.

The room I rented usually went by the hour instead of by the day. This was what the manager had told me as he counted the ten twenty dollars bills I gave him. He usually didn't give out a bathroom key, but since I'd given him cash, I was given access to the shower. I wasn't to loan it out. He didn't have to worry; I wasn't planning on having company over. I took up my place in the windowsill of my room and watched the vacant lot across the street from me. I was convinced of one thing—the two guys that had stolen the car from the kidnappers lived somewhere in the neighborhood. People were creatures of habit, so my theory was if I just staked out the liquor store, I would find the men I was looking for.

The heat in the room was minimal so I had my peacoat, muffler, and beanie on as I looked through my binoculars across the street. I answered my phone when it rang without even looking at it.

"Hello?"

"Jory, where are you?"

"I'm on a stakeout," I told my brother. "How's Sam?"

"He woke up this morning and he wants you."

"Nice try," I said slowly, checking up and down the street. "I talked to one of the nurses this morning. She said he was sleeping soundly and they're gonna move him out of ICU today."

"Where are you?"

"I answered already."

"What does that even mean? You're on a stakeout where?"

"See, I have a theory."

"God, do I even want to know?"

"No, listen—if I can start at where I ended and find the guys that took the car from the kidnappers, then I've got a jumping-off point."

"And you don't think the cops thought of this."

"Since they never even asked me what the carjackers looked like, I'm gonna go with no, they never thought of it."

There was a silence.

"You know I forget to tell you how smart you are sometimes, and you are. That whole line of thought is not bad—however… letting the police take it from there is still the best option."

"So you think it sounds good? Backtracking?"

"Yes. When you lose something, you retrace your steps. You want to know where you were, so you backtrack to the last place. That makes sense."

"See?"

"But that doesn't mean you should do it alone. Tell me where you are and I'll come sit with you."

"No thanks, I've got this."

"The hell you do. The guy who wants you could be watching you right now. You could be killed or worse or… just tell me where the hell you are before I call the police."

"Call them—they can't find a kidnapper who tried to kill one of their own, you think they can find me?"

"Jory—"

"I'm not coming home until I figure this out, Dane, so just… do me a favor and watch over Sam, all right? I took care of Aja, now it's your turn to watch over him."

"Jory—"

"I love you," I said and hung up. When he called back I didn't answer.

IT REMINDED me of living at the YMCA, and then with the four other guys I lived with when I first moved to the city. I had always been cold, both places smelled, and the rooms were dirty. Sitting in a cramped position watching the liquor store, alternating between using my binoculars and not, I realized how boring stakeouts were in real life. They always looked fun in the movies. But lots of things looked like more fun in the movies.

I had to go out for food, but since nothing looked particularly appetizing, I ended up at the liquor store myself, buying water, Red Bull, and lots of PowerBars and pretzels. I had lived through an entire summer once on ramen noodles and pretzels. Both had the same makeup as dog kibble—it expanded with water in your stomach. After three days, though, I remembered why I didn't eat either anymore.

My phone rang constantly, and after I put it on silent I forgot about it. I checked the numbers though, just to keep tabs. Dane called thirty times, Aja nineteen, Aaron called—which was strange since Sam had told him not to—twelve times, Aubrey called fifteen times, Dylan the same, and Chris called seven times from work. Evan called a lot, too many to even count, and I got assorted calls from Sam's family. All that came from the hospital I picked up, as various nurses told me how well Sam was progressing. Doctor Kohara said that they expected him up at any time. Any number I didn't know, I didn't bother picking up.

Saturday night I called Aubrey and told her that I would not be in on Monday but that I had all my files ready to go in my e-mail at work. I had done all my projects from home the week before without Sam knowing. I had e-mailed them all from my laptop at home to the office before I had left. She was thrilled that she was covered, appreciated me pulling my weight, but then fell into begging me to come home.

"Jory, baby—you're scaring the crap out of all of us. Every policeman in the city is on the lookout for you, and Sam... Sam's gonna be awake soon and when you're not there he's gonna—"

"Sam needs me to find this guy, Abe, and I finally realize that it's up to me. Nobody else cares as much as I do so.... But I know you didn't sign on to be the sole proprietor of Harvest Design, so if you wanna just close the office until I—"

"No, honey, I quit Barrington—I want to work with you and Dy full time, if you think that—"

"I would love that. What'd Dy say?"

"Jory, don't you think, considering the circumstances, that we should maybe talk about this in—"

"She was stoked, right?"

"God, your words—what is this, the fifth grade?"

"Yes," I teased her.

"Jory, she thought it was a great idea, so I think that—"

"Thanks, Abe, you're making a good decision. I swear."

"Jory Harcourt, I just found you! I love and adore you and if anything happens to you I just don't—"

"It's gonna be okay, partner. Now look out for Dy and take care of the office. I'll be home soon."

"Jor—"

But I cut her off when I hung up. I didn't answer when she called back.

Around ten that night I was finally rewarded for my vigilance. I saw one of the carjackers stroll into the liquor store while his friend waited outside and smoked a cigarette. I left my phone in the room and took the five flights of stairs down and out the back door to the street. Being a weekend night, the store was crawling with people; the dealers were on every corner, hustlers were clustered in doorways, and a little further down were hookers in various stages of spandex and varying heights of heels. Hard to strut on wet sidewalks in four-inch stilettos. And even though I loved to prowl around at night, it was different in the part of town I was in, and all alone. I realized that between my man, my friends, my family, I was never alone anymore. I had gotten used to being a part of a network of people. It was weird to think it was just me.

"Hey," I greeted the guy standing outside, leaning against the window of the liquor store.

He looked up at me warily. "Hey."

I shoved my hands down into the pockets of my peacoat. "Do you remember me?"

He squinted at me. "No, man."

"I—"

"Oh," he nodded. "Were you at Jerry's?"

"No," I shook my head. "I was the guy in the trunk of the car that you and your buddy stole."

His brows rose, almost disappearing into his hairline. "Oh shit! Billy and me were wondering what the hell happened to you." He looked me over. "What the fuck were you on, man?"

"I was on a lot of shit. But I need to find out where I was before I got put in the trunk of the car. There's a hundred in it for you and your buddy to split if you can show me the place."

He nodded. "Sure, man. But me and Billy gotta hit a club first. You come with us and as soon as we do our trick we'll go, all right?"

"Perfect," I agreed.

"Come on," he said, grabbing hold of the lapel of my peacoat and leading me inside the liquor store. "What's your name?"

"Jory."

"I'm Steph."

I followed him to his friend Bill, who was coming out from the back room of the store when we found him. He seemed just as amazed to be meeting me.

"What club is it?" I asked Steph.

"The Dirty Blonde," he told me. "Do you know it?"

I didn't, but neither had I spent much time in the part of town where I currently was.

"We're meeting our boss there. His name's Rego… it's his club."

I nodded, pointing at Bill's hand. "And those are what—poppers?"

He shrugged. "Sure. We got other stuff too. Tell me what you want and I'll hook you up."

"No thanks." I smiled at him. "Let's go."

There is in me the desire to know things about people. All people—everyone I meet. I have to dissect them and find out what makes them tick. So slowly, gently, as we walked, I asked questions. Steph, short for Stephan, was from Wisconsin. He had moved to the city three years ago to go to college after he graduated from high school. He had, as of yet, not started. He didn't really like the idea of studying. What he did like however was to party with his friends. Because keeping a job with an addiction to crystal meth had proven problematic, he had ended up living with his friend Bill.

William "Bill" Donavan and Stephan "Steph" Baer had met at a club and had been inseparable at once. They were both young and hot so it made sense. Steph was built like a swimmer with long, lean muscles, short curly brown hair and dark blue eyes. Bill was a little taller, built thicker with broad shoulders and heavier muscles. His hair was more of a golden brown and his eyes were greenish-brown, lighter than hazel but close. They fit together, and so when his other roommates had finally evicted Steph from his apartment, Bill had taken him in. The problem was that Bill didn't pay his rent with money; he paid it by working for Rego James.

Mr. James owned several clubs in the city and he also apparently had a lucrative escort service on the side. Rego had no problem with Steph sleeping on Bill's couch, which was basically his couch since he paid the rent there, as long as Steph turned the same tricks that Bill did. They basically did whatever they wanted whenever they wanted, but if Rego needed them to go somewhere or do somebody, they had better jump. It took a lot of money to keep the drugs coming and that was why they had stolen the car. What

Rego had given them from the last party was gone and there was no money for food or anything else. The hundred that I was offering looked really good.

"So Bill, how did you meet this Rego guy?"

He had more of a wary look than Steph did, and for a second I wasn't sure if he was going to tell me when he suddenly smiled. "Call me Billy."

"Sure."

Bill had been in the city since he was sixteen, having left home in his junior year of high school. Fresh off the bus from Knoxville Tennessee, Rego had found him sleeping in the doorway of one of his clubs and had offered to take him for breakfast.

"He took me to his place and that was it—I didn't even know I was gay until then."

I squinted at him, holding back the real questions I wanted to ask. "How old are you?"

"I'm nineteen, Steph's eighteen—he just turned two weeks ago."

"You guys ever wanna go home?"

"No, man," he shook his head. "It's boring as shit at home."

Steph's eyes flicked to mine. "Nobody at home gives a crap."

"Won't you get some money tonight?" I cleared my throat, walking into the club behind Steph.

"No," he shook his head. "We actually owe Rego money, we both had him front us cash."

I nodded, realizing the kind of club I was in. Bar in front with the dance floor, rooms in back, and further back, bigger rooms down long, dark hallways. It was a half step up from a bathhouse. When I had first moved to the city I had been a regular in the meat-market-type places, but because I worked every day for Dane Harcourt, I had not been able to completely lose myself in the scene. For the millionth time I realized how lucky I was to have finished high school and college and have a good job the whole time. I could have easily been Stephan or William if things had gone different.

I followed silently behind them through the dark club to a table where a guy sat, with several other men on couches, close to the back rooms.

"Finally," the guy said, standing up, "Gimme your coat, he's waiting."

Bill shed his coat to reveal tight black jeans and a black spandex T-shirt that clung like a second skin to his chest and abdomen. Not that there was a lot of definition there, but he still had a nice body. He turned to look at me quickly.

"Hang tight, Jory."

I nodded.

"Dance or something," he said before he bolted toward the door and went through it.

"Steph!"

We both turned to look at the man who had yelled for him.

"Get your ass in the back too."

Steph squeezed my arm before he, too, darted away. When I turned to walk back to the bar, the man stepped in front of me.

"Who're you?"

I looked up into the face of a very handsome man. Immediately I was drawn to the thick brows, the big olive-green eyes, and his dark, full lips. The suit he was wearing fit like a glove and the dress shirt was open at the collar.

"Asked you a question."

"Who're you?" I asked instead of answering.

"I'm Rego—now you."

"Oh, you're him."

"Yeah, I'm him."

"I'm Jory."

He nodded, looked me up and down. "You a friend of Steph and Bill?"

"No."

"Rego."

He looked away from me at the man sitting on the couch beside him.

"Is he new?"

He shook his head and returned his eyes to mine. "You don't need a job, right?"

"No. I'm a graphic designer."

He nodded. "Sit with me."

"Sure."

I took off my peacoat and my beanie and sat down beside him, a few feet from everyone else.

"So you do what exactly?"

"Graphic design."

"Rego."

He looked over his shoulder.

"I thought you said you didn't have a blond."

"I don't."

The other man pointed at me. "You can't get any blonder than that."

He chuckled as the music got louder. "He's not mine."

There was a hand on my shoulder and I looked up at an older man standing beside me. "Hi."

"Hi? I love that." He smiled down at me before he looked at Rego. "He's perfect."

"No," Rego shook his head. "He's just here visiting me."

The guy nodded, walked slowly away.

"Hey."

I returned my eyes to him.

"I wanna talk to you."

"Sure."

He got up and took hold of the front of my short-sleeved button-down shirt and led me to the dance floor.

I started dancing, and instead of moving with me, he just watched me.

"Come on." I smiled lazily. "I can look at you and know you can dance."

"Is that right?"

"Yeah."

He nodded and then grabbed me fast. He was bigger than me, stronger, and when I struggled he got his arm around my neck and my arm twisted up behind me. He dragged me off the floor through a side door that I hadn't even seen when I came in. I was shoved hard and had just enough time to get my hands up so I didn't go face-first into the door and then the wall on the other side. My chest was slammed into it hard as he flattened himself against my back.

"I smell hustler on you, Jory, I think you'd like gettin' fucked regular."

I tried to move but he had me again, my arm feeling like it was going to pop out of the socket, his forearm against the back of my neck.

"You are the most beautiful thing I've seen in a long time. You are so fuckin' clean."

"I promise I'm not a hustler."

"But you could be."

"No," I sighed. "I don't have the heart for it."

"Your heart has nothing to—"

"Lemme go," I asked him.

"I don't wanna hurt you, so don't fight me, all right?"

I nodded and he let my arm go but didn't move back, still holding my cheek to the wall.

"Blond hair and brown eyes, Jory, that's real nice."

"Can you let go?"

"I don't think so," he said, working my belt and the snap of my jeans open. "You ever bareback, Jory? I think you'll like it."

"Never happen," I promised him.

"No?"

"No."

"Okay, baby, don't worry, I've got a condom right here."

And I should have panicked, I really should have... but I didn't. Raped was not something I had ever even considered. I figured I might be beat up, maybe even shot at, but never raped. It didn't figure into my plans.

"You don't wanna do that."

"Why not?"

I let my head fall back on his shoulder and just breathed. "'Cause I'm better seduced and taken to bed."

"You—"

"The guys you got—touch my skin, touch my hair, you said I was beautiful and clean—why you wanna make me like all the other guys?"

I felt his breath on the side of my neck before his lips.

"I'm not here to give you trouble."

"Oh, I know... you're here for me to—"

"Kiss me first."

"I don't kiss anybody."

"Why not? You're gorgeous. I bet you could make me come just with a kiss."

His moan was pained as he pressed his groin against my ass and his hands went to my hips. "Jesus, the mouth on you… turn around."

I did as he asked.

"Look at me."

I lifted my head to meet his gaze and smiled. "You have beautiful eyes. I've never seen that color of green before."

He stared down at me and then slowly eased me into his arms. He hugged me tight, his hands smoothing up and down my back, his face buried in my hair. I let him put his hands up under the T-shirt I had on beneath my shirt, run over my bare skin, and then down over my ass. He leaned forward to kiss me but I eased back.

"You told me to kiss you."

"I just needed you to move," I said gently.

"You're not going to let me take you home."

"No."

"Because you belong to someone already."

I nodded.

"But you would if there was no other guy, wouldn't you?"

"I would."

He was stunned; there was no missing it. "You would, wouldn't you, no bullshit. You'd come on your own, I wouldn't have to force you."

"No."

He was having trouble digesting my honesty. "Come with me."

I smiled at him as he slowly let me go, straightened his suit, and led me back through the door to the dance floor. Halfway there, he stopped me with a hand on the back of my shirt.

I looked over my shoulder at him.

"You've got a lot of balls. Other guys've pissed in their pants when I did that to them."

I scowled at him. "Why would you do that to anyone?"

"People don't know what they will do until they're tested. Guys who say they'd never suck dick or take it up the ass change their minds fast sometimes."

"So you see a guy in your club, any guy, and if you think he could work for you, you drag him off somewhere and see what he will and won't do?"

"Something like that."

"So that's what you are? You're a pimp?"

"I'm a business man."

I nodded. "You just got boys?"

"Yep."

I stared at him. "You have a lot of boys working for you?"

He nodded slowly. "Jory what?"

"Keyes," I said, giving him my old name without a second thought.

He looked at me a long minute.

"And you're Rego James."

"Yes, I am."

I tipped my head toward the dance floor. "Are we gonna dance or not?"

"No." He shook his head, hand going to the back of my neck. "Come sit with me."

I let him steer me through the club back to the couch, and he tugged me down beside him.

"What do you want to drink?"

"Bottle of water." I grinned at him.

"Smart choice," he assured me, hand sliding up the back of my neck into my hair. "Natural blond, huh, even with the brown eyes."

"Yep."

"Even your eyebrows are gold," he said, sliding his fingers across my left one.

"I'm gold all over," I told him.

"I bet," he nodded, taking a deep breath. "Why're you looking at me like that?"

"Like what?"

"I dunno."

But it made sense that I would be staring. His profile, the long, straight nose, the dimples when he smiled, the way his hair fell across his forehead, and the absolutely gorgeous eyes…. The man was stunning on the outside, but inside he was a beast. It was mind-boggling. "Can I ask something?"

"'Course."

"Anybody ever brought you up on rape charges?"

"I've never been charged with anything."

"How come?"

"No one ever makes it to trial."

"That's convenient," I chuckled and the men around us looked at me like I was crazy. I was guessing laughter didn't go hand and hand with this group.

"You're a smart-ass." He smiled at me. "And a big goddamn tease."

But I knew how far to take it, since I was playing with fire. I needed him to let Steph and Bill leave with me, and whatever promises had to be made I would make.

"And you smell really good."

I tilted my head to the side so he could reach my neck, inhale me deeply.

"James, I need to dance with your boy," somebody said.

"No," he said coolly, hand on my thigh. "He's just here for decoration, not to touch."

Minutes later, Steph and Bill rejoined us.

"Rego, me and Billy gotta take Jory to see a friend—is it okay if we catch up with you in a couple hour? We'll meet you at your place."

"Sounds good." He turned to look at me as he spoke to them. "Bring Jory with you."

"Sure thing."

The back of his fingers slid down my throat. "I wanna see you, so you better show."

I said nothing because I didn't want to lie.

"I want a number where I can reach you... and an address."

"Gimme a pen." I said quickly, without hesitation.

I gave him my cell number and the address of my favorite Chinese restaurant in Oak Park.

"I want to see you in two hours, you understand?"

What I understood was that I got to take Steph and Bill with me. It was all that mattered.

Outside, Bill grabbed my arm before I could reach the curb to get us a cab.

"What?"

"Did you fuck him while I was sucking that guy off?"

I shook my head.

"I've never seen him wait."

"I've never seen him have to," Steph shrugged. "We both fucked him when we met him."

"I'll give you both a hundred if we can just go now." I sighed heavily. "Please."

All argument instantly ceased and I was thrilled that we didn't have to talk about Rego James anymore.

THE ride to Oak Lawn took forty-five minutes, but as I stood with Bill and Steph in the parking lot of the strip mall, I felt like something had been accomplished. They had stolen the car from point B; I just needed to find point A. I needed a car to get around in and I had to get back and pick up my stuff from the hotel. It was time for the hard work to begin.

I was surprised at how into the detective work Steph and Bill got, and on the ride back, they asked me all kinds of questions that I got to answer honestly, since I really didn't have any idea who had kidnapped me. Back at the hotel, Bill gave me the address of Rego's place and warned me not to blow the man off. If I valued my life, I would show up. I pretended to take it all very seriously and watched them cross the street, back to the liquor store, to buy their drugs.

Ducking back into the hotel, I gathered up all my things, returned the keys, and walked out without the manager knowing anything about me at all. I made sure that Steph and Bill were nowhere to be seen when I caught a cab to the airport to rent a car. I had to get back to the strip mall as soon as I could and start looking for the man that had kidnapped me.

Chapter Eight

I CALLED Caleb Reid because I had an idea.

"Hello?"

"Caleb? It's Jory, are you awake?"

"I'm awake now," he grumbled. "For crissakes, J, do you know what time it is?"

"No, but listen. Do you remember anything at all about the place we were kept?"

"What? Why are you—"

"I found the guys that stole the car with me in it."

"What?"

"The guys that stole the car? Remember? I found them."

"Bullshit."

"No, it's true."

"You found those guys?"

"Yeah."

"Seriously? You did?"

"Yeah, and they led me to Oak Lawn, but now I gotta try and find the—oh, wait... I just thought of something else. I'll call ya in the morning."

"Jory, is Sam still in the hospital?"

"Yeah."

"Why aren't you at the hospital with him?"

"'Cause I gotta figure this out."

"Aren't you still kind of bruised up yourself? You had a concussion, you know."

"That was a week ago, I'm fine now."

"Jory, that was like two days ago. What are you doing?"

"Sam got hurt."

"I know he did. He's in the hospital, that's why I asked you why you weren't there."

"But how did you—"

"Dane called me and told me this whole thing wasn't over and that I should be careful."

"You should."

"So Jory, you—"

"So I'm at the strip mall where the car was stolen and I'm gonna wait until they open and then I'm gonna take your picture around and ask people if they saw you."

"What are you talking about?"

"Well, I was in the trunk of the car but you were in the front seat with the kidnappers, so you they might remember."

"Jory, there was only one guy that I ever saw and I've looked at pictures until my eyes hurt and never found him."

"Sure, but this is—"

"And the sketch they made from what I said the guy looked like didn't come up with anything either. Don't you think if someone saw the sketch on the news or in the paper that they would have called the police and—"

"I think they'll remember you and then that might jog someone's memory."

"What picture do you even have of me?"

"The ones from Dane's wedding. I have them all in my phone."

"You're insane. It's not gonna work."

"It'll work. I'll call you tomorrow."

"Jor—"

But I hung up on him and got comfortable in the car. No matter what he thought, it was worth it to walk from door to door and ask if anyone remembered seeing Caleb Reid.

When Rego James called an hour later and asked me where I was, I explained about being on a stakeout. After fifteen minutes of me explaining things to him, he let out a quick breath and said I was the weirdest guy he'd ever met. It was probably true. I hung up, and when he called back I let it go to voicemail.

I didn't realize that I had nodded off in the car until I jerked awake at four-twenty in the morning. I was freezing and I also had to pee. It turned out to be a mistake to leave the car. When I crossed the street to use the bathroom at the gas station, some guy was hitting a woman in the back. I had the attendant call the police as I went to intervene. The guy had her by the throat, and even though she was already bleeding from her lip and nose, he was going to punch her again. I was afraid if I went for his arm he'd still connect, so I stepped between them and took the hit.

He had a ring that opened up my right eyebrow, and I felt like he had shattered my right cheekbone as well. I felt her fingers clawing for my jacket as she tried to pull me back, out of the way. All I could do was fight dirty since, compared to me, the man was a giant. My knee came up into his groin and when he doubled over, I used the hardest part of my body, my elbow, and drove down across the back of his neck, like Sam had taught me. He went facedown onto the asphalt as the woman grabbed me and hugged me tight. I held her until I heard the sirens, walked her to the attendant, and bolted back across the street. There was blood on my peacoat so I turned it inside out and lay down on top of it in the backseat. My face was throbbing and I still had to pee. Under the circumstances, staggering around the back of the building twenty minutes later was very undignified but extremely necessary. I fell asleep with the engine running, lights out, with the heater on.

My phone woke me three hours later. When I sat up and looked at my face in the rearview mirror, I realized that it was encrusted in blood. I looked lovely.

"Hello?" I groaned, getting out of the backseat and into the front.

"Jory?"

"Hey, Dane," I sighed, sitting down, tired and sore and hungry.

"Jory, Sam's awake and he's asking for you."

My stomach flipped over. "Oh yeah? How's he look?"

"He looks good. Everyone's here except you. Why don't you come?"

"'Cause I'm doing really good. I found the place where the guys jacked the car from and I'm here now. I'm gonna show Caleb's picture around and see what turns up."

"Jory—"

"Last night I had to talk this pimp into letting the guys help me, and you should have seen me. I was scared but—"

"A pimp? What are you talking about?"

"This guy, Rego James, he owns a club down—"

"Rego what?"

"James. He—"

"James? Rego James?"

"Yeah, he—"

"Wait, Sam's trying to say something… hold on."

As I waited I turned off the car, got out, and looked around. There was a diner across the street on the other side and farther down a thrift store. I couldn't wear the peacoat with blood on it and I couldn't use my credit card. I had used the card I shared with Dane for the car rental, but I didn't want to chance that a second time. I had to eat and I had to wash my face. I needed a Band-Aid too, since my eyebrow felt like it was hanging open.

"Jory."

"Yeah? Who's this?" Not my brother.

"Jory, this is Detective Hefron…. Jory, Rego James is a very dangerous guy. Please have no further contact with him and simply come back immediately."

"But I got this far, Detective. I'm running down a lead."

"Jory, just come back and I'll run it down. You don't know what you're—"

"Gotta go, my eye's killing me."

"Why? What'd you do to your eye?"

"It's all busted open—shit, it hurts."

"Jor—"

And I hung up on him too. Didn't want them tracing the call, like in the movies.

I ducked my head down and covered my face with my hand. It was funny that sometimes the smallest injuries, like paper cuts, hurt the most. The cut above my eyebrow hurt like crazy but it really wasn't that big. The scrape on my face, all the big, red bruises, looked really bad but didn't hurt as much as the cut. The waitress at the diner was very nice and got me hydrogen peroxide, Neosporin, and three small butterfly strips and one big one. I had it holding together well, and after I had a short stack of pancakes, bacon and three eggs, orange juice, and lots of coffee, I gave her a ten-dollar tip. She was appreciative, and I felt better. In the thrift store, looking for a new coat, my phone rang.

"Jory."

"Hey, Dane."

"Jory buddy, you're killing Sam."

"What?"

"Sam's losing it, he needs to see you, make sure you're okay. This thing with this guy James… he's really agitated about that."

"Well, tell him not to be, I didn't get raped or anything."

There was a pause. "Raped?"

"Yeah, he threatened to… forget it, don't tell Sam, that won't help."

"Jory." He barely got my name out.

"After I get a new coat I'll start taking the picture up and down the—"

"What do you need a new coat for?"

"There's blood all over my peacoat from that guy hitting me, and I don't wanna look like some homeless person when I talk to these people, so I'll call ya back after, okay?"

"Who hit you?"

Sometimes I talked like everyone knew what was going on even when they were joining a program that was already in progress. "Some guy, it doesn't matter."

"Are you really hurt?"

"No."

"Jory, may I remind you that you have a concussion? No one should be hitting you or—"

"I know. I didn't mean to get hit." *Like I got hit on purpose.*

"Jory, I want you back here now."

"Okay," I said and hung up.

I found a parka that was a size too big for me but clean and in pretty good shape. It was thirty dollars, which the cashier said was really too much for it. Apparently most things in the store went for right around ten. I wore it out, shoving my peacoat in the plastic bag she gave me, and jogged back to my lovely rented Ford Taurus.

I started at the florist and worked my way from one end of the strip mall to the other. I finally got lucky at the bowling alley. The guy remembered seeing Caleb go into the copy shop at the corner. I thanked him profusely and made that my next stop. The copy shop had mailboxes that you could rent and the lady there remembered Caleb because he looked like her first husband. I asked her if that was good or not and she said no, definitely not. It did however etch him into her brain. She was older, late sixties, and whether it was my smile, the fact I was hurt, or the fact that she liked the color of my eyes, I didn't know. Nevertheless, she sat there with me and tried to remember everything she could about the other man with Caleb Reid. Finally, after much searching through many small boxes filled with index cards, she found the card of the guy that had come with Caleb. His name was Greg Fain and his address was in Oak Lawn, three streets away. I asked to keep the card and gave her a fifty-dollar bill for her trouble. She gave me a pen and a key chain flashlight before I walked out.

My phone rang as I was on my way to the house.

"Jory."

"I don't think we've ever talked this many times in one day, even when I worked for you," I told my brother. "What's with you?"

"The fact that you have to ask is beyond me—where are you now?"

"You'll never guess."

"No, probably not."

"I think I found the place where Caleb and I were kept and I'm on my way there now."

"Are you kidding?"

"No, why would I be kidding?"

"Jory, please don't go there by yourself. Please, I'm begging you."

"I have to, what else would I do?"

"Tell me where you are so I can call the police. What if you disturb something or worse... what if there's somebody there. What if whoever's been watching you, trying to kill you, is there waiting. What if it's a trap, Jory? What if—"

"It's not. Whoever was there is long gone. The lady at the mailbox place said she hasn't seen the guy in almost two weeks. I think he's dead, Dane. I think I was right and there were two guys and one guy's dead and maybe I'll find him out there and... oh, I think... I got it—I found it. Shit yeah, I should do this for a living. Jory Harcourt always gets his man."

"Jory!"

"Don't yell, my head hurts."

"You know, I forget sometimes that you're not even thirty yet. You're stupid because you're damn young."

"Please, the police never even got this far," I said, stopping the car, parking across the street, looking at the big gray house on the overgrown lot. "Shit... why does it have to look like that?"

"Like what?"

"All fuckin' creeped out," I groaned, looking at the rusted mailbox nailed shut, the fence with the *Keep Out* sign on it, the knee-high grass and weeds, and the boarded-up windows. "Shit."

"Jory, goddamn it! Tell me where you are and I'll come myself and—"

"Jory?"

"Regina?" I said, getting out of the car and locking it with a chirp of the car alarm. "What are you doing on—"

"Sweetheart, I took the phone from your brother. Can you listen for just one minute? Please."

"Sure."

There was rubbing against the phone, muffled sounds, and bumping, it sounded like she was driving through a tunnel even though I knew she wasn't even in a car. Throat clearing and coughing before the voice I knew.

"Baby," he said, and his voice was rough, full of gravel.

"Sam," I whispered, frozen on the sidewalk, the sting of tears instantly in my eyes. I was so happy to hear him.

"Baby," he coughed softly. "I need you... I need to see your face."

"I—"

"You should be here right beside me, why aren't you?"

"I gotta find the guy that hurt you, Sam. I can't let him ever hurt you—"

"It's how I feel about you. Now you get it. Makes you nuts, right?"

"Yeah."

He knew exactly how to talk to me and I had to smile listening to him being so calm, so matter-of-fact. We were talking like nothing special was going on, just like of course I would be doing precisely what I was.

"So you've been out there on your own what—six days? Seven? Since I got hurt?"

"Yeah."

"All by yourself for a week, huh?"

"Yeah."

"And you found the place, huh? Good job—real good. Now call Hefron and Lange and they'll take it from there. You have no experience in securing a crime scene or what to touch or what not to touch. If you wanna catch this guy, you gotta leave the next step to the professionals, all right? Makes sense, right?"

"I guess."

"I know you wanna see, baby. I know you're dyin' to go in there but don't, please don't. Tell me where you are and I'll call them. You wait there for them and they'll bring you to me."

"I'll call, Sam, but I'm not waiting here. I'm gonna see who else this guy knew. Other people have gotta remember him."

"I need to see you," he coughed softly. "Did Rego James put his hands on you?"

"Yeah, but I let him. I used him because I needed a couple of his boys to show me where the car was. He's kinda pissed at me right now, I think."

"What did you let him do to you?"

"I didn't kiss him."

"I didn't think you would."

"He just touched me, Sam, nothing else."

"Well then, that makes it all better."

"Sam—"

"I want you back here now. I want you next to me now. I cannot believe that my family, your brother, all our friends, and an entire police force can't keep tabs on one twenty-six-year-old graphic designer who thinks he's fuckin' Batman."

He was very funny. "I'll be there soon."

"Now. Do not step a foot inside that house or... oh, never mind—we gotcha."

"Shit," I swore and turned off my phone. Everyone else I could cut off but not Sam. I so wanted to go into the house, but I ended up calling Detective Hefron instead. I gave him the address and he told me that he was already halfway there on the strength of the phone trace. He ordered me not to move. I drove away as I heard the sirens.

AN HOUR later I was stopped before I could go into Sam's room by one of two uniformed police officers. I heard Dane call my name, and I peeked around the policemen to see him.

"Officer, this is my brother, Detective Kage's... partner."

They moved apart and I saw the whole room. Dane motioned for me, and as I stepped inside I saw that it was larger than normal and he wasn't sharing it with anyone else. Sam's parents were there and Chloe, his partner, and Detective Lange.

"Jesus, Jory," Dane said, reaching for my face.

I tipped my head away from him and maneuvered around Regina and Thomas as well to get to the side of the bed. I stood there, frozen, staring down at Sam.

His eyelashes fluttered a second before his eyes opened to reveal the smoky blue I knew so well. My heart felt like it was going to burst.

"Hey." I smiled down at him.

"Oh fuck me," he groaned, reaching for me. "Come here."

I leaned down but stopped before I hugged him. "I don't wanna hurt—"

"Jory." His voice, his eyes, both full of pain. "Baby, please come here."

I let out a deep breath and sank down against him. I gave him all my weight and he held me easily, stroking my hair and pressing my head to his shoulder. He felt so good, so warm, so strong, his body so hard... I felt the shiver run through me.

"Jesus, you scared the hell outta me."

"Me?" I trembled. "You, lying in the street bleeding... God I never wanna live through anything like that ever again."

"Baby, what'd you do to yourself?" He eased me back to look at my face. "Who hit you?" He almost whined and I could tell how frustrated he was—at me, at himself for being stuck in bed, at everyone and everything.

"Some guy was beating on a woman and I just—"

"Jory, goddamnit!" His voice went out on him because he didn't have the strength to yell. "Fuck! You never get in the middle of... you call the police! You call the fuckin' police, baby, that's what they... he could've had a gun or a knife or—"

"But the woman, Sam. She could've been hurt worse than she was."

"Baby, you could've been killed! And Rego James.... Shit! I swear to God, when I get outta this bed I'm gonna chain you up! Nobody puts me through it like you—nobody!"

I smiled down at him. "Maybe 'cause you love me most."

He took my face in his hands and I closed my eyes, letting him touch my cheek, run his fingers over my eyebrow, down my throat, and across my collarbone.

"Dane, call a doctor in here to check him out. I wanna make sure he's okay."

"I'm okay," I assured him, wanting to put my head down so badly. I was so tired.

"Mom, come take this coat off of him, please."

I let Regina gently ease me out of my new old jacket and peel off the shirt underneath.

"I smell bad," I mumbled. "I should go home and—"

"Just lie down a minute, Jory," I heard Thomas order as he steadied me, at the same time lowering the bar on the side of Sam's bed. "Have you got him?"

"Yeah," Sam answered, and I felt his hand in my hair as his other smoothed down my back, pressing me down against him before he enfolded me in his arms. "Lay down, baby, close your eyes."

"But Sam, I—"

"Baby," he soothed me, "you're killing me. Please lemme hold you just for a minute."

My eyes drifted closed and I realized that the warmth radiating off Sam was amazing. The way he stroked my shoulder, rubbed his chin in my hair, pressed my hand down on his chest, all of it was so soothing, so comforting, my body got heavy fast. I never wanted to move.

"Baby," he sighed heavily and I felt his lips on my forehead. "Stay here. Just rest."

I couldn't argue, didn't want to argue, I just wanted to lie in his arms, have him hold me for the rest of my life. I didn't remember falling asleep.

IT WAS the tone that woke me.

"Just fuckin' pray that you have this guy found by the time I can get out of this bed," he said, and his voice was full of a sort of quiet rage. It was scarier than if he'd been yelling. "You leave my… partner out all alone on the fuckin' street for a week 'cause you can't fuckin' find him, and now you tell me that he and he alone found the place where he was held, and the guy that all along he said he heard killed was in fact killed and the goddamn body is still there." He was seething, he was so mad. "This is what you're fuckin' telling me. Jory found the crime scene all by himself."

"Sam, we had no idea that—"

"But you should have! You fuckin' should have! He told you there were two guys… he told you where the car was found… and you guys did shit with that information! He had to bargain with a guy who runs drugs and prostitutes just to get what he needed, while you and Lange were sitting on your asses!"

"Sam—"

"Are you kidding? Do you know who fuckin' Rego James is?"

"Yes, Sam, I'm very well aware who—"

"I suppose you would've liked your wife in his place or your kids or—"

"Sam, I fuckin' get it, all right? Jesus, I get it!"

"Goddamn it, Jimmy, how many of his boys have we fuckin' fished out of Lake Michigan 'cause he strung 'em out and then when they weren't pretty anymore gave them over to some fuck makin' a snuff film or some bondage shit that went way wrong? How many tweakers is he responsible for? How many guys sell their bodies for him? And he had Jory alone in his place without anybody fuckin' knowing shit about it? He could've been raped or…." Sam trailed off, taking a breath. "And he's all beat up. Doc says the eye should've had three stitches for that cut, but as it is—nothing to do now but leave it. Where the fuck were you?"

"Sam—"

"Fuck you! Fuck Lange and fuck those idiots that were supposed to be watching out for Jory instead of jerking off in the car in front of the apartment when he went out the window! How fuckin' hard is it to watch one guy? He's not fuckin' Houdini."

There was a long silence.

"He kind of is," Detective Hefron said quietly.

"I agree," I heard Chloe Stazzi, Sam's partner, say gently. "He's good, Sam. He knows people and how to play them. I mean, I personally have no idea how he got out of Rego's club in one piece. Everything we know about Rego... guy who looks like Jory goes in, he's turning tricks by the next day or worse, never seen again."

"That's what I'm—"

"But what I'm sayin' to you is you need to give the kid more credit. He actually takes pretty good care of himself. He's shitty at knowing his limits, but so are you."

I felt him take a deep breath and clutch me tight. "I'm here at least another week. You guys gotta watch over him, especially now that we know Greg Fain had a partner that killed him."

"God bless dental records, because that was all that was left."

"That guy was soup," Chloe groaned. "It was disgusting."

"Who fills an outdoor freezer with hot water and then puts a body in there?" Hefron asked.

"A guy that hopes the body will never be found." Sam answered, rubbing his cheek against my forehead.

"Why didn't he just bury the body?" Chloe asked.

"Who knows, could be anything." Hefron sighed loudly. "This just keeps getting bigger and weirder instead of starting to make sense."

"What'd you find on Greg Fain's body? Anything?"

"Jory's phone was in the pocket of his jeans, but maybe when he and his partner took it off him he just kept it. I doubt it was actually placed there, like the other items we've found."

"Did you find any other prints anywhere at the house?"

"Nope. There are no prints anywhere but in the shed. There's no evidence at all that either Jory or Caleb were ever in the main house."

"Shit. No blood, nothing?"

"Caleb and Jory's blood in the shed but nowhere else."

"And Greg Fain?"

"His blood's in the shed too, but again, nowhere else."

"How is that even possible?"

"This guy's careful, Sam, really careful."

"And the ME figures Fain died how?"

"He took a bullet to the head—thirty-eight, as far as we can tell. Must've been a helluva mess."

"Which somebody must've cleaned up really good since there's no sign of it anywhere."

"Right."

I shifted to move and Sam massaged the back of my neck.

"Beat it. I wanna talk to Jory."

But I didn't get up; I found myself too exhausted to move. I just took a deep breath and fell back to sleep.

It worked out well, because when I woke up an hour later, Sam was asleep and everyone was gone. Major surgery being completely draining, when I moved off the bed he didn't wake up. I told the officers outside the door that I had to get something to eat from the cafeteria. Since neither of them could move, I was free to take the stairs without any interference.

I got back in my rental car and drove off the lot, and even though I thought maybe someone would be watching me, nobody was. When I made it home, I parked around the block from my apartment. I got back in the same way I had left and was showered and changed and repacked an hour later. Back in the car, I drove back toward Oak Lawn as I called Caleb.

"Hello?"

"Caleb, it's me."

"Jory, you're driving me nuts."

"I know, I'm driving me nuts too. But listen, I need you to be on the phone with me when I go in the house. Will you do that?"

"What are you talking about?"

"I found the place where we were held today."

"Jesus, Jory, who are you?"

"Knock it off."

"You are seriously scary. You found the place?"

"I found it and I told the police and they got the body of one of the guys that held us."

"Are you kidding me?"

"No."

"Jesus, I had no idea you fought crime on the side."

"Shut up. I just ran down a lead."

"Ran down a lead?"

"What?"

"You are seriously fucked up. Your ass should be home hiding in the dark."

"Whatever. Listen—"

"Who was he? The guy that held us, I mean?"

"Some guy named Greg Fain."

"Name's not familiar."

"I didn't think it would be, but that's not what I wanted to ask you about."

"What do you wanna ask?"

"I think you and me would know better'n anybody what to look for in the house."

"Yeah, that make sense."

"So I'm on my way to look around in there, and when I get there I'm gonna call you and as I'm walking around you can tell me if you remember anything."

"Maybe I should just come."

"Are you up to doing that?"

"Yeah, I'm up to it, but Jory, maybe we should wait, huh, and go with somebody?"

"Why? The police have already been all over the place—it would just be you and me with our eyes, we might find something they missed, ya know?"

"Fine. I'll play along. I want this shit over with too."

"Good. I'll have a ticket waiting for you on—"

"I can get my own ticket, hotshot, thank you."

"I didn't mean anything by—"

"I know, J—forget it. I'll call you as soon as I hit town tomorrow."

"Perfect. Don't call Dane, all right?"

"No, I won't."

"I'm still gonna go now so—"

"No, just wait for me."

"I can't—I mean, what if there's something there? I gotta save Sam."

"So now it's about Sam instead of Dane."

"I don't think the guy's ever gonna hurt Dane—I think it's about making Dane suffer, not killing him. He wants to kill me and you and Aja and now Sam... how long are we gonna let this go on, C?"

"C?"

"That's you, asshole."

He chuckled. "You're the only one who likes me this much."

"Shut up, everybody's crazy about you, but listen... I'll call you in like an hour when I get inside the house, all right?"

"You are completely deranged, you know that."

"I know that."

"I really think you should wait for me to get there before you go back."

"I can't."

"Fine. Call me in an hour."

After I hung up with him I continued driving toward Oak Lawn. Dane's number flashed across my display a few minutes later and then the number for the hospital. I answered that call.

"Hello?"

"Jory, where are you?" my brother snapped at me.

"Pretty smart, using the hospital phone. I thought you were Sam."

"I was hoping you would."

"Is Sam up?"

"No, he's not up. Just all that drama this morning exhausted him. Where are you?"

"I'm running down another lead."

"Jory!" he barked at me. "Get your ass back here now."

"If you were in my place and Aja was the one in the hospital, you would be doing whatever you could to keep her safe, so don't gimme shit about this."

"Jory, it's not the same. You're—"

"Doing spectacularly well? I know—thank you."

"Jory, come—"

"I am not a dog and I won't be back tonight. Just take care of Sam for me. Call me if he wakes back up."

"Jory!"

But I hung up so he wouldn't have an aneurysm and drove on back toward the house. I had to get in there to see.

YOU always wonder why people go looking around creepy places at night. In every horror movie I had ever seen it had been my question as well. The fact of the matter was, though, that sometimes you had to go to scary places at night because other people would see you during the day. The cover of darkness was the best time to get the breaking and entering done. So when I parked down the block and ran to the house in the dark, armed with a flashlight and my cell phone, I figured that even though I had an irrational fear of Michael Myers being in the house waiting for me, logically I was safe—it was just dark. This was the rational thought I held on to even as my heart threatened to pound out of my chest.

I slipped into the basement through the window and fell five feet or so to the floor. I was sure that something terrifying was waiting in the shadows to get me, even though rats were probably the only spooky things in the place. I was expecting jars of body parts but found only a washer and dryer, a sink and a counter that folded clothes were stacked up on. Even though I knew that it wasn't the room Caleb and I had been held in, I checked it over anyway, looking for anything that didn't fit. I went to the lint trap on the dryer and found it clean; I went through the small wastebasket and was really disappointed when there was just nothing at all. When I was satisfied that I had seen anything that it was possible to see, I went through the door, using the sleeve of my sweater to turn the knob, and into the kitchen of the house.

It was boring. What had started out as a nightmare quickly became tedious. The house was clean. Like a maid service had been through it clean. Going from room to room yielded nothing at all. The inside didn't match the outside either. It became clear that all Greg Fain had needed was a landscaper. Inside, the house looked nothing like the Bateses' home and more like something that belonged in an Ikea catalogue. Everything was new and shiny; all the bells and whistles were there from brushed steel and wood décor to a plasma TV. The second floor was just as nice, and next to the bathroom was a steam room. As I stood in the master bedroom on the second floor, I had to wonder what in the world had prompted a guy like Greg Fain to get caught up in a kidnapping. But maybe all this stuff had cost a lot of money. Everyone needed money, so perhaps Dane forking over ten million dollars has been his primary motivation.

The only thing weird I found in the bedroom was a frame in the wastebasket beside the armoire. The glass was broken but there was no picture in it. I had no idea what that meant but made a mental note of it anyway. Back downstairs in the den, I looked for any papers that would give me an idea of who Greg Fain was. But again there was nothing. What really was weird was the extent of the nothing. All the desk drawers were empty and along the sides as well. On *CSI* they always found a clue either under a drawer or on the side, taped to the bottom of something, but no such luck in Mr. Fain's office. Nothing inside the air conditioner or telltale drops of blood. It was simply anticlimactic, and I was disappointed. There were no clues to be found.

Still, when I was back outside I felt better. It was a clear night, and not being inside calmed me. I had just watched way too many horror movies in my life to be comfortable in a dark house. I let the shiver pass through me and took a steadying breath when I was alone standing in the backyard. Only then did I see the shed. How I had missed it when I walked around the house the first time was beyond me, but nonetheless, it was there, white in the moonlight. I saw the dead patch of grass where I guessed the outside freezer had been, where they found Greg Fain's body, and I saw all the little flags in the ground where the police had marked it. When I realized that I had to roll the door open on the shed, I knew, of course, this was the place.

Inside was as I remembered—the concrete floor, the metal walls, and the absence of windows. It wasn't necessarily a scary place, just odd to be there without being tied up. I checked over every inch of the room and came up with nothing, not even a gum wrapper or some dirt. It was pristine.

I walked around the shed using the flashlight, looked at the grass surrounding it, and found not a thing even remotely useful or interesting. I walked down the alley on the other side of the fence trying to figure out which way, if any, the kidnapper had driven the car. But it was useless. On the way back my phone rang.

"Hello?"

"J."

"Hey, you're up." I smiled into my phone. "How ya feelin'?"

"Baby, where are you?"

"At the house." I sighed.

"Okay."

"There's nothing here."

"I could've told you that. They pulled everything outta there, J."

I looked at the house as I went over the fence into the backyard and it was only then that I noticed the window. "Oh shit, Sam, there's an attic."

"What?"

"I didn't see a ladder or anything. Nothing was open on the second floor. Did they find an attic?"

"I dunno."

"They must've, right?"

"Probably. Don't go back in the house. Drive here to me."

"I'm gonna go check, Sam."

"Love... don't. I'm gonna call Hefron right now while you drive over here."

The idea of going back in the house made me nauseous. The fear was irrational but nevertheless coursing through my body. Outside I could see if something came at me. I could maneuver or run. In the confines of the house I could not.

"Shit," I said. "Why am I so fuckin' scared of nothing?"

"Jory," he pleaded. "Baby, it's not nothing. You've been fearless so far but really, this is stupid. Lemme check with Hefron and see if they found an attic. Go to the car and I'll call ya right back."

"Okay," I said to placate him before I hung up and willed myself forward, to the back door. I could feel my chest tightening; I was having trouble moving air through my lungs. I was so close to hyperventilating.

In the kitchen, leaning on the refrigerator and hearing it cycle, I calmed down. Normal noises, things that made sense. I still wanted a gun. I had never wanted one before. And even though I was calmer than I'd been all night, my phone ringing scared the hell out of me.

"Shit," I said as I answered it.

"Babe, they didn't find an attic. I told them you had and everyone's on their way back. You're gonna be knee-deep in police officers in like ten minutes, so just drive back to me, okay?"

But I knew his voice too well. He was lying. "Sure," I played him along before I hung up again. It rang seconds later.

"Where are you?"

"Caleb," I sighed, letting out a deep breath.

"Yeah. Who else?"

"Sam's givin' me shit."

"As well he should—you're terminally stupid."

"Do you remember ever being in an attic?"

"An attic? I don't think so."

"When you got taken to talk to Dane on the phone—where'd ya go?"

"I don't really know because I was blindfolded, but if I had to guess I'd say it was a kitchen. It just smelled like a kitchen, ya know?"

Which made sense. The walk from the shed to the kitchen was close and there was a phone in the kitchen. Not that they had used that phone. They had used one of those cell phones you buy and put money on. And they had used cash. The police had run down that lead and found only a dead end. No one remembered seeing anybody; there was no paperwork and no surveillance cameras in the store.

"So you remember being outside and then inside when he moved you."

"Yeah."

"God, I wish you were here to see the shed and the kitchen."

"I'll be there tomorrow morning. You can pick me up."

"I will. What airline?"

"I dunno, I'll look in a minute. Can I just say I've been on more airplanes this past year than I think I have in my whole entire life?"

And as he rambled on I calmed. Even though I was in a dark, creepy house, I was at ease because we were talking about normal things. But when I came around the corner I saw something move. There was no way to stifle the scream.

"Jesus, what?" Caleb yelled.

The living room had double French doors, both glass. I had seen my own reflection. "Crap," I said. "Sorry."

"Are you kidding?" he chided me.

"Shit."

"Maybe you should leave and—"

"No, I'm just freaked out."

"Oh, no shit."

"Should I just call you back when—"

"No. Do not dare hang up. Just—go to the attic."

"Okay," I agreed, hoping that there would be no more girly screaming on my way up the stairs.

I walked all over the second floor—which was technically the third if you counted the basement—looking at the ceiling, looking for the ladder that led to the attic. I finally found it by checking the seams in the ceiling tiles. One was not sealed like the others. I jumped up and hit it until I got it right and it slipped down enough for me to get my fingertips on the edge. As soon as it moved a little, the long cord dropped and I was able to pull on that to get the stairs to fall out of the ceiling. I had been giving Caleb a play-by-play account, and was now ready to go up there.

"An attic... how *Thirty Days of Night* is that?"

"Oh fuck you," I snapped at him.

"What? You know there's not actually vampires up there."

"Shit."

"Ohmygod, boy, calm the fuck down," he chuckled. "Your imagination is spinning completely out of control. At worst you have a crazed maniac with a gun or a knife up there, just waiting for you because he never left the house in the first place."

"You should give seminars on fear management."

He laughed at me as I started up the stairs.

"God, I hate this."

"Which begs the question—why are you doing it then?"

I tried to see everything at once but my flashlight was too small.

"What do you see?"

"I can't see shit."

"Jory, fuck it. Even if the police catch you, who cares? Turn on a light."

I had to agree. I just didn't have the nerve to hunt around in the dark, so I found the switch on the wall and instantly light illuminated the attic. Immediately I pulled up the ladder, making sure the cord was on my side, and tried to breathe. When I turned and saw the man, I screamed and raised my hands. It took me a few seconds to realize I was looking at a CPR dummy.

"Fuck!" I yelled, kicking the wall closest to me as hard as I could. I sat down after a minute and tried to breathe. When I could, I realized that I had dropped my phone. I found it halfway across the room beside a metal chair. I picked it up and spoke into it, telling him I was all right.

"Are you kidding me? Jesus Christ, Jory, you just took ten years off my life!"

It was funny, but I kept my eyes on the dummy to make sure it didn't all of a sudden turn its head and look at me. I was maybe a little paranoid, just a trifle unhinged.

"No more screaming!"

"Sorry."

"God! Just get out of there. I can't take any more of this."

He couldn't take any more?

"Just leave and go camp out at the airport and wait for me."

"Lemme look around first."

"If you can without scaring the shit outta yourself."

I ignored the snide remarks, instead concentrating on the room. It was perhaps the cleanest place I'd ever seen in my life. Besides the creepy CPR dummy hanging on what looked like an IV stand, and the chair, there was nothing. I walked around, making sure I didn't miss anything, but there were no hollow walls or hidden rooms. It was just an empty attic. The only thing scary about the place was me, all psyched up and frantic. I sent Caleb a picture and he was disappointed. His grunt told me everything.

"What?"

"Kinda boring, right?"

And it was.

After a few minutes I climbed back down and left the attic stairs down when I bolted from the house. I definitely needed a partner in crime. I was looking forward to having Caleb there the next day. Following up on leads in dark houses was way freakier than it looked.

I checked the car before I got in it and then locked all the doors and drove away fast before anything happened. I saw the line of police cars that passed me, and there was relief knowing that they actually made it.

"What are you gonna do now?" Caleb asked me, yawning loudly.

"I dunno. I'm afraid if I go home that the detectives working the case might not let me pick you up alone tomorrow morning. I don't wanna go to Dane's or—"

"Why don't you get a room somewhere, and tomorrow we'll get another room together."

"That sounds good."

"Okay. I'll see you in the morning. I'll call you when I get in."

"I thought I was gonna pick you up at the air—"

"You will, but just wait for my call. That way you'll know I'm there and you don't hafta check. Try and sleep as long as you can… you sound really weird."

"I'm just tired."

"See, so… sleep."

"Okay, call me in the morning."

"I will—night."

"Sorry to keep you up all this time."

"It's fine. Later."

I felt better because talking to him was somehow normal. We had been though a lot together lately, and in some ways he was closer to me than anyone. We were like war buddies, and the thought of seeing him was comforting. As I drove toward the airport in search of a hotel, my panic subsided and I started to calm. By the time Dane called I had checked into a room and was lying down, fully dressed, on the bed. I had locked all the doors and felt pretty safe ten floors up.

"Hey."

"Where are you?"

"Why are you up?" I yawned, my eyes drifting closed. "It's so late."

"I want to know where you are."

"I'm fine."

"Not what I asked. Where," he enunciated the word, "are you?"

"I'm safe. Where are you?"

"I'm at the hospital with Sam, watching over him as you asked."

"You should go home and get some sleep. I didn't mean that you should—"

"He's sleeping. You exhausted him with your antics at the house. He tried valiantly to stay awake, but his body's healing and he just can't expend that much energy and not be knocked out. You should think about what you're putting him through."

The guilt wasn't going to work. "Okay."

"Okay? This is all you have to say?"

"Dane."

"What?"

"I have to sleep, I can barely form words."

"Just tell me where you are."

"I'll call ya tomorrow, okay? Caleb's coming to—"

"What? Caleb's in town?"

"Tomorrow. He's coming tomorrow but don't tell him I told you. He didn't want me to tell you." I sighed.

"Why the hell not?"

"He doesn't wanna get in trouble."

"Get in trouble with who?"

"You. He thinks you'll be mad at him for going along with me."

"Which I am. He's supposed to be the grown-up."

I laughed at him.

"When I get a hold of you—"

"I love you," I blurted out. "I gotta sleep now, okay?"

"Jory, did you know my name's on all your credit cards?"

I had no idea what that had to do with anything but I was too tired to care. I might have grunted before I hung up and rolled over. I didn't even turn off the light.

Chapter Nine

MY PHONE woke me at noon and Caleb was on the other end. He wanted to know where I was. After I told him, he said he'd come to me. I appreciated that, since I was barely awake. I got up an hour later and went to take a shower. My body hurt all over and I had a raging headache. I needed food and a bucket of Tylenol and gallons of water. When I answered the door thirty minutes later, Caleb seemed startled to see me.

"What?" I asked him, standing there, waiting.

He walked into me, hugging me tight for just a moment before brushing past me into the hotel room.

"You look like shit."

"Yeah, well... I feel like shit."

"C'mon, let's check outta here before somebody figures out where you are and go eat."

I was all in favor of his plan.

We had a huge breakfast of pancakes, sausage, eggs, and hash browns before driving to a motel and paying for the room in cash. As I drove us back toward the house in Oak Lawn, I told him that I thought we should try and find out if Greg Fain had any relatives living in the city.

"Why?"

"Maybe they'd know who he hung out with."

"And how're we gonna find that out?"

"I think we should start with his neighbors," I said, driving past now-familiar sights on my way toward Oak Lawn. "They might know who his parents were or just who came around the house."

"That makes sense." He yawned, stretching his arms.

"You know, I really appreciate you coming all this way just to help me."

"'Course. I wanna figure this out too. I hate looking over my shoulder all the time."

"Me too."

After a few miles in silence he asked me how Sam was.

"Better. He must still be sleeping or I'm sure I'd be getting threatening phone calls by now."

"He just worries about you."

"Which is nice, but I'm not a kid, right? I actually am a grown-up."

"You're what now?"

"I don't under—you mean like, how old am I?"

"Yeah."

"I'm twenty-six."

He made a noise. "And how old is Sam?"

"He's thirty-eight—three years younger than Dane."

"You worry about that age gap between you and Sam?"

"No. I figure I'm actually older than he is—I'm more mature."

"Yeah, running around in dark houses in the middle of the night is real mature."

"Bite me."

He laughed at me and I concentrated on the road.

I could only imagine what we looked like—me in my hoodie and parka, Caleb in his trench coat and scarf, both of us wearing sunglasses to block out the afternoon light. Still, we must have come off as nonthreatening because as we went door-to-door, people still talked to us. Caleb said it was because I was so cute and I countered with the fact that he looked like the boy-next-door with his *aww shucks ma'am* smile and his Texas accent coming through. I had never really looked at Caleb closely before, but the light brown hair and dark blue eyes were very appealing and the cleft in his chin and the laugh lines made his face interesting. Whatever the reason, people talked to us, and we found out that Greg's mother's name was Joyce and she had moved, Mrs. Ogden thought, to Schaumburg. Mrs. Ogden had lived on the corner for over thirty years and was almost positive that's what she had been told. The snickerdoodles she gave us were very good, straight from the oven. She went on to say that there had never been a Mr. Fain, only Joyce and her son. Once Greg had been old enough to live alone, Joyce had left the house and Greg had lived alone ever since.

We drove to an Internet café and pulled up every Joyce Fain, J. Fain, and plain old Fain in Chicago and Schaumburg. There were more than I would have liked, but as I drove, Caleb made calls, and I realized again how great it was to have a partner in crime. Just one more person working on the same thing as me was a great big help.

"Oh-oh-oh," Caleb said excitedly, and held out his phone after turning it from handset to loudspeaker for me. "Listen-listen."

The answering machine was clear as I listened. The woman's voice quavered just a little as she announced that the caller had reached Joyce with Our Sisters of Saint Andrew's prayer line. We were to leave a prayer request or message and Sister Joyce would return our call.

"That's gotta be her," Cable assured me. "Right?"

I didn't remember seeing any crosses or religious items in the house, but it was dark so maybe I had missed them. Or maybe when his mom moved out, Greg had sent all her paraphernalia with her. Maybe Mom was devout but not the son. "We might as well check it out, but keep calling the others too."

He agreed and stayed on his cell as I drove.

"Why do you think Greg didn't just move in with his mom? Why take over the house and make her move out? Don't people usually take care of their parents, since they took care of them?"

"I think that's how it usually works, yeah."

"So then?"

"Jory, I know the Fains as well as you do," he chuckled. "The inner workings of the family life of one of the men who kidnapped us is a mystery to me."

"Sure—I was just thinking out loud."

"Why don't you ask his mother when you meet her?"

"I don't wanna pry."

For whatever reason he found that very funny.

It was a long drive up to Schaumburg, but Caleb kept busy on his phone while I answered mine. Dane wanted to know what was on my kamikaze mission for the day.

"I had this idea," I began.

"You know, of course, that I will find you. And when I do, you will never-ever get out of my condo without my permission. I hired Aja a bodyguard until this is over and I'm going to do the same for you."

"Yeah, okay," I sighed, realizing that my headache just did not want to let me go. It hurt up the back of my neck and over the top of my head. I felt the tension deep in my shoulders.

"Is Caleb with you?"

"Caleb? No."

"Put him on the phone."

I shoved my phone at him and after a minute he took a breath and squinted as he said hello. He groaned deeply ten minutes later when he hung up.

"Jesus, that man is mad."

"Yeah well—"

"He's mad at you, at me—he's just pissed off all the way around. You know he traced you to that hotel last night already."

"That's because I was tired and I used the AMEX instead of my Visa. He pays the bill on the AMEX."

"That was brilliant."

"Hi, tired, fuck you."

He laughed at me and told me where to get off the expressway.

THE house was at the end of a narrow street with enormous potholes and trees that lined both sides. The sidewalks were cracked with overgrown roots, and the houses were all run-down. Standing in front of the chain link fence with Caleb, I shivered hard.

"What?"

"I dunno, feels weird."

"Why?"

I shrugged.

"C'mon." He smacked my shoulder before lifting the latch to step into the yard.

I followed him up the path with weeds growing through the cement to the front door. He rang the doorbell and knocked on the door. The porch was tiny, the wrought-iron railing framing what was basically a stoop.

"I'll go around the back," he said, taking the four steps back down.

"I'll go with you."

The yard was a mess, full of weeds, with grass that hit my knees. There was a fenced-off garden now dormant in winter and a barren oak tree. It didn't look like Greg had made it to Schaumburg to help his mother with the upkeep of her place. I thought about Sam and his brothers cleaning out their mom's rain gutters, mowing the lawn, painting, raking leaves—it was so different. I wondered what Joyce Fain had done not to receive the same treatment that Regina Kage did.

"God, could it be more grim back here?" Caleb shook his head.

I followed him up the four stairs to the back door, and when he turned the knob the door opened.

"Oh shit," I groaned, stopping Caleb from going inside.

"What?"

"We can't just go in there. She could be taking a shower or something. She'd totally freak if we just showed up in her living room."

"No one's home, J," he assured me. "I just called, remember?"

"Again, this goes with my shower hypothesis."

"Fine," he sighed. "I'll call again and if she doesn't answer we'll go in, all right?"

I nodded.

He scrolled to recently dialed numbers and hit send. I stood beside him as he put the phone on loudspeaker and it rang. We heard the message click on again before he hung up his phone.

"Now?"

The second I agreed, he opened one screen door and then another that led into what looked like an enclosed back porch. It was all glass on four sides, but I had not noticed from the outside because the blinds were drawn. The reason became instantly understandable as we found a woman lying facedown in the middle of the floor. She was lying in a pool of blood. I felt my stomach heave.

"Oh shit," Caleb moaned, taking a step back.

I squatted down and leaned back against the door. "Jesus."

"Look at this."

I lifted my head and he was holding a bloody kitchen knife. "I think this is the murder weapon."

"Tell me you didn't just pick that up," I moaned.

"Oh." His eyes got huge as he stared at me. "Shit."

Unlike me, who owned all the ..ons of *CSI*—the original, not the New York or Miami ones—on DVD, the man had ..... er even seen one episode. Forensics 101: never touch stuff without plastic gloves on.

When he dropped the chef knife, it bounced and landed close to the dead woman. I made it outside in time so I wasn't sick on the carpet.

I SAT at the table across from Hefron and Lange, my head in my hands as I explained for the fifth time what had happened at Joyce Fain's house. I had been fingerprinted, they had taken my hiking boots and clothes, and I was now in an orange jumpsuit that was definitely not made out of cotton and did nothing for my complexion. Even though I knew they didn't think I'd killed anyone, I was still nervous and sick to my stomach. I had thrown up my entire breakfast and had resorted to dry heaving soon after. Even though I had seen two men shot to death those years ago, it was different somehow, seeing a dead woman. The fact that she was somebody's mother was hard for me, so I was trying to think about everything else but her... the jumpsuit, for example. I told myself it shouldn't have mattered—woman or man, my feelings should have been the same—but it did and I couldn't help it. I was cold and shaking and the light was hurting my eyes.

"Tell me one more time, Jory," Neal Lange prodded me.

"When can I see Caleb?"

"We'll bring him in here before we take you guys back to the hotel to pick up your things."

"What?"

"We're taking you both to Mr. Harcourt's residence. He's agreed to house you both for the remainder of the investigation."

"I wanna go home," I told him.

"If you prefer."

"I do."

"And Mr. Reid?"

I shrugged. "I dunno."

"Jory."

I looked up into his face.

"There can't be any more running around town tracking down leads. It's too dangerous, and we will be forced to charge you with evidence tampering and interference in an ongoing criminal investigation should you persist."

"I didn't mean to—"

"We'll charge you with obstruction. Do you get it?"

I nodded. "I won't do it anymore... I don't know how Sam does this every day. I don't know how you guys look at dead people and don't just pass out right there."

He nodded. "It's the job, Jory."

"Yeah... you can have it," I sighed deeply.

I felt like a cold wind was blowing right through me.

"You're shaking."

"That's because I'm freezing."

There was a trace of a smile before he nodded. "Tell me again, Jory, from the time you got out of the car."

So I did.

They told me that Joyce Fain had been dead for at last six hours before we found her. From how she was lying and the lack of any defensive wounds, she had been attacked from behind and her throat cut. There were all kinds of things they knew from the blood spatter and the pool by her head. It would not have been hard to overpower the sixty-eight-year-old woman, as she was not in good health. Nothing was taken from the house, her purse had a hundred and fifty dollars in it, and all her jewelry remained. There was no reason for her to be dead but for the fact that whoever had done it had gone there specifically to do so.

"Jory, you don't look good."

"It's 'cause I'm wearing orange."

He chuckled. "You need food and fluids and lots of sleep."

I nodded, folding my arms and putting my head down on top of them. "Can I go see Sam?"

"Sure."

I closed my eyes. "Thanks."

"What were you hoping to gain by going to see Mrs. Fain?"

"We were... I mean, I—I was thinking that if I got to talk to her then maybe she would be able to tell us who Greg hung out with."

Lange nodded. "That's good thinking."

"Thanks," I said, letting out a deep breath, shivering hard. "I wanna go see Sam."

"Okay, buddy... okay. Jory, look at me. Jory...."

And I tried really hard to focus on him right before I saw spots and the room went dark.

IT WAS bright and so I squinted when I opened my eyes. My groan was loud.

"Nice," Dane growled at me.

I looked around. "I'm back in the hospital?"

"Yes."

"How come?"

"Because you're dehydrated, you have a slight concussion, and your blood sugar is critically low."

"I don't have a concussion. I didn't hit my—"

"It's the same one you had, idiot. You never gave yourself a second to heal, and then you got hit by whoever that guy was when you got between him and that woman, and you—"

"I still have a concussion?"

"It's hysterical that you're surprised."

"Dane, I—"

"They gave you some glucose to help with your blood sugar and more fluid than I thought was possible—two IV's full of fluid—and... you know you always drink like a gallon of water a day, so your body is used to taking in that much. When you stop... that was really stupid."

"Yeah, I know. I just haven't had time."

"What possessed you to go to that woman's house?"

"It made sense, right? I mean, if I had gotten to talk to her I would have asked her who her son hung out with. Maybe we could have put a face to Greg Fain's buddy."

He shook his head. "Well, apparently you and Caleb did a great job destroying evidence and just completely ruining the crime scene."

"Yeah, but no one would have even known about the crime scene without me and Caleb."

"Don't kid yourself, Jory, someone else would have found that woman's body and when they did, they would have tied her murder to that of her son's. As it stands now, Caleb's prints are on the murder weapon, yours are all over the door, and both of your footprints are on the carpet. If they find anything after they pull you two out of the mix, it will be a miracle."

I took a breath and stared at him.

"What were you looking for?"

"We were hoping to talk to her about—"

"No, I mean when you went through her stuff?"

"What're you talking about?"

"Why did you go through her things? What was the point of that?"

"We didn't."

"Well, apparently you did. They found your prints everywhere."

I scoffed at him. "Everywhere, my ass. I touched the door—that's all I touched."

"Maybe that's what you think you touched, but—"

"That's all I touched, Dane."

"Well, Lange told me that they found your prints all over everything. Her books, boxes in the basement, the chest at the end of her bed… they said you tossed the place."

"That's bullshit," I told him. "We went in the back door and that was as far as we got. I don't know where he's getting all that, but if he finds my prints or Caleb's on anything else, he's lying."

"Why would he do that?"

"I don't think he is, I'm just saying… I think he got it wrong. If someone was looking for something, it had to be the guy we're after, not me or Caleb."

He nodded. "Okay. I'll ask him again."

"Fine."

He brushed my hair back from my face. "After you rest a little, we can go see Sam."

"Sounds good," I said, closing my eyes.

"After that, you're coming home with me."

"I don't wanna go with—"

"Do I care what you want anymore?"

"Aww… c'mon, Dane, I—"

"Detective Hefron wants you to go back there with him tomorrow and show him exactly where you were in the house. He's also wants you to look at everything in contrast to Mrs. Fain's cleaning lady. He wants to see if she notices anything different from what you did."

"Fine. Whatever. I wanna see Caleb and make sure he's all right."

"He's all right, Jory. Just rest."

"But—"

"Rest," he insisted, and he had his scowl going so I didn't want to mess with him.

I closed my eyes and told myself I would pretend to rest so he would stop bugging me. But it backfired, and I fell asleep.

THE shaking was insistent and I was irritated as I opened my eyes. This was a hospital; they were supposed to let you sleep. I was surprised to find Aja, looking just as annoyed.

"What's the matter with you?" I asked her quickly.

"Oh, I don't know," she snapped at me. "Between you and Sam, where should I start?"

"Oh."

"Yeah.... Oh, for goodness sake, Jory, my heart can't take all this. Worrying about you, worrying about Sam.... Could one of you," she glared at me, "quit."

"I will, I'll stop." As I sat up I realized that I wasn't hooked up to anything anymore. Very exciting. "Hey, look—I got no strings on me."

"I'm thrilled," she said snidely. "Will you be doing any more running around, Kojak, or are we through with that?"

"We're through with that." I yawned.

She lunged at me then, grabbing me tight, burying her face in the side of my neck. She shivered just once and then squeezed me as hard as she could.

I hugged her back, rubbing circles on her back. "I'm all right."

Pulling back, she stared into my eyes. "Are you sure?"

"Yeah, I'm sure. Do you know when they're going to release me?"

"The doctor was here maybe thirty minutes ago. He said he was going to get the paperwork going so you could leave when you woke up."

"Awesome." I smiled at her. "Then let's get me changed and—"

"Wait." She put up her hand. "You know Dane isn't letting you go anywhere but home with us, right?"

"No, I'll talk to him. He'll change his mind, you'll see."

"I don't know, Jory, he's been pretty upset."

"I know I put you both through a lot, but—"

"Jory, half of the time I don't know whether to hug you or strangle you. I need to know that you're safe and I really can't fault Dane's logic. If he can see you, he knows you're all right."

"I guess."

"He told me he's going to hire you a bodyguard too."

"How's yours? Is he hot?"

"No, not so much." She widened her eyes.

"Not like in the movies?"

"Absolutely not."

I had to smile, she was so cute.

She glared at me and stood up from where she'd been sitting next to me on my bed. "Get up and change. I bought you some clothes to wear."

After I took a quick shower and changed, I walked with my sister-in-law to Sam's room. I complained about the gel she'd bought me the whole way.

"God, do I even get a thank you?" she chided me.

"I said thank you a hundred times."

"Then quit bitching about your hair. It looks fine."

"Fine," I repeated, running my fingers through it again. It wasn't the gel I used. It felt weird, but the glare from her told me I should drop it.

"You are really very vain. Has anyone ever told you that?" she snapped at me.

"I am not," I grumbled, rubbing my cheek with the back of my fingers. "I need to shave."

She snorted out a laugh, which was very undignified. "A little stubble looks good on you. Makes you look like a man instead of a sixteen-year-old boy."

"Oh, screw you," I whined. "I don't look like a kid anymore."

"Whatever you say."

I let her walk into Sam's room first, past the two uniformed policemen, and when I saw him I was surprised to find him out of bed and sitting at the table in the corner, in one of the hospital's ideas of a recliner. He was dressed in sweats, white crew socks, and a T-shirt. I had never seen him look so good.

"There he is," he said, and gestured for me.

I bolted forward, but Dane caught my arm to stop my flight.

"No," Sam said, and my eyes went from my brother's face to his. "Let him go."

Dane dropped his hand.

I gave him a slight smile before I dashed forward to stand over Sam. "You look great." I beamed down at him.

He patted his thighs. "C'mere, you know I love you in my lap."

It was funny. Everyone yelled at once as I put my hand down on the arm of the chair and swung myself over him. They thought I was stupid. When I caught myself, bracing my hands on both arms and slowly straddling his hips, there was a collective sigh of relief. Sam chuckled and put a hand on his abdomen.

"Don't make me laugh yet, all right?"

I nodded as I shifted my ass over his groin, moving around until I felt him get hard. Instantly his hands were like iron on my hips.

"Knock it off, 'cause I can't do shit about that right now."

"I could take care of you," I told him, smiling lazily, biting my bottom lip.

He stared into my eyes and took my face in his hands. "I want you here with me every night from now on, you understand? No more, Jory, no more."

"Okay," I said, leaning forward to kiss him.

He tightened his hold on me so I couldn't move. "You took years off my life, you know."

"No, I didn't. Don't say that."

He let out a quick exhale. "I need you around a long time, you understand? I can't have anything happen to you... I just can't."

"Okay, okay." I grinned at him. "Now can I kiss you?"

"Yes," he said softly, easing me down so that our lips touched. I closed my eyes and his tongue slipped between my lips as I parted them for him. I sighed into his mouth and forgot about everything and everyone else but Sam Kage. Kissing Sam Kage. His hand went to the back of my head, holding me there as his mouth slanted over mine, possessively, roughly. I moaned back in my throat as my hands slid over his chest, touching the rock-hard muscles.

"Okay, stop." Dane's voice cut through my body like ice. He sounded really annoyed.

I pulled back and looked over my shoulder at him as he crossed the room to stand beside us.

"I have no interest in watching my brother make out with his boyfriend. I want to know what the hell you were thinking by going through that woman's stuff!"

I stood up, but Sam grabbed my hand.

"Sit here," he said, patting the arm of the chair.

I perched as I was directed and felt his hand slip up under the back of my sweater to caress my skin. "I didn't touch anything, Dane. I already told you."

"That's not true, Jory," Detective Lange said as he walked up beside my brother. "I checked to make sure I was right, and Caleb's fingerprints are all over—"

"I didn't go through anything," I almost yelled, the only thing keeping me from losing it being Sam's hand on the small of my back. Just that much contact, calming me. "We walked in, we found her lying there." I swallowed hard, remembering. "Caleb accidentally touched the knife and then I ran back outside and threw up."

"Jory, you've gotta be—" Detective Lange began.

"I'm not wrong," I told him and my brother, realizing suddenly that, along with them, Sam's parents were there, and Detective Hefron, and a couple of other people I didn't know. They all had badges hanging from chains around their necks. "I know what I did and I know what I didn't do, and I'm sure I—"

"Shut up," Sam suddenly yelled, and I got up and turned around to look at him.

I couldn't believe he was taking their side and not listening to me, but when I saw his face, I went mute. He was absolutely ashen.

"Sam," I said quickly, leaning down, my hands on his face and arms. "Are you all right? Should I call the doctor or—"

"Sam," Regina gasped, rushing up beside me, her hands on his chest. "Honey, what can we do?"

"Call the doctor!" Thomas barked out.

It was chaos in seconds, everyone yelling, before Sam stood up, brushing away everyone's hands but mine. Me he grabbed tight and hugged to his side, like he was protecting me.

"Shut up!" he roared, and the room went instantly silent. I was suddenly whipped around to face him, his hands digging into my biceps painfully. Even hurt, he was so strong. "You only touched the door and the wall, right?"

I nodded.

He looked over my shoulder but didn't let me go. "Goddamnit," he said and swayed a little, his voice hoarse. "Neal," he said, and let me go as Detective Lange stepped in front of him. "We're fuckin' idiots."

I watched Detective Lange stare at Sam and then his mouth slowly opened before he turned and looked at Detective Hefron.

"It's Caleb Reid," James Hefron said flatly, and let out a deep breath. "Jesus Christ, it's Caleb Reid."

"Wait," Dane said quickly. "What are you—"

"Go to his room," Sam yelled at Lange, who turned and ran, walkie-talkie in his hand, as everyone cleared out but Sam's family, Dane, and Aja.

"Sam," Dane said, stepping closer to him. "What's going on?"

Sam pulled his hair back from his face and looked at me. "Holy shit, Jory."

"What? What's going on? What does this have to do with—"

"It's Caleb, baby," Sam said, putting a hand around the back of my neck to pull me to him. "It has to be. Everything started around the time Caleb came into Dane's life. The first guy killed was right after he met Dane and learned about you. Everything lines up, and I'm sure he purposely touched that knife yesterday to throw us off. He killed Joyce Fain and left the murder weapon in plain sight, knowing that when he brought you back with him that you would see him touch it and vouch for his stupidity. We won't find any other prints on that knife because there aren't any others to find."

It didn't make any sense. "But Caleb was in Texas before yesterday, and they said Mrs. Fain was killed—"

"You told Lange that Caleb showed up at your hotel room. How do you know when he actually got into town? Baby, he could have been there for hours before he showed up to meet you."

My head hurt again. "But Sam, he was kidnapped with me."

"Honey, you don't know that. You never saw anybody's face. If Caleb was working with Greg Fain, that means that he was sitting there watching Greg hit you and hold you down. He killed Greg Fain when he wanted to let you go, and put him in that freezer in the backyard because he probably had no idea what else to do."

"But Caleb's my friend."

"No, he's not." He shook his head. "And he finally tripped up."

"How?" Dane asked, his voice cold.

Sam turned to look at him. "Because the neighbor that saw Jory heaving up a lung on the back porch called the police, because she thought they were breaking in. I think Caleb would have tried to talk Jory into walking around the house and looking for clues, but he didn't have enough time."

"So Jory's fingerprints would have been exactly where his already were?"

"Yeah," Sam agreed.

"You're telling me that Caleb killed Mrs. Fain earlier in the day, went through her house, and then led Jory back there to cover it up."

"Right. My guess is that Greg Fain and Caleb Reid know each other from somewhere and that there are pictures or something that tie them together that Caleb thought were in that house, but weren't. He led Jory back there to cover his tracks."

"But if it is Caleb, why wouldn't he just kill me? He's had hundreds of opportunities."

"I dunno," Sam said, his voice shaky. "But we'll find out."

"It's absurd," Dane said flatly. "Caleb Reid could no more kill a man then... he's not strong enough, Sam, and I don't mean physically... he's just... weak."

"I'm gonna hafta disagree," Sam croaked out and I realized that he was trembling. "It's Caleb, it all makes sense. Why were we only able to find evidence that Greg Fain, Jory, and Caleb were ever in the shed? Why only Caleb and Greg's DNA in the house? How come the car only had evidence that Jory and Caleb had been in it, besides those punks that stole it? Why on earth would Caleb have touched that knife? Everyone knows better'n that. Everyone."

It sounded light to me. "It's all just circumstantial evidence."

"Really?" Sam said indulgently. "Is that what you think?"

I scowled at him. "Sam, there's no hard evidence that ties Caleb to my kidnapping or any of the other murders."

"I bet there is. I bet there's something he missed in that house, and I know that Greg Fain knew me from somewhere or he wouldn't have been so freaked out when he heard that you were with me. We need to search Joyce Fain's house, her car, where she worked, everywhere, and then we need to find out everything about Greg Fain. I—"

"He's gone," Neal Lange said as he walked back into the room. "I got the word out that he's wanted for questioning so he won't get out of the city, but God knows where he is right now."

"Shit," Sam swore, and kicked the chair closest to him. "He must have known that his story and Jory's didn't match. This is the one time it didn't."

Detective Lange nodded. "Yeah. I mean, now that I think about it, it makes perfect sense. The gunshot wound could have easily been self-inflicted, and he knew every move we made because he was in our inner circle. Amazing that I didn't—I mean... all the fingerprints we don't have, all the DNA evidence that only showed him.... Christ, Sam, I'm sorry I totally missed it."

"We all missed it," he growled. "The point is, now that we know we gotta keep everybody safe. You need to get with Dallas PD and check out his parents' home, and his, and see what you can find out. Pull cell phone records and gas receipts and airline tickets... pull everything and then get back to me."

Lange nodded and left without another word. Detective Hefron was right behind him.

"Sam, you're wrong about Caleb," I told him.

He sighed deeply before he looked down into my eyes. "No, baby, I'm never wrong," And then he suddenly squinted like he was confused. "What's with your hair?"

"It's not my gel," I grumbled.

"You're not helping," Aja snapped at him.

"Sorry," he teased her, wrapping an arm around her shoulders and pulling her close.

I looked over at Dane and saw that he was a million miles away, thinking, going through what Sam had said and turning it over in his mind.

"Jory baby, come here."

I went to Sam's other side and let him wrap his arm around my neck and pull me back against him. "You don't leave my sight, you understand? Now that he knows we know, he's got nothing to lose by going after you. There's nothing to hide anymore."

I shivered hard, and felt Sam's chin rest on the top of my head. I felt better for no other reason than he was there and solid once again. I wondered what would happen next.

Chapter Ten

WE WERE sitting having Regina's homemade meatloaf when Detective Hefron and Detective Lange walked into the room, followed by another man. I watched Sam sit up in his bed and swing his legs over the side. He would have gotten up, but the man walked between the two detectives and put up his hand to stop him. When he was close enough, he extended his hand for Sam to take.

"Wow," Sam chuckled, clasping the hand tight and gripping the other man's shoulder. "Big gun."

The other man nodded, the edge of his lip curling just slightly as he looked at him. "Enough's enough, Sam. We are looking at a serial killer after all."

He nodded before the man let go and turned to the rest of us. His pale blue eyes roamed over us all before they settled on me.

"Jory Harcourt."

"Yeah."

He squinted at me. "Why're you wearing a coat inside?"

"'Cause I'm cold," I answered as the reason for my peacoat. It seemed like I was freezing all the time. Ever since Caleb and I had found Joyce Fain dead, I couldn't get warm enough. Aja said that it was psychological and not physiological, but I had dismissed her rationale. And yes, usually Sam was home to hold me and sleep with me and imprint on my mind and body so that everything else disappeared... but I was sure I was really, actually cold. Neither she nor Dane was buying it, however.

"Hospitals are always cold," the man assured me.

"Who are you?" I asked irritably.

He walked over to me and extended his hand as I stood up. "Special Agent Zane Calhoun from the field office in Dallas... pleasure to meet you."

"Special Agent?"

He moved his badge from where it had fallen behind his tie. The letters were big and visible. "FBI. We're helping the Chicago PD with the investigation, as you know, and I've been called in from Dallas, since that's Mr. Reid's hometown. We need to get him into custody as soon as possible before he hurts anyone else or endangers either you or your brother or Detective Kage again."

"But how can you be sure that—"

"That what? That Mr. Reid is a murderer?"

"Yes," Dane answered.

He turned and looked at Dane. "Dane Harcourt?"

"Yes."

He walked around the table and shook Dane's hand before taking the time to introduce himself to first Aja and then Sam's parents. When his eyes flicked back to Dane's, I saw him smile. "I can tell you, Mr. Harcourt, that we have seized hundreds of photographs of you from Mr. Reid's home. His mother has verified that he knew who you were almost six months before he approached Mr. Harcourt at--"

"It's gonna get confusing," I said, cutting him off even though he wasn't talking to me. "Just call me Jory."

His eyes were back on mine and I saw how he was studying me. "All right then, Jory it is."

"So you're saying Caleb was around for months before he let either Jory or me know who he was," Dane said to clarify Agent Calhoun's earlier statement.

"Yessir, that's what I'm saying. At his home in Fort Worth we found a crawl space in the floor where we recovered a knife. Now I'm confident that it will be a match to the one that was used on all the victims. We found a gun in the back of Mrs. Fain's car that, again, I'm confident will be a match for the bullet in Greg Fain's head and for the one taken out of Caleb Reid's leg."

I just stared at his profile as he turned and looked at me. "There was a box of college memorabilia in Greg Fain's storage locker in Hyde Park that I'm guessing Mr. Reid didn't know about, that I'm also guessing Mr. Fain was using as an insurance policy. No doubt he never got to deliver the threat to Mr. Reid, as he killed him before he got the chance."

"Why did he—"

"Kill Mr. Fain?"

"Yeah."

"My guess is that Mr. Fain was highly agitated when he found out about Detective Kage's involvement. Greg Fain had been arrested for selling marijuana to minors five years prior, and on that arrest record Dominic Kairov and Sam Kage are cited as the arresting officers."

"Really? When I was working vice?"

Agent Calhoun nodded.

"I don't remember him," Sam said quietly and Agent Calhoun turned to look at him.

"You can't remember them all, Sam, and my guess is that it's bad but not as bad as it sounds. When I pulled up the report, Greg Fain was twenty-two at the time of his arrest and the guys he sold the pot to were his friends, ages twenty to eighteen. I'm guessin' maybe you and Dom scared the crap out of him then, and when he found out you were involved, the same detective that busted him the only other time he had ever had a run-in with the law... he lost it. No way for Mr. Reid to calm him down, so he did what he felt he had to do and killed him."

"This doesn't seem too easy to you?" I asked him.

"Easy?" Agent Calhoun gave me a look. "It only seems easy because it's so clear. Detective Kage had a hunch and it was the right one. The box in Greg Fain's storage locker had photos of him and Mr. Reid from when they went to Texas A&M together. Only Mr. Reid graduated, but they must have kept in touch over the years. Maybe when

Mr. Reid came here to see Mr. Harcourt, he looked up his old friend and put the idea into his head about kidnapping you to get your brother to pay the ransom."

"I remember Caleb being so surprised that Dane was going to pay a ransom for him as well as me."

"But see, it made no sense that Mr. Reid was kidnapped, and when Detective Kage called me and asked that I stayed involved even after both you and Mr. Reid were recovered... we both felt that it had to be an inside job."

I nodded. "Who did you think it was?"

He sighed quickly. "I thought it was you, Jory."

"Me? But I was kidnapped and—"

"But you got away, and the way you did that, that whole story about car thieves and being left... that sounded odd to me."

"But—"

He put his hand up to still me. "But then Detective Kage was injured, and what you did after that... I knew then you were innocent even before you started running around town looking for answers. Finding the two boys that stole the car, finding the house where you were kept, even finding Joyce Fain... it was nice work and you did it all to keep Detective Kage safe."

I just looked him in the eye. "Why would Caleb want to hurt Dane?"

"The profile we did for Caleb Reid gives us insight into the mind of a classic sociopath. He wants what he wants and he has no remorse or even any emotion at all in his quest to fulfill his own needs."

"What does he want?"

"Well... first, he wants his family to be whole, and with you gone, Jory, the only siblings Dane Harcourt has are the Reids. Second, he wants money—plain and simple. He sees his brother's wealth, sees the woman he married, the lifestyle he leads, and he wants it for himself. Money as a motivator is powerful and everybody gets that. With you dead and Mr. Harcourt grieving, Mr. Reid can ingratiate himself and bring his brother back into the fold."

"Never happen," Dane told him.

"Of course not," Agent Calhoun assured him. "But it's not my fantasy, it's his."

I shook my head, "I still—"

"Caleb Reid killed the first victim right after he met you, Jory. He wrote your name on the wall in your old apartment with blood and fecal matter, and under your name he wrote the word 'fake'."

I shivered hard and looked over at Sam. He had never told me everything.

"Come here," he gestured me close.

I moved to his side and he tucked my head under his chin, rubbing his hand up and down my arm.

"I think fake means fake brother, and that was the piece that was missing all this time."

I nodded slowly.

"The next victim was taken after Mr. Harcourt's fortieth birthday party, which was, I understand, extremely lavish. I'm sure just being there nearly killed Mr. Reid. Next was Mr. Harcourt's engagement party to Miss Greene. He watched his brother throw another party and saw the beautiful woman he intended to marry. And then the wedding itself... it had to have been torture for him. You were there standing up with your brother, and he and his family were merely guests. These were all instances of incredible rage that could only be vented through murder," he finished, and I realized how clinical he'd sounded.

"You know, Caleb isn't some case study, Agent Calhoun, he's a human being."

"Barely," he clarified. "Jory, I can't think of any reason for you still being alive beyond the fact that he must genuinely like you. There's no other reason for it."

I shifted away from Sam but not beyond his reach. "So what now?"

"Now Caleb Reid needs to be found and taken into custody and put under psychiatric care as quickly as possible. Until he's apprehended, you and Detective Kage, and Mr. and Mrs. Harcourt, and everyone else are in terrible jeopardy. Let's not forget that Caleb Reid put a bomb in Detective Kage's car that nearly killed him."

And I had been missing all the rest, dismissing everything that had ever been done to me because I was fine, but Sam... Caleb had tried to kill Sam. I turned and looked at him and felt my eyes get hot.

"Oh shit," Sam grumbled, glaring at Agent Calhoun. "Could ya lay the fuck off, Zane? Don't be such a fuckin' hard-ass when you're talking to Jory."

"Oh c'mon, Sam," he shot back as Sam reached for me, drawing me back into the circle of his arms. "Tell me you're not all thinking about him like he's still affable old Caleb. None of you are putting together the monster inside with the harmless boy-next-door outside. None of you get it. Caleb Reid is—"

"Agent Calhoun."

We all turned to the doorway, where a man now stood.

"Chicago PD has Caleb Reid cornered in a parking structure downtown."

"Which one?" Dane asked.

And when the agent rattled off Dane's address, I was surprised. Why go there?

"He overpowered a security guard," the man continued, "but he just knocked him out. He hasn't killed anyone but he's armed. It looks like he's threatening to turn the gun on himself. The negotiator's there and they're flying his parents in from Dallas as we speak."

"Poor Susan," Aja said softly, leaning into Dane's side as he curled an arm around her. "This has got to be killing her. She's got to be thinking it's all her fault."

"So what now?" Dane asked Agent Calhoun. "How long will you try and talk to him?"

"As long as it takes."

There was a yell in the hall and a woman flew into the room.

"Calhoun—Caleb Reid has a hostage!"

She sounded calm even though she talked really fast.

"Who?"

"A woman, she was there to see the Harcourts... Carmen Greene."

"Oh God!" Aja gasped and nearly swooned.

Everyone moved at once, reaching for her, which gave me my moment. It was like we had planned it.

I bolted out of the room.

"Jory!" I heard Sam roar.

"Grab him!" Agent Calhoun shouted behind me, but I was pretty sure everyone was in the room.

I could not, would not, let Aja's sister Carmen pay for Dane's mistake, or mine. And I was ninety-five percent certain that if I could talk to him, I could get the gun away and let him live. Not that I was the second coming or anything, I just felt like I knew Caleb Reid pretty well. But then, maybe I didn't know him at all.

I hit the door for the stairs, went through, and ran up two flights. It crashed open seconds later and however many men there were went down. I followed them at a safe distance and slipped from the stairwell through the door on the third floor. I walked to the opposite end and took the tiny elevator down to the emergency room, with ten other people stuffed into it. I stepped out into a demilitarized zone—loud, chaotic, and crushed with people. The place was packed and I moved through the bedlam unseen. I was definitely getting good at running. I didn't even have to think anymore.

On the street I flipped up my collar and got a cab as soon as I moved to the curb. I had already missed five calls from Sam, three from Dane, and three from a number I didn't know. I turned it off and gave the driver directions to the building.

I panicked a little when I saw the barricade, but I had sort of a plan by the time I got there. It all hinged on how believable I could be. What was helpful was that I had keys. Because even though the police weren't letting anyone in or out of the parking structure, they were letting people into the building itself. So once I got to the elevator that went to Dane's apartment, I took the private one at the opposite end of the hall to where he parked his car. When the doors whooshed open, there were the guys in their Darth Vader masks and body armor.

"What are you doing here?"

I was hoping that Agent Calhoun hadn't talked to every guy on the SWAT team already. "I was told to report to the negotiator. I'm supposed to try and talk to Caleb Reid until his mother gets here."

It must have made sense. What crazy person reports to a hostage situation?

Grabbed roughly, I was jerked from the elevator and walked through a maze of men in black until we reached a barricade of parked cars. There were lights all pointing toward the opposite end of the parking level, where I could see a car with both the front and back tires flat and a broken-out driver's side window. The front end was smashed into a bearing pole.

"Lieutenant."

There was another man dressed up like Darth Vader's stunt double, two men in black suits, and two more in jeans—one in a turtleneck sweater, the other in a shirt and tie.

"Who're you?" the one in the sweater barked at me.

"I was told by Special Agent Calhoun to come talk to Caleb Reid."

"Bullshit," he said flatly. "Agent Calhoun called us, Mr. Harcourt." He looked over my shoulder at one of the SWAT guys. "Take him back out to the street and put him in a car until this is over."

But I was further than I'd thought I'd be. When I turned to go, I did the swivel move that I perfected during freeze tag when I was eight. Go right, spin back left, and bolt. And it worked like it always did and I made it to the side of the car before I was grabbed hard from the back, my coat firmly in someone's grasp. Not that it mattered, as I had loosened it on the way down the elevator. It slid easily off my shoulders as I flew out ten feet from behind the parked car into the glare of the spotlights.

"Mr. Harcourt, get your ass back here!"

"Dane!" I heard Caleb scream.

"No," I yelled back, hands up as I walked toward the crash. "It's me."

"Jory?" The voice had gone instantly from crazed to calm. He sounded like he normally did.

I nodded, but realized quickly that he couldn't see it. "Yeah! You wanna let Carmen go and I'll come sit with you?"

"Okay," he called back, like I had asked him if he wanted a hamburger or something. Just a nothing decision, not the life-and-death one that it was. I put down my hands and ran toward where the car was as Carmen's head popped up.

I waved her to me as I ran. "C'mon—run!"

The women in the Greene family were phenomenal. She did exactly what I said without any Hollywood theatrics. She just moved.

"Run to the cars at the other end," I shouted at her as she started to slow the closer she got to me. "Don't stop, just run!"

She flew by me and I sprinted toward Caleb, who was crouching behind the car, the barrel of a gun pointed at me. I stopped when I reached him, standing over him, staring down.

"Sit down," he ordered, grabbing my wrist and yanking me down beside him.

I sat beside him, shoulder to shoulder, my back against the side of the car, the cold, concrete ground instantly chilling me through my jeans, the muzzle of the gun shoved into my ribs.

"I'm cold," I mumbled, shivering, leaning next to him.

"Jesus."

I turned to look at his profile. "What?"

He shook his head. "You know and you're still not scared. Jesus Christ, Jory."

And I remembered suddenly the way his face had looked when I was kidnapped in front of him. How terrified and helpless. He had liked me from that moment. Had cared about me from that moment. He would never hurt me, it wasn't in him. "Caleb."

"What?"

But there was someone else who didn't like me. Someone he knew wanted me dead. And my brain had finally figured it out. "On the phone that time… when you called me when I got back… do you know what you said?"

"What are you…." He trailed off. "I don't know what you're talking about."

I nodded. I knew it hadn't been Caleb on my new phone after I'd been kidnapped. It wasn't Caleb who wanted to kiss me when I was cold. "I didn't think so."

His eyes suddenly got huge. "Wait—no—you're wrong."

But I wasn't, and because I was about a second ahead of him, I grabbed the muzzle of the gun and shoved it out, away from me, so that when it went off, the bullet hit the wall a few feet from us. I was more agile and wearing fewer clothes, so I was able to twist and fall on top of him before he could get his feet under him. He fell back and I rammed his face into the side of the car, and then the back of his head down onto the concrete. His eyes rolled back and he went still. I heard the yelling and the pounding feet and then there were hands all over me as I was lifted up and away. Caleb's gun was kicked to the wall, well out of his reach had he been conscious enough to even try for it. I was yanked around hard, and was suddenly face-to-face with Agent Calhoun.

"I'm going to throw you in jail for a very long time, Mr. Harcourt."

"Fine—whatever, listen to me," I rasped out because I was breathless. "I got a call when I got home from being kidnapped, but it wasn't from Caleb."

He glared at me. "I have no idea what you're—"

"Whoever called said they wanted to kiss me when I was cold."

"Again, I have no idea what you're—"

"Caleb would never say that—he's covering."

"Covering for who? What are you talking about?"

"He knew, I don't know when... probably not until just recently, but since he found out, he's been putting himself between us... protecting me." I finished quickly.

"You're not making any sense."

"I'm sure he covered up or pretended like it wasn't happening, maybe hoped... but Caleb's not like this—he's just not. He doesn't have it in him to kill, I know he doesn't, but she does."

"I'm not following you at all."

"It's his mother... it's Susan Reid. She's the one he's protecting... she's the only one he would go to jail for. I promise you—she's the guilty one."

"Do you even know what you're talk—"

"It makes sense. Susan thinks that I'm the thing that keeps her from getting close to Dane, but Caleb knows I'm not the problem. It's him—it's Dane. He's never gonna forgive her for giving him away."

"I'm not—"

"Don't you see—it's everything. It's the media, and her idea, her belief about what was gonna happen. I think she thought that just because she gave him away, later on, down the road, he would forgive and forget. She could bring him back into the fold and everything would be okay. Maybe she clung to that delusion her whole life, and then, faced with his coldness and at the same time his warmth with me and Aja... I dunno. I think somewhere along the way she just snapped."

"But that doesn't explain—"

"It had to be her and Greg. I mean, I heard people struggling that day in the shed. She and Greg must've got into it and then she shot him."

"Why would she kidnap her own son?"

"She didn't kidnap him. He was there to talk to me, to keep an eye on me. He was in on the kidnapping, but not the murders."

He was staring a hole through my head. "I'm not saying I believe you, and you're definitely going to jail for obstruction, but I will look into—"

"Wasn't she coming to talk to Caleb, along with the negotiator?"

"Yeah, but—"

"Can we find out where she is, 'cause I don't want her anywhere near Dane."

He gestured for the SWAT guys to follow him, which they did, carrying me, hands under my arms, as my feet left the ground. I was forcibly shoved into the squad car and made to sit. They didn't cuff me, which was nice, so I could get my phone out and call Dane.

"I'm gonna kill you myself!" he roared at me instead of saying hello.

"Wait, listen…. Caleb was only an accomplice, Dane. Susan's the one who killed all those guys and Greg Fain. She's the murderer, not Caleb."

"What are you talking about?"

"I'll tell you when I get outta here, but promise me—swear on my life that you won't go anywhere with her and you won't be alone with her."

"Jory, I—"

"Please… please. I know you think I'm crazy, but I'm really not. Please, Dane. Please don't go anywhere with her."

"God, you sound frantic."

And I realized how frenzied I must have sounded. "Please," I begged him again.

"Fine, whatever you want, just get back here now."

"I dunno, I think Agent Calhoun wants to put me in jail."

"What?"

"That's what he said," I said. "He's really mad."

"We're all mad, Jory, you're an idiot!"

Which was probably true. I couldn't really defend myself.

"Where's Agent Calhoun?"

"He's yelling at people."

"Where are you now?"

"In the back of a police car."

"Jory, I'm going to—"

Muffled noises and then came the familiar yelling.

"You are never-ever leaving the house again when this is over, do you understand me? You will be a shut-in for the rest of your life! I hope you're fuckin' happy!"

I smiled into the phone. In the midst of everything, Sam was livid with me because I had put myself in danger. "Hi, Sam."

"Jory, goddamnit!" he thundered, his voice firing out of my phone. "I want you back here right… fucking… now… do you hear me?"

"I wish you were better."

"What?"

"I need… you better."

There was a long pause. "If you ever *stayed* here even for a minute, you'd know that I'm being released day after tomorrow. Two weeks in the hospital is enough. I get to come home."

"You do?"

He grunted, but it was his smug, self-satisfied grunt that sent a current of need right through me. "Yes, I do. You sound pleased."

I couldn't even speak.

"Good, now maybe you will come back here and sit and not move until I tell you to."

"Yes."

"Hang up and I will call Agent Calhoun."

"Okay, I'll see you soon and—"

"But—"

"I promise I won't let Dane or Aja leave here until you get back."

My breath came out in a rush. "Okay."

"I'm going to strangle you—you get that, right?"

"I get that."

"You know, I have a theory that because your brain is so small you can't hold more than one thought in your head at a time. That's why you do such stupid shit all the time, 'cause when the new stuff is in there you forget everything else."

I had to laugh because he sounded so serious.

"I'm going to beat you when I get my hands on you."

"I know." I sighed. "I can't wait."

He growled before he hung up and I let out a deep breath and closed my eyes. Everything was going to be all right.

Chapter Eleven

NOTHING ever turns out the way you plan. Case in point: I thought Sam could get Agent Calhoun to let me go. No such luck. He was good and mad, and as far as I knew, had refused to even take a call from my boyfriend. So I got to go somewhere I had hoped to avoid for the rest of my life.

As I sat there in the large but crowded holding cell at the county jail, I had nothing to do but think and that was always dangerous for me. Caleb was going to go to prison for a very long time if I didn't figure out a way to save him. His mother was a sociopath or a psychopath, I wasn't sure which one applied, and since no one but me really believed in his innocence, it fell to me to pull Caleb out of the hole he was in by digging up the truth about her. When I got out, I had to figure out the truth about Susan Reid. I needed to get to Dallas and take a look at her life. When I was free. If I got free…

"Hey, pretty boy," someone called out to me. "What'd you do?"

"Nothing," a voice answered before I could say anything.

I had never considered myself vain, but I had thought that the guy was talking to me. Since I was in jail however, I was kind of glad not to be getting any attention. True to his word, Agent Calhoun had locked me up. I had no idea how long his anger would take to dissipate.

"C'mere."

I turned and looked at the guy who was talking—big guy, muscular but with a beer gut, he had to be at least six-five when standing. Now he sat between two other guys and motioned across from him. The kid had not moved. He shook his head no.

"I said, c'mere."

"No," he said quickly and I could tell he was terrified. He glanced around the room, his eyes searching everywhere until he caught my eye. I stared back and I saw him take a breath. Instantly, he was up and moving, darting down the line of ten men seated along the wall until he was standing in front of me. I looked up into his face, smiling.

"Excuse me," I said to the guy on my left. "Could you slide down just a little?"

The stranger grunted but he moved, making a spot for my new friend to fill.

"Hi," he said breathily, absorbing my face with his eyes. "I'm Carrington Adams, who're you?"

"Jory Harcourt." I held out my hand. "Nice to meet you."

He tried to smile as he shook my hand. "What are you in here for, Jory?"

"Obstruction of justice—you?"

His brows furrowed. "That doesn't sound too bad?"

"It is and it isn't. You didn't tell me what you did."

"Solicitation."

My eyebrows raised and he let out a shaky breath.

"It ain't me, Jory. I just needed to eat and… I went to this party this guy told me to go to and I was just supposed to hang out and drink and talk and… and I got drunk so fast and then I must've passed out and…." His eyes crinkled up like he was in pain. "I just wanna go home."

"And that's where?"

"North Carolina."

I nodded. "Are you okay?"

He just looked at me.

"Hey, pretty boy!"

We both looked toward the back of the room, where the guy that had called him before was. There were five men clustered around him, ready to form a barricade or a wall. Either way, it was dangerous and just plain stupid to go back there.

"Get your ass back here, kid," he threatened Carrington. "Now."

There were catcalls and whistles before the loud, lewd comments began. Apparently the plan was for Carrington to be on his knees for the rest of the night.

He put his head back, let it clunk against the wall behind him.

"It's okay," I told him, "you're not going."

He rolled his head on the wall to look at me. "You're gonna help me?"

"Yep." I smiled at him, turning to look at the guy in the back. "Hey, asshole!"

He glared at me.

"You know Rego James?"

His eyes widened and the others went still, no longer threatening Carrington, all their focus on me.

"'Cause he won't like you touching his boy."

There was lots of whispering, debate I couldn't really hear.

Finally the question was spoken. "He tricks for James?"

"Yep," I said matter-of-factly, "so you better put your dick back in your pants unless you wanna eat it."

No one said another word.

"Jory," Carrington said, leaning close to me, his lips against my ear. "Who's Rego whoever?"

"Don't worry about it. Do you have a plan to get home?"

"Never mind that—do you trick for this guy James?"

"No." I shook my head. "Tell me your plan, hurry up."

"Okay, my mom got me a plane ticket. I just gotta get to the airport."

"You don't need to get your stuff first?"

"It's just clothes, Jory, who cares? I just wanna get the hell outta here."

"Sure, don't worry. We're getting out."

"How?"

"You'll see." I took a breath before turning toward the front of the cell, where a uniformed policeman had suddenly appeared. "It's all about the name you drop and who's listening."

"What are you talking about?"

Did nobody but me watch TV?

"Jory?"

The officer was standing silently on the outside of the locked cell, staring in at me. I tipped my head at him in greeting.

"C'mere.' He crooked his finger at me.

I moved fast to the bars that separated prisoners from policemen. When I was close enough, he reached through and yanked me close to him. Our faces were inches apart as he looked into my eyes.

"That kid works for Rego James?" he asked me, his voice low so only I could hear him.

"Both of us," I said quickly, putting it on. "I was supposed to be along to watch over him, ya know, but we got busted. Will you call Rego?"

He nodded, looking me over. "What's your name?"

"Jory."

"Okay," he said, shoving me back hard.

I went back to sitting next to Carrington.

"Jory, what was all that about?"

"Nothing, just follow my lead, okay? Don't even for a second lose track of me, all right?"

He took a breath and nodded. "Seriously, you ever get to Waynesville, North Carolina,—that's where I'm from, where my home is—my folks'll let you move in."

"We're not out yet," I reminded him.

And I felt his hand on my knee. "I got faith in ya."

That was one of us.

It didn't take long. The officer came and called for us fifteen minutes later. We didn't go out the way we came in. I was given my watch, phone, and wallet back before Carrington and I were led out of the holding cell and through a maze of passageways. Our heads were both lowered so no one could identify us and we walked silently behind the officer, through empty offices and down stairwells. Carrington never left my side as we passed desks of people that ignored us, until a final door opened and we wound up standing outside in an empty alley with the officer. Instantly, we were bathed in a yellow glow as a car rolled toward us, headlights on. When it stopped beside us, we both saw it was a black limousine. The driver's side window rolled down and a hand held out an envelope. The officer took it, turned, and left, disappearing back into the building. When the window rose with an electronic whir, the door opened at the same time. A large man got out and opened the side door for us. He stood and waited, holding it ajar, silent in the cold, dark alley.

I got in the car and Carrington followed me. The door clicked shut behind us as my eyes found Rego James sitting on the black leather seat. He was reclined across from an older man, with a younger man seated beside him. Two young men, both with long black hair and blue eyes, flanked Rego on either side. Carrington and I took seats next to the door as the driver pulled out into traffic.

"You used my name," he said slowly, his voice deep and low. "If I don't show I lose face, so here I am."

I nodded. "Thanks for coming."

He squinted at Carrington. "You're not mine. Who are you?"

"He's nobody," I said quickly. "I just need to drop him off at the airport."

Rego nodded, called out the airport to his driver.

"Have you forgotten about the party?" The man sitting across from Rego asked him.

"No," he said, eying me. "Come here, I want to look at you."

I got to my knees and crawled across the space to him.

"You look like you got beat up."

"It was a while ago."

He nodded and reached for me, taking hold of the front of my sweater and easing me forward between his legs until I was almost against his chest.

"I really appreciate this. The FBI agent was a pain in the ass."

His eyes narrowed. "What?"

So I explained how I was in for obstruction and how Special Agent Calhoun had put me there. "God knows how long he was gonna stay mad. He's gonna bust something when he goes to look for me and finds out I'm gone."

"Special Agent?"

I nodded.

"FBI, Jory?"

I nodded again.

He hit me before I even realized he was planning to. The refrigerator stopped my momentum backward. At least I didn't hit my head.

We were dumped in front of O'Hare, Carrington climbing out unscathed, me being thrown out, bloody, twenty minutes later. He sat beside me on the sidewalk and used the sleeve of his shirt to pinch my nose shut, since it was bleeding.

"You're amazing."

I closed my eyes a minute so they wouldn't water. I didn't feel amazing.

"Your lip's split, Jory, and I think you're gonna have a black eye. He hit you really hard."

It had definitely felt like it. I was surprised I hadn't been knocked unconscious. I had seen stars.

"Now what?"

"Now," I said, taking a deep breath, passing him my cell phone. "You call your mom."

He took it, looking at me. "What should I say?"

"Tell her you're coming home."

I looked out across the parking lot from my sitting position on the curb and was surprised when he suddenly grabbed me.

"You're the best friend I've ever had and I've known you like an hour."

"Promise me you'll never come back here," I said when he let me go.

"I promise," he whispered, and he started shaking as the tears came.

Together we got up and walked into the terminal.

I went to get my ticket for Dallas, and Carrington got his for Raleigh, and when we were done we met at the golf store. I bought a hoodie because I was freezing, and he got a polo shirt and a hoodie as well. We washed our faces, cleaned up so we didn't scare people, and ate dinner, with him asking me a million questions at once. When I watched him get on the plane two hours later, saw him turn and wave, I had an overwhelming feeling of accomplishment. He was safe because of me. Put a line down in my good deed column for the day.

When I was sitting in the boarding area waiting for my flight, my phone rang.

"Hello?"

"I'm going to kill you, Jory."

"You gotta get in line to kill me," I told Rego and hung up.

He called back seconds later. "The FBI, Jory?"

"Just deny you ever saw me. They've got no proof it was you, and that officer was careful. He told us to put our heads down when we walked under the surveillance cameras."

Heavy sigh. "I'm sorry I hit you. I'll drive back around in front of the terminal, come out and meet me."

"You had a lot of guests in the car, I don't wanna interrupt."

"I dropped everybody off, it'll just be us."

"Unfortunately I have a plane to catch."

"What?"

"I'm leaving," I sighed. "When I get back, I'll call you. I really do appreciate you busting me out. When Sam comes to see you, just—"

"Sam? Who's Sam?"

I sighed deeply. "Detective Sam Kage. He's working the case I'm involved in. When he calls you—"

"Jesus, Sam Kage?" he breathed. "Are you kidding?"

"No."

"What are you wrapped up in, Jory?"

"Some kind of witness protec—"

"Lose my number," he ordered and hung up.

Apparently I had stumbled onto the one thing that scared Rego James... the FBI, and a little Sam Kage thrown in for good measure. It would have been funny if I didn't feel like crap. Just watching Sam's calls come in one after another to my phone was painful. I wanted to pick up and talk to him, but I also knew that if I did I was done. I could not have my phone call traced because I could not afford to be found. I needed to clear

Caleb's name and I needed to go to Dallas to do that. The key to saving Caleb was in finding out everything about his mother. I wouldn't stop until that was accomplished.

An hour later, as I sat in coach listening to the flight attendant welcome passengers onto Flight 233 with nonstop service to Dallas-Fort Worth, I sank into the chair and tried to figure out what I was going to do next. My idea was good. Since Susan Reid was in Chicago, I would go Fort Worth and see what there was to find at her house. They had checked Caleb's apartment, but not Susan's house. I was going to save my friend. Just because he loved his mother didn't mean that he deserved to pay for her crimes.

THE airport in Dallas was huge, but being from Chicago, I had no problem with it. In the cab, I chatted up the driver and asked him where I should go to pick up some clothes. He drove me to the Galleria, where I picked up a couple of pairs of jeans and socks, T-shirts, all the essentials, as well as a fleece-lined denim jacket. I didn't want to stick out. I grabbed a beanie, a pair of gloves, and shoved my old stuff into a duffel bag. When I went back outside to wait for a cab, I realized it was dark already. I had been too pumped up to sleep on the plane, and now, as I was finally tiring, I had no room or place to sleep. The good news was that from the grand I had taken out as a cash advance between my American Express and my Visa, I still had almost five-fifty left.

My second cab driver was even more helpful than the first and knew exactly where the closest Internet café was. I sent Dane an e-mail that I was all right. As it was connected to his phone, I knew he'd get the message quickly and be able to relay it to Sam. I wasn't in any danger, since the two people responsible for all the murders were thousands of miles away from me. I wasn't worried about Dane or Sam, though, as they had lots of people, plus one another, looking out for them. What I needed was a motel so I could sleep.

I was driven to a really nice bed and breakfast that had curtains on the windows, tubs in all the rooms, and brass beds. I was in the Magnolia room, and besides the pictures on the walls, there was soap and lotion and shampoo to match. It was very quaint, as was the antique Princess phone and the sink shaped like a flower in the bathroom. I got in bed after a hot shower and didn't even get under the covers. I was too tired to even dream.

Chapter Twelve

MY MORNING agenda was twofold. First I had to call Sam, and second I needed to go to Susan Reid's house and take a look around. See if I could find anything to incriminate her. Knowing something in your heart and proving it were two very different things. As I headed out after breakfast, walking toward the street, I called Sam.

"Jory."

"Hi." I smiled into the phone "How are you?"

Long silence.

"Sam?"

"Jory… Jesus Christ, Jory! Where the fuck are you?"

"I'm fine."

"That's not what I fuckin' asked! *Where* the fuck are you?"

Up to that point I had thought I'd heard every variance in Sam Kage's voice. But cold fury had been missing from the repertoire without my knowledge. I had never, ever heard him so angry.

"I'm sorry," I said quickly. "I really am."

"You have no idea how sorry you're gonna be."

"What does that mean?"

"That means that when I get you—"

"You won't leave me, will you? You're not so mad that you're gonna move out or something?"

"I haven't even moved in yet!" He was incredulous.

I laughed because it was absurdly funny.

"Jory!"

"What?" I chuckled, wiping my eyes. He was a riot.

"Tell me where—"

"I was just worried… I hoped you weren't so mad that you would leave me."

"Are you kidding me? For fuck's sake, Jory, there's not gonna be anything left to leave! I'm gonna fuckin' beat you 'til—"

I sighed deeply. "Beating's fine, just so long as you stick around."

There was a noise, and then an even icier voice.

"Where… precisely… are you?"

"Hi," I said. "Is Carmen okay?"

"Yes, Jory, Carmen's fine," Dane said, clipping his words, using the crisp tone I hated more than anything. "Where are you?"

"I'm all right now, even though the bruise from where he hit me—"

"Hit you? Who hit you?"

Muffled sounds and then, "Who hit you?"

"Rego James," I answered the love of my life. "But I'm fine. It just looks bad." And it did. When I had seen myself in the mirror in the morning light, I looked worse than I thought. I had a black eye and my lip was split.

"When were you with Rego James?"

"In the car."

"In what car?"

"His limo."

"Rego's limo," he clarified.

"Yeah."

"When?"

"Last night."

He growled at me. "And he hit you?"

"Yeah but I kinda deserved it. I freaked him out a little."

"Jory!" He exploded, pushed to the edge.

"Sorry," I sighed, "I'm really... I know I'm makin' you nuts."

He cleared his throat. "Okay... tell me now where you are."

"In Dallas."

He coughed.

"Sam?"

"Are you fuckin' kidding me?"

"What?"

"You left the state?"

"Yeah, I hafta save Caleb."

"Jesus Christ," he groaned.

"Sam, he's innocent, I know he is."

"And so you're gonna do what... find something nobody else could and vindicate him?"

"Yes," I said confidently.

"Jory, there are—"

"Jory!"

Dane had taken the phone back. This was fun.

"Is Aja all right?" I asked my brother.

"What?"

"Is Aja—"

"Aja's fine. She's with her folks and policemen and her very own bodyguard, who could kill most people with his pinky, so you don't worry about her. Right now we need you, and very shortly you're going to get a visit from the Dallas PD, and they're going to take you in for us and keep you safe until we get there."

"Yeah?"

"Yes," he corrected me. "So I suggest you sit tight and wait for them."

He was so full of crap. "Look. I really wanna see Susan and Daniel's house. I have a theory."

"Oh, I'm sure you do."

"Listen, Dane, I—"

The noise cut me off, something moving over the phone.

"Jory, you need to listen to me." Sam again. "I want you to just—"

"I can't stop now, Sam."

"You're just gonna keep doin' whatever the hell you think is right, aren't you?"

"Yeah," I told him honestly. "I hafta save Caleb."

"Jory—"

"He's innocent, Sam, I know he is."

"You don't know shit. You're just hoping that he—"

I grunted, cutting him off.

"Agent Calhoun wants to talk to you."

"Is he gonna put me in jail again?"

"No, Jory, what would be the point? You would just get out."

I chuckled and he growled at me.

"Jory," Sam's deep, resonating voice came over the line. "Tell me where you are."

"I'll call ya later. I just wanted you to know that I was okay."

"Hanging up would be a mistake."

I hung up and climbed into the back of the cab that stopped for me.

The ride was long and boring and when I finally got to the house I was antsy and close to being claustrophobic. I felt the same way I did after a long plane ride, like if I didn't walk around I would just snap and start screaming.

Standing beside the mailbox next to the road, I saw how lush and manicured the front yard was. There were solar panels on the roof, three Golden Retrievers playing together in the front yard, and two hybrid SUVs parked in the driveway. The front of the house was a wall of windows, and I saw someone moving around inside. The trumpeting barks from the dogs brought Gwen, Caleb's sister, out the side door.

"Jory," she called over to me, waving.

I waved back as the dogs continued to bark at me.

"Shut up!" she yelled at them, which—surprisingly—worked the first time.

I watched her closely, unsure of what to do.

"Come here," she motioned me close. "Hurry up, it's cold as shit out here."

So not the greeting I was expecting. "Hey." I waved at her.

"What are you doing here?" she asked, stepping down.

"I was in town for business and I thought I'd come see ya."

She let the screen door slam shut and rushed forward to hug me. "I'm so glad to see you."

"Me too," I sighed, hugging her back.

"Ohmygod." She jerked away, looking at my face. "You are not gonna believe this, but my folks are actually in Chicago right now."

I squinted at her. Was she kidding?

"I know—how funny, right?" She widened her eyes before turning back toward the house.

What about her brother? "Gwen?"

She turned around to look at me as I let the screen door close and then the kitchen door after that. "Yeah?"

"Honey, what about Caleb?"

"Oh, he's doing okay. Why?"

I just stared at her.

"What? Are you gonna see him while you're here too?"

I wasn't sure if she was messing with me or not.

"Jory?"

"What are your folks doing in Chicago?"

"Mom said they had to go see Dane about something." She made a face.

"What?"

She shook her head.

"Gwen?"

She let out a quick breath. "The business isn't going well, J. If Dad wants to keep helping other people go green, he's gonna have to either get a loan from Dane, get other investors, or get a partner. He doesn't like the idea of the investors or the partner, so I think he went to hit Dane up for money."

I nodded. "That's where they are? In Chicago, asking Dane for money?"

"Mom said they were going to see Dane and I'm not stupid. I hear what's going on, ya know?"

I didn't think she was stupid, but she was out of the loop big-time on this one. "So can I ask you a favor?"

"'Course," she yawned. "You want a mocha? I'm making myself one. Casey bought me a cappuccino maker for my birthday last month."

"Casey?"

"My boyfriend Casey," she giggled. "I only talk about him all the time."

"The paragon of virtue Casey." I smiled. "I remember."

She swatted my arm. "Jory, just because you're a huge slut doesn't mean everybody is."

Gwen Reid and Casey Mills had been dating for five years and they had, as of yet, never had sex. The whole no sex before marriage thing had me stumped, but I respected the choice if nothing else.

"So?"

I shook my head. "No thanks on the mocha thing, but do you think you could help me find all the stuff your mom has about Dane's adoption?"

She squinted at me. "Sweetie, all that stuff's in the safe, I'm sure, but… why do you wanna see it?"

"I just really wanna find the agency that put him up for adoption, because I think maybe the Harcourts had another child that I wanna check on."

Her eyes got big. "You think the Harcourts adopted Dane and somebody else?"

It was a juicy lie. "Yeah. I think maybe Dane has another sibling out there, but I can't even dig until I know the agency."

"Okay." She nodded "Let's go see what we can find."

I was led to her father's den and then directed to the safe in the floor behind his desk. Gwen knew the combination and once it was opened we found it the deed for the house, invoices for various supplies and merchandise, birth certificates, picture negatives, five thousand dollars in cash, passports, and an extra sets of keys.

"Sorry, J." She sighed. "I would have thought this is where it would have been."

"Can we check her room?"

"Sure." She yawned, locking the safe. "C'mon."

We climbed the stairs to the second floor and Gwen explained that to the right was her father's room. I looked at her.

"Yeah, I know. But my parents have always had separate rooms. My dad snores like mad and my mom does this freaky throat-clearing thing in the night. It's all phlegmy and gross."

I smiled at her as we passed his room and walked to the next one.

Susan's room was connected to her husband's through a door, just like at a hotel, except there was no lock on either side. Which made sense. Why would there be a lock?

"Cute, right?"

Big is the adjective I would have chosen. Susan Reid's bedroom was all wood floors and a huge four-poster bed done in what looked like mahogany. It was very dark and just a little creepy. The entire wall at the headboard of the bed was comprised of drawers.

"You want me to help you look for any paperwork?"

"That'd be great."

Gwen carefully went through drawers with me, but after a half an hour left me alone to go get another cup of coffee. She promised to bring me back a bottle of water. As soon as she walked out the door, I went immediately to check between the mattress and the frame of the bed. There was nothing there, but that gave me another idea, and I checked underneath all the drawers in the room.

There was nothing anywhere, and when Gwen came back, she told me that she could just call her mom and ask the name of the agency. She felt stupid for not thinking of that earlier, but she had gotten caught up in feeling like a detective, looking for a clue with me.

I explained that telling Susan would be a bad idea because then she would tell Dane and it would be a mess. I didn't want to alert him in case I was wrong.

"Oh." She smiled at me. "Smart."

"Where else could we look?"

"At her office?"

"Perfect, where's that?"

"Downtown. Why don't you go with me? I have class in like an hour and afterwards we can get lunch with Casey and some of my friends. Whaddya say?"

"Sounds great."

"Okay, lemme get my bag."

We left the rural area of Mesquite and she drove me back toward downtown. Apparently Susan had taken a job to help bring in some extra money, to help the business get back on its feet. She was working at a doctor's office as a medical transcriber and manager. The other nurses were happy to see Gwen and interested to meet me. When Gwen left, with orders to meet her right off campus at a really good restaurant that served great Mexican food, I agreed quickly. I was left alone in Susan's office with orders not to move anything. Her friend Nancy gave me a serious look over the top of her glasses, but I grinned and she broke down and smiled back.

Alone in the office, I carefully ransacked it, getting under every drawer, going painstakingly through the files in her desk. I was sure the file cabinet behind me only had the doctor's files in it, but I had to look anyway. When I went back out to the front, Nancy told me that I was right—the large steel drawers were full of patient information and I wasn't getting in there.

"What are you looking for anyway?" she asked irritably. "I'm not sure I want you going through her office without her permission. The more I think about it, the weirder it is."

"I'm just looking for some papers that pertain to my brother. She told me to come get them while I was in town because she's helping me run down a lead with the adoption agency."

"Oh." She nodded, going to a desk drawer and opening it up. "Then you probably need the safety deposit box key. She told me that someone would be by to get it, but she must have meant you."

"What?"

"Nothing. She's just been so scattered lately—I'm worried about her."

"Probably has to do with Daniel's business."

She looked over her shoulder at me before turning back around. "Oh, you know about that?"

"Yes ma'am."

She put a hand on my arm. "It's a shame, isn't it? Them having to take the second mortgage on the house just to get by."

"Her son will help."

"Darling, Caleb's been out of work for months, and Jeremy—"

"Yeah, but Caleb—"

"Will probably end up moving back in with his parents. I told Susan that if he doesn't get a job and pay some rent, she shouldn't let him."

Caleb was out of work before he was kidnapped. He hadn't told me that. "You were going to say something about Jeremy before I interrupted you."

"Well, yes—Jeremy's the oldest, right? He should be the one stepping up to the plate."

"And he's not?"

She winced. "It's not like he doesn't try, it's just.... He missed a promotion he was going after, he and Taylor broke up... he's just not in a good place."

"Taylor?"

"His girlfriend."

"Oh."

"So both her sons are in no shape to—"

"I meant Dane when I said her son would help. He can and will."

Her face brightened. "Will he?"

"Oh, yes ma'am."

She passed me a small set of five keys and squeezed my shoulder. "You'll talk to him, will you?"

"Sure."

"That's great. Susan told me that your brother just dotes on you. I'm sure if you ask him, that will go a long way to helping out."

I nodded.

"And especially now," her brows furrowed as she shook her head, "they need help."

I squinted at her. "Do you mean with just the business?"

She studied my face. "No, but if the business does well, maybe they will too."

Daniel and Susan's marriage was rocky? All the little secrets I was finding out.

"Now, dear, I have no idea what any of those keys are for," she told me. "But they aren't for the doctor's files." She pointed at a flat one. "I think that's the safety deposit box one. She banks at First United Credit Union, a block from us. But just call her and ask, and if she calls here, I'll tell her I gave you the keys."

I couldn't very well tell her not to. How suspicious would that have looked? So I just nodded, thanked her, and left. I just hoped Susan wouldn't feel compelled to call work for some reason. As long as she and Nancy didn't talk, I was fine.

The Credit Union was small and crowded with people when I got there. It was lucky, because the girl who helped me just took the key, walked into the vault, and came back hurriedly with the box. She motioned me to the cubicles behind her and sat me down before she put the box down. She left seconds later with orders to call her when I was done.

When I lifted the lid I found a lot of the same contents that were in Daniel's safe at home. Copies of birth certificates and some bearer bonds, their marriage certificate was also inside, and five hundred dollars in cash. There was also a set of two keys on a Tiffany key ring. It was the one that Aja had given out at the wedding in her gift bags. One of the keys was a large square-top one with the do not duplicate engraving on it. It looked just like the one I had for my security door at home. The other was a house key. I wondered why they were there instead of at her house with all the other sets I had seen there, hanging on pegs in the kitchen. There was nothing else in the box. I pocketed the key ring, locked the box, and called the attendant back.

Back outside on the street in front of the Credit Union, I wasn't sure what to do until I remembered Gwen. Maybe she knew what the key was for. As I walked back toward the office and farther, toward the campus—apparently sometimes Gwen walked to her mother's office and had lunch during the week—I turned my phone on and called Dane.

"Jory," he snapped at me, "where—yes, it's him." He sounded really exasperated.

"Hey, I gotta—"

"Jory, where are you?" he almost yelled but stopped himself.

"I'm on my way to—"

"I'm going to strangle you!" Sam roared into the phone." Where the hell are you? Tell me now!"

"I went to the Reid place and Gwen was there, so she let me look around and then we left and came into town to check Susan's office."

"You're at her office?"

"I was."

"Where... are... you right fucking now?" he finished with a yell.

"Don't swear," I reminded him.

The growl was loud and long and filled with frustration.

"Jory." Dane's soothing voice was like velvet. "Wherever you are right this second—stop."

"But I gotta find out what this key is for."

"What key?"

"The key I found in the safety deposit box."

"You found a key in whose safety deposit box? Susan's?"

"Yeah."

"And you—oh, Jory, I—what? Sure."

"Jory." Sam was back on the phone, his voice low and full of gravel.

"Hey."

"I have to warn you about something."

"What's that?"

"The Dallas PD is on the lookout for you. If they pick you up, they're gonna take you in on a psych eval, and that's—"

"Why? Why would they think I was crazy?"

"They don't think you're crazy, they think you're a danger to yourself and others."

"You told them that?" I couldn't even breathe.

"Look—"

I hung up and stopped where I was, leaning back against the wall, sliding down it into a squat.

He had told the police department I was crazy. All my life people had been saying it to me. And I could take the teasing just as well as anyone else but this wasn't funny, because he had told people when they caught up with me that I needed to be restrained, and I had issues with even the idea. Tied up in bed, tied to a bed... that was one thing. Sitting in shackles or sitting in a rubber room with a straight jacket on was not my idea of fun. I think it was especially scary since I always wondered if maybe it wasn't going to happen at some point. After my grandmother died, it seemed liked there was an endless number of people saying how weird I was, how strange, how crazy. I was delusional and disturbed, manic and incompetent.

Everyone always expected the worst of me, but not Sam. I thought Sam expected the best. But now I knew he didn't. He thought I was crazy too. And it hurt more than I thought it would until Caleb's face flashed through my mind.

Caleb.

Caleb needed me.

I stood up and headed toward campus to find Gwen. I walked down through the quad and saw her waiting for me right where she had said she would be. I was maybe ten minutes late.

"Hey." She smiled and waved. "I thought you had ditched me."

"No." I smiled back. "Just got hung up at the office."

She stood up and put her arm through mine. "Did you find what you were looking for?"

"No."

"Oh, I'm sorry," she said, leaning her head on my shoulder. "Maybe we should call Jeremy and see if he knows where anything is."

Her brother Jeremy, the oldest until Dane appeared out of thin air three years ago. "No, I don't think so. But I found a key—I think it's for a security door."

"Huh." She shrugged. "I dunno, babe. Maybe we should just call and ask her."

"Let's eat first, I'm starving."

"Sure," she said, patting my arm.

She had invited not just her boyfriend Casey but also three other friends. They all seemed nice, they all thought I looked like I could still be in college, and they all had suggestions about what I should have for lunch. I decided to go with Gwen's idea, since it was spicy.

"So, Jory," Casey said as the others started talking. "That's a cool name. I don't hear it a lot."

I shrugged. "Probably for good reason."

He chuckled. "Self-deprecation—nice."

"I try."

"When are you going back to Chicago?"

"Tomorrow probably," I told him.

"Huh. What are you gonna do after lunch?"

"Look for a building."

"I'm sorry?"

I pulled the key out of my pocket and showed it to him. "I gotta find out what this goes to."

He squinted down and took the key out of my hand. "I can tell you what that goes to—it's for an apartment building on Drake." He flipped it over and showed me a stamp on the back. "See the three letters, DGA, engraved there?"

"Yeah?"

"Drake Garden Apartments. I have some friends that live over there."

My eyes flicked to his. "Dude, you're seriously a lifesaver. You just saved me like a day of work."

He smiled at me. "Oh yeah? I helped you out?"

"Totally."

"You said dude."

"That's 'cause I'm the least cool person you're ever gonna meet in your life."

"I somehow doubt that."

"Wait," I assured him. "You'll see."

"Here comes Ty," someone announced.

And the way Casey turned, the breath he took, the way he sat up, I understood why it had been five years of no sex for Gwen.

All six feet, two inches of Tyler Kincaid came around the table and put his hand on Casey's shoulder. His smile was huge, and then he looked at everyone else.

"What's goin' on, people?"

Everyone spoke at once. It was obvious that the gorgeous, blond-haired and blue-eyed man was the center of the group. He was the one that everyone liked, wanted to be with, or simply wanted to be. There wasn't room at the table for him, though.

"Here." Casey laughed. "Sit on my lap."

Tyler arched an eyebrow and everyone dissolved into peals of laughter except me. They should have just saved a lot of time and heartbreak and come flying out of the closet. Tell all their friends that "roommate" was a gentle euphemism for lover, and that they had probably been sleeping together since freshman year.

"You can have my spot," I said, getting up. "I've gotta go anyway. No time to eat."

"No, Jory." Gwen stood up. "Stay. We can grab another chair from—"

"No, baby, it's okay," I told her, leaning forward across the table to kiss her cheek. "I'll call ya before I go, okay? Maybe we can have dinner."

"Okay." She sighed, looking at me. "I didn't ask why you're all beat up."

"Long story," I groaned, as I got up and Tyler sank down into my spot. "I'll tell ya later."

"I'm holding you to that."

I patted her cheek, but before I could turn to leave, Tyler suddenly rose and stepped in front of me.

"I just got here and you're leaving. Why is that?"

I smiled at him.

"Can I give you a ride somewhere?"

"No, it's okay." I smiled at him. "I have to go look for an apartment."

"You're house-hunting?"

"Not exactly."

He wasn't sure about me, and it was there in his face.

I reached out to pat his shoulder. "Thanks for the offer, but—"

Before I could pull my hand back, he covered it with his. Pressing it into his arm. The muscles were hard and corded, and I wondered vaguely if I was supposed to notice.

"Let me drive you wherever you need to go."

"Ty," Casey called over to him. "Maybe Jory—"

"That'd be great," I said quickly, because it would be faster and I had a feeling I had very little time left.

"Good," he said, putting his hand on the back of my neck to steer me forward.

"Ty."

"I'll see ya later, Case," he called back over his shoulder. "You and Gwennie be good."

There was laughter from behind us.

As we walked toward the student parking area, I asked Tyler how long he and Casey had been sleeping together.

He froze in mid-step and stared at me.

"Aww, c'mon, man… gimme a break."

"How'd ya know?" he asked breathlessly.

"Hard to miss." I smiled at him.

He nodded slowly. "Six years, but it's not exclusive. I mean, how can it be? He has a girlfriend."

We reached his Honda Civic and I moved to the passenger side. "So why don't you guys tell everybody and then you can just be together?"

He got in and unlocked the door for me. "It's not as easy as it sounds."

And I was sure it wasn't, but I had no interest in hearing a story I had heard a thousand times. I was sure they were both expected to marry and have kids and probably had parents that would no longer pay for school if their sons came out and told them they were gay.

"Jory?"

"So what does Casey think you and I are doing right now?"

"Screwing, I'm sure."

I nodded. That was healthy.

"So how long are you in town for?"

"I have no idea. I guess it depends on what I find in the apartment you're taking me to."

"Whose key is it?"

"Someone I know."

"What if you find like a decomposing corpse or something?"

It was actually not far from what I had been thinking myself. "I have no idea."

"This is kind of exciting, huh?"

It was something. I just wasn't sure what. I pointed down the street because I saw the sign. "Is that it?"

"Yeah, that's it."

The sign for the Drake Garden Apartments boasted air conditioning, a 24-hour on-premises laundry room and a heated pool. After Tyler parked and we walked inside, I used the large square key to open the security door and we walked into the courtyard. The building was shaped like a U, with all the balconies overlooking where we were standing.

"So where to?"

I shrugged. I certainly had no idea.

"We could go door to door and try the key." He smiled at me.

Even running back over every cool scenario from all the TV I had watched over the years yielded no easy way to figure out which lock the key fit. I had no alternative but to seek out the people in the office.

"You should go," I told Tyler. "I could be at this for hours."

"Oh, no way." He smiled at me. "I'm intrigued. I gotta know what you're gonna do next."

"Then you'll help?"

"Whatever you need."

"Okay, c'mon," I said, walking back the way we had come in search of the office.

Five minutes later I left him by the pool gate, looked into the window of the office, saw the women there, and figured out what I was going to do. I ran back to Tyler and sent him alone into the office, key in hand, armed with what I felt was a pretty good story. I told him to flirt and he asked if I was high. I was actually feeling much more positive than I had in days. He was back in no time with a stunned look on his face and a yellow star-shaped Post-it note.

"What's wrong?" I asked him. "You look weird."

"I just can't believe that worked."

I scoffed. "Of course it worked. You're cute and you look harmless."

"Remind me never to lose the keys to my apartment."

I took the sticky from him. "This is it? Apartment 310?"

"Yeah."

"Thanks, man." I patted his shoulder, turning to head back toward the courtyard. "You were great. How did she know what apartment the key belonged to?"

"Apparently the three random letters engraved on the other side correspond to an apartment number."

"I didn't see any letters on the other side," I said, stopping to turn the key over, inspecting it.

He showed me where I should have been looking, and I saw the small letters that looked like they had been stamped on. I might have noticed eventually, but it wouldn't have helped even if I had discovered them on my own.

"There's no way you would have come up with 310 from those numbers."

"Nope, I'm lucky you were here to help me." I started walking again.

He followed me, close behind, and I could hear the amazement in his voice. "Your story was great. I did it just like you said. I told her my buddy gave me the key so I could crash at his place but he forgot to tell me which one it was. I told her I was really tired since I came cross-country in a Greyhound bus—"

"Greyhound bus is always a nice touch," I assured him, starting up the stairs on the side of the building. "I never leave it out."

"Jory, she bought it," he said, stopping and looking up at me from where he was on the first landing. "What the hell? That was scary."

I chuckled, climbing more stairs. "If everybody in the world always did exactly what they should, think how boring life would be."

"Yeah, sure, but I could be an axe murderer for all she knows."

"You look like you belong on the Disney channel," I told him. "You are all kinds of clean-cut, all-American goodness."

He stopped me with a hand on my shoulder before I could start down the hall on the third floor.

"What?"

"Are you by any chance into clean-cut, all-American guys?"

"I have a guy," I said quickly, moving away from him to check the numbers on the doors.

"He wouldn't have to know, Jory."

"He's a police detective," I answered distractedly, getting closer, watching the numbers ascend.

"So what?"

"He knows everything," I said, finding the door, stopping in front of it, taking a deep breath because here I was on the brink of my discovery.

"And if he did find out? What's he gonna do, kill you?"

"Yeah," I said, sliding the key into the lock, feeling how easy it moved, the glide of it. "And then he'll kill you."

"Knock it off, Jory. He's not gonna hurt me."

But I couldn't even concentrate enough to debate him. I was much too interested to see what was in Susan Reid's apartment.

I figured I would find something small. It was going to be an uphill battle for me to clear Caleb. What I got was more than I could have ever hoped for or imagined. Because in the master bedroom, where there should have been a bed or a chest of drawers or a nightstand or a chair, there were only walls covered with pictures and clippings of Dane Harcourt. There were long strips of paper, maybe two feet by five, thumbtacked to the walls, and on them were photographs of a ribbon, a card, some ticket stubs, and various other items—a cocktail napkin, a matchbook—all put together in a mosaic that was horrifying and stunning at the same time. It must have taken weeks, months, just to take all the pictures, and the patience to see a task like that completed was hard to imagine. That it had been painstakingly done was an understatement, and Tyler's low whistle of awe said all that I could not at that moment.

We walked closer to get a better look, neither of us touching the prints, just our eyes moving over the surface.

"Somebody's got a little obsession going, huh?"

Absolutely. "There's something weird about it, though."

"Weirder than it being here at all?" He chuckled.

"Yeah," I said, leaning closer, wanting to allay my curiosity. "Weirder than that."

His hand closed on my shoulder. "Don't touch it, Jory."

I couldn't figure out what was wrong, but maybe Sam could. I turned on my phone and dialed him.

He didn't greet me, he just made a demand. "Tell me where you are… please."

"I can't do that. I don't wanna psych eval or a straightjacket."

"Oh for crissakes, Jory, you know I would never—"

"I expect you, no matter what… to always have faith in me."

"Jor—"

"Everybody else can be surprised that I'm not dead or roll their eyes and be like 'dumb-ass Jory', but you… you're the one who's supposed to know I'm smart and good and not just someone else waiting to hear the latest stupid thing Jory did."

"You're right," he said hoarsely. "I'm sorry."

I took a breath.

"I think you're amazing. You are smart and sexy and I'm going out of my mind 'cause I can't put my hands on you."

He always knew the right thing to say. "Okay."

"Okay?"

"Yeah."

He growled. "Tell me where you are."

"I'm at the Drake Garden Apartments."

"And?"

"Apartment three ten."

Deep exhale. "Good. Lemme call it in. Don't touch anything."

"No, I won't. Tyler won't either."

"Who the fuck is Tyler?"

"One of Gwen's friends."

Quick, exasperated exhale of breath. "Dane and I are coming with an army of people, but so help me, if I do not find you sitting on the floor when I get there, when I finally do catch up with you—you will be more than sorry."

His threats did nothing for me. "There's something weird, but I can't put my finger on it."

"Define weird."

"I dunno."

"So you're already inside the apartment?"

"Yeah."

"How did you figure out which one it was?"

"I'm gifted."

"Christ, you really are."

I smiled into the phone. "I miss you."

Another frustrated growl. "Just wait, all right? Just stop… I need to see you."

"Just see me?" I teased him.

"Your brother is sitting in the car with me."

I laughed at how uncomfortable he was. "Sorry."

He groaned.

"I'll be here. Hurry up."

"Baby, don't touch anything. If you touch something or ruin evidence—then Caleb's screwed."

"I know. I'm just gonna walk around."

"Baby—"

"Hurry up," I said, and hung up.

"Jory?"

I looked at Tyler.

"Maybe I shouldn't be here, huh?"

I nodded. "Probably not."

"Call me later if you need a place to crash," he said, taking my hand, turning over my palm and writing his number in pen on my skin.

"Thanks," I said, patting his shoulder.

"For the record," he said, walking backward away from me. "You are seriously hot and a rush to hang out with, and if you wanna see me later, just call."

I had a man. What did I want with a boy?

"Did you hear me?"

I waved and started back through the apartment.

What was I expecting? So many thoughts ran through my head. Scenes from *CSI*, or *Silence of the Lambs*, even *Seven*. What was I expecting—a severed head? Perhaps nothing so dramatic, but the apartment was pristine and I found that strange.

In the smaller bedroom there were the same kinds of things that were in Sam's second, unused bedroom. Gym equipment and a computer and a twin bed shoved up against one wall. But if this was the place that guests slept and where the free weights lived, where was the furniture that should have been in the master bedroom? Walking back out, I went through the kitchen and found nothing out of the ordinary; the living room was the same. Somebody just like me lived there, and yet the wall in the bedroom and the lack of furniture spoke to something else all together. It didn't add up.

The bathroom was clean, but from the products in the medicine cabinet and on the counter and under the sink, a guy lived there. The bathroom had no feminine touches, but there were a few articles of women's clothing hanging in the closet of the master bedroom. There was nothing under the bed in the second bedroom, hardly any food in the refrigerator, and very little in the pantry as well. It was a bachelor pad, plain and simple, but whose?

I used my sweater sleeve and unlocked the sliding glass door that went out on the balcony. There was nothing out there but dead plants and wicker furniture.

"Freeze!"

Not Sam.

"Hands on your head!"

I did as I was told, and seconds later I was face down on the ground with my hands cuffed behind me, being frisked. When I rolled my head sideways, I saw the shiny black leather shoes.

"Mr. Harcourt."

I let out a deep breath. "Agent Calhoun."

"Take him to County now. Put him in lockup."

I didn't have a chance to say anything. I was half-carried/half-dragged down three flights and taken out the opposite way of how I had come in. The two officers that had taken charge of me complained back and forth that they did not work for the FBI but instead for the city of Dallas. I was put not into the back of a black and white, but in the back of an SUV. I was locked in and they told me to sit tight. I waited to move until they walked away.

I look helpless. I'm not a big guy, and when people meet me they think subdued first, until I open my mouth. So the two police officers had no clue who I was. So they didn't check to see if I had climbed out of the backseat and out through the driver's side door. The windows were tinted; I locked it after me and calmly walked around the side of the building and down the street. A block away, I ran. At least, since they had taken my phone, I wouldn't be in trouble for not calling Sam.

Chapter Thirteen

MOST people think I'm stupid. It comes with being younger than thirty, blond, and kind of an airhead. So while it's true that I have the attention span of a goldfish—oooh castle, oooh castle—I can actually use my brain for complex reasoning. I didn't go to the hardware store or anyplace else to get the handcuffs off. I got a cab (with handcuffs on) and asked to be driven to a store that specialized in adult sex toys. When I got there, I told the cashier that my boyfriend had lost the key for the cuffs we had bought the day before. She laughed, her manager laughed, the guy in charge of the viewing booths laughed, but the stock clerk got the bolt cutters and separated my hands before another stock clerk, coming back from break, picked the locks on each cuff for me. They were impressed at how real they looked as they tossed them into the steel wastebasket behind the front counter. I gave the manager a fifty and asked him to buy everybody lunch. He invited me to go line dancing with him after work, and I graciously declined before ducking out of the store.

I caught a cab to the Galleria and found a pay phone. I dialed my own number.

"Jory, goddamnit! Where the fuck are you?" Sam asked when he answered on the second ring.

"Do you have my phone?"

"Obviously," he growled. "What the hell happened? You were supposed to wait!"

"Ask Agent Calhoun."

"No, I know he—screwed up. He said… shit… are you cuffed?"

"Not anymore."

"Jesus," he deflated. "Baby, you—"

"I gotta get out of here, Sam. If I stay, I'm gonna get hurt."

"Jor—"

"I'll see you at home, okay?"

"No, it's not okay! I need to—"

"I'm not gonna fly." I was thinking out loud. "They might be looking for me at the airport, so I'll drive or take the bus or—"

"No," he said flatly. "Just meet me at the hotel and I'll—"

"I don't want you to get in trouble for harboring a fugitive."

"Love, you are not a fugitive. The only thing Agent Calhoun wants to do is hold you for questioning."

"The way he talks—he scares the shit outta me."

"I know, but he—"

Aaron Sutter suddenly popped into my head. "Shit—I just thought of something."

"Baby, just please—meet me at my hotel. Dane and I are staying at the airport Hilton. I'm in room nine-twelve. Please—just be there."

"I think I have a better idea." Aaron had a private jet—he could send it for me, and would, I was sure, if I asked him nicely enough.

"No, don't call anybody else. Do not turn to anyone but me right now, it'd be a mistake."

There was no denying that the man knew me well. "But Sam, I—"

"Baby," he said, and his voice was like honey. "Please."

I let myself take a breath, and as I did, the sound of his voice seeped into me.

"Don't leave without me. I need you."

I let out a deep breath. "I'll go get my stuff and meet you at your hotel."

"I'll get your stuff—just go to the hotel. I'll call and tell them to give you a key."

"Are you sure you won't get—"

"Jory, just go to my room and wait for me. Please, I'm begging you."

I was useless when it came to saying no to Sam Kage.

"Tell me where you were staying so I can grab your crap."

I told him and hung up after he extracted another promise to meet me at his hotel. The man was determined to see me, and as always, my stomach fluttered just thinking about him. I wondered vaguely if it would ever change.

I SMELLED bad, I felt grimy, and so I took a shower after I was in Sam's room for an hour. When I opened the bathroom door a while later, stepping out into the room, I found him standing by the window. He still had his coat on, like he had just gotten there.

"Hi." I smiled over at him and I couldn't keep the sigh out of my voice.

He didn't answer, just crossed the room and grabbed me, yanking me forward, crushing me against his big, hard body.

I felt myself shaking but I was powerless to stop. It felt so good to finally be safe. He was warm and solid and his lips on the side of my neck felt like heaven.

"Look at me."

When I lifted my head, his mouth was on mine. It was a devouring kiss, nothing gentle about it, his tongue tasting me, claiming me. He lifted me off my feet and carried me to the bed, where he fell down with me still wrapped in his arms. I expected to be ravaged, but instead he straddled my hips and sat up. He pulled off his coat and scarf and threw them on the floor as he looked down at me.

"God, you look so good," I sighed, taking in the sight of him… all better, healed, back in one piece. "How do you feel?"

"Me?" He scowled. "Jesus Christ, J, you look like shit."

I tried to get up, to move away, but he held me down easily.

"Stop screwin' around, you know you're gorgeous. I just mean that you look like you've been through it and… Christ, I'm never gonna let you outta my sight again."

His eyes were so dark and beautiful. "Okay."

He grunted before he lifted my chin to look at my neck. "Jesus, baby, you're covered in bruises. How did—"

"But you still like me, right? You still want me?"

"What are you talking about?"

It took me a minute to answer. "I'm not pretty right now."

He lay down beside me, his hand reaching out to touch my cheek. "Jory, I love the outside of you, I do... you're beautiful and just seeing you gets me going. But honey, really... I'd never stick around if that's all there was."

I nodded, my jaw clenching tight.

"I love you, Jory. I love your good heart and your kindness and the way you bring out the very best in everyone you meet. I need you, because without you I'm empty and mean."

"No, you're not," I said, leaning into his hand.

He eased me back down onto the bed and kissed up my neck.

"I can feel your heartbeat right here, under your skin."

I felt my breath catch in the back of my throat. Just having him close to me was causing rippling heat to run through my body.

"You scared the hell out of me, again."

"I'm sorry," I said, staring up into his eyes. "I just knew that Susan Reid was the one who—"

"I know, I know, but listen," he said softly, his voice deep. "Don't go anywhere without me from now on. I'd love to be your sidekick."

I smiled up at him. "I think we both know who the hero of the piece is, Sam."

"No, I don't think we do," he said as he leaned over and kissed me, slowly but thoroughly, taking his time, his tongue exploring my mouth. It wasn't full of the usual heat and urgency, but I felt it sear through me just the same.

I whimpered when he pulled back.

"You need me."

"Yes," I agreed wholeheartedly, wriggling around under him.

He smiled suddenly. "What are you doing?"

"I'm trying to get rid of the towel."

"I can see that." He grinned lazily. "But baby, you are in no shape for me to—"

"Oh yes, I am," I assured him, grabbing his hand, sliding it down over my groin, just terry cloth separating our skin. "Does that feel like I'm not ready?"

"Babe," he said gently, "you—"

But I pushed up, shifting him off balance enough so I could roll over on my stomach and breathe.

"And now what?" he asked as his hands rubbed over my ass.

"Sam... please... show me you're all better. I don't wanna be the strong one anymore."

There was no movement.

"Sam?"

"You've been doing all this to try and protect me 'cause I was hurt."

"Yes."

"So if I'm better, you'll stop playing detective?"

Playing? "Now wait." My voice dropped low. "I've done pretty well to—"

"Shut up," he growled before he yanked the towel away, leaving me naked beneath him. "Guess what I brought you?"

"I'm sure I have no—"

"Don't move."

His weight was gone for only seconds before it returned. The sound of the cap opening let me know what he had retrieved from his duffel bag on the floor.

"You weren't worried about me," I teased him. "You just wanted to fuck me."

He grabbed a fistful of my hair and yanked my head back hard. "No, J, you want me to fuck you. I have been sick just thinking about you dead or raped or God knows what else."

I shivered, I couldn't help it. My brain understood that we were having a serious conversation, but my body was just processing the dominance and the strength he was exerting over me.

He let go of my hair and I pressed my face down into the pillow. I felt his slick fingers pressing inside my body and let out a low moan.

"I'm all better now, J, so you need to do exactly as I say from now on. Do you understand?"

I nodded, unable to speak, feeling his hands slide over my ass, spread my cheeks.

"You need to remember who you belong to."

"I know who I belong to," I whimpered, trying to move back into him.

He kissed the back of my neck, moved to my shoulder before he bit down and thrust deep inside me. I lifted my head and he repeated his movement.

"Sam...." It came out as a rasp of sound as his hand slipped under me.

"God... I missed you... I just got you back...." His voice had a catch in it, faltering at the end.

No comforting words could be given, as there was only heat, the familiar smell of his skin, and my drowning, aching response to him.

"I hate that I need you."

And I wanted to explain to him that what he saw as a weakness was really a gift. Most people never needed anyone.

"Jory...."

All that came from me was my panting breath, groans of pleasure, and his name spoken over and over again. It was all I could manage, my senses drowned in sizzling heat, his touch, and the primal sound of his voice. I was so happy, my body so ready, having gone so long without him. I had none of my usual stamina to hold my orgasm at bay.

He set a pounding rhythm that pulled a guttural moan from me. Filled and stroked at the same time, I felt the throbbing deep inside me, rising, peaking, my skin burning under his as I begged for what I wanted and needed.

His confession that he wanted to sink inside me, touch my heart, brought blood rushing through my veins, my muscles tightening all at once as the wave burst over me. I felt the jolts of pleasure move through Sam, his body shaking with them until his breath caught and it was my name that was called out. In that brief, white-hot, heart-pounding, flooded-with-euphoria moment… everything seemed perfect.

He lifted off me quickly, careful that I wouldn't be crushed, and I heard his zipper and then the jingle of his belt buckle.

"All done with me, are you?" I said, smiling into my pillow.

"Never done with you," he said hoarsely. "Flip over."

And when I did, he wrapped me in his arms and held me to his heart. I kissed his throat, felt his wildly beating pulse, and lifted my lips to his stubble-covered jaw. He slipped a denim-clad leg between my bare ones and smoothed his hand down my hip before pulling the comforter up over me. I was naked, he was fully dressed, and I knew without asking that he was pleased. His dominance was without question.

"You love this," he chuckled, his voice husky as he stroked my back, letting his hand trail down over my buttocks to the leg draped over his thigh. Hand under my knee, he pulled me closer, wanting just that much more contact, wanting me flush up against him so my groin was against the zipper of his jeans. "You love it when I overpower you."

I would cry if I opened my mouth. There was too much relief, too much happiness, all of it threatening to flow right out of me if I let it. There was a flood of emotion inside all the way back to when he was lying in the hospital bed. I would be strong for Sam, and keep it to myself.

"Let me have it, J. I know you're pissed that I wasn't strong enough not to get hurt. It shook your whole world and made you afraid, 'cause you hate the idea of being vulnerable, of having something taken from you." His voice was caressing, so gentle, as were his lips on my eyelids, my cheeks, on my forehead. "Here you let me back into your life and I almost go and die on you… your heart, that you take such pains to keep safe, I nearly annihilate every chance I get."

I swallowed hard, willing him to stop talking.

"Don't be mad at me anymore. I'm sorry I got hurt. I promise it'll never happen again. Just don't leave me. Don't ever leave me."

I tried to breathe, but it was so hard.

His fingers traced over my jaw and then he lifted my chin and bent forward at the same time. He reclaimed my mouth, kissing me deeply. I kissed back with everything I had to give, and he rolled over on top of me, pinning me under him to the bed.

"Goddamn, Jory… I don't think I've ever wanted you this bad." His voice was low, almost a growl.

"No?" I teased him, biting my lip.

He rose off me fast, rolling off the bed, fumbling with his belt, yanking and pulling at his clothes, shedding everything as fast as he could. I was chuckling as I watched him because he was so intent, and then I saw the scar and caught my breath.

"Oh, no-no." He smiled, climbing back in bed under the comforter, wrapping me up in his arms, crushing me against his chest. "You don't get to use my recent surgery as a reason not to do me."

I was shaking. I had almost lost him.

"I'm not pretty enough for you anymore, huh?" he teased me, his mouth on my collarbone, slowly licking and biting his way up from my shoulder to my jaw. "I'm disfigured."

"Sam," I barely got out. "You could have—"

"You know, instead of thinking about what could have happened, why don't you channel all that fear to passion and blow me—I mean… blow my mind." He chuckled.

I just stared at him.

"What?" He smiled wickedly, his eyes dancing.

He was unbelievable. He actually had his mind on only one thing.

"I don't know why you're looking at me like that." He continued to grin at me. "I'm not any different from every other guy on the planet."

I grunted, and he laughed as I pushed up against him to get him off me. He let me roll him over to his back.

His eyes were heavy-lidded as he stared up at me. "Come here."

I moved over him, lifting up before slowly lowering myself over him, seating myself as deep as I could, burying him inside me.

His breath caught and it was very sexy the way he responded to me, his hands clutching my hips, his body rigid under mine.

"Oh… God," his voice cracked.

"Tell me you missed me," I pressed him before I leaned forward to kiss him.

"You know I… oh… Jory…." He sounded like he was in pain as I eased myself up and down over the long, hard, slick length of him. "Your body is so hot."

I smiled, he moaned. It was exquisite torture and I enjoyed the plight of my willing victim. When he roared my name, fisted his hands in my hair to pull me down for a kiss, I rode the crashing wave with him, his senses momentarily flooded with pleasure that left no room for rational thought. He thrust up into me, pulling me down at the same time, his fingers digging into my thighs, making sure I couldn't get away.

"Jory!"

I smiled when his body went limp under mine, his groan making me chuckle.

"You're too cute," I sighed.

"Shit," he muttered. "I had things to say."

"Say them," I said, lifting off him, causing him to grimace and grin at the same time.

He patted his chest. "Lie down."

I snuggled down into his shoulder and he wrapped me in his arms, tucking the blanket around me. I never felt as cared for as I did when I was in Sam's arms. "So tell me what—"

"I love you."

"Why?"

"Because you're mine," he said, his thumb sliding over my lips before he tipped up my chin and bent to kiss me.

It was a slow, deep, sensual kiss that I felt slither through my entire body.

"Mine."

I was boneless in his arms, his warm skin and the hand stroking though my hair lulling me quickly into a very relaxed state. I was utterly spent and completely at his mercy.

"You know that, without you, I have no home," he said suddenly, his lips on my forehead, his arms tightening around me, plastering my body to his.

I willed myself not to cry. Sometimes the things he said were just too much. His honesty, the heat and strength of his words were overwhelming. "I really love you."

And there was no doubt that he did.

"Did you hear me?"

"Yes."

"Good." He chuckled, kissing my eyebrows, the bridge of my nose, whatever passed under his lips as I continued to lift my chin. "Now you gotta focus here, because I have a ton of stuff to tell you, and Dane's gonna be here in probably another five minutes or so. I just barely convinced him to let me see you alone, and Agent Calhoun is…."

I shifted against him and he made the contented noise I loved before he continued talking. It was no use explaining to him that my brain had shut off paragraphs ago. I drifted off and didn't worry about bringing it up. I was safe in his arms and that was all that mattered.

THE way Agent Calhoun kept glancing at me, I felt more like Jason Bourne than Jory Harcourt. He looked almost afraid of me. In some sense it was well-founded. I had broken out of jail, eluded him pretty well, and slipped through his fingers earlier in the day. When I had explained how I had gotten out of the handcuffs, he was especially amazed. Sam was really impressed that an excuse of bondage would prompt people to help me.

"Only you," he said, and his fingers trailed up the back of my neck into my hair. He couldn't take his hands off me. "People will do anything for you."

Which wasn't true, but the way he was looking at me I didn't want to argue with him.

"So your hunch was right, Jory," Agent Calhoun said slowly. "It looks like your friend Caleb Reid is actually innocent and his mother is the criminal."

I leaned forward and looked at him, giving him all my attention.

"The knife we recovered at Mr. Reid's residence had his mother's prints on it and nothing else."

I tried not to smile.

"He finally confessed that he'd found out a few months ago what his mother and Mr. Fain were doing, and he was going to the police when Mr. Fain threatened to kill you. To keep you safe, he pretended like he was kidnapped, and when it went too far, he ran and was shot. He wanted to tell you the truth, but he had no idea what to do." He let out a deep sigh. "He's an idiot, but he's an innocent idiot."

"Isn't he still an accessory?" Dane asked Agent Calhoun.

"Oh, he's going to be charged with obstruction and being an accessory and—"

"But there are extenuating circumstances that will be taken into consideration," Sam assured me, rubbing my back. "Don't worry, baby, we won't let Caleb go to jail."

I nodded and looked at Agent Calhoun. "Whose apartment was that today?"

"Campbell Haddock."

"Who's that?"

"Apparently he was having an affair with Susan Reid."

"And where is he?"

"He's dead," Agent Calhoun said as his eyes rested on mine.

"How?" Dane took my question.

"There was a freezer out on the patio—did you see it?" he asked me.

I shook my head.

"Well, it was under a vinyl tablecloth and there were lots of potted plants sitting on top of it... I'm glad you didn't see it."

I nodded. "He was in there, huh?"

"Yes."

"How was he killed?"

"He was shot."

"And you think what? Susan Reid killed him?"

"The bullet came from her gun. Same bullet that came out of her son... the gun itself is missing. It's circumstantial, but coupled with everything else... it could mean a lot."

"Why would she kill her lover?"

"I have no idea. Maybe he caught her doing something, maybe he found her gun... we won't know unless she tells us."

"If she tells you."

"Right."

"So she killed those guys."

"She and Greg Fain."

"Why would he help her?"

"That we don't know, but we'll find the connection."

"Okay."

"Jory."

I looked at Dane.

"You should be very proud of yourself. You alone saved Caleb—you alone believed in him. He has you to thank for the rest of his life."

And I was happy for Caleb, so happy, but there was something not right back at that apartment. "What did you think of all the pictures on the wall?" I asked Agent Calhoun.

"Run-of-the-mill crazy, I'm sure they'll be studying Susan Reid for years."

And I was sure they would be, but still, something was wrong.

"God, I can't wait to go home." Dane exhaled deeply, and I realized from looking at him and how tired both he and Sam seemed that I had put them both through hell.

"I'm sorry," I said honestly, my voice wavering.

"How can anyone ever be mad at you when your heart is always in the right place?" he asked gently, smiling at me.

"Like this," Sam snapped, turning an accusing finger on me. "You ever pull any of those bullshit stunts again and you will learn the true meaning of pain."

I smiled at him as Dane chuckled.

"I myself hope you mess up," Agent Calhoun assured me.

There was no love lost there.

Chapter Fourteen

A DAY can make all the difference in the world. Two weeks can do even more. Amazing that just fourteen days later, I was safe and healed and completely ensconced back in my life. I was at work with Aubrey, Sam was doing the cop thing, and Susan Reid, not Caleb Reid, was sitting in a maximum-security psychiatric hospital for observation. It was all very normal, if you were me.

Dane dismissed Aja's bodyguard, they moved out of the condo and into their stunning three-story house in Highland Park, and he loaned his father the money he needed to get his business back on its feet. It was all he could do in the way of comforting Daniel Reid. He'd had no idea that his wife, Dane's mother, was capable of the atrocities she'd committed in her desire for vengeance. Somewhere along the line her love for her son had turned to hate. She was no longer speaking to anyone, so her true motive—the how and why of the crimes, why she had not just killed me instead of others—was locked in a vault inside of her. There was no telling when and if she would ever explain her murderous actions.

Caleb was out on parole and had to visit a psychiatrist and attend group sessions and perform an ungodly amount of community service, but he was free to live his life. He was going to work with his father and Jeremy, the three of them changing the name of the company from Reid Global to Reid and Sons. They would start over, and with Dane as their safety net and many new prospects, it seemed like they were well on their way to success. All wounds healed, with time.

I saw Caleb before he went home and he hugged me so tight and long that I finally started laughing. He did too, and when we pulled apart he leaned in and kissed me. I was stunned, and he just smiled sheepishly. He didn't want me to get any ideas about him, he just didn't know how else to express the depth of his feelings. I alone had believed in him and trusted him and knew his true heart. He loved me and that was all there was left to say. It started raining as I left the airport, and it felt like a blessing.

I could have lived in Seattle as much I loved rain, but I was in the minority. The constant gray skies, wet clothes, and puddles bummed most people out. The fact that it had been raining straight for a week and a half was taking its toll on the moods of everyone I knew. Half the problem, in my opinion, was cold feet. Your shoes got wet, so then so did your socks or nylons, and walking into work, your feet froze. What everyone needed were galoshes. I had a bright yellow pair just like I did when I was five, so my feet were never wet. Dane was certain that only gay men could pull that look off but I disagreed. Sam had an olive-green pair that I bought him and no one ever gave him any crap. Dane felt that had more to do with my boyfriend's size and muscles than anything else.

Whatever the reason, I got Sam into the habit of keeping two extra pairs of shoes at work. He told me that all the married guys had galoshes and dry socks. I was very pleased with him. But my goodwill had changed in the face of our constant arguing. It had all started with Aaron Sutter.

Sam wanted to accept Aaron's offer to have dinner with him because he felt that if Aaron saw us together, interacting, he'd get that we were an exclusive item that worked. I didn't want to go to dinner on that premise. I wanted us to go to be friends. Sam said that it would be a one-time-only thing. We'd eat and say good-bye and that would be it, forever. I found the whole thing immature and childish. He found it cathartic. I wanted no part of lording something over Aaron Sutter. Sam said Aaron and I needed closure; I told him to get over it. So Aaron kept calling Sam and I kept telling Sam no. We were at an impasse.

We were also fighting about my assorted gay friends. Sam liked Evan and Loudon, but that was as far as it went. And I knew why he was comfortable with them. Unless someone told you, figuring out that Loudon was gay was just like guessing about Sam. And because Loudon acted straight, he could deal with Evan being his diva self. So Sam was fine going out with them, being seen with them—the problem arose with my extended circle. My friends who used exaggerated lisps, made statements with their clothes or lack thereof, and who had adorable expressions for everything—including pet names for Sam and me. *The girls* they would call us, or *Jory and his girl*, or *the Diva and her man…* all this bugged the hell out of Detective Kage. The fact that my phone rang sometimes in the middle of the night drove him crazy. That I was needed to sit with someone or rescue someone or be there to offer a shoulder to cry on, all of this was beyond Sam's grasp to understand, or he acted like it was. I explained that because he was older than me, our friends were at different places in their lives. Most of his were settled down with kids; most of mine were still partying like rock stars into the wee hours of the morning. When I brought up our age gap, he asked me if I thought it was a problem. I replied honestly that I had never thought so before. He had no comeback and I had nothing else to say. It was something to contemplate, and we did so at opposite ends of the apartment.

It had been easier with all the breaking up and making up that we had done in the past to not consider the bigger picture of living together, and what the happiness and horror of that could be. Faced with the reality of trying to blend two very separate, very different lives, with people that populated both places… it was harder than either of us had ever imagined. The fact that we had moved in together the moment we got back from Dallas had been a spur-of-the-moment decision that I was beginning to regret. We had acted in haste, and it showed.

Sam's friends were doing the best they could with me. It was awkward. They accidentally said things like *that's so gay* when it was something bad, and then immediately looked at me and winced or flinched or muttered expletives under their breath. They never looked at Sam, only me. Like I was the only homosexual in the room. One evening I overheard two of his friends' wives saying that it was just a phase. Sam had been straight first and eventually he'd find a nice girl and settle down, once he had this "gay thing" out of his system. Like I was the flu instead of someone he loved. When I told him what had been said, wanting him to address it, he told me not to worry about it, that they would all come around. I wasn't going to hold my breath.

Being both stubborn people by nature, I wasn't going to give up Saturday night dancing with my friends and he wasn't about to give up dinner and beer and pool with his. So we had gone our separate ways, and I felt hollow inside all night long even as I forced myself to enjoy what I was doing. When I broke down and called him to tell him how much I loved and missed him, he acted like he couldn't be bothered. He was having a good time, not giving me a second thought, and there I had been, fretting the entire night. I hung up on him, turned off my phone, and didn't stumble home until after three in the morning. I didn't make it any further than the couch before I passed out.

Sunday morning he was gone when I woke up at noon, still in my shoes and jacket from the night before. I was hurt that he hadn't woken me, hurt that he hadn't moved me, and hurt that he had abandoned me so easily. When I called him it went straight to voicemail. I made sure I was gone before he got home. I had dinner with his family and he ended up being the one in trouble for not calling to say he was working and couldn't make it. I went to my office afterwards and then to Evan and Loudon's for late-night dessert. Evan scolded me for being a baby, told me to just get up the guts to make the first move toward reconciliation.

"What courage?" I asked him. "It's easy to be the one that gives in."

"No," he assured me. "That's the hard part."

Aja agreed with Evan when I talked to her on the phone.

"Don't cut off your nose to spite your face," she said.

"What does that even mean?"

"You know what it means. "

"Well, yeah, I know what it means, but what? I have to give in or I'm too stubborn for my own good?"

"Something like that."

"But why do I have to give in every time?"

"You don't, not every time. But maybe this one time or this first time you do or should."

I groaned.

"Don't be such a baby."

Which was exactly what Evan had said.

But I just couldn't back down or give in or let it go. It was juvenile and stupid but I played the cat-and-mouse game with him, with no end in sight. I took the silliness to a new low by rearranging my schedule. I knew he had to get up early to go to work and so I stayed at the office past the time I knew he could stay awake and still be expected to function the following day. I came home when I knew he would be gone, returning home to sleep and then get up late and shower. I worked for myself, so my time was flexible; I just moved everything around to accommodate the freeze-out of my lover. This went on for three days, into the following week.

So he was working late and I was not returning his latest phone call when my friend Tracy called me. He needed to bring a buddy to his self-esteem workshop because they were having group that evening and people were supposed to share with someone in the room that knew them. The idea was that a person from your life, a friend, could call bullshit on something you said. Only a friend could really say if you were telling the truth or not.

I tried so hard to weasel my way out of going to group once I knew what I was getting into, but by then it was much too late. I was good and stuck at the YMCA with him.

Group is exactly what it sounds like. You sit around in a circle and talk about what's going on in your life. In Tracy's case, he had to say what he did the week before that made him feel empowered. He seemed nervous, the way he was shifting around in his chair, doing that thing where he chewed on the inside of his cheek and squinted his left eye. I was squinting at him, and he interrupted his monologue about how he had not gone home with the first guy that asked him at the club on Saturday night.

"What?"

I shook my head.

"No." He took a breath. "I'm being taught that when I feel upset I need to confront the person immediately and find out the situation, instead of assuming it's all my fault."

"What do I always tell you?" I asked him.

He scowled at me.

"C'mon, tell me."

He rolled his eyes. "You always say that I don't know my own worth and that I shouldn't go home with just anybody—I'm special, they should be special."

"Precisely." I sighed, turning forward, stretching my legs out in front of me and crossing them at the ankles.

"Tracy," the group leader said to him. "How do you feel about what—I'm sorry, I can't read your name—is it Jordan?"

"It's Jory," I told him.

He smiled and looked back at Tracy. "How do you feel about what Jory just said?"

"I don't know. I know he means it, but I don't feel special. He can say it because—I mean, look at him, he's like perfect."

I shot him a look that I hope conveyed the full extent of my annoyance.

"C'mon, Jory, you know you are."

He was exhausting. "So are you. Do you ever—T, you are the sweetest, nicest guy with the best heart and—"

"Jory, nobody cares about my internal organs—they only care about the outside and outside… I'm not you."

I shrugged. "So what?"

"Jory, I go to the gym as many times a week as you and I'll never have your body."

This was so boring. "You need to meet somebody nice, not somebody at the bar."

He threw up his hands and turned to the group leader. "You see, always we go back to this."

"And what is that, Tracy?" the leader asked.

"He wants me to meet somebody nice, meanwhile he screws the entire city of Chicago."

"Is that true, Jory?"

I just looked at him. Marc, the group leader, seemed like a nice guy, easygoing, with a gentle voice. But I was not there to be psychoanalyzed. I was there to support Tracy. "No."

"Perhaps we have some of our own self-esteem issues to work through."

I looked at Tracy.

He looked back at me before his face suddenly cracked into a huge smile.

"You're such an asshole," I assured him.

He laughed so hard he fell over into my lap. Everyone was looking at us.

After the session, when everyone was hanging around talking, I was leaning next to the door waiting for Tracy when Marc and another guy approached me.

"Jory."

I waited for whatever he was going to say.

"We would love to invite you to join our group."

I nodded. "Thank you."

"So we meet every—"

"Oh no, I'm not gonna come." I smiled at them, moving off the wall as Tracy started toward me. "It's just nice that you invited me. Excuse me."

I stepped by them and Tracy smiled before he put an arm around my neck, pulling me in close.

"Thanks for coming, J, you were a really good sport."

I grunted.

"I didn't mean to embarrass you."

"You didn't." I yawned, giving him a brief hug before shoving him back away from me. "But for the record, it's just me and Sam now, okay?"

"It is?"

"Yeah. I'll have you over for dinner so you can really meet him."

"That'd be great."

I smiled, then gave him a pat on the shoulder before I turned to leave. I was on the street heading toward the subway when I heard my name called. When I looked around, I saw Aaron Sutter standing beside his car, in the rain, under an umbrella. I jogged over to him and when I was close enough, he reached for the lapel of my peacoat and yanked me forward.

"Hi." I smiled at him, running my hands through my wet hair. "What are you doing here?"

He just stared at me, at my face, absorbing me with his eyes.

"Aaron?"

He dropped the umbrella, put his hands on my face, and kissed me. It was so spontaneous, like he never was, that it caught me off guard. He usually asked if something was okay or not, announced all his intentions, and received permission or not. That he was just suddenly kissing me, on the street, out of the blue, his tongue sliding over my lips seeking entrance… it was a shock.

"Aaron." I said his name as I took hold of his wrists and pulled his hands off me. I took a step back before he could recover. "What's going on?"

"Jory," he sighed, his eyes soft. "I'm sorry for everything. I'm sorry all the way back to the first time I took you to bed and was careful instead of how I really wanted to be. I'm sorry for not telling you everything I was ever thinking, and I'm sorry for ever making you feel like you were less than perfect just the way you are." He smiled quickly, bit his lip before raking his hair back from his face. "See, I want you back, and I'll do whatever you want to make that happen."

All I could do was stare at him.

"I should have told you that all I did when I was away was think about you. I mean, I missed talking to you and laughing with you and arguing with you and being in bed with you and just all of it. You make my life fun, you make me laugh at myself, and you infuse my house with this warmth that is just gone now. I mean, even my butler misses you. He told me I wasn't such an asshole when you were there."

I laughed at that. I had really liked his butler; he was very sarcastic with a dry but wicked sense of humor.

He reached out and captured my face in his hands again. "Jory, I don't give a shit about anything else, I don't care if you fall down drunk every night we go out, as long as I get to take you home with me."

I took another step back from him. "What are you doing here?"

He looked at me oddly. "I just unburdened my soul to you and you want to know what I'm doing here?"

"Yeah."

His voice had a thread of chill to it. "I called Dylan, she said you were here giving Tracy support."

I nodded.

"Could you please respond to what I just said to you?"

I took another step away from him. "I appreciate what you said and I'm flattered, but you and I are over as anything else but friends."

"Jory."

"C'mon, Aaron." I squinted at him. "You know that."

"Jory—"

"If you really look at us… you know I'm not the one for you."

His eyes were scared. "Come home and talk to me."

One more step back and I was successfully out of arm's reach. "I can't do that, you know I can't. There's no way."

His entire expression hardened. "Why? Because of that detective? How does he rate a second chance but I don't? I didn't leave you for years and then just show up one day out of the blue. I never had you take a bullet for me! I never hurt you the way he did!"

"Because you can't," I said, because it was better that he knew so he could be done with me.

"What?"

"You could never hurt me the same way he could."

And we were both silent, letting my words seep in, and he saw suddenly the size of the chasm between us. I had to make him see it so he understood that there was no way to get back across.

He took a breath through his nose, stood rod-straight, and looked at me with flat eyes. "I could never hurt you like that because you never loved me enough to let it."

I nodded slowly.

"God, Jory, you really love him."

"He's the only man I've ever loved."

And with that, he left.

He didn't offer me a ride, which was a relief, and he didn't look at me again. He just got back into his car and left me alone, standing on the sidewalk in the rain. There was no other way for it to have ended.

I REMEMBERED halfway home that I still had my cashmere trench coat at Dane's office. I was way too cold, soaked through every layer I had on, to catch the subway and not end up getting pneumonia. So I took the detour downtown to Harcourt, Brown, and Cogan. I still had my key card for the after-hours elevator and another for the front door. When I got off on the twenty-fourth floor, I went immediately to the glass door and knelt to unlock the bottom. I was surprised when it swung forward. Someone was dead. Dane would murder whoever had forgotten to lock the door. I was betting on his latest new secretary, Kristin. She had seemed perky when I talked to her on the phone and Dane had called her energetic. It wasn't one of his better compliments.

Walking by the front desk where Piper usually sat, I saw a light on toward the back. It wasn't in Dane's office, so I realized someone was burning the midnight oil. Maybe it was Miles Brown. I slowly took off my lace-ups, not wanting to track water across the marble floors. I would slip up behind the architect and scare the crap out of him. He screamed like a girl, and I knew this from the many other times I had taken years off his life by jumping out at him. It was a lot of fun. But when I started down the hall, I realized Sherman Cogan was in his office instead. When I poked my head in, he turned from where he stood beside the wall and looked at me. His smile was instant.

"Hello there, stranger," he said warmly. "Come for your old job back?"

"No." I shook my head, slipping into his office. "Just came for a new coat."

"I see—looks like you could use one. What did you do, stand outside for an hour?"

I shrugged, walking over beside him to look at the blueprints on his wall. "It's pouring out there."

"Don't I know it." He chuckled, looking back at the blueprints. "That's why I suggested to Melissa that she meet me here for dinner. We're going to the Chop House."

I nodded.

He turned and looked at me. "Would you like to join us? Melissa was just saying to me a few weeks ago that she never gets to see her Jory anymore."

I liked Melissa Cogan a lot—she was funny and smart and could talk to me about chili dogs and sports and four-star restaurants and the ballet all at the same time. "Not tonight, I feel like a drowned rat. But soon. I'll give her a call."

"Do that," he urged me, patting my squishy shoulder before looking back at the blueprints.

"What is this?"

"Project Miles is working on. I didn't feel like walking back and forth from my office to his, so I had the guys make me an oversized set and tack them up in here."

"From what, a digital file?"

"No," he scoffed. "Listen to this—those guys at Delmar Construction only had one hard copy, can you believe it? How do you have only one set of plans to turn over?" He rolled his eyes. "So I had Jill take pictures of the other set and put it up in here."

I went cold.

"Hilarious, right?"

I bolted down the hall to the office of Miles Brown, opened the door, and turned on the light. There on his wall was the exact duplicate of what was in Sherman's office, except the one I was looking at was in pieces and the other was in long sheets. And I was an idiot, because it had been staring me right in the face the whole time.

"Jory?" Sherman called out to me. "Buddy? You all right?"

The answer was no. I had made the biggest mistake of my life.

THE drive out to Glendale Heights gave me time to think and put things together and just breathe. When I was almost there, my phone rang and I saw that it was Sam.

"Hi," I answered quickly, distractedly.

"Hi? This is all you have to say?"

"Sam, I really don't—"

"So where is it you live now?" he cut me off sharply.

"Sam—"

"What? It's a legitimate question. I haven't seen you since Sunday morning. It's Thursday night."

"No, I know, but could we talk about this later 'cause—"

"If you wanted to know, if you cared at all, I'm at Hooligans with Pat and Chaz."

"Okay," I said, trying to get him off the phone.

"Where are you?"

"I'm on my way to Glendale Heights."

"For what?"

"To see Susan Reid."

He scoffed.

"What's funny?"

"That you think that you have clearance at eight o'clock at night to see someone under criminal psychiatric evaluation. You're a goddamn riot."

"Oh." I was deflating. As usual, I hadn't thought that far ahead.

"I'm curious, though—why would you need to see her anyway?"

"It's a long story, but I think maybe—"

"Look, I know we fought but this ain't the way to fix it. Ignoring me is not going to make anything go away, it's just prolonging the big blowout."

"Are we gonna have a big blowout?"

"Oh fuck, yeah."

"And then what?"

"Then what—what?"

"What happens after the blowout?"

"I dunno… God willing we'll have hours of makeup sex and then go on."

"Oh."

"Oh?"

"No, I just thought… I don't know what I thought."

"You thought what? This was the end?"

"I dunno."

"Oh for fuck's sake, Jory, can you stop being such a goddamn drama queen? We're gonna fight, we're gonna disagree, it doesn't mean shit. You're gonna hafta deal with my friends. I told Pat and Chaz—which is why I'm here, by the way," he clarified, "that they don't hafta kiss your ass—"

"Sam."

"'Cause that's my job, after all," he said, his voice deep and sexy.

"Sam."

He chuckled. "But they better be good to you, or we're done. So they get it, they like ya, they're just not sure how to bond, so we'll fish next weekend and see how it goes."

I wasn't sure I'd heard correctly.

"Jory?"

"Pardon me?"

"Pardon you what?"

"What'd you say?"

"When?"

"About next weekend."

"Oh, we're gonna fish."

"Fish?"

"Yes."

"Like with a pole and stuff—all day sitting outside?"

"Yep."

"Oh God," I groaned.

He chuckled and the sound rolled right through me. I missed him like crazy. "Baby, I know your friends like me, I just need to get comfortable with them too. I'll work on it, you'll work on it, and we'll go on."

"Jesus, Sam, you're such a grown-up."

"Somebody has to be."

I let it go. "I thought maybe you wanted out."

"Never want out."

"Okay."

"I wanna be in."

Already I knew where this was going. "Uh-huh."

"Like inside you."

"I got it."

"When?"

"When what?"

"When do I get my makeup sex?"

"Was that the blowout? I thought you said it was gonna be big."

"Fuck the blowout. I want you back in my bed tonight. Do you understand?"

"I understand." I sighed. "After I talk to Susan Reid. I'll just go out there and sit and wait. Maybe they'll let me in. I'm cute and nonthreatening. It could work."

"I cut you off earlier—tell me why you're going there."

"You're gonna kill me."

"Oh God, what," he asked me, his voice lowering.

"I think I made a mistake."

"How?"

"I think maybe Susan Reid is innocent."

There was a silence.

"Sam?"

"Oh fuck that, Jory!" he erupted with a roar. "That's bullshit! Can you please just kill the drama before it kills you? Why the need to create—"

"No," I cut him off. "Listen. The stuff in the apartment wasn't up in pieces, it was up in sheets."

"I have no idea what—"

"That's what's been bothering me all this time. It was too neat, but I couldn't figure out what was wrong. If you were gonna create a shrine to someone, why would you create it, then take a picture of it and print it out in long panels that covered a wall. You wouldn't—it would just be up wherever you started it."

He was quiet.

"Don't you see, Sam? That's why there was no furniture in that one room, that's why it made no sense—it was staged. I bet Campbell Haddock's bedroom set went to Goodwill or somewhere like that. It was so clean in there, I bet it was professionally done. It was staged, it was all staged to frame Susan. I have no idea why she's letting it happen, but she is by not speaking. So I'm on my way to see her right now."

"Wait," Sam stopped me and his voice had changed. He had slipped into his cop tone. "Turn around and go home. I'm serious when I tell you that it's past visiting hours and they won't let you in to see her without cause and definitely not without her lawyer. It needs to be set up, so let me do that. I'll call everyone and we'll go in the morning."

"But—"

"Listen to me just this once, all right?"

And I didn't want to do it alone, because what in the world was I ever going to say? "Okay—I'll wait."

"For once he listens," he groaned.

"I'll meet you at home," I said, and then thought of something. "Or if you want, I can come and join you and your friends at—"

"I'll see you at home."

"Thank you for listening to me and loving me even though I'm difficult."

The familiar growl that was just for me.

"I love you."

"I love you too baby... you kill me."

It was all I needed to hear.

AFTER I took a long, hot shower I called Dane before I started making myself some dinner. He wasn't sure I knew what I was talking about, but to humor me he promised to call his lawyer and see about talking to his mother. I told him I was sorry for being wrong, again, but as he wasn't absolutely convinced that I was yet, he said he would hold off on accepting my apology. If nothing else, he assured me, my heart had been in the right place.

I was in the kitchen making soup, having tossed together a salad, when there was a knock on the door. My hands were full and it was open so I called out the invitation to enter. I was surprised when Steven Warren, my next-door neighbor, poked his head in.

"Oh, hey." I smiled at him. "What are you doing here?"

"Well, I don't know if you knew, but Lisa and I moved to Downers Grove."

"No, I had no idea." My life had been much too busy lately to even be aware of what was going on around me.

"Yeah, so since I didn't really get a chance to say good-bye—seemed like you had a lot going on—I drove by tonight and saw your light on and figured I'd stop."

"Great," I said cheerfully, motioning him inside. "Come in—come in."

He closed the door behind him and stood there, looking nervous.

"Please, when you get settled, call me. I'd love to see the new place—bring a gift, see Lisa."

He nodded. "Sure."

"Are you hungry?"

"Oh no." He smiled quickly, putting up his hand. "I can't stay—Lisa's got dinner for me I'm sure. I just wanted to say good-bye."

"Thanks." I smiled at him, wiping my hands on the dishtowel before starting across the room to him. "I'll miss you guys."

"Me too." He smiled at me, and it was a strange smile, bittersweet.

I walked into him, wrapping my arms around his waist as I rested my head on his shoulder. His sigh was deep, content, and when I shifted to step back, his hands clutched me tight, his face buried down in my shoulder.

"What's wrong?"

"I just… there was always stuff I wanted to say that I never got a chance to."

"Like what?"

He shook his head. "It's too late."

I smiled as his hands slipped down my back, sliding up under my T-shirt. I heard the door click open at the same time.

"Who the fuck are you?"

I lifted my head and smiled at Sam. He looked like some angry Norse god standing there, larger than life, his face a study in fury. "This is Steven—you remember, from across the hall? He just came by to say good-bye—he and his girlfriend moved to Downers Grove."

He nodded, turned, and held the door open. "Better get going then. That's a long-ass drive."

Steven nodded, stepped back from me, and told me he'd call as soon as he and Lisa got situated. I made him promise to.

"Who the hell was that?" Sam roared at me once he slammed the door after Steven.

I was confused. "That was Steven, I just reminded you."

"What the hell was he—"

"No-no-no," I cut him off, pointing at his feet. "Are you high? Take off your boots—I don't want water all over my clean floors."

He growled and yanked off his hiking boots.

"Where are your galoshes?"

"Jory, why was that asshole in my house?"

"He came to say good-bye." I scowled at him, walking back into the kitchen. "Were you listening to me at all? I wonder about you sometimes… are you hungry? I made—"

But he was suddenly behind me, having crossed the room that fast, spinning me around to face him. I gasped, it was so startling.

"His hands were all over you!"

"He was just hugging me good-bye."

"And he needed to touch your skin to do that why?"

"I dunno, everybody does that."

"I know! I fuckin' hate it."

I scoffed. "He doesn't want me, idiot."

"I saw his face, J, he wants you bad."

"Believe me, I'm not what he wants. If he did, he would have told me, just like Aaron did."

"What?"

I talked way too much.

"J?"

"I… shit."

"Tell me what happened."

"Sam, it's—"

"Tell me now, please."

The "please" was never a good sign.

"J," he said again.

So I explained about my interlude in the rain with my ex. I left out nothing, even the kiss.

"Uh-huh." He nodded, his eyes hard.

"It doesn't mean anything, Sam."

"Only because you don't care. If he had his way, he'd have you."

"Yeah, but—"

"You need to stop being so accommodating to everyone. You need to learn to say no."

"I say no a lot."

"Bullshit."

"Sam, I—"

"You're way too nice."

"Sam."

"Like this asshole in here tonight."

"Sam."

"That guy—"

"Steven," I supplied his name again.

He growled. "That guy Steven wants you bad, and you're too blind to—"

"Don't get yourself all worked up."

"Jory, you need to be more careful. You—"

"Yes, dear." I yawned, smiling at him.

"Are you fuckin' listening to me?"

I leaped at him, wrapping my arms around his neck. "Not really. Welcome home."

He grabbed me, hugging me tight, breathing me in. "No one else can have you, you're mine."

"Everybody knows that, Sam."

"The fuck they do. You're too nice… everybody thinks they got a shot with you."

I tapped his shoulder and when he met my eyes, I gestured at the jar on the counter.

"Shit," he groaned, fishing in his pocket for a quarter. "Do me a favor; wrap your legs around me while I dig for change."

I chuckled as he bent and kissed me, rubbing a hand over my ass. I heard the quarter hit the many others already in the jar.

"Happy?"

"Ecstatic."

He grunted as he walked us out of the kitchen and down the hall toward the bedroom.

"And yeah to your earlier question," he said, his voice low and rough. "I'm hungry… but not for food."

"I picked up on that," I said, my body liquefying as he pressed me tight against him. "Kiss me."

He didn't have to ask me twice.

He ate dinner with me later, him in his sweats, and me in my pajama bottoms and T-shirt, and we talked while we ate. After dinner I sent him to the couch to watch TV while I cleaned up. He turned on the stereo instead, and Astrud Gilberto filled the apartment. It was soothing, and when I joined him I brought a hot mug of tea for him as well as myself. The afghan on the end of the couch looked warm and inviting, so I wrapped up in it before I sat down. I started talking to him again, but when I asked about his day I didn't get a response. Looking up, I found him gazing around the room.

"What are you doing?"

"Just taking it in."

I glanced around. "It's our apartment, Sam."

His eyes flicked back to mine. "Yeah, but it feels different when you're here."

I scoffed at him. "You don't need to butter me up, you already got what you wanted."

He scowled and I gave out a snort of laughter.

"What are you trying to say?"

He was silent a minute, thinking, and then his eyes once again rose to mine. "The best cops I know come home from seeing blood all day and suffering all day and talking to people on the worst days of their lives to homes where they're loved and needed. You don't even know how many times I think about you when I'm up to my eyeballs in shit."

I reached for his hand and his warm fingers laced through mine.

"Just coming home, walking in our bedroom and you're sleeping all warm and safe in our bed… I just… I can breathe. My home is a sanctuary now, and I won't give that up because you're pissed at me about something my friends said or because I hate the way… Stacy?"

"Tracy," I corrected him, smiling, putting my mug next to his on the coffee table.

"I won't give up my home because I hate the way Tracy calls me 'lover'."

"I told him I didn't like that either. The only one that can call you lover is me."

He squinted. "Yeah, don't call me lover. It's just lame."

I nodded, looking down at our fingers twined together.

"Look at me."

I raised my eyes to his.

"I don't love anything or anyone as much as you. You're my whole life."

I opened the blanket and climbed over into his lap. He held me tight, his face in my throat as his hands slid up under my shirt to my skin.

"You're freezing," he told me.

"I love you," I said back.

"I know." He chuckled, kissing a line up my throat to my jaw then over my chin before settling on my lips. I parted them and his tongue swept inside, kissing me deeply, taking his time as he opened my mouth wide.

"If Aaron Sutter ever kisses you again, he'll be sorry," he said as he broke the kiss, leaving me panting.

"He won't—we're done."

"Why?"

"I told him you were the only man I'd ever loved."

"That would do it," he smiled evilly before he kissed me again. He was so smug, but that was okay with me. Him knowing I loved him was a very good thing.

When I was wriggling in his lap, little noises coming out of me, shoving my crotch against his flat, cut stomach, he put his hands on my thighs to still me.

"Stop. I wanna talk to you about Susan Reid."

But I needed to connect with him, and there was only one way that I wanted to. "Sam," I breathed, my hands unbuckling his belt, fiddling with the snap and zipper. "Please."

"No, listen... we need to—"

"No." I shook my head, opening his jeans, spreading the flaps, my hands sliding under his briefs. "You, wanting me, loving me.... That makes me so hot, you don't even know."

"Jory... baby... I...."

I curled my cold fingers around his hardening cock.

"God." His voice was raw and deep. "I can't even think."

Which was what I was after.

I leaned over to the end table, opened the lid, and retrieved the bottle there. I would have to remember to collect all the lube that was around the house before we had people over. You didn't want someone searching for a pencil to keep score with and come up with a tube of lubricant instead. How would I explain that to Sam's father?

"What are you giggling about?"

"I don't giggle," I assured him, chuckling. "School girls giggle, men laugh."

He rolled his eyes at me, but not before he shoved his jeans down to his knees.

"Say something good," I said, my voice hoarse and low. I didn't even sound like me.

"Come here."

I sank over him, straddling his thighs, my legs folded up beside his hips. His hands felt so good on my suddenly hot skin.

"I want to have dinner with you every night unless either you or I have an emergency or something else, all right?"

"Okay." I agreed as I began gently pressing down into him.

"I like coming home to my home."

"Me too."

"It's not home if you're not in it."

My eyes locked on his. I watched his pupils dilate as he filled me up, and my spinal column turned to mush as he stroked a hand over me.

"Baby, you feel so good."

"You missed me."

"Yes, but not just because of… this."

His power of speech was leaving him with every second that I pushed down deeper.

"You… I…."

I smiled because I had reduced him to guttural muttering. I increased my rhythm, gentle replaced with jolting, quick motion, and his breath caught sharply.

"My sweet baby."

This, the litany repeated from whisper to yell. And I had the connection I so desperately needed.

Chapter Fifteen

I HAD to pee. I sat up in bed, and for a second, I had no idea where I was.

"Go back to sleep."

I looked down at Sam, who was on his side next to me. Seconds before I had been in the warm cocoon of his arms and now I was sitting up, cold, weighing the need to relieve my bladder against how icy the floors would be, how freezing the air in the bathroom would be, and how much bitching Sam would do when I tried to warm myself with his skin when I got back in bed.

"Or go pee already."

I grunted and got out of bed. I would actually write it down this time, the need to purchase a pair of old-man slippers. Socks just weren't going to cut it. There needed to be much more insulation between me and the hardwood floors in the middle of winter.

I whined all the way to the bathroom and all the way back, and I realized that I didn't even remember getting in bed. I had been so exhausted after making love to him the second time that he had probably had to carry me. Not that he ever minded.

"Where are you?" Sam yawned loudly, which brought me out of my head and into the present.

"I'm right here." I smiled, coming back around the bed, ready to dive in until I heard a floorboard squeak in the living room. "What was that?"

Sam went from groggy to fully awake in seconds. When he slid his gun out from under his pillow, I put up my hands in disbelief.

He glared at me, whispering, "Don't make a big deal out of it."

I opened my mouth to give him a piece of my mind, but he put a finger to his lips for me to shut up and went immediately to the doorway.

"Don't," I whispered to him. "Just stay here."

He shook his head. "It's okay, baby."

But I was terrified. My luck was not good lately. Anything could be out there, and I hated it when he went into dark rooms alone. I gave him a three-second head start and followed him. The front door was wide open, and that scared me to death. How did we not hear the door open?

"It's clear," he yelled out to me as all the lights in the living room and kitchen flicked on.

I pointed at the front door.

"Yeah, I know. Just—calm down. Sit on the couch and let me look around."

I did as I was told, feeling like I was in a horror movie where something was going to jump out at me at any second.

"I don't see anything," he called to me from the second bedroom before checking out the door that led to the tiny square of concrete that was listed as the "patio" when I moved in. All you could see from it were the other "patios" of my neighbors.

I waited for him, frozen on the couch as I looked from window to window in the living room. When lightning paled the sky, I thought I saw something move. My yell brought him, fast, down the hall.

"What?"

I pointed at the window that led out to the fire escape. All the others were much too high up a sheer brick wall for anyone to ever be in. Unless you were a vampire.

He darted across the room but stopped when he got there. "J, it's wet over here."

I felt the shiver slip down my spine. "Is it open?"

He turned to look at me. "Yeah."

"Shit," I said, getting up to join him.

"Stay there," he ordered me, throwing up the window.

"Don't you dare stick your head out there," I yelled at him.

I watched him decide, saw the muscles cording in his jaw, his shoulders tensing before he suddenly relaxed and closed the window with a bang.

"Thank you."

"Aww, babe," he said, walking over to me, putting an arm around my neck and pulling me close to kiss my forehead. "It'll be okay. I'll call it in—you'll see. Everything's gonna be fine."

I nodded, trembling against him.

OUR apartment was swarming with policemen. Most of them were wearing those jackets that said POLICE in bold yellow letters, but some were in ties and suits and those shiny black shoes, while others were in uniforms and hats with shower caps over them to keep them from getting soaked from the rain. The crime lab guys were there dusting and taking photographs, outside on the fire escape, inside by the window, and down on the street. Someone had been in the apartment, they were sure of it; they just didn't know who and there were no fingerprints to be found.

Sam spent his time between being on the phone and talking to Hefron and Lange. I was surprised that Patrick and Chaz were there instead of Chloe, and even more surprised when Patrick came and sat with me, not talking at all, just sitting beside me, shoulder to shoulder, stopping anyone from getting too close to me.

"Back off," he said continually.

It took hours, and I was nodding off when Sam came and sat with me. He put an arm around me and leaned me against his chest.

"How're you holding up, baby?"

I nodded.

"Jory," Patrick said slowly, drawing my attention. "Did ya ever think that maybe all Sammy's friends don't care so much that you're a guy and more about the fact that you're so goddamn young?"

I looked at him.

"Yeah. Ya missed that, huh?"

I turned my head to look at Sam and found him scowling.

"He's not that young," he growled at his friend.

"Oh, screw you, Kage." He shook his head, flipping him off. "You're the only guy in our group who's got a nice, young piece of ass."

"He's twenty-six, Pat."

But Detective Patrick Cantwell was already rising up off the couch. He reached out and ruffled my hair before sauntering across the room to talk to Chaz.

I turned and looked at Sam.

"What?"

"They all think I'm gonna leave you crying in your coffee 'cause you're old."

"I'm not—fuck you, J, I'm not old! I'm not even forty."

"No, you're not."

"I won't be forty for three years!"

"Two years," I corrected him. "You already had your birthday this year. You're thirty-eight."

He stared at me.

"What?"

"You remembered when my birthday was?"

"Of course… it was in August."

"I had no idea you—"

"You're twelve years older than me."

His brows furrowed and I got a growl. "I'm not old."

I couldn't wipe the smile off my face to save my life.

"Leave me," he muttered under his breath. "Never happen."

But I could tell from the way he was acting, from the scowl on his face, the muscles flexing in his jaw, and the way he was gripping his cell phone that maybe our age difference had him a little spooked as well. I couldn't have that.

"What're you doing?"

It was perfectly obvious that I was comforting him. My hand was in his lap under the blanket and my lips were pressed to his throat.

"Quit," he shifted uncomfortably, trying to push me away. "You're gonna give me a boner and I'm wearing sweats."

"You're not old."

"Thank you, but I know that already."

"You're the hottest guy I know," I said, slipping my hand down under the elastic waistband of his sweats.

"Stop before you—"

I bit his jaw lightly before I licked it better, moving my lips back towards his ear.

"Baby," he groaned, wrapping his arms around me fast, crushing me against his hard, muscular chest. "Stop—I can't put you over the kitchen table right now so… quit. I appreciate what you're trying to do, but my ego is not that delicate. All I gotta do is watch your eyes when you see me to know that I do it for you big-time."

I closed my eyes, surrendered all my weight to him.

"There ya go, just relax. I gotcha."

We sat together on the couch, me in his arms, my eyes closed, drifting in and out as he talked on the phone to Dane and Agent Calhoun and his captain and his partner and so many, many other people. It was four in the morning before he finally put me in bed. He kissed me good night, promised that he'd be right back, and tucked the down comforter around me. There was an officer outside our front door, two posted outside the front door of the building, a patrol car parked on the street, and another officer walking the halls of the building. No one was getting anywhere near me. I wanted him to stay. He had to go. He was going to talk to Susan Reid with Dane. I argued that I, too, should be there, but I had done enough. I needed to rest; it was all anyone expected me to do. I was really much too tired to argue.

I realized when I heard the front door lock that I was more like a prisoner than anything else. Scary to think that I was no more able to do as I pleased than Susan Reid. Hard to imagine a time when it wouldn't be like this. The last thing Sam had said was to concentrate on setting a date for us to fly to Canada and get married. I dreamed about that.

Chapter Sixteen

I SO wanted to know what was going on, but when I called Sam as soon as I woke up he didn't answer. I got Dane on the second ring, and he said that, yes, Sam was with him and that neither of them could talk. He hung up on me before I got out another word. It was just plain rude.

I checked outside and it was still pouring, still dark, and still overcast and gray. The police cruiser was there and I saw it through the rivulets running down the window. Outside the front door were two uniformed policemen. I told them I would make coffee and they were both very appreciative.

Walking around the apartment, I realized how cold it seemed, how shadowy. Maybe Sam was right; maybe moving back into his place was a better idea. Logically, I knew someone could break into Sam's apartment too, but before someone bought it, maybe taking it off the market and moving back in was a better idea. Dane had never understood how moving into a rental and selling the place Sam owned was smart. And it wasn't, I had just been too stubborn to agree with him. When Sam got home, I would tell him that I had reconsidered and that his place could be our place again. I just couldn't shake my feeling of unease, and I doubted that it would ever go away.

I delivered the policemen outside my door steaming hot mugs of coffee and told them that I would make muffins shortly, since I wasn't going to work. I had firm orders from Sam to sit my ass home—this was the note that I had awoken to on my nightstand. Apparently even if I tried to leave the apartment, I wasn't going anywhere—the policemen had orders. So I resigned myself to being home, called Aubrey, called Dylan, and finally Aja just to see what she was doing. She was dying to know what was going on as well, since she, too, was at home under police protection. I told her I was baking. She was doing conference calls. She won for more productive.

I took a shower after I watched TV for a while and delivered the muffins to the officers. I was creeped out, though and dragged a chair into the bathroom and wedged it against the door so no one could come in without me knowing. That was the very reason why I had a see-through vinyl shower curtain. Norman Bates was never going to get the best of me.

The hallway closet door was open when I walked out of the bathroom. I felt the hair stand up on the back of my neck. I bolted to the front door and out into the hall. The policemen looked at me like I had two heads. They did what I asked though, and came in and took another walk through the apartment with me. But just like previous sweeps, there was nothing. No one. I asked if they could sit inside with me and they agreed.

An hour later they had to change shifts. They went out, but not before pointing to the police cruiser that had pulled up on the street. They promised to send the replacements in. I was very thankful. When I closed the door behind them, I shivered hard. I needed Sam to come home or I needed out of the apartment. Caged was never good for me. Running, moving, either being so much better than just sitting around and waiting. And I was freezing, which wasn't helping my mood.

I went to get a sweater, and when I came back down the hall, something moved out of the corner of my eye. I turned, and there was a bird flying around by the ceiling. In the middle of winter there was a pigeon, now sitting on top of one of the beams in my ceiling. What the hell? I looked toward the windows; I saw that the one that opened out onto the fire escape was open just a crack. I turned and froze, standing face to face with Caleb Reid.

"Jesus," I croaked out, backpedalling before he raised the gun.

There was a knock on the door.

"Tell them you don't want them inside, Jory," he told me, his voice soft, controlled like it never was.

"Yes," I called out.

"Mr. Harcourt, do you want us to come in?"

"No, thank you," I managed to get out.

"Okay, then, we'll be right out here."

Fat lot of good that did me. Shit.

"I was in the closet," he said suddenly, smiling.

And I understood. He had opened the window to make Sam think he had gone out that way. Neither of us had thought to check anywhere else in the apartment after Sam did his initial sweep. And the police who had come had concerned themselves with the same window, the same path.

"I watched you sleep last night."

I felt my skin crawl, tried to control the tremor that ran through me without success.

"Scary, right?"

I nodded.

"I went out on the fire escape while you were in the shower. Sorry I let the bird in."

I was just staring at him, realizing that his pupils were completely dilated. He looked like he was on something, I just had no idea what. "Tell me what you're gonna do."

"Come closer, I want to look at your eyes. I never look at them."

My life depended on me moving forward, but I still couldn't.

"Where's your mother, Jory?"

"I have no idea."

"So you're an orphan."

"Yeah."

He nodded. "But not really… you have Dane."

I tried to breathe.

"And you're the only one who does."

Looking at him, I saw how empty he looked. Like he was all used up. I had never noticed it before.

"Say something."

"Like what?"

He stepped closer to me. "Why did he pick you?"

"I have no idea."

"You've never asked?"

"No."

"He destroyed my family, you know."

"How?"

"My dad—he stopped loving my mom."

"Why?"

"Because she gave away his son. He can't ever forgive her for not having any faith in him."

"They were both in high school. He needs to cut her some slack."

He smiled slightly, but it was bittersweet. "Yes, he should."

I waited for what he would do next.

"She wanted him back so desperately."

Every woman that ever met Dane Harcourt wanted something from him. Not surprising that his own mother was no different.

"And you, Jory, you're the reason he wouldn't. Why did he need his old family when he had you?"

The calm, controlled voice was way scarier than if he'd been yelling at me. I felt the goose bumps rise on my skin.

"He hates me—my dad, my mom... all of us."

"No."

He nodded slowly. "You're right, it's worse than hate. He feels nothing for me, for any of us."

Which was the truth.

"I thought maybe my dad had a shot with him—he didn't know, after all."

I was silent, not wanting to provoke him.

"He'll give him anything... it was so easy for my dad to ask for the money. Dane will do anything but spend time with him, or me. It's like he'd pay us to stay away from him."

Time required interest, which Dane didn't have. Caleb was right. Money was easy to get; sitting around just talking, hanging out, that was asking for too much. Dane only spent time with those he truly loved.

"And he never touches me first. If I never hugged him again, he wouldn't care. But you.... Just how soft his eyes are when you walk into the room... it takes my breath away."

It was a weird thing to say. It wasn't something a guy would think, it was something a woman would think... or an estranged mother.

I watched the tears slowly slide down his cheeks.

"And now there's Aja too. There used to be just you, but now she's here."

He wasn't really talking to me. I wasn't sure if he could even see me.

"I just wanted my life, Jory.... I wanted him back."

Crap. "Caleb?"

He looked confused. "No, Jory, it's me."

My stomach flipped over. He didn't think he was Caleb. Jesus, who did he think he was?

"I thought when I found him… since his parents were dead… I thought he would need us—need me. But he didn't. He didn't need any of us… because he had you."

When did he go from being Caleb to being whoever he was now? He had started out as Caleb but now….

"Why did you have to be there, Jory dear?"

Dear?

"Funny… you really are such a good boy."

He sounded just like… Susan. "Shit," I swore.

His head tilted like he was interested in what I was going to say, interested in what conclusion I would draw.

Holy crap. He thought he was his mother.

We stood there facing each other, him with his gun at his side, me ready to dart in the opposite direction of wherever he pointed the weapon.

"Why kill all those guys?" I asked him, trying to strike up a conversation.

"I didn't mean to." He smiled at me coldly. "I just—Caleb likes you, and he was supposed to help."

"Did Caleb do anything?"

"He called you after you got away from me."

"He didn't kill anybody."

"No—nobody."

"You're strong. They thought a man killed those guys."

"A man did."

I put it together. "Greg."

"Yes. Greg killed them, but when he found out about the detective—your man—he got cold feet."

I nodded. "You blew up Sam's car."

"I thought if I killed him that you'd be too overwhelmed with grief to do anything else."

"But he didn't die."

"No, and then you came looking for me, so Greg had to be there for you to find."

"He was somewhere else first," I put it together.

"Yes."

"You killed Greg's mother."

"And Caleb knew it."

So surreal to be talking to Caleb with him answering like he was his mother.

"He covered for you, grabbing the knife."

"Yes, he's stupid, but he's not a complete fool."

"Why would Greg Fain help you kill people?"

He arched an eyebrow.

"Please tell me."

His eyes narrowed. "His mother was a nun before she was raped. Who do you think bore the brunt of all her rage?"

Which answered my questions about why mother and son didn't live together.

"Who do you think was filthy and never loved?"

"I get it."

"Perhaps," he said, looking at me, "being an orphan is not such a bad thing."

"I'm not an orphan anymore."

"You're not going to be anything anymore," he said, raising the gun.

"Please don't, Susan," I pleaded, using the name he would recognize at that moment.

"I have to, I hate you. I want you in the ground."

I thought of Sam. I thought of Dane. My heart hurt. I could feel how tense my muscles were, heard the blood rushing like a train in my ears, tried to pull in air and found I could not. There had to be more. More love, more work, more time, more everything. I lunged forward without thinking, heard him yell from so far away.

His right shoulder exploded in blood and he screamed like a wounded animal as he crumpled to the floor in front of me. I went to my knees beside him, whipping off my T-shirt, balling it up before pressing it to the wound, holding it there.

"Mr. Harcourt, stand clear!"

But how could I? Caleb was looking at me with such wounded eyes.

"Ohmygod, Jory." His voice was shaky; I saw the color drain from his face, saw his eyes get glassy, the beads of sweat on his forehead. "Are you all right?"

I nodded before I was suddenly grabbed from behind and thrown backward onto the couch. I watched the two officers that had been outside move in unison, one kicking the gun across the room, the other with a shoe on Caleb's chest.

"No!" he howled as he was flipped over onto his stomach, his good arm twisted up behind his back. It looked rougher than it needed to be, more brutal, faster.

The two officers were on top of Caleb, holding him down, one pressing his face into the floor, the other cuffing him so tight, sitting on his legs. There was no way he was moving; there was no escape this time. I heard thunder in the hall before the front door was thrown violently open. More officers came through it, guns drawn, announcing themselves by yelling until they realized everything was fine. I heard that the scene was secured and was comforted.

I watched in a daze as they spoke into the radios on their shoulders, calling to tell whoever what had happened. I was eased to my feet, walked to the couch, and sat down. I was wrapped in a blanket before I was asked if any of the blood on me was mine.

I shook my head. "No."

They left me then as Caleb screamed my name. When I didn't hear it anymore, I closed my eyes and leaned back, letting the fear and cold and nausea roll through me. I couldn't stop shaking. I thought I had been cold before… turned out I was wrong.

THEY needed somewhere to take me. I didn't want to talk to anyone, so I elected to go to a hotel instead of someone's house. The room was checked, and double-checked, but I wasn't worried anymore. Everyone that wanted to kill me was in police custody. The officers that had brought me over were the same ones from outside my door earlier. The older one, Officer Fadden, had shot Caleb. He stopped me before I got inside and thanked me for worrying about him and his partner. I hadn't called to them to rescue me because I didn't want them to get hurt. Apparently they both knew it, and so did everyone else.

"Detective Kage will be here soon," he promised me, squeezing my shoulder.

I nodded, feeling like a zombie, and walked into the hotel room. A long time later I heard the bathroom door open even with the shower running.

"Baby."

I didn't answer.

The shower curtain moved slowly and I looked up and found Sam.

"What are you doing in here?"

"I have blood all over me... it's in my hair."

"Jesus," he breathed, yanking the shower curtain all the way open so he could turn off the water.

I was sitting in the tub, knees drawn up to my chest, hugging them to me.

"Baby, the water's freezing."

"Is it?"

"You let it run cold."

I couldn't really tell the difference.

He grabbed towels and effortlessly picked me up before sitting down on the edge of the tub with me in his lap. He wasn't careful as he dried me, going for fast instead of gentle. "How long have you been in here?"

"I dunno," I barely got out through chattering teeth.

"Shit." He sighed, standing up, carrying me out of the bathroom to the bedroom.

"I wanna move into your place. Don't sell it—let's go there."

"Baby—"

"Caleb watched me sleep last night after you left... I'll never feel safe in that apartment again."

He made a noise deep in his chest before his voice came out, hard and gruff. "As soon as they release the crime scene, I'll have movers there first thing, okay?"

I trembled hard and he threw back the sheet and blankets before he put me in bed, covering me completely, even my head. "I was so scared, Sam."

He didn't answer but I heard the jingle of his belt buckle, the thump of boots hitting the floor, the sound of fabric as it slid off his skin.

"You were right.... I should have been more afraid this whole time."

The covers lifted as he slid into bed beside me. His bare chest was pressed to my back, his arms wrapped around me, his face down in my shoulder as he eased my ass against his groin. Nothing sexual about any of it, just him wanting to warm me, hold me, make me feel safe. And it worked like magic, because with him I was bulletproof, and the heat radiating off the man was incredible.

"You're like a block of ice, J. I gotta get you warmed up."

I shivered hard, feeling his body heat start to seep into me. "I know a way to warm me up."

He held me tighter in his arms. "Don't tease me—just rest."

"Okay."

He cleared his throat. "When they called me…. It was a mistake to leave you."

"No. You had to talk to Susan. Tell me what she said."

"I will later."

"I thought I was going to die, you know?"

I felt him tremble.

"I didn't want to die, Sam."

"They told me you tried to save Caleb—ended up using your shirt to try and stop his bleeding."

"Is he gonna be all right?"

"Yes."

I was relieved. "Why did he come after me?"

"He was always going to. It was inevitable."

I nodded.

"You're amazing."

I ignored the compliment. It didn't seem like the time to give any or take them. "Is Caleb at the hospital?"

"Yes."

"He's not gonna die, right, Sam?"

"Right."

I was quiet, savoring his warmth, and he tucked my head under his chin as he hugged me tighter.

"Close your eyes."

I did, even though I was sure there was no way I could ever sleep again.

"I'll be right here. I won't move."

Which turned out to be all I needed to hear. Safe there in his arms, I was out in seconds.

Chapter Seventeen

SOMETIMES people try and make decisions for you because they feel they know what's best. I have an issue with this kind of thinking. For instance, two weeks later, when Susan Reid wanted me to go with her to the hospital to see Caleb, Sam and Dane made a decision not to tell me. Unfortunately for them, Gwen called me, told me what her mother wanted, and I went alone to meet her at the psychiatric hospital in Evanston.

We sat together, Susan and me, in the area just outside the heavy metal door and talked. I apologized for thinking she was crazy. I told her I would have sent her a card but Hallmark didn't make one for mistakenly assuming someone was a homicidal maniac. There was no flower that conveyed that sentiment either. She gave me a trace of a smile as I passed her a dozen yellow long-stemmed roses. They were for friendship, and she thanked me.

"Why did you do it?" I asked her gently.

She took a settling breath, the tears welling in her eyes. "I'd already lost one of my sons and my husband... I couldn't lose anyone else."

"But Caleb... he could have killed again. If not me, then eventually Dane."

She shook her head. "I don't know, Jory, I wasn't thinking straight. I'm still not.... I just... I lost my life when I gave Dane up, I just didn't know it."

I nodded.

"I was obsessed with getting him back, making him a Reid... I didn't think of what it would do to Daniel... or to Caleb."

"Sure."

"Caleb was always the most sensitive, so attuned to me, and when I told him... I think he felt like I'd been lying to him all those years."

I watched her face, the worry lines around her eyes and the shadows under them. She looked completely drained, the weight of the world just crushing her.

"And Daniel... he's asked me for a divorce. After so long, he can't even bear to look at me anymore. And I know it's my fault. If I had never given Dane up or kept the fact that I did to myself, taken it to my grave... none of this would have ever happened."

How could I argue? It was true on some level.

"Dane didn't want us, and that made Caleb angry.... I just had no idea that he had it inside of him to kill people. I never knew."

"They told Sam he has two complete and separate personalities."

"Yes. When he was killing those poor men... when he's Caleb, he could never do that. The part of him that is your friend, Jory—he truly loves you."

I knew that. The problem was that the other guy in his head wanted my brains splattered on a wall.

"They don't expect him to ever make a recovery. He's been this way far too long."

"So why are we here?"

"To talk to him. He asked for you."

"What will happen to him?"

They said that after he's released from this observation, after they determine his fitness to stand trial, then he'll be moved to a facility in Wisconsin, long-term."

"How long is long-term?"

"I suspect forever."

"I'm sorry."

"It's for the best. I don't want him to hurt anyone else."

"Can I ask you something?"

"Of course."

"Why were your fingerprints on the knife they found in Caleb's apartment?"

"He showed it to me once, had me hold it…. I had no idea I was being set up at the time. It's not a place your mind goes to when you're just chatting with your child."

"Sure." I nodded.

"Something else?"

"Yeah. Were he and Greg friends?"

"Great friends. I loved Greg too. If Caleb ever comes to realize that he himself killed Greg, that will probably kill him."

I wanted to comfort her, I just didn't know how.

Tears rolled down her cheeks. "Oh Jory, the way you're looking at me… my God, the capacity for love you have, for kindness. You're such a good boy, Jory. Your mother did such a good job with you."

I didn't tell her it was all my grandmother's doing. Annie Keyes had loved me fiercely and desperately with everything she had up until the day she died. My mother was gone; the only person she had left to love was me. I still missed my grandmother, and I wished she had been able to meet Sam and Dane. She would have been crazy about both of them, especially Sam. Stubborn and gruff were her favorite kind of people.

"Jory?"

"Sorry." I smiled at Susan Reid. "I zone out a lot."

She sighed, curling her fingers around mine. "It's scary in there. I need to let you know that."

"It's okay," I assured her, patting her hand before I eased my hand free.

She was comforted, and we rose at the same time to go to the door.

I had to empty my pockets, and when the door locked shut behind me after we were buzzed in, I had a moment of uncertainty. There were orderlies everywhere, huge, muscle-bound guys that squinted at us as we walked by. The guards at the nurses' station were armed with batons and the nurses moved nowhere without an escort. After we checked in, an orderly took us to Caleb's room. I was expecting a big room with a bay window; the reality was a tiny room with bars across a sealed pane of glass. There was no escape to be had that way. A breeze on his face would be a luxury for Caleb.

He was sitting in a chair when we walked in. On the desk in front of him was one of those 64 packs of crayons and lots of paper. My guess was that a pen was out of the question for the immediate future. There were books, thick ones that most people said they would read before they died. But Caleb had time now to take on all the great Russian novelists. In fact, all he had was time.

"Jory," he said, and I moved quickly into the room. My name was slurred, and that broke my heart.

"Hey." I smiled at him, moving to kneel beside the chair so he wouldn't have to look up at me.

His hand went instantly to my cheek, but it was like he didn't have control over it completely. It trembled and he moved it robotically, poking at me rather than the smooth glide of his skin over mine.

"Jory, what did I do?"

The look in his eyes... helpless, lost, forsaken. I couldn't breathe. I stood up and he grabbed my hand with both of his, his face imploring me for an answer.

"I'm not sure, buddy, but they'll figure it out."

"Don't go, okay? Stay here and talk to me."

Talk about what? How I still felt one way about him but feared him at the very same time? How Greg had made the car bomb that had blown up Sam's car, but that Caleb had been the one to plant it, since Greg was already dead? Everyone was amazed that I could separate the Caleb I loved from the murderous man that had nearly killed the love of my life... but I could. I had never actually seen Caleb try and hurt Sam, I had only seen him try and hurt me, and hurting me I could forgive. And it was funny that I could, but my brother could not, Dane having completely shut himself off from the Reids, dealing with his father through his lawyer, paperwork being the only contact the two men had. Dane, as well as Aja, had a standing restraining order for Susan Reid. Her giving him up at birth he could have cared less about. The fact that she had lied to protect Caleb and he had come after me, that was bad; but that he might have eventually come for him, thus putting his wife in the line of fire... this was unforgivable. I had consoled Susan with the promise that someday he would thaw. I had a feeling that when he had his own children, when he felt that bond, he might turn to her or his father and look for reconciliation. But until that time they would both have to wait and hope.

"Jory?"

Zoned out again; it was troubling, that. I looked down at Caleb. "I gotta go, buddy—but I'll come back."

He nodded and gave my hand a tug to get me close to him. But I couldn't hug him, I wasn't that strong. I patted his shoulder instead, and the sigh rose up out of him.

Stepping back, Susan Reid was suddenly on me, grabbing me tight, startling me a little with the ferocity and quickness of her movement. I was good and creeped out, there was no denying it.

"You've been better to me than my own son."

It was still no time for compliments, and I didn't want that one anyway. She was not allowed to be critical of Dane. I pulled free and stepped back beyond her reach. "I'll call you."

"Please," she said with a longing that made me cringe. Because we both knew I wouldn't. This was the end of the road for Susan Reid and me.

I turned and went to the door. What made me look back was beyond me, but I did. I shouldn't have. I told myself I would be back to see Caleb, sit with him, bring him books or paints—whatever you took to a hospital, whatever they would allow. When my eyes flicked to his, I froze where I was.

Caleb's eyes, which seconds before were liquid with tears, were now narrow slits of ice. His head was dipped forward just slightly so that he was looking sort of up at me, his jaw clenched, his face a study of rage. The hatred was etched in every line, in the slightest quiver of his upper lip, like he was ready to snarl or bite. I had no doubt that if the medication would have allowed him to rise, he would have lunged for me and strangled me to death right there in that room. I reached out and grabbed the doorframe.

"Jory?"

I couldn't even turn to look at Susan. I was suddenly terrified that every time I closed my eyes for the rest of my life I would see Caleb's eyes at that moment. See him rising at the foot of my bed every night, remembering his words that he had watched me sleep. He would become my own personal bogeyman if I let him.

I bolted from the room, not caring if it was weak or not. I went to the front desk, collected my things, and walked with the orderly, even though I wanted to run, scream to be let out. I kept my emotions in check, outwardly calm and unaffected, inside just churning as the door was opened and I was released from the padded side of the door that kept people in to the hard metal side that kept people out. I didn't stop until I was outside under the awning, watching the rain come down in streams. I took deep, gulping breaths of air, calming slowly, joyful with the knowledge that I could go and never return. I was free.

WHEN I was young, there would be those nights when I was scared. Things that went bump in the night, I was sure were coming for me. My imagination was boundless, and I was able to make even the most ridiculous terrors seem plausible. On those occasions, I was certain that I would not live to see the dawn. Into the nightmare would come some seemingly mundane noise—the cycling of the refrigerator, a barking dog, the flushing of a toilet—just something that would remind me that there was a world outside my paranoia. It was comforting and I appreciated it, and so when Sam called to remind me that I was running very late for his captain's wife's birthday party downtown, the note of irritation in his voice soothed me. He was annoyed at me, and that grounded me.

I felt even better when I got to the enormous hotel ballroom where the party was being held. There were lots of people, so I could blend easily into the crowd. I looked for anyone I knew, and when I spotted Patrick at the bar, I knew Sam had to be close. I leaned in on the very end and was rewarded with a view of my man. I was not the only one looking.

There was a cluster of women looking over both him and Pat. I would have waved to Sam to get his attention, but the hand on my back took precedence.

"Hi, Jory." Ersi Cantwell, Pat's wife, smiled at me when I turned my head.

"Hi there." I smiled back, leaning in to kiss her.

She gave me a peck on the cheek before sighing heavily. "My God, every time we come to one of these things it's the same. Do you see the vultures checking out my man?"

"Yes, ma'am, I do." I chuckled. "They seem interested in Sam as well."

She gave me a dismissive wave of her hand. "Gimme a break, they have no chance with Sam... Sam's gay. Patty, on the other hand...."

I gestured at the sparkling red dress that hugged her hourglass shape. "Sweetheart, in that dress, why on earth would you be worried?"

She was gorgeous. With her hair up in a ponytail, wearing sweats and doing the laundry, she was gorgeous. And now she was worried about someone snatching her man when she was all done up, looking like a million bucks? I didn't understand women at all.

"You are so good for my ego." She squinted at the women on either side of Sam and Pat now. When both men were led to the dance floor, I was surprised. I'd never seen Sam dance.

Ersi and I leaned on the bar as Stephanie Diaz walked up beside us. She looked confused.

"What?" I asked her.

"Are those your men out there?"

Ersi grunted.

"Why aren't you guys... oh," she said after a minute of watching Sam and Pat on the dance floor. Her face scrunched up like she'd tasted a lemon. "Never mind."

Ersi snorted; I couldn't hold back the grin.

"Wow." Stephanie whistled. "That is some bad dancing."

I pointed over at Chaz, who was dancing with some other woman I didn't know. "Who's that?"

"His ex-partner's wife."

I tipped my head. "She's cute. She seems to like Chaz."

She pinched me hard.

"Owww." I chuckled, turning to her as she leaned into me, her arm around my shoulder.

"She more than likes him, she always has."

I turned to look at her face. "Whaddya wanna do?"

"Kick the crap outta her, but Chaz would be mad."

We were silent for a few minutes, all three of us.

"You know, Jory," Ersi said distractedly. "Sam told us that you were worried we didn't like you."

I turned and looked at her.

"It's not true." She sighed. "We both like you a lot. You act like us... you act married... and we both think that's wonderful. I just wanted to tell you that. I know a couple of the girls think it's just a phase, Sam being with you and all, but me and Steph— we know it's the real deal. We can tell the difference."

I stared into her eyes and she smiled. When I looked at Stephanie, she had the same soft expression in her eyes. They both actually liked me—when had I missed that? My gaze returned to Ersi.

"Just so you know, okay, so we're all clear."

"Thank you."

"You're welcome." She sighed, looking back at her man. "God, I hate these things."

But they had never had me along before.

"Move," I ordered her, standing up and shedding my trench coat, suit jacket, and tie. I unbuttoned my dress shirt and took it off, as well as the cotton T-shirt underneath.

"Not that I don't appreciate the floor show," Ersi teased me, arching one eyebrow, "but honey, what—"

"Just," I gestured for the iridescent red satin shirt that she was wearing to cover the sweetheart neckline of her dress. "Gimme that."

"Jory, I'll look like a whore without the shirt on."

"You'll look hot," Stephanie assured her. "You've got perfect boobs, girl—show 'em off."

She blushed and took the shirt off, giving it to me. It fit tight, but that was okay. It was supposed to be open low, to show off my skin.

"Okay, girls—let's hit the floor."

Stephanie gasped, digging in her heels when I tried to pull her along with Ersi and me.

"No." She shook her head. "I don't look as good as you guys. I'm so fat."

"The word is 'voluptuous'," I assured her. "And baby, that ass needs to be shakin'."

She bit her lip.

"Sweetheart." I arched a brow for her. "It's disco."

She laughed, put her drink down, and squeezed my hand tight. They were both trusting me and I felt like I could fly.

Ancient disco songs are irresistible to me, and it is my belief that if you're truly happy and enjoying your partner—or partners, as the case may be—that nothing else matters. Bliss will wash away everything else. So even though at first my girls looked uncomfortable out on the floor with me, when I started to sing along with the lyrics, did the Travolta move before grabbing each of them in turn and spinning them out and then back into me, they started laughing. I saw them both start to get into it, watching me the whole time, their eyes sparkling with surprise when they saw that I could seriously dance. I bent backward, arching almost to the floor before slowly raising back up. I got pulled back close to them with a hand on the front of my shirt.

"Jory... honey... look at you move," Stephanie said appreciatively.

"Here," I said, putting her hands on my hips as I swayed them.

She sighed playfully and stepped into me. Seconds later there was a pat on my ass. Looking over my shoulder, I saw Ersi dancing behind me. I moved back into her and she stayed where she was and danced. Sandwiched between two women, I showed off, letting them see how fluid my body could be. Since everybody knows all the repetitive lyrics of the old songs, we all sang out the words at the top of our lungs.

I glanced around and saw Pat's eyes riveted on his wife as she writhed beside me on the dance floor. Chaz lifted his hand to me with a blank stare as his mouth dropped open. His wife with her head back, eyes closed, feeling the music, had all his interest. I pointed my finger around so he wouldn't miss any of the other appreciative stares on her. I saw the surprise on his face, and couldn't contain my smile. I turned my head to find Sam, but he was nowhere to be found. I wasn't worried, instead concentrated on grinding it out with my girls, all of us in tight front to back formation, hands all over each other.

Most straight men either don't like to dance or don't dance well. And even as I was aware that I was grossly generalizing, it was certain that the officers in Sam's unit and his captain did not. In no time the other wives and girlfriends abandoned them, preferring real dancing to either sitting it out or the simple plant your foot, slide the other over to it, and repeat. Women, as a rule, like to dance, so we had a group out on the floor three songs later, all of us being wild and freaky and just having a great time. After the DJ played his entire vintage disco collection, he got the Electric Slide going for old time's sake. Sam's partner, Chloe, came and danced right next to me.

After that Ersi and I did some club dancing, making it look pretty pornographic even with all our clothes on. When the detective came to claim his wife, he pointed a finger at me and promised that he was watching me. I got a slap on the back of the head as warning and a huge smile from his wife. I had put a spotlight on how hot she was, and got a kiss blown to me in appreciation. When I looked up to find Stephanie, I saw her leaning on the bar, her husband with a protective arm around her. Both women had been claimed, and I was pleased with myself.

"It's Jory, isn't it?"

I turned and found Sam's captain's wife. "Yes ma'am."

Her smile was shy. "Is the Hustle part of your repertoire?"

I gave her a wide smile in return. "Oh yes, ma'am."

She beamed at me as I took her hand and led her to the floor. As we started to dance together, the DJ, ever vigilant, put the song on. After that I went through moves that I had learned and was pleasantly surprised when the captain's wife kept up with me. The seventies were apparently her era, and the steps came rushing back easily. She dissolved into throaty laughter when I dipped her. Back on her feet, she hugged me so tight before leaning back to kiss my cheek.

"Oh Jory, you're delightful."

I spun her out and back as the next song started.

I excused myself to go find the bathroom a half hour later, promising to be back even as there were whistles and catcalls as the captain joined his wife. He squeezed my shoulder as I slid by him and we shared a quick smile before I bolted off the floor.

Walking quickly back from the bathroom a few minutes later, I was yanked hard into one of the darkened rooms. Before I could form words of protest, before I could even push back, I was pinned to a wall by an equally hard wall of muscle.

"You move nice," he growled, his mouth close to my ear, sending a wave of goose bumps down my side.

"Sam," I sighed, drawing his name out.

"Kiss me."

"No—stop," I ordered, terrified for him, trying to push him off me. "Get away before somebody sees you."

"And if they do?"

"Sam, you—"

"Look at me."

When I lifted my head, he bent and kissed my chin, jaw, and finally my lips. The kiss went deep, and I felt how excited he was as his body pressed against mine. The sound that came out of me, I couldn't stop it, and the mouth grinding down over mine was ravaging. He was taking his time, and even though I couldn't breathe, I didn't care. He put his hands on my face, holding me still, making sure I couldn't get away. My knees went weak.

"God, you taste good," he growled against my throat when he finally pulled back.

"What are you doing?" I asked breathlessly. "This is a work function, you're gonna get in trouble."

"For doing what? Kissing my partner?"

"Yeah. People will freak out."

"The hell they will. Every woman out there is thinking that if he moves like that on the floor, what must he be like in bed."

I laughed at him. "You're insane."

He grunted. "And all the guys are thinkin' damn... I wish I could move like that."

It didn't matter what anyone else thought; the important part was that I had obviously turned on my man. The way he was pressing against me, the way he bumped my chin with his nose, making me lift up so he could reach my throat with his mouth, the labored breathing, his hands under my shirt, sliding over my bare skin... all of it let me know that I was wanted, desired, needed.

"And some guys out there are wondering what it would be like to just once sleep with a man."

"Is that right?"

"Or more precisely... sleep with Sam Kage's man."

I closed my eyes and arched up into him, my skin burning up, aching to be touched.

"You are gorgeous and everybody wants you."

His hands were all over me, and I heard my breath catch.

"But you're mine... only mine."

I felt the heat in his words, the possessive growl that annihilated me.

"It was the first thing I ever thought when I saw you lying in the street."

My eyes snapped open and I looked up into his face, which I could just barely see in the darkness.

"I remember you were there on the ground with that stupid dog, and I thought... he's mine. He belongs to me. It was the weirdest thing... and it didn't make any sense, but that's why I followed you around and that's why I could never let you walk away.... I knew right then, right there, in the middle of the street, that you belonged to me... and that you were supposed to be with me."

"You did?" My voice was barely there. The lump in my throat made it hard to even make a sound.

"I did. I knew. I never felt anything like it before. I never had that reaction to anyone… that's why I had to see you and talk to you. When something happens like that, you hafta see what it is. You hafta find out."

"And what did you find out?"

"That you were the one."

I wrapped my arms around him, hugging him tight.

He pressed me into him, his leg wedged between my thighs, face buried in my shoulder, arms holding me tight. I was completely enfolded, and instead of it being smothering because he was so much bigger than me, it was bliss. I loved being held like I was everything.

"Come on," he said after several long minutes. "Let's go back in so we can say good night and go home."

I scoffed. "None of those people are gonna let me go home."

"That's bullshit. Pat took his girl and left, same with Chaz…. I get to take my boy home and go to bed too. Fair is fair."

I smiled at him. "Who was the girl you were dancing with?'

"I have no idea."

"You can't dance at all," I assured him.

"Yeah, no shit, that's why I don't do it."

I nodded, moving to walk by him.

He grabbed my arm and spun me around to face him. "Where were you before you got here? Why were you late?"

I winced.

"Oh shit," he groaned, his eyes narrowing as he looked down at me. "What'd you do, J?"

"It's what you did."

"What did I do?" he growled at me.

The furrowed brows, his deep dark eyes, the way the muscles in his jaw worked… all so usual, all to be counted on, depended on, his annoyance with me, the love that permeated it all.

"What the hell are you smiling about?"

I shook my head, my lips pressed tightly together.

"What?" he demanded, his hand slipping around the back of my neck.

"I just—I had a weird day, and seeing you… I feel better."

His head lifted, he was unsure how to respond. "Oh."

I sighed deeply. "How 'bout we go home and you cook? I'll make it worth your while."

He eased me close to him and nodded.

Back in the ballroom, several women came to grab my hands and lead me back to the dance floor, but Sam's grip on my shoulder was solid and unrelenting. I was not leaving his side for the rest of the short time we would be there.

"Whose shirt is this?" he said as we walked back to the barstool where my things still were.

"It's Ersi's."

He grunted. "It's sticking to you."

"That's 'cause it's hers, not mine."

"I hate it."

I pulled my trench coat on over it, buttoning up so I was covered. "Better?"

He just grunted at me.

"Are we going or are you just gonna stand there and scowl at me?"

In answer he walked me over to his captain, who complimented my dancing as his wife rose and hugged and kissed me. I wished her a happy birthday, as I had forgotten to earlier. She thanked me for coming and for the lovely bouquet of wildflowers and roses that had been delivered to her home that morning. It was stunning, she told me, the most extravagant that she had ever received. And I knew it was. I had used Dane's florist, after all.

"I just loved them, Jory."

"Well, Sam and I are so pleased," I told her, making sure my partner was included in her thanks, as his name had been first on the card.

She turned to him. "Oh Sam, I'm so happy that you finally brought Jory with you. He's simply enchanting, I just adore him."

"Everybody does," Sam said gruffly, his fingers sliding through my hair.

As we walked out, I looked at him.

"What?"

"Finally?" I asked, needing clarification.

His sigh was long and loud. "Whenever there was a thing like a Christmas party, or a Fourth of July party, or her birthday last year, or the policemen's ball, or whatever, she always asked me why I didn't bring anybody. I always told her that I wanted you to come with me but you couldn't make it."

"Oh."

"But it was always the next time and the next time, because the timing was never right and you weren't with me yet. I mean, you were gonna be, eventually, but still... I think she got the idea in her head that I was stalling."

"Which you were."

"Which I was."

"I see." I chuckled as he held the door open for me so I could walk out first.

"So tonight when she saw you and got to dance with you and talk to you, I think she was just so happy that you were real and not a figment of my imagination."

I nodded.

"What's the matter?"

"I just worry... I don't want your career to be screwed because of me. I don't want people to think about you as the gay detective. I just want them to know you as a good detective, as just Sam Kage."

"If they do, they do, J. There's nothing I can or would change about it. I get to take you home with me tonight and every night and that's all that really matters."

"Okay."

"And Christ, did you bond with Ersi and Steph or what?"

"I did, huh?"

"Oh shit, yeah."

"I'm really happy about that."

"You guys looked amazing out there together."

I smiled at him as he led me toward the parking lot.

"But I gotta tell you—the girls were hot, you were hotter."

"I think you're a little biased. Pat and Chaz would both say different."

"No, J, make no mistake… you were really something. I'll explain it to you when we get home."

From the low sound of his voice, I understood that his explanation would have nothing to do with words.

As we walked toward the car Sam threw his arm around my shoulder, and it occurred to me as I walked beside the man I loved that, without him, I had no home.

"I'm very lucky," I said, because I meant it.

"Me too," he said back, not really listening to me as he steered me around parked cars.

But I had to explain it to him. Explain that he was so brave to risk everything for love, because loving me had changed how he saw himself, had changed his relationship with his family and friends, had put everything he knew into question. He loved me more than himself, and that was so rare to find. I was still raw from earlier and realized that I was barely holding it together. I started to tear up, and Sam stopped suddenly and pulled me into his arms. He hugged me tight, molding me to him. I told him, as I did often, that I loved him and he said he knew, had always known, even when I told him I didn't. After a moment we walked on, his arm back around my shoulders, leading me like he always did.

In the car, when Sam's phone rang I told him to let it go to voicemail. I had a bad feeling about who would be calling him. And he would have not answered, but when he checked the number, he saw that it was Dane. I sighed as I watched him listen, saw his brows furrow, his jaw muscles clench, and his knuckles turn white on the steering wheel. I was in trouble. When he stopped the car in front of the building, I didn't wait; I got out fast, darting toward the stoop in front of his, now our, apartment.

"Jory, goddamnit!"

I ran faster, flying inside the front door and hitting the stairs fast. I heard him below me as I shoved the key in the dead bolt lock on the front door. Inside, I dropped my stuff on the couch, and flew down the dark hall to the bedroom. I stripped out of my clothes and ran to the bathroom. I clicked the door closed as I heard the front door slam shut.

"Jory!"

"I gotta take a shower," I called back as I turned the water on and got in, the hot spray hitting my face.

I heard the growl of frustration through the door, but he didn't come in. Apparently I was safe for the time being. But I had to come out some time.

When I finally opened the door, he nearly fell in on me.

"Hey." I smiled up at him.

"You dripping wet is not gonna distract me," he said, cupping my chin in his hand, raising my eyes to his. "Your brother said that you went to see Caleb, and his mother was there too... is that true?"

"Have you ever known Dane to lie?"

"I was just giving you an opportunity to talk to me. I don't doubt Dane for a second."

Shit, I thought. "Shit," I said.

His fingers tightened on my chin, his eyes boring into mine. "Please... never again without me."

I nodded.

"I'll make you something to eat while you tell me everything that happened from the moment you got there. Don't leave anything out."

After I changed and joined him in the kitchen, I got to watch the various emotions slide over Sam's features as I talked. When I ended with the way Caleb had looked at me before I left, he nodded as his eyes locked on mine.

"Did that scare you?"

"I just... I never thought that he could hurt me, but he could."

"He's sick, Jory."

Nice that he was trying to comfort me. "You know, Sam, when you contacted the families of the guys that Caleb killed... what did they say?"

"Closure's good, ya know?"

"Do they blame me or Dane?"

"People can't be blamed for the craziness of others, J. What would they begrudge you, your life? That's stupid."

I just stared into his eyes. What was I supposed to say? "Hey, why do you think Caleb went to Dane's apartment that night when he left the hospital? Why did he grab Carmen?"

"I have no idea."

"Just c'mon... venture a guess."

"Okay. I think he panicked. I mean, he was already planning on setting up his mother, but he thought that we had figured it out."

"You did figure it out. I was the idiot that saw more there than there was. You knew he was guilty, I was the only one who thought he was innocent."

"You thought the best of him because he was your friend. Just let it go."

I had no choice.

"It's too bad that Susan's last choice was a bad one."

"What are you talking about?"

"Well, if she had told Dane about Caleb, not gone to jail for him and protected you and Dane... maybe she would've had that chance with him that she was looking for."

"But she thought she had already lost Dane."

He leaned forward, staring at me across the counter, him in the kitchen cooking, me sitting on a barstool watching him. "But she still had you, and having you... she would've gotten Dane eventually. All she had to do was protect you and she would've had your brother in the palm of her hand."

"But she didn't."

"No, she didn't."

"Are you mad at me?"

"No," he said, passing me a plate with a very large cheese and ham omelet on it. "I just want you to get it finally. I want you to realize that you are not a superhero, you are not bulletproof. You need me to protect you, and I need to do it. All I want is to stand between you and the world... please just let me."

I nodded.

"You agree, but then you just go off and do whatever the hell you feel like."

But I had learned my lesson. I was tired of being scared. I would let Sam take care of me.

"So what?"

"Give me another chance, okay?" I asked him. "I promise to start making phenomenally good choices from here on in."

He squinted at me. "Who are you kidding? I just want you to let me know what's going on so I'm not blindsided and so I can be there every time to dig you out."

I let out a deep breath. "Absolutely."

He shook his head like I was exhausting. "You want salsa on that?"

"Yes, please."

I cleaned the kitchen as he went and collapsed on the couch.

"Oh, by the way," he called over to me. "I got a call from vice today, from a Detective Adams."

I turned from wiping down the stove and looked at him.

"Do you know who that is?" he asked, leaning over the back of the couch to look at me. His smile was sly and I had no idea what was causing it.

"No."

"Think hard."

"I have no idea."

He grunted. "What if I told you that his first name was Carrington?"

"Oh." I smiled at him. "You got it wrong. The detective's name is probably something else, and he was calling you about Carrington Adams. He was the guy that got out of jail with me."

"You mean he was the guy you got out of jail."

"Yeah."

"Uh-huh. Well, guess what, baby? That guy was a cop."

"No, he wasn't."

"Yeah, he was. Turns out he was undercover. He's a vice detective investigating several different pimps in the city and you got him out of jail."

It took me a minute to process what he was saying. "Oh shit."

He grinned at me.

"So he was never in any real danger."

"Nope."

"Oh shit."

"I think you owe like a dollar in the swear jar."

I leaned back on the counter. "So where did he... I saw him get on a plane."

"You saw him walk through the door to a jetway, you never saw him get on a plane."

"He must think I'm like a total idiot."

"Nope, he thought you were undercover too—maybe vice, possibly on a task force, but he was sure you were on the job."

"Hilarious."

"He said that Rego James is on his way to prison."

I nodded.

"He also said that you took quite a hit from him that day."

"I don't remember."

"The hell you don't, you just don't want me to get mad about something I can't do anything about."

Precisely.

"You know Detective Adams said that you were really brave and really hot."

I laughed as I came out of the kitchen, turning off the light as I crossed to the couch to stand over him. "I'm sure that's exactly what he said."

He put his hands on my hips and pulled me down on top of him, easing me into his lap. "Okay, so maybe he left out the hot part, but he did say that you were brave and that he felt like you would have protected him with your life. He was really impressed, Jory, he said it over and over."

I straddled his hips, pushing against him as he pulled my shirt off over my head and tossed it at the chair beside the fireplace.

"You did an amazing job with everything you know, I don't think I told you enough... you were really something the way you figured things out. I think I might talk to you when I can't solve something. Maybe you can help me with my cases."

"Don't patronize me," I teased him, loving the way his fingers were tracing my spine.

"I'm being serious," he told me, staring into my eyes. "But we gotta talk about this later."

"Why?"

"'Cause right now I can't think."

And just that statement and the way he was looking at me heated me right up. When he lifted me, stripped off my sweats, and then pinned me under him on the couch, his lips on my neck, his skin against mine, his hands sliding all over me, I wondered how I had ever thought of living without him. I wondered what I would have done if he had given up on me and gone away, as I'd told him to so many times.

"I was never gonna give up," he told me.

"What?"

"You just asked what you would have done if I'd given up."

"I guess I was thinking out loud."

His smile was gentle as he eased me forward. "Baby, I was never going to give up on you. You belong to me. You're mine."

And the possessive declaration was something I loved to hear.

"Lemme tell ya again."

I didn't argue.

Chapter Eighteen

FOR Michael, I had been patient. For Beverly, I was tolerant. For the sake of peace, in the spirit of getting along, I had stayed calm, kept a smile plastered on my face and bit my tongue. But now I was free. The gloves were off because the wedding was over. The bride and groom had retired alone to their lavish penthouse suite upstairs, while most of the guests were still enjoying the open bar that would be serving until midnight. Because the bridal party was supposed to be there in the morning, to have brunch with the newlyweds before they left on their honeymoon, Sam and I had a room at the hotel. I had watched the wedding from my seat beside his mother, but Sam had been a groomsman. It was this honor/burden that had started the whole mess.

Beverly Stiles, Michael Kage's fiancée and now his wife, had nine bridesmaids in her wedding. They had all been wearing dresses with diamond-cut backs that flowed in long lines of voluminous black fabric to the floor. What came to mind when you saw them was movies from the 1940s where the women were all elegance and glamour. It was like a fashion show instead of a wedding, and when Amanda Rinehart had walked down the aisle ahead of her best friend, the bride, there had been gasps.

She was a stunning woman, tall and graceful and oozing confidence that you could feel. With her jet-black hair pulled up into a French twist, her sapphire eyes and flawless, creamy skin, no one could take their eyes off her. She looked like a model, but I knew she had just been made partner at the law firm where she worked in Manhattan. And she could cook too. She was, Beverly said, a triple threat. She had beauty and brains and made her grandmother's Italian meatballs from scratch. Any man in their right mind would want her.

The bride had confessed to me before the first day of the four-day marriage juggernaut that she was worried about Michael falling for her best friend, as had every man she'd ever dated. I told Beverly that Michael Kage loved her and her alone. She did not need to worry. Turned out I was half right. Michael had made no bigger a fool of himself over Amanda Rinehart than any of the other men. Even Sam had noticed her, and was nicer than usual. I didn't like it.

When Beverly came to me the morning of the bachelor/bachelorette parties and asked if I could help her get the wedding programs reprinted, I asked her what was wrong. I had designed and printed them over a month ago, so the last-minute panic had me confused. It turned out that there was nothing wrong with what I'd done; the change had only to do with Amanda. She was insisting on walking with Sam.

"I'm sorry, what?" Dylan needed clarification again. I had told her twice and she was still looking at me like she didn't believe me. We were at our office later that same day.

"Beverly wants the programs reprinted because Amanda says that the best man is too short to walk her down the aisle." I repeated for the third time.

She did the thing where her eyebrows scrunched up in the middle. "Let me get this straight. The maid of honor is stepping down as maid of honor two days before the wedding because she doesn't want to be taller than the best man."

"Right."

"And the bride is gonna let this princess have her way?"

"Apparently."

"Are you kidding?"

"No."

"What's going on?" Aubrey Flanagan asked as she walked into the office the three of us had shared for the past year and a half.

So Dylan told her, and she gave me a funny look.

"What?"

"Who does she want to walk with?"

I arched an eyebrow for her.

"Oh, no way," Dylan chimed in. "The prima donna wants to walk with Sam?"

My shrug was my answer.

"The bitch is hot for your man," Dylan teased me. "Better watch out, Jory—the man used to be straight, after all."

I shot her a look and Aubrey started coughing. I flipped them both off.

That night, at the bride and groom's last night of freedom out on the town, the men and women had apparently bumped into each other. I hadn't been able to go as I was pinch-hitting for Dane at a dinner Aja was having for a visiting speaker on educational reform. My brother was out of town, so his wife had asked me to go with her as her date. Thus occupied, I had apparently missed Amanda's impromptu pole dance at the strip club, which met with thunderous applause from everyone in attendance at Michael's bachelor party. The lap dance she gave Sam afterwards was the talk of the table the following evening at the rehearsal dinner. It suddenly made sense why I had been attacked when he got home the night before. She had started his libido raging and I had been the recipient of his attention. Knowing that she turned him on did little to improve my mood.

The fact that I had agreed in advance, along with Sam, not to mention our relationship in front of Beverly's very Christian, very conservative Midwestern family was not helping matters. None of her family or friends knew what I was to Sam. No one had any clue that the rings on our fingers signified the wedding we'd had in Canada a year before, or that, as far as the city of Chicago was concerned, we were domestic partners. That Michael had agreed with Beverly that it was the best thing to do in front of her family had saddened me, but in the end, I understood. It was her day, not mine. Who was I to ask her to let me have my way? Why should my agenda top hers?

"So, Beverly will let this girl go from maid of honor to bridesmaid so she can walk down the aisle with Sammy, but you and Sammy can't be a couple at her wedding?"

I looked at Jen as she sat beside me at the table.

"Huh," she grunted. "That's funny."

Turning to watch Sam and Amanda slow dance with the other couples on the floor, I didn't think it was so funny. It was, in fact, the exact opposite.

Just the bridal party was invited out for drinks after the rehearsal dinner, so I went home and packed for the following night. Sam stumbled in after two with smudges of lipstick on his collar and reeking of Amanda's perfume. When he tried to grab me, I sent him to the shower. I found him a half an hour later, passed out naked with only a towel wrapped around his waist, in the middle of our bed. I covered him up and went to sleep on the couch. I was woken in the middle of the night, and my irritation slept longer than my desire for him. I was carried back to bed, and his kisses and his hands coaxed my anger right out of me.

I woke up there alone in the morning. He had more things to do with the rest of the bridal party and didn't want to wake me. He had made me coffee, though, and the note on the nightstand that told me where he'd gone was under a mug of it. I felt better until I got to the wedding.

Everyone around me, except Sam's mother, commented on what a beautiful couple he and Amanda made. And I knew that Sam's dad didn't mean to hurt me with his comments, he loved me after all. But there was, I knew, in the deepest, hidden part of his heart, the hope that maybe—just maybe—someday Sam would come to him and say that being gay was over and he was ready to find a wife and have kids.

"Jory."

I turned my head to look at Regina and found her smiling at me.

"Angel." She smiled, patting my hand as we waited to leave the church. "No one looks better beside Sam than you. The two of you make the most beautiful couple I know."

I nodded and squeezed her hand.

"Think about what your ring means to you. Going to a wedding, any wedding, should always make you think of your own and reaffirm your love."

Even if no one in the place knew I was married?

"It only matters what you know," she told me like she was reading my mind.

I felt better, even though Amanda spent the entire reception practically in Sam's lap. She danced with him and led him to and from the floor with her hand in his; she fed him things off her plate and laughed like a hyena over everything he said. When she caught the bouquet, since it was basically tossed to her, she begged Sam to go up and catch the garter. He flat-out refused, and no amount of cajoling or begging or whining was going to move him. He smiled when he said no, his eyes twinkled, but he wasn't moving. Married men didn't catch garters, and even though Sam didn't tell anyone at Michael's wedding that he was, in fact, married, he wouldn't have lied if he'd been asked directly. Denial was not part of Sam Kage's repertoire. When the best man caught the garter, Amanda took one shot with him before walking over and climbing back into Sam's lap. They took many suggestive photos, to the catcalls and whistles of the crowd.

"Good for Sam for not being a hypocrite," Dylan commented when I told her what was going on downstairs. I was in our room, changing, when she had called to check in on me. "I mean, the man is married, after all."

"Is he?"

"Jory Harcourt!" she yelled over the phone. "That's a terrible thing to say! Of course he's married! He's married to you! I was there when you guys exchanged your really weird really sweet vows."

I laughed, remembering Sam and me standing in front of everyone and the justice of the peace in Toronto. I told him that I would love him forever and I would stick like glue no matter what. His smile, the look in his eyes, told me everything, even before he promised to use the swear jar for our kids' college fund, to never let me get away from him again, and to love me until he was dead. It was a little maudlin, but Dane said "okay" really loud and everyone laughed before Sam grabbed me and kissed me breathless.

"Don't be a drama queen, okay, Jory? Sam loves you desperately. You just need to go back down to the party and remind him that this woman, this Amanda whoever, ain't got nothing on you. I've seen you all dressed up, my friend… even my husband thinks you're hot."

I couldn't hold in the laughter. Leave it to my best friend to jolt me out of feeling sorry for myself. I was really very lucky. "Yeah? Chris thinks I'm hot?"

"Chris," she called out, "come tell Jory you think he's a sexy piece of ass."

I lost it completely. She was a mother, for God's sake.

Everyone that was staying overnight had moved to the bar by the time I got back downstairs. The bridal party was still drinking, along with some family members, friends, and various stragglers. They were all sitting toward the back, all still in their wedding finery, bridesmaid's dresses, tuxedos, suits, and gowns from the formal affair, definitely showing signs that the festivities were coming to an end. High heels had come off, ties were discarded, and shirttails were hanging out. It was about comfort, since no one but me had left to shower and change. I walked to the bar, ordered a snifter of brandy—it was late after all—and then walked over to the table where Sam was.

"Jory," Sam's cousin Joe greeted me drunkenly, taking my hand the way he always did. The Kages were a big touchy-feely group. "I was wondering where you were."

Sam's head turned from talking to Amanda and his eyes hit mine.

"Hey." I smiled at him, taking a sip of my drink.

He looked me up and down before he rose and moved out of the cluster of chairs around the table to stand in front of me.

"I was thinking I'd go out while you stay here and hang with everyone."

He took the snifter from me and took a sip of the brandy as he stared down into my eyes.

"Okay?"

Slight shake of his head as he passed me back the glass. I took another sip and licked my lips. It was really good brandy.

"Sam, come sit down," Amanda called over to him.

His eyes were on my mouth and he said something.

I had to lean closer because I could barely hear him. "Sorry?"

"I said I didn't get to tell you how good you looked in your suit before."

"Oh, thanks."

"Every time I got over to your table, you were off dancing with another one of my cousins."

"You've got a lot of cousins," I teased him.

His smile was slow, lazy, and very sexy. "And they all liked you."

"Those nice Catholic girls from New York are scary, Sam."

He chuckled. "Oh baby, I know."

"So you liked the suit?" I fished.

"I did. I wanted to see it come off."

I smiled at him. "Maybe I'll just go up to the room and wait for you."

"No waiting necessary," he said gruffly, taking the glass out of my hand and setting it down on the table before taking hold of my hand. "Night, everybody."

He tugged me out of the bar after him and then to the elevator in the lobby.

I chuckled.

"What?" he growled at me.

"Why are you all mad?"

He gestured at me like I was nuts. "I'm not mad, but look how you're dressed to come down to the bar? What were you thinking?"

I was in a pocket T-shirt and old, faded jeans, I didn't see the problem. "How am I dressed?"

"And you're all clean and… your hair's wet."

"Which has what to do with anything?"

The muscles in his jaw clenched as he squeezed my hand.

"You can stay down here if you want. I didn't come down here to rush—"

"You're being such an ass," he said, shoving me into the elevator as soon as it opened.

Before the doors could close, there was a hand to stop them. Amanda was there, along with three other women.

"Sam, where are you going?" She laughed and the others smiled.

"Wedding's over," he told them all. "I'm tired and I just wanna lie down and relax."

All eyes were suddenly on me and my hand in his.

"Night, Amanda." He smiled at her. "Ladies. We'll see you all at breakfast."

Amanda nodded, so visibly stunned that in that second before the doors shut I felt sorry for her. She had set her sights on Sam Kage, only to watch him slide right through her fingers. It had to be a new experience for her, to not get what she wanted.

I had no time for my thoughts to linger on her as Sam turned on me, pinning me to the wall before he kissed my chin, jaw, and finally my lips. The kiss went deep, and I felt how excited he was as his body pressed against mine. The sound that came out of me I couldn't stop, and the mouth grinding down over mine was ravaging. He was taking his time, and even though I couldn't breathe, I didn't care. When he pulled back, I leaned with him, trying to keep my mouth on his.

"You're such a brat," he said into the side of my neck, gently biting me before he pushed me out of the elevator. "Why would you ever be jealous of anybody?"

"Who said I was jealous?" I asked over my shoulder, getting out the key for our room.

He scoffed. "Please. I know you."

At the door I turned and looked at him, up into the smoky blue eyes of the man I loved. "You like her."

"Yeah, I do," he agreed. "She's smart and funny and she's got a great laugh."

If one enjoyed the sound of hyenas; it was a bit too Discovery Channel for me.

"And let's face it… she's smokin' hot. She—don't gimme the look, J, she is, you know she is."

I grunted. All my friends were prettier.

"But… will you look at me, please." He was chuckling now, obviously enjoying me being jealous, amused to no end.

I returned my eyes to his as his fingers slid over my jaw, tipping my head up.

"I like you better. In fact—I like you the best."

His statements were always so simple and always so perfect.

"Don't be stupid," he grumbled, snatching the plastic card from me to open the door and shove me inside our room.

"Quit pushing me around," I snapped at him.

His snort of laughter made me smile in spite of myself. I loved it when he manhandled me and he knew it. I turned to face him as he stepped in front of me, his hands on my face.

"Stop trying to pick a fight with me, there's no reason to. You know you never have to worry… you're it for me."

And the way he said it—so matter-of-fact, like I was just so annoying—was better than any long-winded declaration I could have ever had. The truth was that the sun shined, the rain fell, and Sam Kage loved me. Doubting him or worrying about his feelings was a stupid waste of time.

"Kiss me." His voice was soft and coaxing.

I smiled and heard his breath catch as my lips touched his.

"I love you."

And I knew that, of course.

End

MARY CALMES currently lives in Honolulu, Hawaii, with her husband and two children and hopes to eventually move off the rock to a place where her children can experience fall and even winter. She graduated from the University of the Pacific (ironic) in Stockton, California, with a bachelor's degree in English literature. Due to the fact that it is English lit and not English grammar, do not ask her to point out a clause for you, as it will so not happen. She loves writing, becoming immersed in the process, and falling into the work. She can even tell you what her characters smell like. She works at a copy store but has been unable to incorporate that into a book… yet. She also buys way too many books on Amazon.

CPSIA information can be obtained at www.ICGtesting.com
Printed in the USA
BVOW071617250912

301349BV00006B/225/P